Also by Marie Harte

The McCauley Brothers

The Troublemaker Next Door
How to Handle a Heartbreaker
Ruining Mr. Perfect
What to Do with a Bad Boy

Body Shop Bad Boys

Test Drive
Roadside Assistance
Zero to Sixty
Collision Course

The Donnigans

A Sure Thing
Just the Thing

Chapter 1

"*IT WAS THE PUNCH HEARD 'ROUND THE WORLD! OR, AT LEAST, around the motorcycle world. Harrison 'Gear' Blackstone and Brian 'B-Man' Gandanna are quits! That's right, you heard it here first. Rumor has it Gear and B-Man have been fighting over the future of Motorcycle Madnezz for months, and now it's finally come to a head.*"

"*That's right, Katie. But my sources tell me the problem really lies with sexy Sahara, Gear's fiancée. Or is that ex-fiancée? The pair hasn't been spotted out together in months.*"

On the television, the on-air hosts continued to gossip about the angry, bearded giant shoving cameras out of his face while he stormed to a tricked-out motorcycle—complete with a skull-painted body and ape-hanger bars—and roared away, leaving a chaotic mess on the set of yet another doomed reality show.

Sadie Liberato watched Motorcycle Madnezz's employees staring from the departing giant to a flustered couple. Probably B-Man and Sahara. B-Man sagged to the ground, his eye puffy, blood gushing from his nose, and sporting a split lip. Near him, the busty blond shrieked and cried and generally became histrionic as she blathered about true love and lawsuits. The screen then cut to a replay of the bearded giant smacking the crap out of B-Man. And all while the camera crews, the garage employees, and millions of Americans watched from their TVs.

Talk about living a nightmare. Considering she'd only paused her channel surfing in hope of seeing some eye candy—and because there was nothing else on—Sadie had to admit the drama made a nice break from the boredom of watching men tinker with bikes. Meh. Motorcycles. Wrenches. Who cared?

"Will this be the end of Motorcycle Madnezz? *I can't imagine my Thursdays without Gear and B-Man. What about keeping up with Sahara's amazing style? What will we do? Unless Sahara's mother returns for a much-welcomed cameo, giving the guys a chance to patch things up. Or Smoke and Chains take on Torch and Skid in a motorcycle showdown, like they did last year. Remember, Don?"*

"I do, Katie. We should—"

Sadie muted the television and laid her head back on the couch. She had her feet propped up on the coffee table and her lanky frame sprawled on her ugly yet comfy sofa while she thought about how dull her life seemed compared to the craziness of the TV show…and how much she preferred it that way. A cheery commercial for Party City Halloween came on, and she groaned at the reminder, having procrastinated about getting her costume ever since her brother, Elliot, had forced her to accept a costume party invitation.

So *of course* her brother chose that moment to reenter the living room. Elliot saw the ad, then turned to her, glaring. Any hope that he might cease nagging her about the stupid party vanished the moment he opened his big mouth.

"The party is in three more days. Don't make me dress you, Sadie. Because I can, and I will. So if you don't want to go as a pasty Smurfette, a flying monkey, or a killer clown, I suggest you get a move on with the costuming."

"We have thirty-three more days until October 31st. Tell me again why I can't skip this Halloween party when it's not even Halloween." Sadie glared at her younger brother. Though Elliot had a few inches on her, he hadn't grown so tall that she couldn't still maneuver him into a headlock. Thirty-one to her thirty-two, and still as annoying as he'd been as a toddler constantly stealing her Monopoly money.

"First of all, anything that gets you out of those *clothes*"—he pointed at her sweats—"gets my vote. Second, you're turning into the store hag. Limp hair, no sense of style, and you growl at all our customers. Growl...like a dog. And third, your clothes."

"You said clothes already," Sadie growled. She tightened the band holding up her hair, which *wasn't* limp, and then heard herself growling. He gave her a knowing look. She cleared her throat. "Well, you did."

She glanced down at her sweatpants and raggedy matching sweatshirt, then compared her state of dress to Elliot's navy slacks and white button-down shirt. He had his dark hair slicked back, his square jaw cleanly shaven, and he smelled amazing. Some expensive cologne, no doubt a gift from his latest ex-boyfriend. Her brother, Prince No-Commit, held a matching suit jacket over one shoulder.

"You look like a model in a *GQ* ad," she complained.

"Screw that. I look *better* than a model in a *GQ* ad. And speaking of models, my new friend, Pierre Gallant—only the hottest up-and-comer to score a Calvin Klein account—and I have a date tonight." He grinned. "What do you think of this?" He posed some more, and Sadie shrugged, not surprised her brother had nabbed a supermodel. He'd done a little modeling himself right out of high school, and for a few years he'd traveled the world.

Unlike Sadie, the homebody of homebodies.

"You look handsome." What else was new? Her brother could wear a sack and look stellar. As luck would have it, he and their sister Rose had gotten their good looks from their parents. Hell, even their cousin Ava was a beauty queen. Sadie did average, even cute, passably well. She'd inherited her mother's sharp tongue and her father's height and muscle. A lot of good that did her outside the gym.

Elliot smoothed down his shirt, plucking at a stray thread. "I know I look handsome. It's an innate gift." Without missing a beat, he added, "And it's important you go Saturday night. A friend of a friend invited me—"

"So you go."

"—to put a face with the outstanding food we'll be providing. With the number of influential people and big-shot locals in attendance, we're easily going to build more business. But I need you with me, talking up Sofa's, not catering tables. That's what I hired Theo, Gina, and Tory for. We cook it; they serve it; we mingle."

She frowned. "I thought Theo had left for boot camp already." Theo Donnigan was a cute kid, twenty-one years old and full of excitement about his recent enlistment in the Marine Corps. Theo went through jobs the way Elliot went through boyfriends, so the Marines seemed like a final destination after a slew of quickie career choices.

"It got postponed. He leaves right after Christmas."

"Elliot, I—"

"Your 'sad little life' needs to change." Elliot used air quotes around his favorite and often-used expression. Sadie had visions of dunking his fat head Saturday night. *Please God, let there be apples, a barrel, and a lot of beer.* "It's embarrassing. You're thirty-three years old."

"Thirty-two."

"You dress like Aunt Caroline."

Her aunt was an awesome woman but dressed as if refusing to let the eighties die.

"I'm telling her you said that."

"Go ahead. She knows. My point is, you should be dating, enjoying life, laughing more. You mope around when not snarling at men...and you only meet them because they come into the shop. You do nothing but hang out at the gym all the time."

"First of all, there's nothing wrong with wanting to be fit. I don't just hang around the gym, you moron. I work out. Secondly, I snarl at *all* our customers. I hate people. Oh, and you forgot about me scaring small children and kicking puppies in my spare time," she added with a healthy dose of sarcasm.

"I wouldn't be surprised." He shook his head. "Men suck. We all know that. We cheat, we lie, and you can't trust us. But sometimes you get lucky. Look at Rose." Their younger sister constantly smiled now that she and her husband were expecting. Then again, Rose had smiled all the time before that. "Joe is a hell of a guy, and he'll make an even better father." Elliot smirked at her. "Think about it. We're going to help raise their kid. Do you want to be known as the lonely, kooky aunt? Or the sexy, handsome uncle?" At her look, he amended, "I mean, sexy, gorgeous aunt?"

"You want your niece or nephew calling you sexy? Because, ew." She tried to wind down the conversation, unmuting the television and stretching her arms. "Gee, it sure is getting late. Shouldn't you be heading out with Mr. *GQ*?"

Elliot opened his mouth to say something, then paused, his attention riveted to the television, which now showed an interview with the crying blond. "Now that's just sad. *Motorcycle Madnezz* was one of my favorites."

Sadie watched as a reporter chatted up busty Sahara. B-Man stood next to her, looking like the walking wounded.

"You like watching them build custom bikes? I didn't know you were into mechanic stuff."

"I'm not. The MM guys are hot." He waggled his brows.

"How can you tell under all that bruising?"

"Oh, B-Man's not bad. And some of the mechanics have a tough kind of biker charm. But Gear is so sexy. He's gruff and has no time for the cameras, and he's *intense*. B-Man is the show's charm. Sahara, the glam." He sighed. "You should dress like that. She's gorgeous."

"Are those even real?" Sadie asked, snarky as she stared at the woman's large chest.

"Who cares? She wears them well. She's Gear's fiancée. Or maybe ex, now that everyone's breaking up. Damn it. I am so sorry I'm going to miss tonight's episode." He checked his watch and frowned.

"See? Even TV personalities don't last. Dating sucks. Men are assholes. And I'm done with all of you." Seeing how happy her sister was, Sadie had given dating another shot a few weeks ago. Another chance to find her Mr. Right. But on her first and last date with the jerk, he'd conveniently left his wallet at home during their dinner out, tried to cop a feel that went nowhere fast, then left her to use a public restroom…and never returned. Good riddance, but still.

"You might be done with us, but we're not done with you." Elliot leaned down and pinched her cheek, which he knew irritated the crap out of her. "I'm not kidding about going to the party, Sadie. Our business needs it, and I've had it with your attitude." He paused, giving her the green-eyed glare of death. And yes, he'd named it. "You *will* go with me, you *will* be charming, and you *will* help us grow our customer base. If you want to be miserable, at least be rich and miserable." He sniffed. "Or I'm telling Dad."

Hell. She did *not* want to deal with her father. Big Tony wanted his children happy. Straight, gay, single, or married, it didn't matter to him how she lived her personal life. But screwing around with financial responsibilities, with business? That would not go over well. And she knew Elliot would spin things his way.

"Fine. I'll go. But I won't like it." Sadie tried one last excuse and in a whiny voice said, "The smart thing would be to have Rose go. She's not that pregnant. Only six months, and she's barely showing. She's gorgeous, charming, fun."

"Everything you're not." Elliot ignored the finger she shot him. "But she's a master at organizing, and we need her running the staff."

"Staff? Try two teenagers, an almost Marine, and our sister. That's what you call staff? Man, talk about delusions of grandeur."

She could almost hear his teeth grinding and basked in the brief moment of victory.

"My point, dear sister, is that you need to suck it up. Hell, have fun for once. Maybe you'll find a guy you like."

Sadie grimaced. "You really have a way with words." But he had a point. Maybe she should find a guy. Something physical might clear her mind and cheer her up. Hmm. Did she really want to take a turn on a hookup app? No, better to find someone anonymous at a party, get her goody on, and leave. At the thought, she grinned.

"What's that look?" Elliot frowned. "I don't trust that smile."

"No problem. I'm just thinking I'll take your advice."

"What? Why?"

"I'm going to find myself a man at your party. Hell, maybe I can sell my born-again virginity to a billionaire investor who's into baked goods and tall girls. He can take me to his dungeon and whip me while I seduce him into letting us name a cookie after him."

Elliot rolled his eyes. "Sure thing, Fifty Shades of Insanity. So long as you're there Saturday and you're charming. Or just not angry. Okay?"

"Deal."

Elliot leaned close—to kiss her cheek goodbye, no doubt. For all that he annoyed her, he'd also do anything for her, and she loved the brat. She angled her cheek toward him.

Then the rat bastard stole the remote and turned up the volume. "Oh my God. Look at what Gear did to B-Man's face! That's gonna leave a mark." He shoved her back by her forehead while he held the remote up over his head.

"Don't you have someone to bone?" she said nastily, trying to push away his arm.

"Oh, I can be a few minutes late. Pierre won't mind." He shot her an amused glance. "But Sadie, if you plan on Shading your way to a billionaire, you really do need to do something about that hair."

"Yo, suckfest. What about that one?"

Harrison "Gear" Blackstone silently counted to ten before answering his younger brother. He noted his sister standing by a dress dummy, trying to pretend she wasn't listening in on the conversation. Just an ordinary day at Fair of Dreams—costume shop to the stars, or so Iris liked to brag after having once dressed the local weatherman for a party.

"I am not going as a gladiator," Gear enunciated to his brother. "I don't want everyone staring at my bare arm and asking about the Sahara tattoo I'm missing." *No, I'll leave all the ass-kissing to Brian, that lying, cheating, fuckhead of a backstabbing—*

"I still don't understand why Sahara wanted you to get a fake tattoo of her on your bicep," his sister said. "Your other arm is full of them, but your bare arm looked stupid with her face on it. You know I'm right."

"Of course I know."

"The minute you showed it on camera, you were sunk. I mean, now you have to get a real one to show it was real all the time, or you're just a poseur." Iris blinked. "Er, well, you're not a poseur. I mean, you don't... Because she, um... You..." She coughed. "Brian... Ah..." Her voice trailed off as Gear stared at her.

A moment of awkward silence filled the dressing room. Then Thor said, "So no to Spartac-*ass*?" He guffawed, holding up the costume with one short-as-fuck skirt. "Gear, you of all people could pull this off. The ass part, I mean."

"I'm sorry, *Thorvald*. Are you seriously trying to make fun of *me*?"

His brother glowered. "It's Thor, knuckle-dragger."

"You wish." Gear laughed, cheered when Thor hung the outfit back on the rack, then moved to another one, muttering under his breath. So easy to get one over on his brother. Thor might not be as mighty in presence as a Norse god, but the guy had a brain like a computer. If anyone could figure out a way for Gear to escape the mess that had become of his life, Thor could. "Oh, come on. I'm kidding. It's not like you haven't heard that since birth."

"True," Iris had to add. "He's just upset because the new girl in the shop laughed when she heard his name." To Thor, she said, "You should be over that by now."

"I am." Thor gave them a smug look. "Please. I might not be Chris Hemsworth, but I'm rich, handsome, successful, smart, driven—"

"Verbose," Iris interrupted. "Arrogant."

Gear cut in, "And crazy if you think I'm wearing

anything you've been holding up." He sighed. "Do I have to go to this party?"

"Yeah. You do," Iris said, no-nonsense. "It's in your contract that you go, but not that you have to be seen all night. You show up wearing that"—she pointed to a costume for the Joker, Batman's archvillain—"show your face, growl, and act like the complete jerk you are on *Motorcycle Madnezz*."

"I'm not a jerk."

"Uh-huh, keep telling yourself that," Thor said drily.

"After some time on camera, duck away, change into something with a mask, stay for the rest of your mandated time, then check out with the producer before you leave. And bingo, you've followed the terms of your contract."

The last terms. Thank God the contract had been up for renewal. Delaying the agreement had pushed back filming, but it also had allowed him to take a hard look at what his life had become. The dream of running one of the best custom shops on the West Coast had come true, but at a cost.

Just thinking about the shit Sahara and Brian had put him through—letting him take the blame while they gloried in looking like sunshine and fucking roses—made him want to hurt someone. Two someones. He'd been raised not to hit women, or he'd have decked Sahara. That he hadn't been hurt by her so much as pissed told him they'd been over for a while. But the betrayal he felt at Brian's deception… That still stung. The fucker.

"Stop it. You're scaring away my good vibes," Thor complained.

"Good vibes?"

Iris cleared her throat. "What our brother is trying to say is that he's been envisioning a future for you filled with good things. A happy life, a fine woman to love, three children, one of whom you will name Thor Junior, and a return to the fold."

Thor nodded, smiling. "Like you read my mind."

Iris snorted. "More like I sat through Mom's latest lectures on positive thinking and the way of the hippie."

Gear chuckled. "Glad I missed that one."

Iris gave him a mean smile. "Oh, you'll be getting it when they see you for brunch on Sunday. It'll happen. I'm *envisioning* it for you." She snickered. "Ah yes, I see you coming back, adding to the show. Making your wicked bikes a part of the act. Gear the Magnificent rides again…"

"Not no, but *hell no*." Gear had run fast and far from the family business years ago. His gift with all things mechanical had transformed into a love for the motorcycle—only the finest mode of transportation known to man. His mistake had been in sharing that art with his family, letting them use his funky motorized bikes in the jousting part of their medieval show.

Since then, his father had been on his ass to come back home and leave his glamorous TV life behind. His mother kept trying to zen Gear into believing life would be good to him if only he believed.

"Click your heels together, and wish upon a star," he muttered, remembering her nuttier advice. He loved Orchid Blackstone, but by God, the woman had dropped some crazy drugs in her day. Probably why she tolerated his father though. Otis was one scary mother-fucker, a badass biker to the bone with the clichéd heart of gold. It would have been cheesy if it wasn't so obvious anytime his dad glanced at his mom, his big heart in his eyes.

For years Gear had itched to leave all their positive energy BS behind. Then when he did, he landed in a black hole steadily sucking away his identity, creativity, and happiness. Hell, maybe Orchid and Otis were on to something after all.

"I know that look." Thor shook his head. "No, you are not joining back up with the Blackstone circus."

"Steampunk fair," Iris corrected, sounding irked. Gear knew she had a pet peeve about anyone talking down on the family business.

Thor ignored her. "Gear, you will avoid the temptation to join up with Satan's jesters. You and Otis nearly came to blows the last time you tried to help out."

"True," Gear had to admit.

"You will get out of this mess. We'll find a way, Bro, don't worry. And you'll be even better for it. The parental unit will only drive you insane." Thor shot a sly glance at their sister. "Look at what they've done to Iris."

"I would flip you off, but that's negative." She threw a tiny pillow at his head instead. "Now embrace the love I just sent you, and piss off."

Thor laughed. "You haven't had a good insult for me in, like, five years. Try again, or—" An alarm on his phone interrupted him, and he turned it off. "Damn. Gotta get to class. Talk to you guys later." Thor darted away with a light punch to Iris's arm and a high five for Gear. As usual, Professor Blackstone would be late to lecture.

Gear grunted. At least some things hadn't changed.

His brother still tried to boss everyone around with his superbrain while being unable to understand how time worked. His sister continued to design amazing costumes for the show while picking on their younger brother, and their parents remained loving, crazy, and humming with positivity while they recovered from Renaissance Daze and prepared for next season.

"So this party," Gear said with a sigh. He sat on a stool and watched Iris trace chalk over the fabric on the dummy. "I really don't want to go."

"I know, sweetie." She paused. "They keep replaying that punch on TV. It's like it happened yesterday." It had happened two months ago. "Man, you knocked Brian into tomorrow. Nice. He's such an asshole. Didn't I tell you he was no good? But did you listen to me?"

He groaned. "Please. Not again."

"Biggest mistake you ever made was letting that bitch convince you to let her partner up with you guys. You know the only reason they didn't go it alone as soon as she signed on is because you're the talent."

"And they're the charm," he said, having heard that since they'd started *Madnezz* three years ago. "I know."

"Nope. They're not charming. She has giant fake boobs and bottle-blond hair, and he has a straight, white smile under that fake tan. That's all they have going for them."

He grunted. "Thanks."

"So you're going to go to the party, and you're going to ignore the rumors about you cheating on her first, that Brian was just defending her honor, and that you've been trying to break up the business to steal clients for a solo show. Instead, you're going to hold your head—"

"*What?*"

"You really need to watch *Entertainment Tonight* more often." She sighed, filled him in on what that conniving ex-fiancée of his had been up to, and heard him out as he swore, punched *through* the wall, then punched it again.

After he'd knocked a second hole through the drywall and bloodied his knuckles, he sat back on the stool, breathing hard.

"Sorry to have been the one to tell you, but it could have been worse."

"How?"

"Well, you could have married her, then found out she and Brian would get custody of your love child as well as access to half of everything you own. Now you don't have to split the kid too. Just start over without them."

"Start over? With what? There's nothing left." God, he wanted to destroy something before he broke down at the hopelessness of it all. His entire life spent working toward a goal, only to have it crumble because he'd put his faith in the wrong people.

Fuck.

Iris put a hand on his shoulder. "You listen to me, Harry." Only she could get away with calling him that. "You've always been up-front about who you are and what you want. The people who are your friends know this. So you see who's still around after your house of cards tumbles. And then you pick up, start over, and kick those fuckwads in the ass with the best new chop shop on the West Coast."

He felt himself smiling. "It's not a chop shop, Iris. Those are illegal."

"Whatever. Get it done. And if you still hate me calling you Harry, wait until I start calling you Harrison. Or,
you know, your *other* name. That which should never
be said."

He shuddered. "Fine. I swear. I'll man up and deal.
But I won't like it."

"Don't. Get mad, get even, but don't get played for
a fool again."

He nodded. "Yeah. That." And that's why Gear
would go to the damn party. Because the studio would
throw Brian and Sahara at him, using his loss to drum
up ratings for the new show without him, making him
a scapegoat for the crap he hadn't done so they could
salvage viewers. He'd go tonight, but on his own terms.
Sahara he'd ignore. Brian... With any luck, he would
refrain from blackening Brian's face all over again.

Gear sighed. "What should I wear to the party?"

"I thought you'd never ask." Iris cheered, came over
to hug him, then shoved away Thor's awful choices and
found him two costumes. A villain for the press, the
other to hide in.

He smiled at the second, warming to the idea of the
party more and more.

Chapter 2

Saturday Night

THE PARTY WAS IN FULL SWING, THE MANSION outside Seattle, just past Newcastle. Anyone with this much space and a house this large had to live away from the city where land could be had, but at a premium. Joaquin Torano—a friend of a friend of Elliot's, apparently—liked to live large. Big party, beautiful guests, in a massive colonial complete with marble flooring, gold inlaid columns, and a ballroom that had been cleared to host a hundred-plus guests with room to spare.

A large, muscular man with tattoos, ear gauges, and a Mohawk standing inside the foyer bro-hugged Elliot, gave Sadie a refreshing once-over to let her know she was indeed a woman, and then let them continue inside.

The music grew louder the farther they walked into the party. But not so loud Sadie couldn't hear Elliot's apparent shock. Or rather, his *continued* shock.

"I have no words." Elliot stared at her as if Sadie had grown two heads.

"You keep saying that...which is kind of ironic, don't you think?"

"Just...no words."

She sighed. "What?"

"You're...hot. I mean, really sexy in that getup. Ew, I think I threw up in my mouth a little." Elliot pretended to gag. Dressed as the Phantom of the Opera, he looked magnificent. The half mask he wore emphasized the vivid green of his eyes and the square line of his jaw. But now, inside and adjusting to the festivities, Sadie saw more beautiful people, making Elliot appear almost normal.

"You know, I can look good when I put my mind to it."

"I see that." He smiled.

She glanced around at men and women in costumes a lot more revealing than hers. She'd been annoyed enough that she'd decided to go as a warrior princess, complete with a fake sword she considered using on her brother. Sadie's costume showed a lot of skin but kept the important parts covered. Nothing less than what she wore at the gym, to be honest. A short skirt of fake leather and a matching halter top that bared a good bit of her toned stomach, complete with a scabbard at her back. Fake-gold armbands tightened around her biceps, while quality leather boots with tufts of faux fur around the tops looked authentic enough to be part of the costume. In reality she'd borrowed them from Rose.

Sadie had left her hair long with a single braid on each side of her face, and she'd darkened her eyes and lips with black makeup. A few fake war-paint lines under her eyes and across her cheeks apparently made her look authentically man-eating—or so the drunk guy brushing by her thought out loud.

Not bad. If he hadn't been so sloshed, she might have considered trying him on for size. She had a leather satchel belted to her waist containing some money, a few condoms, and her phone.

"Oh my God. Is that who I think it is?" Elliot dragged

her around the packed dance floor and up a half level toward the rear of the home leading out onto the patio, where the crowd was thin enough to see a small gathering under bright lights. Space heaters and tall tables had been placed around a slate-slabbed yard, while strategically placed minibars provided drinks.

"Who are you talking about?" She rubbed her arms, feeling the chill before Elliot squeezed them in next to two couples by a space heater. Before she could ask again, her brother shushed her.

To the small group near them, he asked in a low voice, "Is that Gear in the Joker costume? And B-Man with Sahara?"

"Yeah," came a low reply from one of the men. "See the camera guy standing just behind the tall Batman? And the other one, the lighting guy there, is wearing scrubs, but he's no doctor. Dude is working to keep the lights on in this clusterfu—"

"Foley," the redhead next to him chastened.

"Come on, Cyn. This ain't the place for reality TV. I just wanna party."

Sadie glanced at the guy and blinked. The large man had dark hair, a muscular build—the way she liked them—and amazing gray eyes. Dressed as a sexy cop, he exuded menace more than law and order. Très sexy. Before Sadie could close her mouth, Cyn, the stunning redhead wearing an orange prisoner jumpsuit that clung to her curves, whispered something into his ear. He chuckled, and Sadie turned away, knowing she could never compete with a woman that pretty. Not that she'd ever try to break up a relationship, but with that woman, she'd stand no chance.

"Look, Sadie," Elliot whispered with excitement. "It's the guys from *Motorcycle Madnezz*."

"Oh, right. Birdman and Glock."

"B-man and Gear," he growled.

"Whatever." She wanted to turn away, but their dialogue sucked her in.

Gear, the bodybuilder mechanic from the TV show, wore white makeup and a green wig, and had a Joker grin painted in red over his lips, making him seem both perpetually smiling and sneering at the same time. The purple pin-striped suit he wore seemed painted onto his larger-than-life body. *He looks damn good* was all she could think, wondering when she'd become so desperate that now maniacal clowns turned her on.

"Jesus, he shaved off his beard." Elliot fanned himself. "I'm in lust."

"I know." Cyn sounded in awe until her boyfriend grunted. "I mean, I'm surprised about the beard." She coughed. "It's so sad they broke up, isn't it, Foley? Gear and Sahara were perfect for each other."

He shrugged. "Too bad about the show. They sure made some killer bikes."

Next to them, another guy agreed while his girlfriend called Gear some unflattering names. Her boyfriend started to argue with her, defending the mechanic.

"People, we're getting ready to roll." A man holding a large mic over the TV combatants glared at the onlookers. "Quiet."

The growing crowd around Sadie and Elliot grew silent.

Elliot gripped Sadie's hand. "They're starting. Oh my God. Best. Night. *Ever*."

Illuminated and surrounded by heat lamps, standing

across from each other with the mediator seated on a barstool between them, the three leads of *Motorcycle Madnezz*—Gear as the Joker, with B-Man and Sahara as Adam and Eve—faced off. B-Man showed off pecs and a set of tight abs, clad in shredded shorts covered with vines. He had to be cold. Gear looked hot under the collar and even more impressive despite being covered up in a suit. And Sahara… *Eve, really?* The woman wore a see-through toga that barely covered her ass when she moved. A fake snake lay around her neck and over an arm.

Sadie knew she was being harsher on the woman than the men, but Sahara seemed so obviously out to stir up trouble. Glaring daggers at her ex while she clutched B-Man's arm and gloried in others fawning over her… She reminded Sadie too much of the girls in high school, the same idiots who'd tried and failed to make her life a living hell. Had she been a less confident person, Sadie would have folded. But she'd never much cared what others outside of family thought of her.

To my detriment, because it's a Saturday night and I'm at a Halloween party with my brother. Oy.

To make sure she didn't look as ridiculous as Sahara, Sadie gave herself a subtle once-over, checking out her costume. Nah. She looked just fine.

"So, Gear, B-Man," the slick emcee began, "do you want to tell us what happened two months ago? What started the fight?" The emcee had teeth too white to be natural. He looked styled, eager for news, and tacky in a gladiator costume showing off a shaved chest and a tan a little too orange to be natural.

B-Man had his arm around Sahara's shoulders

and hugged her tight. It spoke of comfort, a platonic embrace, yet Sadie had a feeling it meant something more. "Sahara, you tell him."

Sahara shifted and flashed her ass at the crowd behind her. The emcee leaned toward her. So did the lighting guy, while a few masculine whistles and groans came from the crowd. Sahara batted her thick lashes and sighed.

Sadie barely bit back her own sigh—of disbelief. "It's like you can feel the testosterone leaning closer for a whiff of her p—"

"*Sadie*," Elliot hissed.

"I was going to say *perfume*." Probably. She tried not to be too vulgar in public.

A few of the people standing near them chuckled before Elliot shushed them. If her brother wasn't careful, he'd get his ass beat. And she'd be first in line.

Sahara's voice came out husky; she sounded vulnerable. "I didn't want this for us, Gear. For any of us." She sniffed and turned to the crowd. "They say when you make your life public, ugly things happen. Relationships end." She sniffed again, and Sadie could feel the woman's tears building, no doubt ready to roll down Sahara's perfect cheekbones in slow motion, glistening under the eye of the camera. "But I never thought that would happen with Gear and me. Oh, baby, I'm so sorry." Yep. There it was. A single tear tracked down her cheek.

B-Man murmured encouraging words while the interviewer handed her a hanky. Gear rolled his eyes. Oddly, of the three participants, she found the clown-faced villain to be the most real.

"Give me a break." Gear huffed and turned to the emcee. "You know why I'm here, Tool?"

The interviewer's face tightened. "That's Todd."

Sadie coughed, then bit back a laugh when Elliot stepped on her toes in warning. She put a finger over her lips. "I know, I know. Shh."

"*Todd*," Gear drawled, looking out of place with that square jaw and large red mouth. Sadie wouldn't have recognized him as the once-bearded giant had Elliot not said something before. "I'm here because it's in my contract to be here. I'm here so I can face this two-timing bitch and my fucker of an ex-best friend and give you some goddamn ratings."

The censors had to love this guy.

The crowd hollered and whooped until a few of the television people got them back under control.

"Dream on," B-Man snorted. "We know who cheated first, and it wasn't us. We're just friends anyway. Nothing to talk about except I feel so bad for Sahara. We know about your weekends in Taos with that chick you met at a fan show in Dallas. Hell, man. You and I talked about you flying her out for a hang and bang. I thought you were joking. With a woman as fine as Sahara, why go somewhere else?"

"Taos? What the hell are you talking about? What do I ever do but work on the show, covering up for your lack of talent?"

B-Man managed to look both sad and angry, and Sadie wondered if she'd had him all wrong.

"Oh, he's good." Elliot practically purred the word *good*, and she waited for him to tap his steepled fingers together like Mr. Burns from *The Simpsons*.

Excellent, B-Man. Exxccellent. "He's lying, but he's so good at it."

Sadie was strangely hooked on the train wreck of an evening. Like the rest of the gathered partygoers, she was eager to be titillated by infidelity and a television camera. Real or not, it made for terrific entertainment. Especially since she doubted any of it was real.

They hurled insults at one another, most of them from the emotionally drained Sahara and B-Man asking why Gear had done what he'd done, while Gear called them everything under the sun that could and did offend.

"Say what you want." Gear was smiling, and his painted mouth looked horribly deformed. Demonic. Sadie liked it. "You want her? You can have her. But fair warning, Sahara's one desert that never stays dry. Your new girlfriend's a climber, sleeping her way to the top one dick at a time."

"Hey." Sahara looked more angry than hurt, seemed to realize that fact, and started crying again.

Gear added in a more reasonable tone, "She's more interested in what you can do for her than what she feels for you, Brian."

"That's B-Man to you," Brian snarled. "And fuck you, Gear. You shit all over the show for months. Always wanting it your way. You treated her like crap. She never deserved it, and neither did I." Now B-Man's eyes were shining. "We were best friends, bro. How could you do me this way?"

"That's rough," Foley, the handsome cop next to Sadie, murmured. "Bros before—"

"You say hoes, you sleep alone," his girlfriend warned.

"Ah, noes. I was going to say noes, as in, never cheat on your bud."

"Good answer."

"We grew up together, Gear," B-Man was saying. "You're like my brother. We learned how to build an engine together."

"What script are you fucking reading from? Otis taught me how to build an engine, asshole. And fuck you. Brothers don't sleep with their friend's woman." Gear glanced at Sahara with blatant disgust. "Although to be fair, it's tough to resist a woman who never shuts her legs. Or her mouth."

A few women in the crowd gasped. "Asshole," one shouted. "Nice slut-shaming, Gear. You jerk."

Not too popular with the ladies, was he? Frankly, Sadie didn't care for his attitude much either.

"Yeah?" B-Man said, his gaze darting from the crowd to Gear. "Well, a *real* man doesn't sleep around on his fiancée. You're such a dick."

The crowd cheered him while jeering at Gear.

Gear gave an angry laugh. "That's right. Throw it all on me. While I'm working my ass off, you're sleeping with my fiancée and making plans to cut me from the show. Stab me in the back again, why don't you?"

"Nice story." B-Man huffed. "She loved you, man. You ruined it all. Not me. And not her."

Sahara remained quiet, looking at B-Man as if he'd hung the moon.

Sadie waffled once more, thinking B-Man in the right. Gear sounded like a chauvinistic jerk, and the cheating accusations could have come from him being caught, so he made up stuff about his friend and fiancée.

Having dealt with a cheating ex, she was inclined to believe B-Man's story. Yet...the makeup couldn't hide Gear's furious hurt. Until it smoothed out and his painted mouth sneered again.

Not sure what to believe, Sadie watched, enthralled and hating herself for it. Wait. Was that a flash of disdain in Sahara's eyes before they turned grieving once more? And there, the smug satisfaction on B-Man's face before he shook his head. He started arguing with his best friend again, asking him to come back. That despite it all, they could try to rebuild and forgive. And damn, but he sounded genuine, while Gear's anger and smirking Joker face came across as rude, backstabby, and unforgiving.

"He needs some PR help," Elliot whispered. "Seriously. He's worse than you during the holiday rush."

"Shut up, Elliot." Sadie sighed, no longer entertained. "This is just sad. Let's go back inside and get something to eat. I'm starved."

"Yeah. What she said," the redhead agreed, and her boyfriend joined her.

The four of them walked back inside the mansion, and Sadie appreciated the warmth generated by the hordes.

"Hi. I'm Cyn, and this is Foley," the gorgeous redhead said by way of introduction and turned to Elliot. "I've seen you before."

"Yeah, you look familiar to me too. I'm Elliot Liberato." Elliot shook their hands. "This is my sister, Sadie."

"Hi." Sadie nodded at them, still thinking it too bad Officer Hottie had a woman.

"I'm not sure how I know you, but I'll figure it out." Cyn smiled at Elliot, engaged Foley in the conversation, and as usually happened with anyone who spoke with Elliot for any length of time, immediately became his new best friend.

"I'll be back. Just going to get a drink." Sadie was promptly ignored as the three of them laughed at something Elliot said.

With a sigh, she left them in favor of one of the appetizer tables, which sat on either side of the spacious ballroom being used as a dance floor. The decor looked terrific. Orange and black tablecloths were being constantly cleaned. She spotted Tory wiping up on the south side and gave her a wave.

Tory smiled back. More of Joaquin's people milled around the outskirts of the dance floor, holding trays for revelers not wanting to load up. But not Sadie. She moved to the opposite side of the room, so as not to interrupt Tory, and filled a plate with tiny crab cakes, shrimp pâté, mini egg rolls, and—yes!—Elliot's famous tiny corn dogs and a side of cheese curls.

She had to hand it to Joaquin, who catered to the lower class, like Sadie, as well as his hoity-toity guests, of which she'd guess more than half the invitees to be. He'd done well to hire Sofa's Catering, because she, Elliot, and Rose made the perfect team to handle a shindig like this one. Delicious eats, but not too fancy that commoners couldn't enjoy them.

Sadie grinned, liking the thought of being low man on the totem pole. God save her from famous idiots like the ones on *Motorcycle Madnezz*.

A wave at Theo and Gina, refilling her table, had the pair approaching.

Theo's eyes grew wide as he eyeballed Sadie's costume.

"Oh man. You are like every geek boy's dream of Xena, Warrior Princess." He blinked at her cleavage, which she didn't think impressive in the slightest. "Nice, er, top."

"Xena who?" Sadie asked.

Gina frowned. "Yeah, who?"

Theo groaned. "Today's youth. So sad, Gina." Gina was maybe a year Theo's junior.

"Yeah, well, what's her excuse?" Gina asked with no deference to Sadie—*her boss*—whatsoever. "Sadie's thirty-four."

"Thirty-two," Sadie growled. "Ah, whatever. Get back to work, you two. And remember, if anyone asks about the food, mention Sofa's. A lot."

Theo gave her a thumbs-up. Gina nodded and trailed him back toward the kitchen, asking about this Xena person.

Sadie continued to watch the crowd, but as more drunken sailors, cops, robbers, and monsters continued to approach, asking about touching her *sword* and other body parts, she gradually left the open area. She found a shadowed area off to the side that afforded privacy as well as a tall table gone unnoticed by the masses. Perfect for her to set her plate and drink on while she ate and watched the party.

As far as costume parties went, Joaquin had scored. The dance floor remained packed, and the DJ was top-notch. Dance and dubstep vibes competed for most heavily populated track. The plethora of minibars meant no one had to wait long for a drink, and the amazing catering company—ahem—made sure to keep the tables fully stocked with goodies.

While continuing to snack on high-calorie goodness,

Sadie felt no guilt whatsoever. Tonight was her night to enjoy fat foods and, with any luck, a talented boy toy for some mindless pleasure. She'd seen a bunch of contenders. Men with muscular builds engaging in guy behavior. Smack-talking with friends, checking out scantily clad women, and acting not all that bright.

Perfect.

Sadie didn't want a date with Einstein. She wanted some quick nooky to end her dry spell. With any luck, she'd enjoy herself before kissing her nameless hookup goodbye. Maybe Elliot had been right to insist she attend.

"Hey, Xena. Be my Valentine." A drunk guy smelling of BO, Axe body spray, and cheap beer leered close by.

Crap. She'd been found out. "Hey, um, what are you supposed to be?"

"Hercules." He flexed, and she had to admit his arms impressed her. Too bad she'd have to hold her nose while praying she couldn't taste his breath during a kiss. Gross.

"Nice to meet you, Hercules." She took the hand he held out and tried to contain a grimace while he gave the back of it a sloppy kiss.

"Hey, pretty thing, you want to go fuck in the corner?" He nodded over her shoulder to the discreet alcove nearly hidden by a wall of potted bamboo behind her.

Though Sadie loved frank talk, the whole "let's fuck in the corner" was a bit much even for her. Could she be that desperate? He smelled like Elliot's dirty socks. As much as she wanted to be that kind of girl, the one who felt no guilt for a shameless hookup, she just couldn't. Not with Hercules.

"Sorry. I'm waiting for a friend. And he already called dibs on the corner."

"Well, shit. Can't blame a guy for tryin'." He stumbled back, gave her a salute that nearly had him tripping over his own feet, then turned and hit on the next woman he ran into.

Sadie sighed and returned to people watching, sipping from her cosmopolitan now and again. To her amusement, she spotted one hell of a hot devil getting accosted by a drunk and giggly genie very close to falling out of her bikini top. The devil wore a half mask hiding his face, a dark-red cape over broad shoulders, and black from head to toe. He held a plate of food in one hand and a bottle of beer in the other as he tried to gently nudge the woman back, but her hands were everywhere.

Oh boy. Talk about grabby. He swore when lady fingers grabbed at what appeared to be a generous package.

Sadie felt for the guy, even as she had to laugh at his desperation. He had his hands full, for sure. It was like looking at a picture of herself as she'd stood on the dance floor. Minus the crotch grabbing, of course. She'd have skewered any jackass who tried. Devil glanced around, and she felt the heat of his gaze when it landed on her. Despite the half mask, which covered the upper half of his face, his stare penetrated.

His lips curled into a dark smile before he turned to the genie and said something.

She pouted, took a good look at Sadie, then flounced back into the crowd.

The devil took his time walking toward Sadie, now striding as if he owned the place.

She nodded at the vanished genie. "Problem?"

"Yeah. I'm not a fan of being molested while trying to save my food and beer. I mean, at least let me eat before you knock me down and mount me." His voice sounded like gravel licked with fire.

She laughed. "You have a way with words."

He stared at her, then slowly grinned. And man, the sight of that square jaw and those full lips grabbed hold and wouldn't let go. "So I've been told." He paused. "You mind if I share your table? I'm dying to sink into these crab thingies."

This close, she could see that his eyes had been darkened by black makeup but were actually hazel in color. *Wow*. Talk about a handsome…devil. She chuckled aloud at her pun. "Why not? You earned it."

His smile showed even, white teeth, but his eyes seemed serious, a bit mean despite his mirth. Underneath the humor, he had the menacing air down pat. Hmm. She mentally added him to her maybe-do list.

"What's that look?" he asked.

"Are you a demon or a vampire? With that costume you could be either or a mix of both."

He flashed fang-less teeth and shrugged huge shoulders. When he stood by her side, she realized he was half a head taller than her own five eleven. "I've been called worse, so I figured the devil was appropriate." He stuffed a whole crab cake in his mouth and chewed, so she did the same, liking his style. "What about you? What's with the Xena getup?"

"I've been told I clomp around and growl at people like a barbarian. Thought I'd run with that theme."

He held up his beer for a toast. "Nice."

She clinked his bottle with hers and took another sip.

"So, Devil, why are you hiding and not trying to get lucky like half the bozos in here?"

"I could ask you the same." He continued to eat, watching the crowd as much as he watched her.

"If you'd seen my last 'suitor,' you'd understand. For the record, body spray does not mix well with baked-in BO."

He winced. "I smelled my share on the dance floor. Joaquin packed 'em tight tonight."

"Yep." She finished the snacks on her plate and downed her drink, wishing she'd grabbed more to eat.

"So how'd you get in here? You know Joaquin?"

She understood the question. It was a closed party.

"In a way. He's a friend of a friend of my brother's." Gee, that sounded sad. Like she couldn't get in unless dragged along with a sibling.

"Yeah, me too. A friend of a friend."

The music's tempo jolted the partyers to new heights of enthusiasm.

"Great DJ," Devil said, his foot tapping to the beat.

She found herself doing the same. "No kidding." She eyed the tiny corn dogs on his plate. He had half a dozen. She wondered if he'd miss one... "Hey, is that B-Man over there?" she asked.

When he turned his head, she stole an appetizer off his plate and shoved it in her mouth. Oh yeah, Elliot would be thrilled to see her display her "house manners" in public.

The devil turned back to her. "Not him." He frowned at his plate, then at her full mouth. "Did you just steal my food?"

"Nope," she answered around a mouthful.

He stared at her for a moment, then burst into laughter. It was a full-bodied laugh, holding nothing back. Charming and real. She put Devil at the top of her list.

She swallowed, wishing she had something more to drink. As he finished off his plate, he glanced at her clean one, then at her. When he sighed and handed her his beer, she took it gratefully.

"No backwash, I promise." She opened her mouth to show him hers was clean, then downed half the bottle. "Damn, that was good."

He blinked. "Ah, you want more?"

"No, no. You drink that. I'll go get some."

She moved to go, but he grabbed her arm. They both paused. Together, they glanced down at his large hand on her wrist, and he dropped her arm. "Ah, that's okay. You stay here. I'll get you something. Beer? More chow?"

She nodded. "Um, both, thanks. I'll save your place."

He left, and she watched his progress as he cut a swath through the crowd. Yes, the devil made his own path. This time, no one bothered him as he returned posthaste. To her surprise, she was glad. The guy smelled good, a hint of subtle cologne that went straight to her head. He had a kickin' body and a great smile. But that air of *Don't fuck with me* really turned her on—ah, made her amenable to his presence.

Talk about a wordy mouthful. At the thought, she found herself glancing down his body to see what *else* might be a mouthful.

Jesus, Sadie. Get your head out of the gutter, girl.

"You okay?" Temptation leaned closer. "You look a little flushed."

"You can tell in this lighting?" she teased, trying to get it together.

"Good point." He handed her a beer, placed his own down on the table, and then put a plate overloaded with goodies on top of their empties. "This is to share. To *share*," he said slowly.

"Yeah, yeah. Man, I'm starved." She fell on the plate as if the Russians were coming.

To her amusement, he fought with her for the cheese curls as much as for the mini egg rolls, and they devoured the snacks in good company.

They talked with their mouths full, making fun of the drunken genie as well as several unsuccessful hookups on the dance floor.

"Oh, now that had to hurt," the devil said. "Rejected by a zombie and her warty witch friend."

"Yeah, but he's not taking it personally." Sadie took another sip of beer, loving the fact he hadn't gotten her a sissy glass to drink from. "See? He's turning from the undead to slutty doctor chick."

"Slutty? Isn't that non-PC?" he sneered, and she thought he sounded familiar, but the loud music made it difficult to tell. "Because I say the wrong thing about a *woman*, not a 'chick,' and I'm a caveman asshole setting women's rights back twenty years."

"Well, I can say *slutty*. You have to say *sexually adventurous*." Sadie grinned. "Kind of like telling a gay guy he's a raging homo. Now I can say that, because my brother earned the title. But you try telling him that, and he'll knock your head off. And call him anything else, and *I'll* knock your head off." She hefted her fake sword before leaning it against the wall. "Don't try me."

He shrugged. "You have a sword. I have a pitch-fork...somewhere. I think I left it by the bar." He glanced across the room. "But hey, I have no plans to tangle with your brother. I'm here to sin until this thing is over. Nothing else, and no fights." He paused, and she swore he added something else under his breath.

At that moment, her brother appeared in the crowd, his gaze searching.

"Shit."

"What?"

She took Devil by the waist and turned him, noticing how he tensed but ignoring it. "Sorry. I'm having fun not mingling, and my brother is right over there looking for me."

He relaxed and glanced over his shoulder. "Which one?"

"See the Phantom? He's a pain in my ass, much as I love him. I didn't want to come to this tonight, you know."

"Yeah? Me neither." He stayed where he was, still watching the dance floor. "Uh-oh. He's looking over here."

"Crap, crap, crap. This is a primo spot!" She did what any smart woman in her situation would do. She turned Devil so he completely blocked her from Elliot. "I need to blend in. Work with me, would you?"

"Sure, what—?"

She wrapped her arms around his thick neck and dragged him down for a kiss.

At the taste of his lips against hers, she shuddered, not having expected he'd taste better than his beer, or that up close and personal he'd smell like man and sex and chocolate. *Chocolate?*

Jesus, she must have had too much to drink.

Then he dragged her closer and deepened the angle of their kiss.

Sadie forgot about her brother, about the last crab cake on the plate, about how much she didn't want to be at the party.

And fell into the arms of a man who kissed like the devil himself.

Chapter 3

SADIE COULDN'T BE HAPPIER SHE'D DECIDED TO attend this stupid party. *Whoa, momma.* Devil's invitation was all in his lips, his hips, and his personal pitchfork pressing insistently against her belly. Someone moaned. She thought it might be her, and then he dragged her closer, cradling her against him where it would do the most good.

She gasped into the kiss, feeling as if she'd gone from zero to Mach 10 in a heartbeat.

They broke the kiss and stared at each other, his eyes narrowed, assessing.

She did her best to catch her breath and figure out how a simple kiss could light her fuse so easily. Even though she hadn't had sex in months, she'd never gone up like dry kindling in a desert before.

"Huh," he said.

Sadie just blinked at him, trying to focus.

"That was... Damn." He didn't even try to hide his erection as he ground against her. Instead, he closed his eyes and softly swore, then opened them again. "A room would help get to the bottom of that kiss."

"You think?" She gasped as he swooped in for another hungry taste. Damn it. Just as good as the last one.

"I have been known to think. Sometimes."

"You sure you're not a vampire?"

"No, I'm the devil." He grinned. "Why?"

"Because at this moment, you are the epitome of Vlad the Impaler." She nudged him with her hips.

He grimaced. "You're going to hell for that." She shifted, and he groaned. "Or I am. Because if you do that again, I might not make it to a room."

"Oh." She sucked in her breath when he leaned close and kissed down her cheek to her ear.

He whispered, "So pretty thing, you wanna go fuck in the corner?"

She pulled back and stared.

He chuckled. "Sorry, couldn't resist. I heard some drunk-ass hitting on women earlier. Surprise, surprise, he seemed to strike out."

"Yeah, he didn't get a hit with me either. You, on the other hand…"

"I'm temptation made flesh," he said, being overly dramatic. Yet the deep timbre of his voice and the way he looked at her made her feel as if he'd put her under a spell.

"You can say that again." She pulled him back for another kiss.

Better than the last two. Well, hell. Sadie yanked her mouth away, grabbed him by the hand, and dragged him behind the plants. They wouldn't be visible to the partygoers unless someone sought them by deliberately skirting the foliage. The shadows deepened, and she saw his eyes gleam before his face became a black blur.

Perfect.

"Right here," she whispered.

"Yeah? Hot damn. Sex in public. *Okayyyy*." He gave a dark laugh. "Hell. I don't have a—"

"Condoms are in my satchel." She grabbed one and shoved it in his hand. "Use it."

"Fuck me."

"No, fuck *me*."

He groaned and reached for her at the same time she reached for him. She'd never been so out of control before. And she didn't care. Tonight was her night for some fun, and she'd take it any way she wanted it. *I am Xena. Hear me roar*. She got down to business, her hands over his chest, his belly, and lower.

"Wow." She felt warm flesh, a thick cock ready and willing to please.

He growled, "Put it on me," found her hand, and wrapped it around him with a curse. Then he shoved the condom into her other hand.

She trembled, on fire to have him. Should she do a quick shimmy out of her panties? But first, the condom. She ripped the package and hurried to put it over him. Dear Lord, talk about a happy, *happy* Halloween. She rolled it over him and felt his hands on her breasts. He cupped and squeezed, gently, then with firmer insistence.

The devil wasn't grabby, but he sure did set her on fire.

She felt his mouth at her throat, his hand over hers, forcing her to hold on to his sheathed cock.

"Pump me," he muttered into her neck, then nipped and sucked.

She moaned, holding what amounted to a miracle of nature in her hand. She wanted him inside her, felt her body ready for him. Easy and quick, she figured he'd shove up into her, give her a good ride, then dart away.

Except the devil had other plans. He continued to

suck her neck, then her chin, then her mouth. Kissing away her will to do anything but comply.

"Yeah, you wet for me, princess? Your pussy hungry for some cock?" His low whisper made the crude words hot. She heard his lust, and she sure as hell felt it.

"Yes. In me." She started to tug under her skirt to pull at her panties, but he interrupted her by lifting her as if she weighed nothing.

He pushed her back to the wall. "Wrap your ankles behind my back," he ordered.

She didn't have to be told twice. "My underwear is—"

"Not a problem." He slid his hands under her thighs, one hand and the wall holding her in place while he nuzzled her cleavage and inched a thick finger under her panties and into her. "Fuck, you're hot."

And so wet. She hadn't realized how excited she was until he showed her. But that finger wasn't enough. The music pounded, the crowd's cries growing louder. The noise, his scent, the feel of his presence all around her. She was under a spell for sure, having sex in public. Sadie Liberato, party whore.

But she couldn't bring herself to care about possibly ruining her reputation, about being kicked out, about being caught by her brother. Because Devil pushed her panties aside and started sliding inside her.

So big, so full, he continued to push until he could go no farther.

"Jesus," she moaned. "So big."

"So tight." He swore, grabbed her ass in both hands, and *moved*.

She sucked in a breath, perilously close to orgasm. "I-I'm going to come."

He moaned and slammed into her, and she came like a shot, the pleasure overwhelming. But he didn't stop, just rode her through the best damn orgasm of her life. She wasn't sure if she screamed, breathed, or simply endured, completely fogged over by the ecstasy of a friggin' orgasm thrumming through her system.

Her devil slowed his pace, no longer so intense as he took her, feeling incredibly huge as he continued to pump inside her. "So... Fuck, that's good. Better than good. Amazing." He kissed her, still thrusting, his entire body tense. Then he gripped her hips hard enough to bruise.

She toyed with the hair at his nape, and he shivered.

"Sorry. Came twice, so fast. Good thing you brought condoms."

"No kidding." Was that her? All breathy and feminine sounding?

Sadie blinked, aware a stranger, a man whose name she did not know, remained inside her. The insanity of it all kept her mute.

He withdrew, then fiddled with the condom and his clothes, she assumed, while she straightened hers. Her panties would never be the same. And neither would her sex life. Hmm. Maybe she should frame them, have him sign her ass before he left. The thought made her want to laugh a little hysterically.

Before she could tell him she had to go, noise from behind the wall at her back stopped them both. A glance beside her showed a hidden door, the crack all but invisible unless you happened to be fucked up against it.

"I don't believe you." A woman's muffled shriek came through.

Next to her, Devil froze.

"You went off script. What did we talk about, Brian?"

"Get off my dick, Sahara."

Sadie wished she could see her devil. "That sounds like B-Man and Sahara from that motorcycle show," she whispered.

"Shhh."

Another man shushing her. What the hell?

He moved closer and caged her with his big body, holding her back to the door while he pressed his ear to the crack. So close, she felt his breath against her neck and did her best to hold in a whole-body shiver. God, the man was sex personified. He had to be human though, right? No way she'd been seduced by the actual devil.

Oh man. Now she felt the need to go to church in the morning.

"What did you think would happen when you brought up that Hallmark crap about building engines together?" Sahara continued. "Gear has never had a schmaltzy bone in that big body. He built engines with Otis because his old man busted his balls to. The only thing you did right was bringing up that chick from Taos. You're sure she'll go along with our story?"

"Yeah. That's something, then." Brian sounded hopeful. The douche. And here Sadie had felt bad that he'd had his friendship ruined by Gear—who wasn't as big a jerk as she'd previously thought. "But at least now I'm not a home-wrecker. He is. You're still beautiful and loyal. He's the bad guy. You heard Todd. Ratings were beyond what they hoped. We stick it to Gear, start our own show, and the asshole won't bother us anymore. I always told you I'd make the better partner, Sahara."

"So you did," Sahara said, then added something else

Sadie couldn't make out. Except… Oh. The sex sounds coming through the door were impossible to mistake.

She and her devil pulled away at the same time. They moved together toward the bamboo, and Sadie saw the mess of his face.

Her black makeup was on his lips and cheeks. "Hold on." He stood still as she used a napkin by her discarded plate to clean him up. "Okay, now do me."

His lips quirked. "Thought I did that already."

"Ha-ha." She waited under his hesitant touch, curious that he seemed so gentle now. "I won't break. Go on. Rub it off."

"Rub one out, more like," he muttered, but she saw his grin. "Xena, you are one sexy warrior. I just did you, and I want to bend you over and do you again."

To her shock, she wanted to let him. Sadie cleared her throat and kept it light. "You say the sweetest things."

His rough laughter warmed her. "Yeah, that's me. Mr. Sweet."

She shook her head. "Speaking of sugary sweet, can you believe what we just heard? I watched them out there on the patio earlier." She ran down the conversation for him. "At one point I almost thought B-Man was telling the truth. But there was something not right about him. And I really don't like that Sahara chick. What a bitch."

His eyes seemed to warm.

"I mean, it's clear she cheated on the guy. I really hate cheaters."

"Yeah, me too."

She heard his underlying emotion. "You've been screwed over before, I take it?"

"Yep."

Sadie sighed. "Me too. I really feel for this Gear guy. You ask me, though, his asshole ex-bestie did him a favor. Any woman who'd sleep with her guy's best friend isn't worth keeping around."

"Good point."

"Me? I've been cheated on before. At the end, I was happy to see him go. But still, it makes you question your judgment. Who you can trust." She paused. "And why am I telling you this?" Maybe he really was the devil in disguise. Sadie didn't like to share feelings. Sex? Sure. Hearts and flowers, not so much.

"You're telling me because I get it." He nodded. "My ex was a waste. But my friend was worse. I mean, who does that? Screws their friend's fiancée in the guy's own damn bed?"

"That's low." Sadie stared back at the plants. "Man, what I wouldn't give to pound those two through the floor."

"I bet you could take 'em." He winked. "You sure the hell took me."

Sadie felt her cheeks heat. "On that note, I'd better go."

"Seriously? No phone number? No 'I'll call you later'? No name?"

"I know your name. Satan. The devil. You know me. I'm Xena." She kissed him on the cheek, then brushed away a black smear of lipstick. "Have a happy Halloween." She heard the shutting of a door behind her and turned to see B-Man and Sahara. B-Man stopped when he saw Sadie, but Sahara scowled, and then her eyes narrowed. No doubt wondering how much Sadie might have heard.

Sadie glanced behind her and saw only the wall of bamboo. Her devil had disappeared. Smart guy.

"Did you hear enough?" Sahara smiled through her teeth. "Had your ear up to the door, did you? And what are you doing back here? It's off-limits to regular people."

Regular people? "First of all, it's kind of loud in here. It's a par-ty," Sadie said slowly. Though to be fair, the sound was muted in this corner, and yeah, with an ear up to that crack in the door, you could hear everything. "Second, who died and made you boss of the party? Or are you fucking the host too?" The look she shot B-Man made it clear Sadie knew about their affair.

"So you *were* listening at the door. Brian, go get Joaquin." He gave Sadie a wary glance and left to do the skank's bidding. "Bitch, do you know who I am? I'm Sahara Blankenship from *Motorcycle Madnezz*. So watch how you talk to me."

Annoyed on behalf of herself and people cheated on in general, Sadie growled, "You know what? You can shove your attitude up your ass, Blankenship."

The woman's bright-blue eyes widened in shock, then narrowed in anger. "Slut."

"Shrew. Or is that too big a word for your empty little head?" Sadie scoffed. "You're nothing but a whore hanging on to fame one desperate finger at a time. Plastic boobs, tummy tucks, and Botox aren't enough to save your never-there future."

Sahara shrieked with rage and darted forward. Sadie held her ground, not expecting the cheater to do anything but threaten. To her surprise, Sahara slapped her. Then froze, as if surprised she'd gone through with it.

The slap stung. Sadie, who'd taken some awesome self-defense classes at her gym and liked messing around with martial arts and kickboxing for fun, finally got to put her skills to use. She gave the woman a cold stare, then punched her in the face.

Sahara went down, hard. And stayed down, moaning.

Not done with the fight and pumped with adrenaline, Sadie grabbed the woman by the hair and yanked her head up, liking the runny mascara and tears, as well as that bruising eye. "Watch how you talk to Xena, you cheating witch."

"Oh my God. Come on." Elliot magically appeared and dragged Sadie away.

Surprised, she'd automatically let go of Sahara's hair. Sadie would have loved to have taken a hank of bottle-blond tresses as a souvenir.

Her brother sounded frantic. "We have to get out of here before someone sees what you did! She'll sue, you moron. Get moving."

Sensing he might have a point, Sadie hustled away with Elliot, wishing she could have shown her devil what she'd done. He'd have gotten a kick out of it. Or to have shown Gear. For sure, the villain would appreciate her moves on his cheating ex.

She sighed. As usual, she'd been a goddess in motion and no one cared.

Elliot continued to ramble as he hurried through the crowd, dragging her with him.

"Now this is a party," Sadie said with a laugh. She'd met the devil, had incredible sex, and punched a conceited bitch in the face. A trifecta of amazing. "Where are we going next weekend?"

Gear stared in shock and awe at the quickly departing Amazon who'd punched Sahara in the eye. *Oh my God. I'm in love.*

He still couldn't believe it. He'd walked away from Xena when he'd seen Sahara and Brian, because he couldn't be near them without doing exactly what Xena had done.

Shit. She really smacked the crap out of my lying, cheating ex.

He was grinning from ear to ear, watching from his hiding spot behind the bamboo wall, far back enough Brian hadn't given him a second glance as he'd run to do Sahara's bidding. Xena's brother had been smart to whisk his sister away from the litigious whiner crying on the floor. Man, Sahara played the part, all right. It was a good thing the altercation had taken place in private, or Sahara would have milked the performance for all she was worth.

Another thought occurred. If he stuck around and someone realized who he was under the half mask, he'd end up getting blamed somehow for the punch. Just more ammo to make him appear the creep.

He mingled with the crowd and made his way back to one of the show's producers. "Hey, Jim. I'm outta here."

Jim frowned at him. The guy smelled like a brewery but was known to be able to hold his liquor. "Gear? Is that you? I thought you were the Joker."

"A villain, the devil, it's all good, right?"

"Uh, okay." Jim glanced at his cell phone. "It's only been two hours…"

"Which is one hour more than I agreed to. I've been here long enough, I think. Contract fulfilled. And I—"

Just then, Sean, the lighting guy, raced to Jim and whispered in his ear.

Jim perked up. Had he been a dog, his ears would have pointed up, his tail straight out. Scenting fresh prey. "Seriously? Punched by a warrior princess? You have to be kidding me! Get the cameras."

They raced away, forgetting Gear. He had a feeling problems might follow his sexy warrior if he didn't head them off. And hell, he owed her. Not just for the incredible sex, but for doing what he could never do to a woman. He grinned. Best party ever.

Directed by a few of Joaquin's security, he found the guy smoking in a back room, away from the party. They'd met briefly an hour ago, and the rich dude seemed okay. "Um, Joaquin? Can I talk to you?"

"Sure, man. Come on in. Want a hit?" The guy blew a stream of smoke, and the smell accounted for his mellow mood. "Sorry I bailed on the party. Just wanted a minute to myself." He frowned. "Do I know you? You sound familiar."

"I'm Gear." Gear removed his half mask. "We met earlier. I was the Joker then."

Joaquin's eyes brightened. "Oh right. *Motorcycle Madnezz*. Dude, you guys rock!" He stood and crossed the room to shake Gear's hand.

Not having expected the guy to like him, considering everyone seemed to think him a dickhead for cheating, stealing, and whatever else went wrong on the set, Gear basked in the brief moment of acceptance.

"Thanks. Glad you like the show." He cleared his

throat. "I wanted to let you know some chick decked Sahara, and I have a feeling Sahara's going to be on you to get the woman's name."

"Seriously? B-Man told my security something about that, but I thought it was a joke. A catfight and I missed it? Damn." Joaquin leaned back against his desk and puffed on his joint. "So I'm supposed to know this woman's name, huh?"

"Something she said made me think you do. I'd appreciate it if you didn't tell Sahara what you know. It'll only end up in a lawsuit, and man, the chick did me a solid. Finally, Sahara mouthed off to the wrong person, and she put a stop to it. To be fair, Sahara hit her first. Though I'm sure that detail won't make it into her recollection of the event."

Joaquin grinned. "Bet it was awesome to see."

"Oh yeah." He coughed. "I mean, I didn't see anything."

"Gotcha." Joaquin laughed. "Man, that is so epic. At *my* party. Bet your producers get more film over it."

"Jim's doing that now." Gear made a decision and went with it. "So this chick… She was dressed as Xena, Warrior Princess. Tall, dark hair, amazing body. Her brother was dressed as the Phantom of the Opera, and—"

Joaquin's eyes widened. "Shit. That's Elliot. My caterer. The warrior must have been his sister. Can't remember her name, but yeah, she's a hot one. All toned and shit. Totally right." Joaquin paused. "She decked Sahara?"

"Allegedly."

"Right, right. Thing is, man, if there are witnesses, nothing much I can do."

"No, see, that's the beauty of it. Sahara mouthed off

in a private area, off the dance floor behind a bunch of bamboo plants. No one saw it."

"Good. That makes it easier." Joaquin laughed again. "Elliot's sister clocked the motorcycle queen. Classic."

Gear felt better than he had in a long time. "She's my hero, for sure. So can you tell me where I can find her? I want to thank her in person."

"Sure. Try Sofa's, a bakery in Green Lake. They catered for me. Did a bang-up job too."

"Awesome. Thanks a lot. I appreciate it." Gear held out a hand, and Joaquin took it.

"So, you blowing *MM*?"

"Huh?"

"Are you leaving the show, or is all the bullshit just for ratings?"

Gear frowned. "I'm done. No more for me. Time to get back to building motorcycles, period."

"Yeah? 'Cause I been thinking about getting some custom work done. I collect cars, but your motorcycles are killer."

"Thanks. Look me up when you feel like a bike. Shit. Not at the shop. I can give you my cell."

"Yeah, do that."

He wrote down his cell phone number on a notepad Joaquin handed him. "I'm out of here. Great party, man. Legendary."

"Right. That's me. A legend." Joaquin started laughing again, and Gear thought the weed must have kicked in. He left the millionaire giggling and skirted a sobbing Sahara being comforted by Brian while Todd of the fake tan interviewed her in a quiet corner of the ballroom.

A thought struck, and he went back to his rendezvous

spot. Yep, she'd left it behind. He carefully grabbed the fake sword leaning against the wall. Now he had a reason to seek Xena out.

He smiled and left the party, the devil pleased with the hellish night his Amazon had unleashed.

After he arrived home, his sister called to check in.

"What's up, Iris?"

"Oh my God. Tell me you had nothing to do with Sahara getting belted in the face."

"It hit the news already?"

"It's making headlines. I saw it on the local news and YouTube. The link is already going viral. Even Thor texted me asking about it, and you know he's rarely on the computer unless he's working."

"Damn." He explained that a woman he'd met had done the damage. "Sahara was bitching her out, slapped the chick, and finally got her ass handed to her. Man, it was *awesome*." He laughed, remembering Sahara's shock. "The user finally got what was coming to her."

"Yeah, well, your barbarian friend might get what's coming to *her* if she's not careful."

"There were a bunch of women in similar costumes at the party. And the crowd helped cover her escape, I think. I hope. She was really cool, Iris. Funny too."

"Aw, Satan made a friend. Come on, thank me for the costume. I told you changing into a second one would save your butt."

"You did. Once I got rid of the Joker, I was anonymous. It was great. Plus my producer saw me there, so he can't claim I left right after the interview. Okay, so that's my night. Now I'm getting some sleep so I can function tomorrow."

"Coffee with the family at noon, remember? You know Otis and Orchid are going away for the week. So they'll want to see you before they go."

"Sure, fine. Whatever." He yawned, not faking his exhaustion. The idea of the party, attending it, dealing with Sahara and Brian, had stressed him out. Until a certain savage blew his mind.

He disconnected the call and dropped into bed, still smiling as he drifted into sleep, his dreams full of strong women, swords, and deep-green eyes.

Chapter 4

Sadie was so tired of hearing her brother caution her about keeping quiet about that punch. It wasn't like she planned to shout it out to the world. Granted, she probably shouldn't have hit the woman, but she'd been hit first. And it had been *so* satisfying, as if in punching Gear's cheater, she'd punched her own ex for doing her wrong.

"Cut me some slack, Elliot. The woman was being bitchy. She freakin' slapped me. I'm claiming self-defense. Plus, I told you I heard what they said about setting Gear up to be the fall guy. She deserved it."

Elliot had his hands full as he shaped spider, skeleton, and goblin sugar cookies before turning to the butter scones waiting for his attention. Sadie had her own work putting together Sunday salads. She had to make enough to last the day without overdoing it. They could always use any extra dressing in the following day's menu, but wilted greens went in the compost bin.

"That's the only thing saving your ass this morning," Elliot muttered. "Good gossip." He put three trays in the oven and cleaned up his station in their kitchen.

Sundays at Sofa's—the coffee shop/bakery that had expanded into a catering business—saw the siblings spending time together before they opened at eleven. Every weekend Sadie, Elliot, and Rose mixed, prepared, and frosted the most delicious treats—from healthy salads to sandwiches and baked goodies. Sadie would never admit it to the pair, but she loved their family time. She would forever associate the smell of baking cookies with Elliot's bitching, Rose's exuberance, and laughter.

Elliot was her best friend, and it wasn't easy sharing him with everyone. She and Rose had always been too different to be *close*-close. Sure, Sadie loved her little sister to pieces. Yet Elliot was the one who could see that sometimes a cup needed to be half empty, not half full, and was that much funnier because of it. Rose was too Pollyanna for Sadie, who enjoyed, say, punching a woman in the face. Or talking while eating, or having sex with a man she thought of as Devil, because she didn't know his name.

She grinned at the reminder. "Elliot, let me just say thank you."

He gave her a wary look. "For what?"

"For the most fun I've had in a while. The last time I was even half that entertained was watching our cousin and Landon fumble their way to a happily ever after while you and Jason, ex number four hundred and ten, committed to dating exclusively." She didn't miss her brother's flush. "Oh, come on. You're not still pining for that twerp, are you? He was so incredibly passive-aggressive. You need someone who says it like it is, not someone who sulks and throws hissies if you don't know how to read his mind."

Elliot sighed. "Yeah, but he was great in bed. I'll miss his—"

"TMI. Ugh."

He gave her a wicked smile. "I was going to say

creativity. So tell me more about last night. Because no way smacking some woman made you this happy. Oh, and where is that sword? I need to return it to the shop later."

"Hmm. About that… I may have left it behind when I was carried off by the Phantom of the Opera," she said drily. "But don't worry about getting the deposit back. What's more important is that we know the truth. That our food kicked ass last night."

"I told you we should go." Joaquin had texted her brother about four events in the coming months he wanted them to work. "I mentioned to him that from now on, we just cook it and deliver. We're stretched too thin to serve as well."

"Good. Because if you think I'm going to hold a tray and beg people to eat your gluten-free Holy Hell rolls, you're out of your mind."

"Like I'd let you," Elliot snorted. "I'd be afraid someone would say something wrong and you'd punch them."

Sadie grinned. "Rose was so shocked. Like, did she not expect me to have a violent streak? You've seen me on the heavy bag at the gym."

He shrugged. "What can I say? Rose is our square peg. She's too damn nice for our family." He sounded as puzzled as Sadie felt. "I told her not to come in at all today."

"No, *I* told her not to come in at all today. How is it you're still struggling to realize I'm the oldest and the one with mad skills in the kitchen?"

"Yes, your dishwashing is beyond compare." He rolled his eyes. "Might I remind you that we're partners, but I am the brains and marketing master behind our success?"

A success that paid, if not well, enough to keep Sadie comfortable. She had little in the way of needs. A gym membership at Jameson's, subscriptions to Netflix and Hulu, and an addiction to frilly underthings and white chocolate raspberry truffles. Just one truffle alone cost four bucks.

They worked in companionable silence while Emery managed the counter out front. Like Theo, he was a part-timer, a college kid with a great sense of style—what Sadie liked to call preppy grunge—and a terrific sense of humor. He thought Sadie was hilarious.

"Did you set up next week's schedule yet?" she asked. "Because I know Emery has midterms and Tory's got a dance recital."

"I think you should do it. You know more about everyone than I do."

Yeah, because I have no life, just watching the rest of you from the sidelines. She didn't say it, but she knew he had to be thinking it. They'd had this discussion before.

"Oh, and before we veer completely away from the topic of the party last night, just what were you up to?" he asked.

"What?"

"I looked for you. Despite there being several barbarian hussies—"

"Warrior princesses, you mean?"

"—out there, we both know you don't dance. So I didn't bother looking for you on the crowded dance floor. But I looked everywhere else, and I didn't see you. Where were you hiding? Behind those trees all night?"

"Trees?"

He waved a floured hand. "The bamboo plants. It was a nice hiding spot. But the point was for us to mingle. That means we talk to other people."

She studied him, wondering when he'd get it through his thick skull that she wasn't lovely like Rose, charming like him, or interesting like their cousin Ava, a shrink. Sadie was just Sadie. She had no aspirations to get famous or rich. Didn't have much in the way of interests besides working out, and mostly liked her life, boring as it was.

When she remained silent, he threw up his hands. Mr. Dramatic. "Oh, forget it."

She nodded. "Elliot, let me ask you something."

"This should be good."

"Why is it that I'm an unhappy person?"

"You are?" He frowned.

"Well, if I'm not dating or trying to make millions, I'm apparently unhappy and unfulfilled. I like being single. I like my little apartment that's affordable, comfortable, and mine." Sadie had no pets, plants, or debts other than monthly rent on an apartment owned by her father. She could move at any time. She was—in a word—tether-less.

"I don't think you're unhappy. But you're not happy, either." Elliot paused to study her. "You're comfortable, yes. But you're not challenged. I'm not saying you need a relationship to complete you, but you're missing something that will make this conversation make sense in the future. When you find it, you'll know."

"That was enlightening. Not."

"What can I say? Some advice you pay for, the crap is

free." He gave her an evil smile. "And for making me do all the work last night, and for being the reason we had to leave early, you get the front this afternoon."

"You're an ass, you know that?" An ass with a majority ownership of Sofa's, giving him leeway over business decisions. They'd all come to that agreement of who should be in charge before going into business together. A wise recommendation from their father.

Sadie cleaned up her workstation, washed and dried her hands, then snuck up behind her brother. She mussed his perfectly styled hair while he swore and tried to shrug her away. "Yeah, that's what you get, McBossy."

"Bitch," he snarled and patted down his hair.

"Whore."

"Wimp."

She raised a brow. As far as insults went, that was lame.

He blew out an exasperated breath. "Fine. You win. And you're still out front."

She flipped him off and left to help Emery, now that the majority of the afternoon prep had been done.

To say she enjoyed their crowded shop would be a lie, because in general she didn't like dealing with people. But she did like staying busy, and she served more than her share of lattes, espressos, and Americanos. She also dished up plenty of Sunday salads, critter cookies, and Boo-Baguette sandwiches. When they had a small break, she went out to clear tables and smiled at two cute little kids playing straw wars.

Sadie loved children. She always had, and as she watched their mother gently chastising them, then laughing at the faces they made, somewhere deep inside her, something mourned.

Sadie pretty much knew she'd never have them, never commit enough to any man to make a baby. She didn't want to raise a child by herself, and she'd never met a man she liked enough, or rather, who'd proven *trustworthy* enough, to father them.

Now depressed when before she'd been feeling good, she scrubbed harder. Needing to take her mind off her limitations, she sought refuge in cleaning. With the tables shining, she grabbed the cleaning bin from the storage room in back and tackled the bathrooms, which she normally left for the newer employees. But Emery was busy, and she needed the distraction.

It didn't take long before both the men's and ladies' rooms smelled lemony fresh and clean. Nothing worse than a food establishment with nasty restrooms.

Feeling a sense of accomplishment and never bothered by doing menial tasks for the greater good, Sadie cleaned up, inside and out. Refreshed, she managed to smile at her next customers. And as the day wound down, she planned to work in a trip to the gym to feel better.

Besides, Sunday nights at Jameson's were typically pretty empty.

She belatedly realized Elliot was out front chatting up someone with more enthusiasm than he normally had and glanced up from the food counter.

"Yo, S. I'm outta here." Emery slung his backpack over his shoulder. "See you tomorrow."

"Later, Emery." He left, swaggering past Elliot and his companion, then did a double take and backtracked. After a few words and a huge smile, Emery departed.

Sadie stared, curious. She didn't recognize the tall man with her brother, but a glance at thick black hair, broad shoulders, and big hands had her taking a second look. She was a sucker for big hands on a man. Weird but true.

She left the counter, seeing no one else around but the tall guy with her brother. As she drew closer, she noticed the big guy holding something.

At her approach, he turned his attention to her, and she was caught by his piercing gaze. Hazel eyes, neither green nor brown but an incredible mix of both, fringed by thick lashes, studied her from top to bottom. She'd seen those eyes before…

Then he smiled, and her racing heart plummeted to her feet. Holy crap, was this guy hot or what?

"Xena, I presume?" He handed her a sword. *Her sword.* "You left something behind last night."

"Just call me Cinderella." She accepted the prop and scrutinized him, minus the devil regalia and half mask. "Satan, is it really you?" she teased to cover her shock.

He laughed, and she recognized the husky timbre immediately.

"Sadie." Elliot huffed, though she caught his grin. "Sadie, this is Gear Blackstone. Gear, my sister, Sadie."

"Wait. Gear? That guy from the stupid motorcycle show?"

Gear sighed. "Yeah, that one. Surely you haven't forgotten me already?" The blistering look he shot her reminded her girlie parts all too easily how well she knew him.

So of course her gaze automatically went to his fly.

He chuckled, and she met his gaze, mortified. Sadie didn't do embarrassed often, so she had to give the guy props for being able to get to her. "Thanks for returning it," she mumbled.

Elliot watched her and Gear, his eyes narrowing. "You two know each other?"

"You could say that." Gear stuffed his hands in his pockets. Dear Lord, he filled out a pair of jeans to perfection. He wore biker boots and a faded Carhartt jacket over a Led Zeppelin tee. "I saw what happened. I talked to Joaquin, and he won't mention your name if asked. He was pissed he missed the fireworks. You are okay, aren't you?" He looked over her face.

"Just a slap. Didn't leave a mark at all."

"Good." Gear broke into a huge smile that warmed his eyes and jackhammered her heart. "It was incredible."

"So you're Gear. My devil." She had a difficult time processing the fact that Satan was in fact someone she'd once seen on TV.

"Your devil." His smug grin should have annoyed her. "And you're my Xena."

Elliot whipped his stare from Gear to her and back, as if watching a Ping-Pong tournament. "Your Xena?" he repeated.

She nodded, wary at the look on Gear's face.

He stepped into her personal space before she could blink and kissed the breath out of her.

"Hot damn, Sadie. That was fuckin' awesome." Gear burst into laughter. "You clocked her. I mean, that punch was straight-up beautiful." He turned to Elliot. "You should have seen it, man. Sahara was treating Sadie like shit, and Sadie didn't take it. No, she dished it out." His wide smile remained.

"You're Gear." She still couldn't wrap her mind

around the fact she'd slept with a reality star. Not that she cared about fame, but Devil had seemed so far away from *Motorcycle Madnezz*.

"Sorry. I wasn't trying to hide anything. I mean, I was. But I just wanted to be anonymous, away from people talking shit. I hadn't meant for…ah…" He paused, and they both turned to Elliot, who watched with his mouth agape. "Hey, man, can I talk to your sister for a minute?"

Elliot backed away, still not blinking. "Sure, sure. I'll be in the back cleaning up."

Once he'd left, Sadie turned back to Gear to see him staring at her. "What?"

"Ah. There's Xena. All attitude and tight fists." He reached out and cradled her hand in his, then straightened out her fingers and studied them.

Taken aback by the heat in the man's palm, and the crazy way her entire body seemed to want to lean in his direction, she had to clear her throat before speaking. "What are you doing?"

"Just lookin' at you." He squeezed her hand in his and let go. When he looked into her eyes, his own seemed to glow.

Jesus, I'm seeing things. He is not *the devil!* Sadie blinked and the glow was gone.

He frowned. "You okay?"

"Ah, yeah." *Just acting like a moron.* "Sorry, but you look so totally different without that lumberjack beard."

"Lumberjack?" He stroked his smooth chin, and she couldn't help but notice his square jaw and lean cheeks. The guy had a rough-meets-sexy-meets-fuckable look.

Sadie's skin had goose bumps, her nipples tightened into peaks, and heat blossomed between her legs. Damn. Talk about lethal.

"I can handle lumberjack. That's better than most of the names I've been called lately." He grimaced.

"Yeah, about that. You need to call out Sahara on those lies."

He shrugged. "What good would it do? You weren't sure of me until you overheard her, remember?"

"That's because you come across as a macho idiot."

He blinked. "I do?"

Sadie huffed. "Gear." She tested his name on her tongue and liked it. "You're hot when you're angry, but that doesn't show well on TV against a charmer like B-Man and an 'angel' like Sahara. Trust me, I know all about alienating people. And buddy, you have me beat, hands down."

"I know." He groaned. "It's a crappy situation. But it's over, thank God. Now I can get on with my life."

Doing what? she wanted to ask, but something kept her silent.

"So, ah, I just wanted to return your sword and let you know how much I loved that punch."

"Not half as much as I loved giving it." Sadie gave him her mean smile.

"Oh yeah. That's sexy."

She blinked in confusion. "Huh?"

"That inner bitch of yours. Hot. As. Fuck." His gravelly words destroyed her composure.

"Yeah?" She smiled at him, feeling…well…girlie.

"Yeah." He moved closer.

Something in the back clanged, and they sprang apart.

Sadie slapped a hand to her racing heart, so intent on Gear she'd forgotten all about Elliot.

"Ah, well, thanks for bringing the sword. Now Elliot will stop bitching at me about getting back the deposit."

Gear nodded, his gaze fastened to her face, her mouth in particular. When he met her eyes again, she recognized the same hunger that blossomed inside her. "Good." He coughed. "Not that you should be charged too much. That thing's a piece of crap."

"I know."

"Next time you need a costume, go to Fair of Dreams. They do quality work."

She nodded. "Okay."

They continued to stare at each other.

"Sadie, you ready?" Elliot called, now behind the counter, watching the two of them like a hawk. "Oh, you're still here, Gear? Sorry."

"No problem." Gear started to turn away, then stopped and asked her, "You want to go to dinner sometime?"

Sadie considered that idea and threw it out the window. "No way in hell."

Gear snorted. "I would have been okay with a simple no, but okay."

"I mean, no because you'll have paparazzi watching you, right?" She looked over his shoulder through the windows. "No one followed you here?"

He relaxed. "Oh. No. I think shaving off my beard has saved me. That and I took my brother's car instead of my bike. So, ah, if you want, we could eat at my place. Or yours."

Suddenly Sadie felt really, really hungry. "Just for dinner, right? Something casual. A one-off."

He frowned. "You need me to define this? It's just... dinner." *And hot sex* went unsaid.

"Just making myself clear. Because I'm not looking for a boyfriend."

His smile brightened the room. "Cool. After my disaster of an engagement, I don't want a girlfriend anytime soon either. But I do like to eat." He leaned closer and whispered, "And after last night, I'd love to eat you."

Her cheeks burned. She croaked, "Sounds good." Amazing. Incredible. Exciting.

"Yeah, good."

Elliot cleared his throat.

Gear didn't glance at him. He grabbed his phone from his back pocket and gave it to Sadie. "Gimme your number." At her look, he tacked on a rumbled *please*.

She chuckled and gave him her contact information. "Just follow the KISS principle, and I'm sure we'll get along just fine."

"Keep It Simple, Suckass?"

"Keep It Simple, Stupid, but yeah. I like your version better."

"Thank my dad. He's a real wordsmith."

She smiled. "Call or text. And if you don't, it's no biggie."

He quirked his lips. "Actually, it is a biggie. And I think you know I'm not lying."

"Shut up." She wanted to kiss him. Not punch, insult, or kick him to the curb. This man had that something she'd once found and lost long ago. He intrigued her. And God knew he turned her on. "Well, if you really intend to feed me, I like pizza, hot dogs, burgers, and beer. Not all together, but any of them work for me."

He just stared at her.

"What?"

"Nothing. I'll text you. I'd better go before your brother stares a hole through my head."

"Elliot," Sadie yelled. "Give me a minute. Sorry. He's a fan of the show. I think he might have cried when rumors started about *Motorcycle Madnezz* ending."

"What about you? Ever watched it?"

She hoped she wasn't insulting him, but Sadie believed in being honest. "Hell, no. I turned it on once or twice for the hot mechanics. But to watch simply for the bikes? Custom or not, boring. Sorry."

He chuckled. "Don't be. See you soon." He leaned in for a there-and-gone kiss and darted away.

"The Flash of kissing," she complained and put fingers to her lips to keep the sense of him there.

"You fucked Gear Blackstone, didn't you?" Elliot accused from right behind her.

She jumped and spun around. "Don't *do* that."

He stared at her, his eyes growing so wide it was almost comical. "Tell me something."

"What?"

She waited for him to lecture her about screwing around on company time, about putting a good face forward. About her responsibilities to Sofa's…

"What was it like?"

Her slow grin must have said enough, because Elliot followed her home and praised her up and down for being the best sister ever. An inspiration, even.

"I am Xena, Brother. Hear me roar."

———

Monday night, Iris stared at her brother, not sure what to make of him. Yesterday at family coffee, the irate, pigheaded, grumbling brother she'd come to expect since he'd become part of *Motorcycle Madnezz* hadn't been there. After watching that disaster of an interview at the Halloween party, she'd expected the family would need to do damage control to prevent him from ripping Brian's arms off.

Instead, Gear had sat calmly. He listened, he laughed, and he agreed with their father on too many issues to consider his attitude normal.

She glanced from him to Thor, who shrugged. She mouthed at him, "*Drugs?*"

"*Maybe*," he mouthed back.

"Gear, what is going on?" she asked, dying to know. "We saw that interview where they made you out to be the true villain of the piece."

"Justified, considering you had him go as the Joker." Thor huffed. "If you'd let him flex for the cameras in his Spartac-ass costume, he'd have public opinion on his side right now. Just sayin'."

"Quit calling it Spartac-ass," she snapped. "Gear, seriously. What's going on? And did you have anything to do with Sahara's attack?"

"*Alleged* attack," he said with a grin. "There were no witnesses."

"You didn't…?" Thor asked.

Gear's grin vanished. "Hell no. Much as I wanted to smack her, I'd never hit a girl. And I'd never get someone else to take her out either." At Iris's pointed look, he sighed. "Fine. Not girl, woman. But yeah, I saw it go down. It was a sight I'll take to my grave." He nodded, his smile back in place. "Not only did Sahara get socked in the face, but the chick who delivered it is hot as hell and mean as shit. Like, wet-dream hot."

"Ew." Sometimes Iris could use a little less of Gear's detailed descriptions.

Thor straightened. "Tell me more."

Iris fetched them bowls of simple spaghetti and wondered about this "hot-as-hell chick." Gear's taste in women had been questionable before, but dating Sahara had taken him down a dark path. Iris had never liked the gold digger, and the more she came to know of Sahara—and sadly, Brian—the more she regretted ever encouraging Gear to do that show.

"Not much to tell, really. After that awful interview, I circulated around the crowd as the Joker. It was weird. A lot of the guys didn't seem to mind me either way, but the women hated me. Anyhow, I took Iris's advice and changed into my devil costume. With the half mask and no beard, no one recognized me. It was great except for the drunk women groping me all over the place."

Thor sighed. "I knew I should have gone. Any men groping?"

"No, or I'd have pounded them into tomorrow," Gear growled.

"Too bad. Next time invite me to this Joaquin's. Sounds like it was fun."

Gear shrugged and stuffed his face full of noodles. After a moment, he continued. "It would have been a kick-ass party if not for the show crap. Anyway, I was looking for a place to chill and eat, and man, the food was awesome." He wore a goofy grin that alarmed her.

"Gear?"

"Right. Anyway, killer food, killer music, and then a killer right hook." He laughed again, sounding more carefree than he'd been in ages. "I found a place out of the way to kind of hide out and eat. Right next to this woman dressed as an Amazon. She looked good, I mean, real. Muscle on her, she was sexy, and she didn't come on to me or anything. Maybe because I wasn't Gear Blackstone, just the devil. But it felt good. We talked, made fun of the morons on the dance floor. Then we overheard Sahara and Brian admitting to setting me up. I have to tell you, it felt good. Finally someone else hearing the truth."

Thor nodded. "Vindication."

"Exactly."

Iris was more curious about this woman than every-thing else he'd said. Gear seemed almost…enamored.

"So where Sadie and I were, we were hidden from the crowd by a wall of bamboo trees. When Brian and Sahara came out, I darted away. Didn't want to deal with them, because if I had, I'd have ended Brian. I mean, *ended* him."

Iris believed it. Of her two brothers, Gear had a lot more in common with Otis than Thor did. And her father put the *bad* in badass.

"So what happened?" Thor asked, his dinner forgotten.

"Sahara being Sahara tried bitching out my friend. Turns out Sadie doesn't give a shit about *Madnezz* or Sahara. And when she told Sahara to stick her head up her ass, Sahara cursed her out, then slapped her."

"She *hit* your friend?" Iris asked, dumbfounded.

"Yep. A solid crack on her cheek. I'll be honest. I thought it was all for show. You know Sahara's full-on hissy mode?" At their nods, he added, "But it wasn't. Then it was too late. Sadie clocked her. Gave her a mother of a black eye." He sounded cheerful, and consumed food like he hadn't in months.

Thor watched him with a thoughtful expression. "So you watched sexy Wonder Woman—"

"She was dressed as Xena, though her name's actually Sadie."

"Xena hit Sahara. But she never knew who you were?" Thor asked.

"She didn't until yesterday. She left her sword behind, so I returned it." To Iris he said, "It was a piece of crap. Nothing like your stuff in the shop."

She preened a little. "What happened when she realized who you are? God, Gear. If she's found out, your name will be dragged through the mud even more. I just know people will think you put her up to it."

He gave her a dark grin. "Put her up to what? Like I said, no witnesses. And no one but Jim and Joaquin saw me in the devil costume."

"Sadie could tell. She'd get a ton of money if she went to the tabloids," Iris said.

Gear seemed to consider that, then shook his head. "Nah. Not her. I admit I messed up with Sahara. She had a great body and skills with… Well, never mind that. But I learned my lesson. Trust me. If anything, Sadie wants out of the limelight."

"How's that?" Thor frowned. "She knows who you

are. How can you be sure she won't tell all or just make up stuff like Sahara and Brian did?"

Gear shook his head. "Nope. I asked her out yesterday. She turned me down until I said we'd eat in."

"You asked her out?" *Are you insane?* Iris wanted to shake her brother, to get him to settle down away from the press and the mess his career had become. But Gear only did what Gear wanted to do. Not even Otis could get the dunderhead to listen if he didn't want to.

"I know what I'm doing. Besides, she doesn't want a relationship, and neither do I. What's wrong with me enjoying a woman's company for no other reason than fun?"

"Not a thing," Thor said over her spluttered protest. He shot her a look to keep quiet, so she did.

After Gear left an hour later, she turned to Thor and punched him in the arm.

"Ow. How is that enlightened behavior? That's not very positive, Iris."

"Shut up. How can you stand by and watch as he ruins his life all over again?"

Thor shrugged. "It's his life. And I don't think he's ruining anything. Look, the show is over for him. He knows that and still has to come to grips with what that means. Public sentiment is against him. As much as Gear has never cared what people think of him, it can't be easy to have strangers paint you as the villain all the time. If this woman makes him happy, who is she hurting?"

"Well, I don't trust her."

"Okay."

"And I'm going to make sure he doesn't get hurt again."

Thor sighed. "And just how will you do that?"

"I have my ways."

"Of course you do." After helping with the dishes, Thor hugged her goodbye.

Iris took out her favorite set of tarot cards, her own design. She did a reading for her brother, nonplussed at the results. So was he going to be blessed or cursed? Right now, the future didn't seem so certain. Change featured prominently in his future, something she already knew.

But one thing was for certain—Iris would move heaven and earth to keep her big brother's heart safe from being crushed. And heaven help anyone who stood in her way.

Chapter 5

WEDNESDAY NIGHT, GEAR WAITED FOR SADIE TO arrive, happier than he could say that she'd accepted his invitation. Astounded to find photographers outside his house in West Seattle, he'd arranged instead to meet at his parents' place in Ballard. He couldn't believe anyone considered him newsworthy. Even at the height of *Madnezz*, he'd thought people nuts for constantly commenting on what he wore to work or how long his beard had gotten. Who the hell cared? He created custom bikes for a living.

After he'd gotten used to the money from each episode, he hadn't minded the media attention so much. Paid sponsorships for clothing lines and his personal brand on a bike? Nice. Now, the only things he would take away from his time with *Madnezz*, courtesy of his expensive lawyer, were his paid-for house and his shares in the garage, provided the network settled on their last compromise. The garage, his designs, the clients—they would all belong to the network. And yeah, he was an asshole for signing his rights away and not getting a lawyer to oversee the initial contract. His own fault for listening to Otis that once.

"Lawyers are scum-sucking sacks, boy. You know what you want. Why pay some rich asshole to tell you what you already know?"

"Great advice, Dad," he mumbled. He'd put aside

some money for his future, for those rainy days when his finances took a hit.

It had been raining over his head for some time. He had a feeling he'd need to use up most of his savings to start anew, and that bugged the shit out of him. Why should Sahara and Brian use the foundation he'd laid to get rich while he had to walk away from his brand, his merchandise, hell, his fucking garage?

He'd miss the mechanics, Smoke most of all. But he'd be damned if he'd beg to stay or try to convince the guys he hadn't been lying and stealing from the show. If they didn't know his character after years of working side by side, they never would.

His mood started to sour, so he forced himself to relax and check the place out, something to occupy his mind until Sadie arrived.

He'd changed the sheets in the spare room he normally used when he stayed over. Condoms in the drawer, a few lit candles for the mood. His mother was a fanatic about cleanliness, living with Otis. So he understood how she'd gone off the deep end. He had no worries about cleaning up the rest of the house. With Otis and Orchid visiting distant cousins in Spokane for the week, he had the place to himself.

The place...and Sadie Liberato. Man. Talk about a hot piece of ass. Amused that she'd probably consider that a compliment and not some affront to womanhood, he figured to mention that to her after he got her naked. Because, just...damn. The woman was a work of art.

Gear didn't have a type when it came to women. Or maybe he did, because the last few he'd dated, even before Sahara, had wanted a man to take care of them.

He'd liked being the big, strong type. Until all the neediness had worn thin. But Sadie didn't seem to have a needy or meek bone in her body.

Shit. They'd fucked at a party where anyone could have come upon them. She hadn't been ashamed, sorry, or weird about it afterward. She guzzled beer, didn't sugarcoat her opinions, and openly admitted to a fondness for pizza and burgers.

He was half in love with her already, and that wasn't counting their intense physical connection. Because, *day-um*, just thinking about how hard she made him, how powerfully she could kiss, or how hot and tight her pussy had been had him ready to go right now.

He groaned and tried to relax, wishing he hadn't worn jeans because he could feel his zipper making an impression on his dick. He'd been in lust countless times in his life. He liked to fuck. But he didn't turn into walking wood from one encounter with a chick. Because every time he thought about Sadie, he first remembered her dark-green eyes looking mean. Then he recalled her snug fit around him, those long, muscular legs and tight biceps. The woman had tone, and he loved it.

Swearing under his breath, he tried to ease his jeans from his cock and wondered if he had time to jerk off before she arrived. So at least he'd look like less of a desperate fool with a constant hard-on.

The doorbell rang.

He counted to ten, thought about his mother, his father, Thor's foray into bisexuality. Then he thought about Sahara and Brian going at it in his own damn bed. And he lost his hard-on.

He answered the door. "Yo." *Real smooth, Gear.*

She frowned at him, and his erection returned full force. He swallowed a groan.

"I've been waiting here for like ten minutes."

"Try ten seconds."

"Yeah, well, let me in."

Charm was not her middle name. And he liked her all the more for it. He stepped back, and she walked past him. He caught a whiff of sugar and cherries.

"You smell good."

"I smell like bear claws, but yeah, I agree. I smell good." She grinned.

She'd kept her hair down long, the brown so dark it looked black. She'd worn little to no makeup, and her fresh look only enhanced her blatant sexuality. Sadie Liberato wasn't pretty, to tell the truth. But she was fascinating, intriguing, and more than attractive. Harsh yet soft, with a full mouth made for kissing. And with any luck, sucking.

He groaned.

"You okay?"

"Dirty thoughts, but they'll keep." He took her jacket, a bright-pink outdoors coat. "Pink?"

He caught her glancing at his crotch and saw her smirk. Not offended by his arousal—good.

"I like pink. I like brown and green too. And guess what else? I'm hungry. Where's the food? Or was that just an excuse to bend me over the couch and do me?"

He choked, not having expected that image to knock him for a loop, but why she should surprise him, he didn't know. Sadie was unlike most women he'd dated. Blunt and raw, she didn't seem to play games. Then again, Sahara hadn't seemed like such a deceitful witch at first either...

"You okay?" She sighed. "I'm being too me, aren't I?"

"Nope. Not yet, anyway." He smiled and took her by the arm, dragging her to the kitchen.

"Nice place."

He laughed. "That's kind of you. But it's not mine. The incense, altar, and Buddha statues belong to my mother. And you can put all the manly biker art and animal sculptures and paintings on my dad's shoulders. I'm a simple guy. My parents like clutter. It's clean, but it's busy."

"Ah, yeah, it is. But it's charming." She smiled, and he liked that she meant it.

"What would you like to drink?"

"I'll have water, actually."

"No beer?" He took one for himself after filling her glass.

She swallowed down half, then said, "It was hot in the kitchen today. Heater problem. We're calling in the furnace guys tomorrow. In the meantime, I got seriously dehydrated."

"You okay?" He frowned.

"Oh yeah. I try to make sure I get eight glasses a day. Otherwise I get burned out faster at the gym."

He leaned back against the kitchen counter and watched her. "You work out a lot, huh?"

"I like it. It keeps me sane."

"Keeps you looking amazing too." He gave her a thorough once-over and smiled.

"I do have a nice ass." She turned to show him, no embarrassment whatsoever. "My glutes are like rocks, thanks to a ton of squats." She turned back around and drained her water. "I like physical activity." She frowned. "That's pretty much all I do for fun, I guess. According to Elliot, I need to get a life."

"Yeah, I hear that from my brother and sister too. All I do is work. The gym is a close second, I guess."

"Sahara a third?"

"Yep. Or at least she was a third. What can I say? I love what I do. Did." Hell, there went his good mood.

"You can vent over dinner. Is that pizza I smell?" She batted her eyelashes at him, and that easily, he laughed.

"Supreme, minus the onions." He waggled his brows. "Can't be kissing you smelling like onions."

"Please, no. One thing I'm sensitive to is smells." She leaned in and sniffed at his collar, and his entire body tightened up. "You smell good."

"Yeah?" He cleared his throat, glad she stepped back so he didn't grab her, showing her he really was the Neanderthal he'd been accused of being. "What do I smell like?"

"Hmm. Soap, sandalwood, and a hint of lemon."

"Not bad. The soap had sandalwood. The lemon is from the lemonade that spilled over the counter earlier." He grabbed two plates and handed her one. "Pizza from my favorite place. Leo makes a killer pie."

"My father would agree. He's Italian on my grand-ma's side, Sicilian on my grandpa's. Me? I'm a half breed. My mom was a mutt. I think I even have some Scottish somewhere in my family tree."

"Don't look at me being a purebred." Gear took two slices for himself and motioned for her to join him at the kitchen table. He pushed the bowl of organic fruit aside, then plunked the pizza box in the center of the table and sat. "I'm Irish, German, Russian, Native American, and

Romani. Try saying *gypsy* to my mother and watch her throw a shit fit."

"Ah, more PC for you to deal with. How tragic."

"You don't sound sincere. I wonder why." He wolfed down his piece in seconds, surprised to find himself so hungry when he hadn't been able to eat all day, thinking about Sadie.

"Hey, I live unfiltered. Supposedly why I have *so many* friends." She didn't sound upset over her sarcasm, and her smile made everything inside him buzz with excitement. Which was nice but weird. He wanted to have sex with her in the worst way. But liking her this much, it was as if he wanted something more. Which she'd straight up told him she didn't want. And he certainly didn't, not after the mess with Sahara still a pain in his ass to deal with. He had to put that behind him and move on.

Nothing like the present. "I like unfiltered," he told her. "You're honest. I haven't had a lot of that lately."

"You picked the wrong friends."

"Tell me something I don't know."

"I would, but I'm trying to make a good impression. I don't get many of those."

"Ha." He grabbed another beer and refilled her water.

"Thanks." She sipped and watched him over the brim of her glass. "So what's the deal? How did you get bamboozled by your best friend?"

He finished his third slice, pleased to see her enjoying her second. "I've always been more into bikes than people. My dad's an ex-biker."

Her eyes widened. "Like from a gang? A Hells Angels type?"

"Yeah. He was a real thug before he met my mom. Otis and Orchid. The biker and the hippie chick. It's so weird that they work." Gear shook his head. "Anyway, my dad got me hooked on bikes and fixing things early on. I love making things work—mechanical things, I mean. I met Brian in elementary school. We weren't really friends until a few years later, when he started liking bikes, and girls. I never seemed to have a problem getting girls." Which still surprised him. He'd never had to try all that hard. Then again, look at who he'd attracted.

"I can see that. You have good bone structure, you're big, and you're sexy. Until you talk, that is."

"Thanks *so much*, Sadie."

She laughed. "Well, it's true."

"Pot calling kettle, hello."

"Hey, I make no bones about being antisocial. I just don't like people."

"Me neither." He smiled. "Anyway, back to Brian. He was always the more outgoing one. I could get chicks, but he made them want to stick around after fu— Ah, after we'd be together."

"You're not a good lay?"

"No." He blushed, feeling stupid. "I'm a *great* lay, and quit laughing at me."

"You are so red right now."

"Eat your pizza and shut up." That she did, her eyes sparkling, eased his worry he'd somehow offend her, the way he always seemed to offend women until they got to know him. "No, I'd fuck their brains out. Then they'd expect me to be as sensitive in real life as I am in the sack. In bed, I know how to please. Out of bed, I don't have time for games or pretty talk."

"Gotcha. I've been warned."

He glared at her, and she tried to hide a grin. "So Brian and I hung out. The girls stuck around because he's funny and fun and a bunch of things I'm not. The guys hung around because I talk bikes and parts and know my shit. And Brian would make it even better, organizing parties, setting up sessions where I'd show the guys how to fix stuff. Fast-forward several years. I have my own shop. Brian is a marketing wiz, and we remained friends.

"Brian convinces me to send in a taped segment of my own *Motorcycle Madnezz*. Sahara was my makeup and style person, then somehow became my girlfriend." Gear scratched his head. "Still not sure how that worked out. But I don't think I was what she really wanted. After a few years, we got engaged."

"Did she get you drunk and force the ring on her finger?"

"Maybe." He shrugged. "Brian was always talking her up. It was easier to say yes with her and him pressuring me to make a commitment to help ratings, to be honest." He pushed up his sleeve. "See this arm, the one that supposedly has a tattoo of Sahara?"

"No tattoo. Not like your other arm."

"She lied about me having one, so I had to have it applied before taping if I wore short sleeves. That's why I wore long sleeves all the time. Everything Sahara did was about the show. I just wanted to make bikes."

"Bummer." Sadie grabbed his beer and took a sip. "Thanks."

"Gee, have some." He snorted. "More pizza?"

"I'm stuffed. I can't believe you're having more."

"What? I'm a big guy. I need to eat."

"Not complaining. Go for it. Mind if I grab a beer?"

"Go ahead." When she sat again, he asked her, "So how is it you're single? You can say what you want, but a guy will go along with anything for a hot chick. And as blunt and mouthy as you are, there's no denying you're hot." He paused, knowing this was the time to insert his compliment. "In fact, you're one hot piece of ass."

Sadie gave him a slow smile. "You're not just saying that?"

He laughed. "Trust me. I think that, I don't say it. The one time I did, I got slapped. But I figure you like honesty, so there it is." She glowed, and he saw a hint of vulnerability he never would have associated with Sadie. His tough chick didn't seem to realize her value as an attractive woman. "Come on. You have to know you're sexy."

"To you, but then, you're weird."

"Hmm. Starting to see why you don't have that many dates."

"See?" She nodded, still smiling. "I'm confident in who I am and what I want. Women like Sahara have tried and failed to get me to feel bad about myself. I don't care if my arms make me seem manly, or the fact that I'm fine with a one-night stand somehow classifies me as a slut. I like sex. Problem is, it's tough to find great sex. But you..." She looked him over. "You rang my bell Saturday night. I'm curious to find out if that was just luck on your part or the fact it had been a while for me."

"Yeah, me too. I was wondering the same thing about you." He confessed, "I'd been on the outs with Sahara for a while. I mean, we argued all the time. But it was like four months ago that we were last together. Guess I should have clued in that not being with her didn't bother me at all, and her not bugging me for sex was a sign of something not right." He sighed. "So did I just ruin the mood talking about my ex? Told you I'm not good unless I'm between sheets."

"I'd say you were good up against a wall, so you can add that to your repertoire." She smiled. "I think it's time we went into your bedroom and found out. You game?"

―⁓―

Sadie liked Gear. A lot. He'd been blunt and real with her, and he seemed to like her being the same. Most guys wanted flattery, doe eyes, to feel like "the Man" with her. Gear just wanted honesty.

"Am I game?" He gave a harsh laugh, drained the rest of his beer, and stood. "Baby, I've been hard since you texted me back earlier. I keep thinking about Saturday. Hate to break it to you, but I don't normally bang a woman against a wall at a party. I'm not into public scenes."

She noticed he wasn't joking about being hard. A huge bulge distorted his jeans. "So, ah, the bedroom?"

He glared down at her.

"What did I say? You look angry."

"No, this is my sex face." He gave a menacing grin, and she grew immediately wet. "Here's the deal. I have a box full of condoms in the bedroom. You say no, we're done. I don't play around. You want it rough, you tell me you want it rough. I want to see you naked. I want to eat you out and swallow you down when you come.

And I don't think one time is going to be enough. You okay with that?"

She nodded, unable to speak. When Gear took charge, he *took charge*.

"Great. So you going to nurse that thing or what?"

She slammed the rest of her beer, wiped her lips with the back of her hand, and stood. "Let's go."

They walked down the hall to his room in silence, and Sadie felt as if she'd become a combatant in some weird game. Gear radiated intensity, and she felt a little discomfited. She'd been with men before. Hell, she'd been with Gear before. But he seemed so much bigger, so much...more...somehow, right now.

Once in his bedroom, he closed and locked the door behind him. "Sorry. Habit," he apologized. "I'm the oldest with two nosy siblings."

She understood that. She watched him light a few candles. "Nice."

"I can do romance. Sometimes." He winked at her, and everything was okay again. "Now strip, Xena. Let's see those weapons you were hiding Saturday night."

She chuckled. "I'd say you were the one with the big gun. Have to say, I was impressed. You filled me right up."

He groaned. "Quit talking before I come in my pants." So saying, he stripped off everything but his boxer briefs. And *wow*, was he a sight to see.

Gear had definition everywhere. Thick thighs, that sculpted V-shape from a muscular torso. His biceps were twice the size of hers, his forearms huge like his hands. This was a man who worked with his body for a living. She studied the tattoos on his left arm, from his wrist to his shoulder.

"Pretty."

He made a face. "Please. Not pretty. Sexy. Tough. Handsome. Pretty is for wimps. Now quit stalling and get naked."

"One thing I have to know. Are the condoms to prevent a baby or disease?"

He wiped a hand over his face. "Does it matter which if I'm wearing one? But to answer your question, I'm clean." He gave a mean grin that turned her on even more. "Always wore one with my ex too, because I wouldn't have put it past her to try for a kid to keep us together."

"You don't like kids?" She toed off her shoes and socks.

"I like 'em well enough. Plan to have some after I get married. But not before." He nodded at her. "Can you hurry up? I'm hurting over here." He palmed his erection. "I might implode if I don't get some relief."

"Why didn't you say so?" She whipped off her shirt and shucked out of her jeans. But when she started to unhook her bra, he shook his head.

"No." He stared at her, muttered under his breath, then stepped close. "If I'd known you were wearing that under your clothes, I totally would have eaten you before the pizza."

She smiled. Her decision to wear the red lace panties and bra set had panned out. Sadie liked the little luxuries when she could afford them. Expensive soaps. Truffles. And pretty lingerie. But other than that, she was a fairly plain person.

Fortunately, Gear liked both the plain and the luxury. So far, so good. The same excitement she'd felt for him on Saturday she totally felt right now. It wouldn't take much for her to climax, especially when he watched her like that, touched her like that.

His hot hands gripped her shoulders, but he held back from doing more than looking. "This has to last. You're not going home for a while."

"Put up or shut up."

He barked a laugh and looked her over some more. "So why ask about the condom? I'm wearing one, so that's good, right?"

"Well, if you had some problem other than not wanting to make a baby, I wouldn't want to go down on you, would I?"

He seemed to stop breathing. In a thick voice, he said, "We'll get to that later too, hmm?"

Then he kissed her, and her world spun, sparkles of color and feeling swirling behind her lids as she moaned and tried to press closer.

He controlled the kiss, the embrace, and *her* with his strength, which she found impossibly sexy. The kiss moved from her mouth to her cheek and then her neck. He sucked the spots that sent tingles throughout her body then zinged straight to her sex.

When Gear's chest grazed hers, she sucked in a breath, exquisitely sensitive.

"Oh yeah. You have great tits," he rumbled. "A kickin' ass, and that pussy. I gotta have some."

For a man not great at romance outside of bed, he said all the right things to Sadie. She didn't want pretty, not in bed. She wanted gritty, real desire. She leaned her head back when he sucked her throat and cupped her breast.

His thumb rode her nipple, and her arousal shot off the charts.

"Oh yeah, I need to suck these." His hand slid down her belly, and she blinked her eyes open to find him watching her. When his fingers slid beneath her panties and found her wet folds, the heat in his gaze set her on fire. "You feel like silk. So fuckin' hot. I'm still hungry, Sadie."

"Me too," she managed, stroking his firm shoulders.

He continued to watch her as his thick finger slid inside her. She closed her eyes.

"No, watch me."

She opened her eyes and saw his intensity as he started fingering her, thrusting that digit in and out. "I'm so wet," she admitted.

"I know. Jesus, you're fine." He kissed her again, this time fucking her mouth with his tongue while his finger made her hotter and hungrier for the rest of him.

Just as she teetered on an orgasm to end all orgasms, he pulled away.

She moaned and reached for him. "Don't stop."

"Don't move."

She froze at the harsh command.

Gear put his hands on her waist and slid her panties down, holding each foot so she could step out of them. He kissed her, right between her legs, and sighed, before continuing up along her belly. He stood and removed her bra, letting it slide down her arms slowly.

He shook his head, not saying anything. But then, he didn't have to. She read the approval on his face and in the tense body so close to her own. He palmed her breasts, kissed each nipple with a reverence that surprised her, then moved up to kiss her mouth. He pulled her body to his, and the press of skin to skin made her tremble as she returned his desire.

They were moaning and panting, touching each other everywhere. Sadie grazed his abdomen and sought the heat of him lower, clutching that thick rod through his underwear. He was wet and long and so damn thick.

"I want you," she said and pulled back to see his face. "Get naked, Gear."

His heavy-lidded eyes and raspy breath pleased her, as did his hand stilling her own, his grip powerful. "I take these off, I'll fuck you and come too quick. I want to take my time."

"I'm close to coming. Don't take too long," she whined—and hated herself for sounding so needy.

But Gear smiled. "Get on the bed."

She did, watching the shadows and candlelight filter over a face too brutal to be called classically handsome. Yet he compelled all the same. She wanted to lick him all over. And by the direction of his gaze, he had the same thought.

"Gear?"

"Time to eat, baby." He smacked his lips and gave a deep chuckle. "Now spread those pretty thighs wide and enjoy."

Chapter 6

GEAR COULDN'T BELIEVE HOW HARD HE WAS. OR HOW much he wanted to watch Sadie come. To hear her beg and plead, his name on her lips.

He saw nothing but loveliness as he stared at her. So long and lean, muscular yet soft under his roaming hands. She squirmed and tugged and ran her foot along his shoulder. Her low moans were music to his ears.

He wanted to suck and kiss every part of her. But that would have to wait. He removed his underwear finally, unable to stand having it against his skin. Then he settled between her legs and blew a breath over her pretty pussy.

She had a strip of dark hair over her sex, but her folds remained bare, slick from her cream, her clit full and ripe. Begging for a taste.

He spread her with his hands and blew another breath over her. She moaned and shifted, then arched up, so close to his face he could dart out his tongue to touch.

"Please," she begged. "I'm so close."

He answered with a kiss, and the taste of her went straight to his head. He took her clit between his teeth and gently bit down, overjoyed to hear her cry out his name. He licked and sucked, nothing but his mouth over her. And damn, she was wet. As excited to have him as he was to fuck her.

Thinking he should have put a condom over himself

before starting this, he could only hope he wouldn't embarrass himself and come before he could put himself inside her. He groaned and continued to tongue her, clutching her hips to keep her still while he lapped up the taste of ambrosia. Fuck, he could do this for hours. So damn good.

She clawed at his shoulders, humping his face, and he attacked with greater intensity. The amusing thought that the warrior woman underneath him would fight for her orgasm made him want to smile. And made him want to fuck the fight out of her.

"God, Gear. I'm coming. Right now," she moaned as he licked and put more pressure on her clit.

She cried out, a rush of honey coating his mouth, and he devoured her until she shuddered and pushed him away.

"Too much," she rasped, overcome.

He kissed her thighs, gave her a moment, then kissed her clit again. He had to lick her, to take her inside him once more, loving her scent, her taste.

When he finally raised himself to his hands and knees, he saw her dazed smile.

"I think I died." She flopped her arms back, bringing attention to her beautiful breasts. Perky, full, and just the right size for her frame, they demanded a few kisses of their own.

He crawled up her body, still not speaking, and gave her breasts the attention they deserved.

"Gear," she breathed, stroking his hair and making him crazy. His cock dragged along her belly, the greedy thing more than ready for some respite. "When are you going to fuck me?"

He pulled away, breathing hard, and managed a

"Now" without losing it. How, he had no idea. He'd never been so hard.

He sat up on his knees and saw her attention on his erection. With no time to waste, he dove into the drawer and fished out a condom.

"Wait."

He froze. If she said no after all she'd put him through, after tasting so damn good and being so incredibly responsive, he might cry.

"Let me." She scooted out from under him and took the condom. She had it in hand, then surprised him by lowering, belly down, on the bed.

"What—?"

"You need to get cleaned up first." She shocked him by licking the tip of his dick, then sucking the head.

His eyes rolled into the back of his head, and he gripped her hair to hold her still. But the damn witch used her tongue. "Stop before I come down your throat. *Stop*," he growled, desperate for relief but wanting his first time to be inside her.

She pulled away and smiled. "I'll be gentle. I promise." The mischievous look in her eyes had him laughing and swearing. She laughed with him and, true to her word, had the condom on quickly with minimal fussing.

She leaned close to kiss his lips, and he wondered if she liked tasting herself on his mouth. He thought it the sexiest thing to know she'd tasted his cock.

Without waiting another moment, he manhandled her onto her back and mounted her. "I'm not going to last."

"Don't. I didn't." She yanked him down for a kiss, her tongue making him insane. "Fuck me."

He couldn't wait a second longer. Especially knowing

how wet she was. He'd come to the end of his ability to hold back. Gear moved between her legs, stared into her eyes, and entered her with one deep, hard thrust.

She gasped and arched up, into him. "More."

He grunted and began fucking her. Nothing gentle or timid about it. He needed to give her what she'd been asking for. And it didn't take him long. He was harder than he'd ever been, so it made sense that his orgasm would be as intense.

"Coming," he warned, barely able to remember speech. "So hard." He groaned and growled as he fucked her, and then he was there. At heaven's gate, as he shoved one final time and spent. He jetted into that damn condom, unable to get deep enough inside her.

For a minute he saw nothing but black as pure bliss settled over him.

Then he was aware of her petting him, stroking his shoulders, his hair, while he inhaled her scent at the crook of her neck, bent over her, shuddering.

When he could function again, he pulled his head back and saw her smiling up at him. Something broken in him felt whole again. And he smiled back.

"Hi."

"Hi." He pushed her hair back. "I think I died too."

She laughed. "Died right inside me. You are so big." She sighed. "Man, I hit the jackpot."

"Me too." He kissed her, needing to pull out but loath to leave her. So he kissed her some more. She started to move under him in a way that told him she was ready for round two. "Hold on."

He left to dispose of the condom and returned, sliding on top of her once more.

But Sadie wasn't having it. She shoved him onto his back and straddled him. Not so stupid he couldn't see the advantage in this position, he let her run her hands over him while he stared up at the nicest breasts he'd ever seen.

"I know. Smaller than you're used to, huh?" She grinned.

She didn't seem fishing for a compliment, but he gave her one anyway. "Better than any I can remember." He cupped her, and she bit her lip, a soft moan escaping. "You are fuckin' amazing. I love your tits. Your pussy. Your mouth." His cock jerked, waking up again. "Give me a few minutes, and I'll be ready to go again."

"Oh goody. You're not a one-time wonder. No, make that a two-time wonder." She pinched his nipples, and his cock gave another twitch under her. Nestled against her slick pussy, he wouldn't have far to go before entering her.

"Ah, better put a condom on just in case."

She smiled and grabbed one. But instead of putting it on him, she moved aside and played with his dick. Stroking the semi-hard shaft, then grazing his balls. She cupped and petted him, and he watched her single-minded focus with pure pleasure.

"Have I told you how much I love your body?" She stroked him, small pumps that woke his dick right the hell up. "You're so hard all over."

"Mmm. You make me that way." Hell, he sounded like one of his mufflers, low and grumbly. But it was as if his vocal cords needed a restart.

"I mean, you obviously have muscle. But not too much. You're not a beefcake or gym flunkie." She snorted. "Those guys have to be compensating for something." She had yet to take her gaze from his cock. "But not you."

"Sadie…" He closed his eyes and bucked into the mouth over his dick. "I think you have an oral fixation," he said hoarsely. "Thank you, God."

She laughed around him, then started blowing him. When she stopped after getting him hard again, he swore.

She gave him one final kiss and pulled completely away. "Sorry. I was playing."

"Play some more."

"Well, I'm not as talented as you are. Because your mouth is just sinful." She sighed and lay next to him, still caressing his body while he lay like a lump, unable to do more than bask in her touch. "I thought maybe the first time was a fluke. I came really hard. But you proved it wasn't just a lucky night for me." She leaned over and sucked his nipple into a tight bud.

He'd had enough. He yanked her on top of him, her knees on either side of his head.

"Playtime's over."

"Well, how about we do some mutual kissing? That way we can save some condoms for later."

"Wow. Great minds really do think alike," he teased, staring up at her sexy, sexy body. "Hurry up and turn around, and be prepared to swallow a mouthful." He waited, tense, for her to disagree. But his girl didn't protest a bit. Instead, she took him down, *all the way* down, her expertise with oral something he'd one day write a poem about. And Gear didn't do poetry.

Then all thought left, and Gear did nothing but *her*.

Sadie was in a daze for the rest of the week. Everything reminded her of Gear. Elliot begged for details, but she'd only tell him Gear's shoe size did indeed fit the man. In all ways. To which Elliot had called her a lucky bitch and complained about rinky-dink Pierre. Rose wanted to know if Sadie was on drugs. Even the other employees had teased her about how nice she'd been acting to them and the customers.

Gear had texted her the day after, then called twice since Wednesday night. But Sadie didn't know what to do. That date had been to satisfy her curiosity, nothing more. He'd been amazing in the sack. He sure hadn't lied about that. But the clear affection, liking her for herself, and his unselfishness in bed and out threw her for a loop.

She'd answered his text briefly with a smiley face and a thank-you. But she hadn't returned his calls. He wanted to get together again.

She wanted the same thing, a lot more than she should. She hadn't been lying when she'd told him she didn't want a boyfriend. So why was her first thought upon waking about him, and her last thought in bed about sex with him? She wondered what he was doing, how his deal with the TV show had gone, wanted to call just to talk.

"Talk about what?" she muttered as she threw together ingredients for their Shrieking Snickerdoodles. Late Friday afternoon, the crowd had thinned, but she knew they'd be slammed this weekend. Green Lake had moved up their usual Halloween festival to the second weekend in October this year.

Pumpkin carving for the little ones, face painting, crafts, a hayride, and a hay bale maze. They did it up for the kids. Add to that the beautiful fall weather, sunny but crisp, and the orange, red, and yellow leaves falling. Like a freakin' postcard. The scent of apples and cinnamon filled the back room as they worked on a new cider recipe Elliot planned to unveil tomorrow. Sadie and Theo would work a tent at the festival, and she actually couldn't wait. It was no wonder Halloween was her favorite holiday, fall her favorite season.

Gear her favorite person.

"*Ack.* I have to quit thinking to myself."

"Um, isn't that counterproductive?" Rose asked, patting her slight belly as she watched Sadie with concern. "If you don't think to yourself, who do you think to?"

"Oh shut up, Pollyanna," Sadie said, not unkindly. She'd been calling Rose that since her sister's fourth birthday. "We can't all be married to the best guy on earth, having the best baby in the universe."

Rose smiled, her beauty a feminized version of Elliot's. She looked just like their mother—black hair, light-green eyes, beautiful with a petite frame that all but screamed *I'm gorgeous and fragile, want me from afar*. Sadie's sister was the ideal woman, in Sadie's opinion. What Sadie would never be. During her adolescence, she'd gone through a bitchy, jealous phase. But it hadn't lasted.

Sadie loved her sister too much to make her cry. And as the oldest, she'd had it drummed into her head to protect her younger siblings. After their mother passed, she'd been even more dedicated to helping them. She'd thoroughly vetted Joe before allowing him to marry Rose, even if Rose thought the engagement had been her and Joe's idea. And Elliot... Sadie had given up on his love life, at least until he showed some sign of being ready to commit. She'd thought Jason might finally be The One, until she'd caught him and Elliot fighting over the dumbest things and watched Jason play the martyr.

Um, no. Elliot deserved a straight (gay) shooter. She grinned openly.

"What? Are you still thinking to yourself?" Rose asked.

"I try not to think as much as is humanly possible."

"You're right about that," Elliot said as he joined them in the back. "So are you sticking around tonight, Rose?" They were late decorating the shop, and it was past time they Halloweenified—Sadie's word, thank you very much—Sofa's.

Sadie answered for her sister. "No. She's been on her feet too much and her back hurts." Before Rose could refute that, Sadie pointed out, "You rub your belly like that and frown when your back aches."

"Oh right," Elliot agreed. "Go home, slacker. We can decorate without you."

"No way." Rose frowned. "It's family tradition."

"Fine. But you have to sit down and not complain about everything I do wrong. Or I'll tell Joe you refuse to take time off," Sadie warned her. "He's a pain in the ass. He'll make you sit one out."

The mulish set to Rose's mouth told Sadie she'd won this round. She and Elliot high-fived.

"You're both so immature." Rose flounced out toward the front and yelled at Theo to move away from the register because she could "*count change while pregnant, by God.*"

Sadie shared a glance with Elliot. "A little snippy, isn't she?"

He nodded. "I get the impression Joe is coddling her too much. Why don't you talk to him about treating our sister like a woman?"

"Huh?" She grabbed the dough from the mixer and starting rolling cookie balls, then setting them on trays. Elliot joined her.

"Rose and Joe need a date night." At her blank look, he sighed. "To act like adults and do all the adult kissy things you and my secret boyfriend, Gear, have been doing."

Sadie flushed. "Oh. Well, I don't think they should do that. Might not be safe for the baby." Elliot's brows rose, and she snickered. "Secret boyfriend, huh? You wish."

"You're damn right. I can't believe you snagged the man." He quieted as they worked, then blurted, "So what's the deal? Are you dating, just shagging, or what?"

"Saying the word *shagging* does not make you an honorary Brit."

"I know," he said sadly. "At least I don't try to fake an accent. Pierre's was horrible."

"That didn't last long," she said of his relationship with Mr. *GQ*.

"It wasn't supposed to. And stop trying to change the subject. What's up with you and McHotPants Biker Guy?"

"I'd say that's a mouthful, but you'd just run with it." Sadie ignored Elliot's wide grin. "I don't know. We had a great time Wednesday night. He texted and called. He wants to go out again."

"Go out as in…?"

"You know. Bumpin' uglies."

"Which is all you want from a man, if I'm not mistaken." He seemed to be looking at her a little too intently. "Right?"

"Right." *Wrong. No, not wrong. He's just a great lay. With an awesome smile. A personality that totally meshed with mine. A—Stop it.*

"When are you seeing him again?"

"I don't know if I am." The disappointment that followed pissed her off.

Elliot wisely refrained from saying any more. Before long, the store closed. Rose went home to get Joe, an honorary Liberato by marrying into the family. Elliot and Sadie remained behind, tugging down the shades in the large windows to keep the shop's decorations a surprise. They even pulled the shade on the door, to mask what locals had come to claim was their favorite part of the holiday—Sofa's Spookville.

"So who are you seeing now?" she asked her brother.

"No one."

She feigned a heart attack. "Seriously? It's been at least *six days*. Shouldn't your boy parts be shriveling up from disuse?"

He flatly stared at her. "You know no one likes you."

She guffawed. "Poor little Elliot, all dressed up and no one to bone."

"Hey, at least I don't go around bitch-slapping people."

She shook her head. "Again, the insults. Just lame."

He groaned. "I know." He hid his face over his arms on the table. "I can't come up with anything clever around you lately. It's embarrassing."

She laughed at him. "Lightweight."

Someone knocked on the glass door.

Elliot sprang up as if powered by springs. "I'll get it." He raced to the door and let Gear inside.

Wait. *Gear?*

"Hey, man. How are you?" Elliot's secret crush asked.

"Great. How about you?" Behind Gear, Elliot looked at her and made kissy faces.

Asshole.

"I've been better. Been getting the cold shoulder from your sister." He gave her a sad face. "Way to make a guy feel bad about himself. Dodging me. Ignoring me. What? I didn't give you enough orgasms?"

She felt her face heat up and threaten to explode. Next to Gear, Elliot laughed so hard he cried.

"Awesome. You're invited here anytime. Want a cookie?"

Gear brightened. "Sure. What do you have?" He followed Elliot, passing right by her. He said nothing but gave her a pat on the butt, then continued to ignore her.

She watched in astonishment as he and Elliot chatted like old friends.

"Um, you know he has a secret crush on you, right?" she told Gear to embarrass her brother.

Gear nodded. "He told me. Can't fault the guy for good taste."

Elliot flipped her off.

"What are you doing here?" she asked, blunt as always.

"Elliot invited me to help decorate the place. Since Halloween's my favorite holiday, I had to say yes." He paused. "Plus my sister was bugging me to pick up my parents from the airport, so I needed an excuse to stay away."

"Seriously? You at an airport? Wouldn't that be like holding rancid meat out to hungry wolves?"

He frowned. "Wait. I'm rancid? More like prime rib, I'd think."

She sighed. "Answer the question."

"My sister isn't happy with me right now, so yeah, she's trying to dangle me like bait to click-happy photographers and fans. She also thinks I'll look like the good son doing favors for my family, and that if I'm shown in public more being friendly, it'll help my cred."

Elliot coughed. "No. You'll still manage to come off as a bigger asshole than you are."

"That's what I told her." Trust Gear not to be offended by the truth.

Damn it. She *liked* him. "Yeah, you're right. But this is—"

"Usually family decorating night," Elliot interrupted. "We're all big fans of Halloween. Used to decorate the house like crazy when we were kids and Mom was alive. So now we do the shop real big."

"Oh, I should go then if it's a family thing."

"Yes," she said at the same time Elliot said, "No, we're expanding tradition. Last year we let Joe help."

"Joe?" Gear's eyes narrowed on *her*.

"My sister's husband," Sadie growled. *Oh, Elliot. When I get my hands on you…* She knew exactly what her brother was up to. The meddling gigolo liked the idea of her and Gear hanging out and wanted to give the guy a chance. Was he nuts? Talk about a bad pick. Gear just broke up with his fiancée. He had relationship disaster written all over him. And the press wanted to rip him apart. *Yeah, perfect boyfriend material, Elliot.*

Not that Sadie was looking for a boyfriend. Though it would help if she stopped thinking about it every time Gear entered her mind's eye.

Gear frowned. "I don't know. Maybe I should go."

She started to nod when he added, "I think my being here is bothering Sadie. See, she's hooked on me, and I scare her, so—"

"What?" Sadie glared. That didn't sound like Gear. Then again, he liked to speak the truth. God, could he see what she'd been trying so hard to ignore?

"Yeah." Elliot sighed. "She's usually fearless, but when it comes to a guy she really likes, she has a tendency to—"

"You know what? Stay," she barked at Gear, feeling stupid and embarrassed—*again*—and not sure why excitement seemed to dominate her other emotions. "I would have talked to you, but I wasn't sure what to say on the phone." Okay, that sounded weak, even to her. "But I didn't invite you tonight because I thought my baby brother would throw a fit. We usually just have family. But this will be fun." She arched a brow at Elliot, pleased to see his frown.

"I really hate being referred to as a baby."

At the same time, she and Gear both said, "Ah." She turned to him.

"I use that same tone to annoy my brother and sister. You know, Elliot, you'd love my *baby* brother and *baby* sister. You all have so much in common."

"Dick," Elliot muttered.

Sadie couldn't help laughing. She and Gear did seem to have a lot in common. And then there was the sex…

"I'll get the cider," Elliot said. "We'll have it with the cookies while we celebrate." He went into the back, and soon his Halloween track started playing.

Sadie smiled, then locked gazes with Gear, and her smile froze while her heart did a tap dance inside her chest.

He wasted no time. Gear walked right up to her, dragged her into his arms, and kissed the breath out of her. "Such a pain in my ass," he growled. "Next time, pick up the damn phone."

She growled back, "Next time I will," and meant it.

Gear laughed and hugged her. "You crack me up. Now, angry woman, let's see these amazing decorations that even my sister knows about. I heard her mention Sofa's Spookville to my brother the other day but had no idea they meant you guys."

"When we bought the shop five years ago, it was right around Halloween. We made a major celebration out of it and decorated in a big way. The kids loved it, and so did all of our customers, so we decided to make that our big thing every year. We still make a big deal out of the winter holidays, and we sell a ton during Christmas and Hanukkah. It's always a toss-up between what sells most, Elliot's apricot rugelach or my gingerbread cats."

"Cats?"

"They fly better than reindeer, but they're harder to control. It's a long story."

"Ah, I'll take your word for it."

She grinned. "But Halloween is just fun. Monsters and sweets and decorations and costumes." She leaned closer to whisper, "And sex and brawls at parties."

He drew in a breath when she nipped his earlobe and in a low voice replied, "Unless you want me to fuck you right here, with your brother watching, I suggest you not do that again."

She felt invincible. Nothing like owning a powerful man with a nip to the ear. Then she wanted to brain herself for feeling anything because of a guy. When she'd gone head-over-heels in love with Adrian way back when, she'd thought a happily ever after was right around the corner. Then he'd screwed her over sideways for a shot at her then-friend Annette. But had Sadie learned? *Noooo*. Because five serious boyfriends and many years later, she still ended up with wackos and losers, her dinner-ditcher from a month ago a prime example.

Just because Gear rang her bell not once, but every time—a half dozen, to be exact, because yeah, she was keeping track—was no reason to think he was anything more than a friend with benefits. She gazed into his eyes and felt herself falling down the proverbial rabbit hole.

"What's that look? You seem guarded."

"Isn't that a big word for a motorcycle jockey?" she teased and stepped back.

He snorted. "Funny for a woman who's afraid of said jockey. Though I'm not averse to riding you. Ha. Okay, sorry, bad pun."

She grimaced. "That was worse than Elliot's lame comebacks. And I'm not afraid of you."

"Uh-huh. Keep telling yourself that. But if it makes you feel any better, I'm afraid of you too."

She blinked. "What?"

Elliot, the jerk, chose that moment to rejoin them. "You two done making goo-goo eyes at each other yet? It's a little bit disgusting. Unless, of course, Gear feels like taking off his shirt while gazing lovingly at you."

They both turned to stare at him.

"*Such* a little brother," Gear said with a sigh.

"Yeah, seriously annoying when he gets whiny."

"Hey." Elliot gave a mock glare, then laughed at

them. "You two are giving me the exact same 'I'm annoyed' look. It's funny."

Gear opened his mouth to retort, then froze. "Is that Oingo Boingo on the speakers? 'Dead Man's Party'? That's, like, my favorite song."

"It's, like, mine too," Sadie teased, except she really meant it. So weird that Gear happened to like the same things she did. And so suspicious.

Elliot read her glare and held up his hands in surrender. "Hey, I didn't coach him to say that. It's not my fault you two like the same lame music."

"I could give him a noogie for you," Gear offered. "Always works to piss off my brother."

"Hmm. That works on Elliot too. He hates for anyone to touch his perfect, perfect hair." They both stepped toward Elliot.

Joe and Rose chose that moment to enter from the back. "Hey, guys. We're here," her sister announced.

"Saved. Thank God." Elliot pretended to cry while he hid behind Joe, a mountain of a man with a sense of humor that enabled him to tolerate not only Elliot, but Sadie too. For that alone, she liked him. But he treated her sister like gold. So she loved him like a brother.

Introductions were made, and the shop took on new life, with orange, black, and purple all over the place.

Gear laughed at something Joe said, and Sadie felt herself spiraling in a storm of hope, anger, disbelief, and happiness.

"I am so screwed," she muttered as she drank her cider.

"Yeah? Well, so am I," Rose answered next to her. "I just learned earlier today that we're having twins."

Chapter 7

GEAR LOOKED OVER AT SADIE, WHO WAS HUGGING HER pregnant sister and laughing like a loon. What the hell?

Joe explained, "I think Rose told her we're having twins."

"Ah. Congrats."

"Thanks. But then, Sadie could be laughing for any number of reasons." Joe looked at Sadie fondly. "They're all a little wacky, but such a fun family."

"Wacky, huh?" Gear wouldn't call Sadie wacky. Sexy, angry, passionate, mean, lovely... Okay, not lovely in the conventional sense, but her personality happened to mesh with his perfectly. He hadn't been lying. The woman freaked him out.

"In a good way," Joe hurried to add. "She and Elliot made me run the gauntlet to prove I was good enough for Rose. They'd do anything for each other. And they're all really close. Hell, closer than my family. But that's another story." Joe sighed. The big, tall blond in the room, he didn't quite fit in with the Liberatos. But Gear did.

He was an idiot for comparing himself, he knew. Hell, Joe had *married* into the family. Gear was just a—what? A fuck buddy? A friend who gave Sadie sex? A mistaken hookup she was humoring until someone better came along?

"So I have to know, the show..." Joe started.

Gear groaned. "It's real. The drama with Sahara, B-Man being an asshole…all too true. It was supposed to be a show about bikes. Somehow, my ex turned it into a soap opera with hairy mechanics."

Joe laughed. "Funny. I almost didn't recognize you without the beard. How come B-Man never had one?"

"The fucker can't grow one," Gear said with relish.

"Ouch." Joe chuckled. "So I hate to ask, but you being here is too good to be true. Can I ask you a question about my bike?"

Motorcycles were in Gear's wheelhouse. "Sure." It would be a relief to talk about something close to his heart, something not confusing. Unlike Sadie.

When Elliot had responded to his text earlier, Gear had thought Sadie had finally answered him. Then Elliot had revealed who he was and why he'd answered instead of his sister.

She's scared of you because she likes you so much. Don't screw her over, or I'll end you. Oh, and come by the shop at 7. Be prepared to stay. Cookies on us.

Nothing more, but the message had given Gear a strange sense of hope. For Sadie to be scared of anything, that had to be a good sign. Right?

He tuned back in to Joe's question about not getting a good throttle response. "I already checked the carburetor tuning and engine tuning, and they're fine."

"How about the air filter and fuel filter? The spark plugs?"

Joe shrugged. "All good."

"Then check the acceleration cable. That one always gets overlooked."

"Oh, yeah, okay. I'll do that." Joe smiled. "Good call."

"It's an easy thing to forget, but rust can build inside the cable. And if that's still not the problem, check out the clutch plates. Otherwise, take it in."

"Hey, Mr. Boring," Sadie said as she joined them. "And I mean Gear, not you, Joe."

Joe smirked. "Thanks for clearing that up."

"This is a Halloween party." Sadie poked Gear in the chest. How pathetic was he that any part of her touching him felt good? "I appreciate you scaring the rest of us away with shop talk, trying to be all Halloweeny—"

"Is that a word?"

"—but it's time to get Spookville rolling."

Gear grinned at her. "Missed me, did you? Is Joe taking up too much of my time, Xena? Gonna fight him too?"

She shook her head. "That ego. It's too bad you didn't shave that off with your beard."

"Ouch." Joe stepped back. "She goes for blood, man. Be careful."

"Oh, I've seen her deliver. She packs a punch." He gave her a thumbs-up. "And I am still *so* damn impressed with that hit. Nice form, solid contact. I'd give you a ten, for sure." He laughed. "So where do you work out, anyway? I'm thinking of changing my gym membership since most of the garage works out there. Change of scenery is right up my alley."

Elliot cut in. "It's Jameson's Gym, here in Green Lake. Mac Jameson runs the place. It's an awesome spot. You can actually work out, or you can hit on the many fit, attractive people there."

"Don't listen to Elliot," Sadie cautioned. "He's already been warned by the management to stop breaking hearts. He's putting a real downer on the place."

"Hey, not my fault they can't keep up." Elliot eyed Gear up and down. "Once you go queer, hetero you'll fear."

"And won't go near," Rose added from the back counter, setting a tray of cookies down. "What do you think? I made that up myself."

Gear grimaced. "Such a…ah…poetic family."

Joe snorted. "You should see what Rose can do with a few thee's and thou's." He lowered his voice. "She took one too many Shakespeare classes in college, you ask me."

"Seriously," Sadie agreed.

Her sister joined them, and Gear noticed the obvious resemblance between the three, though Elliot and Rose could have been twins they looked so much alike. Both outwardly beautiful, while Sadie wasn't as refined. Not pretty or delicate, but real and tough and bendable.

Bendable? God, he needed to scrub his brain, the things that popped into it lately.

"What's wrong?" Sadie asked, frowning.

"I'm getting a low-sugar headache," he lied. "I'm sure some cookies and cider would help. Hint, hint."

"This is what you get when you let just anyone in the door, Elliot," Sadie lamented. "Weak help."

"Those spiderwebs look awesome. And maybe a bat or two," Gear prodded, drooling over the decorated cookies sitting too far away.

"Good choice. Sadie made the shortbreads. Elliot frosted them, though." Rose smiled and patted her rounded tummy. Joe gave her a kiss on the cheek, and Gear felt the couple's clear love for each other. It gave him a moment's pause, longing for that same connection he'd never thought to find. He glanced at Sadie, then away.

Joe and Rose moved to fetch the cookies and thermos of cider, and Sadie leaned closer to whisper, "I know. So in love it's sickening. But it's kind of sweet, in a diabetic overload kind of way."

"Yep. A real poetic family. You should write for Hallmark."

She grinned.

He chuckled, ate and drank, and did what he was told. Elliot used him as muscle, hauling boxes out of their large storeroom as well as Joe's truck.

It took a few hours, but when all was said and done, the place looked great. Strings of orange lights criss-crossed the exposed ceiling. The many glow-in-the-dark cobwebs had been strung over corners of the room. A skeleton named Stan sat with a life-size witch at a corner table, and the witch looked both cartoony and a little creepy. So real that, had he not known she was fake, Gear might have thought a real person sat with Stan.

Spookville happened to be the name of their haunted dollhouse, complete with eight creepy miniature rooms. A few werewolves, ghosts, and a vampire here and there chased doll children and adult action figures through the open rooms. They'd closed off the Victorian dollhouse in a huge clear-plastic box, and strobe lights timed with a soundtrack of lightning and thunder illuminated the house.

"That is just cool," he said when they'd finished. They'd had to clear two tables to make room for it, but the family seemed to think the loss of seating worth it.

Sadie looked more animated and excited than he'd ever seen her. "Isn't it great? I love that thing."

"She didn't love it as a little girl, though," Rose

informed him. "She'd use all our dolls and toys and have mock wars over who owned the house, who had started a fight, and who would karate chop who. My Barbie never lived through the night."

"Not when Boba Fett, a secret space ninja vampire, would suck her dry. *Mwa-ha-ha-ha*," Sadie added in an evil voice.

"Okay, now I'm scared."

Elliot laughed at that and slapped Gear on the back. "She's a real fan of Halloween. Which makes it so odd that she fought going to that party."

"It wasn't Halloween yet, and that party was all about schmoozing, not scaring people," Sadie said, defending herself.

Gear added, "I didn't want to go either."

Elliot nodded. "Yeah, but you had a good reason. Your betrayers were there."

"You know, I like the dramatic flair you've got. You ever think of acting, Elliot?" Man, his parents would love the guy. Gear could just see them putting Elliot front and center, a new knight of the Round Table during Renaissance Daze, their seasonal renaissance fair outside the city.

"I would be an awesome actor. Alas, I am too tired, slaving away all day while my lazy and pregnant sisters force me to work my fingers to the bone."

"That makes me sound like I'm pregnant…which I'm *not*." Sadie eyed her brother and sighed. "What Elliot actually means is he's a control freak who can't stand to let us handle things. No way he'd leave us to take acting classes."

Elliot perked up. "Quite right, sister dear."

"What did you put in the cider? You're acting weird."

He smiled. "It's called being in a good mood. Try it sometime, hag."

"Ass." Sadie chugged her cider, bit the head off a bat, then grabbed Gear by the arm. "I'm out of here. See you tomorrow, losers."

"Love you too, Big Sis," Rose yelled.

"Bye, Sadie. Bye, Gear!" Joe yelled with her.

Sadie tugged Gear with her out the front door.

"So, lot of love there, huh?" he teased.

"Oh, they're great. But they were eyeing you like a seal pup in a shark tank. It was about to get ugly."

"Great image you painted there." He had to laugh. "You guys are a riot."

"You say that now, but if we'd given it any longer, you'd be facing the inquisition. 'What are your intentions? Where do you see yourself in five years? What are your finances like? When are you two getting married?' Trust me. I've been there, done that."

"Yeah?"

"Well, it was a while ago. A few years, maybe, but it's always the same. I date a guy longer than a few weeks, he gets the spiel. With you it would have been sooner, because we never have anyone but family around for Halloween decorating." Her eyes narrowed. "What did Elliot do to get you here? Did he say anything?"

"Oh, something about paying me to babysit his hag of an older sister."

"*What?*"

He grabbed her flailing hands and put one in the crook of his arm. "It's cold. We can continue to chat in my car."

"Again with the car? For a hotshot motorcycle guy,

you should be wowing me with something better than a…Camry? For shame, Gear."

He laughed. It was hard not to when around the crazy woman. "It's my brother's. I told you. They're still camped out at my place."

"They—the press?"

"Yeah." He corralled her into the car and turned up the heat. "So your brother calls you a hag, and you haven't beaten him senseless yet? What's his secret?"

"He's a nag, but he means well." She sighed. "You had a good reason not to go to that party. But I was just bored. Bored about being bored. Sometimes I get too inside my head and don't want to do anything. Which is not to be confused with me liking my own space. I'm an introvert, so I've been told."

"Yeah? Me too." He finally started to thaw out. "Damn but it's cold out."

"You can say it. Colder than a witch's tit. One of my favorite expressions."

He tried not to, but when she said *tit*, he immediately remembered holding hers. Sucking hers. As usual, his body reacted.

"Tit, huh?" He glanced at her, heard her sudden intake of breath, and knew they were on the same page.

"Dirty mind."

"Yep. Always." He tapped the steering wheel. "You know, it's been a while for me. Two days, as a matter of fact. My balls are totally blue."

She tried to hide a grin. "Blue, huh? Well, my pussy's hungry. Let's say we go back to my place and fuck."

He blinked, not sure he'd heard what he thought he had until she laughed. And didn't stop laughing.

She caught her breath. "Sorry. You're too easy. I'm not usually that blunt. Well, not out loud. But I wanted to shock you. Did I?"

"Well, yeah, but in a good way. I'm on board."

"Ha. With what? My hungry pussy?"

"You keep saying it, and I'm gonna feed it. Meow."

They looked at each other before Sadie sighed. "I'd better stop talking before I turn our foreplay into something ugly and cheesy, huh?"

"Yeah. Let's just go have sex."

"Well, if I must." Her eyes sparkled.

Gear had a difficult time finding something not to like about her. "Your place okay?"

"Sounds perfect. And don't worry about my car, because I walk to work."

"In the dark?" He frowned. "That's not safe."

"It's Green Lake."

He followed the directions she gave him to her place, which was just a few minutes away. "It's Seattle. Don't be stupid."

He could almost *feel* her dander go up. "Oh?" she said a little too softly. "So you're calling me stupid?"

"Yeah, if you walk alone in the dark in this city. Even I don't go around by myself unless I have to. Every neighborhood has problems. Hell, my brother nearly got mugged in Ballard last week."

Her ire faded. "Seriously?"

"Well, it was my sister who assaulted him, we later found out. But that woman is scary when she's on her period."

Sadie just stared at him before a grin creased her lips. "You are such a prick. No wonder we get along."

He nodded. "Great minds think alike."

She agreed. "So can I ask you something?"

"Sure." They parked and got out, and he walked with her into her building and up to her floor. She didn't say anything else until they entered her apartment.

"So this thing between us. It's still casual, right?"

He watched her lock the door, then face him with an unnaturally calm pose. He could tell she was nowhere near calm because she tapped her foot, and her breathing seemed a little fast.

"Casual, just the way you want it," he agreed.

But she didn't look satisfied.

Join the club, hot stuff. He had no idea what to make of her. Gear wasn't looking for a new fiancée, girlfriend, or flavor of the month. Yet Sadie felt like all three combined, and it was odd.

What made her even more compatible was that she seemed as uncomfortable about getting close as he was. Every argument she threw up was one he'd already used. It made dealing with her both easy and challenging, and he looked forward to seeing her again the moment they parted.

Something to think about at another time, though. Right now he had a woman to make love to. Or fuck. Lady's choice.

He waited for her to say or do something.

She watched him, unmoving.

"Well?" he asked. "Is this where we draw guns or what? Come over here, and have your wicked way with me."

"You sure do like to boss me around."

"And you like it." He gave her a mean smile, heard her swallow, and knew he'd lost the game before they even made the rules. "I bet you ten bucks you're wet right now."

She lifted her chin. "I'll take that bet and raise you another ten that you're hard right now."

"Like that's a big leap. Baby, I was hard ten seconds after seeing you flaunt your ass at Sofa's."

"Flaunt my ass?" She smiled. "More like gently waving it before you. So glad you noticed."

"Yeah, yeah. Now come over here and blow me."

Her smile widened, and true joy shone from her eyes. "I love the way you talk. You're so lyrical."

"Poetic, just like your talented family." The moment she got within reach, he dragged her close and started kissing his way down her neck. "Hard and fast, or slow and thorough?"

"Hard and fast," she rasped, yanking him down by the hair and kissing him, giving him enough tongue to make him regret giving her a choice.

"Fuck. Fine." He palmed her ass, grinding her against him. "Take off your pants and bend over the couch."

"Right now?"

"No, tomorrow." He rolled his eyes. "I'll get the house tour later. Go to the couch, Sadie."

She raced over and got rid of everything from the waist down. Man, she had a nice ass. So round and tight.

He bit back a groan, walked over to her, and took his pants and underwear down to his thighs.

"Condom?" she asked, her voice low, thick.

"Always." He already had one halfway down his cock. "This is gonna be fast. Touch yourself while I fuck you. Let's see who can come first."

"I say me," she breathed and started fingering herself.

He wished he could take a picture, yet knew she'd slap him if he tried. But God, Sadie Liberato, bent over with that fine ass… He was ready to bust from just looking at her.

Nudging her ankles wider, he warned, "I'm coming in." Then he was there, right at the heat of her sex and thrusting. The position made her unbearably tight, and he had to fight not to come *too* soon.

"You're too big," she moaned.

"Want me to pull out?" he said between breaths.

"God no. Fuck me."

"You got it." He pulled nearly all the way out, then slammed back inside her.

She made the best sex sounds, all breathy and moany, right there with him as he took her. The sounds of rasping and the slap of flesh were all to be heard as they rose on the climb toward orgasm.

"Fuck. I'm coming." He jetted inside her a moment before she squeezed him tight.

"Yes," she hissed, rocking back into him.

He saw stars as he moved inside her, committed to giving her everything he had. Feeling primitive and raw, he withdrew, took the condom off, and gave serious—crazy—thought to shoving inside her, bare. Just to know what she'd feel like with nothing between them.

"What are you doing?" she asked, still trying to catch her breath.

"Tring to remember my name," he quipped. "Where can I toss this?" he asked while straightening back up.

She waved toward the kitchen, and he found a trash can under her sink. The place was small but tidy and had a clean, uncluttered Sadie look to it. Spartan. Hell, even her house suited him.

She joined him in the kitchen, half naked and apparently not bothered by it. With her body, she had nothing to worry about. But still…

"You aren't modest at all, are you?"

"Not with you. Why? Should I cover up?"

He tried to stop staring at her toned thighs and gorgeous pussy, but he couldn't. "You have the best body I've ever seen. And I'll be honest. I've seen a lot."

"Flatterer." She sauntered into her living room, then wrapped herself in a blanket before flopping onto…

"That is one fugly couch."

"Thanks. It reminds me of my mother, whom I lost at a young age. It's one of the only things I have left of her."

He felt like shit. "Hell. I'm sorry."

"You should be. For all you know, that was a true story."

He narrowed his eyes at her. "Is it?"

"Hell no. My mother had better taste than this." She snorted. "But you should never judge a girl's furniture."

He just stared at her.

"What?"

"Move over."

"Shouldn't you be leaving? You know, a fast hump and dump?"

He grabbed the TV remote from her hand, lifted her up, and settled her on his lap while he flicked through channels.

"Hey. That's mine."

"I'm a guest." He batted her grabby hands away.

"Well, you can't stay late. I have to be up early

tomorrow to set up for the festival." She told him about Sofa's stand, where they'd be selling hot cider and goodies.

"Are you there all day? I'd call and ask you about it tomorrow, but we both know you never answer your phone."

"Shut up about that already." He'd swear she sounded embarrassed. "I said I'd talk to you the next time you called."

"Gosh, Sadie. I'm the luckiest man on earth," he said in his best Lassie's-the-best-dog-in-the-world voice.

She shook with laughter, then yawned.

"Ah, I win. I outlasted the mean chick."

"We're playing a game?" she asked.

One where I win the girl if I'm careful. Oh shit. Do I want to win the girl? Then Sadie kissed the underside of his chin and snuggled close. Sugar and cherries hit him hard.

"No games, Sadie. I'm not good at playing them."

"Me neither. I'm a lightweight. It's sad."

He smiled and rested his chin on top of her head. "I wouldn't call you a lightweight. More like welterweight. Maybe light middleweight."

She chuckled. "You're a funny guy."

"Don't sound so surprised." He kissed the top of her head.

"Mmm. I like that. You're warm." After a pause, she rubbed his pecs, and his heart gave a strangled leap. "If you're free tomorrow, you should stop by. I'll give you free cider."

"Well, for free cider, I might have to."

She nodded, her breath warm against his chest. A few

moments passed, her breathing growing deeper, more even. "Gear?"

"Yeah, honey?"

"Am I boring?"

He frowned. "You? Boring? You're the least boring person I know. Scary, cantankerous—and yes, I know what that means. I do read, you know. Oh, and obnoxious. But boring? Hell no."

He felt her smile against his chest. "Good. You aren't either. And I'm glad Sahara cheated on you."

The hurt he felt surprised him, mostly because he hadn't expected Sadie to be cruel.

"Because you deserve so much better than her."

He relaxed, stunned to go from feeling high to low and back to high again. "Boring, Sadie? You? Never." He stroked her hair, loving that she left it long, out of a ponytail.

She fell asleep in his arms, and he wondered how he could feel such bone-deep contentment with a woman he'd met only a week ago. A woman he didn't want to leave, even though he knew it would be best for both of them in the long run.

But Gear had never been all that smart. So he carried her into her bedroom and tucked her in. The soft-blue room needed further exploring, but not now. He kissed her goodbye, fit her into a compartment in his brain, and his heart, and left, locking up as he walked out.

Once at home and in bed, he set his alarm for ten. He had things to do in the morning. And people to see. One dark-haired siren in particular.

Chapter 8

SADIE WOKE UP REFRESHED, SEXUALLY REPLETE, AND looking forward to the festival. Not just because she loved Halloween, but because she'd invited Gear to swing by, and she had a feeling he'd show.

She sighed as she and Theo set up their stand under an overhead tent. The weather, fortunately, shone bright and crisp. Even if it had rained, she knew she'd have been smiling.

How could she be so wrapped up in a man clearly wrong for her? Not like she had a *right* guy in mind, but Gear had so many issues. One of which was *a lack of reciprocity when it came to emotional connection*. That was the phrase her shrink of a cousin liked to use on her when nagging about Sadie's exes. It wasn't as if Sadie sought men she couldn't bond with. She'd tried not to. But the majority of them had been perfect on the outside and empty within.

Unlike Gear. The ex-TV star seemed as far from the glamorous life as could be. He didn't put on airs. Didn't act better than her or her family. And he had been so sweet last night. After that earth-shattering climax, she'd expected him to leave. It was just about sex, after all.

Except it wasn't.

He'd stayed, kissing the top of her head, holding her close, making her feel protected. She should hate him for that. Adrian had been protective, a real presence in her life. And he'd hurt her. Badly. Yet unlike Adrian, Gear hadn't done anything to advance his cause. He'd already had her. She was already impressed. And she had a feeling he'd assumed she'd been asleep when she'd played possum in his arms, listening to his calming heartbeat.

He'd been so tender tucking her in, kissing her again, sighing before he left.

What did that mean? Did he *like*-like her? Or was he stymied, trying to find the words to break it off because he sensed how much she was trying *not* to like him? For all that he acted like an asshole in public, she sensed in him a genuinely nice guy.

Oh God. If he was trying to find a nice way to break it off with her, that would be terrible. She'd rather he just dumped her ass.

"You're too quiet. What's up?" Theo asked.

"Nice. Good morning to you too."

"Look, I had to deal with Hope moping around this morning while her boy toy is in Portland at some conference. And that after being bitched out by my mother for upsetting my father about something I did. I'm supposed to think about my actions. But I don't know what the hell she's talking about."

"So ask her."

"What? And admit I'm insensitive as well as clueless? No thanks."

"Ah, to be twenty-one again."

"Can you remember that far back?" He grinned, and she could already see this one breaking hearts. Like his older brothers, the Donnigans who'd given those amazing self-defense classes at Jameson's Gym, Theo had looks and a killer smile. His oldest brother, Landon, had managed to snag her cousin, a feat in itself. Ava analyzed everything to death, but Landon had turned her brain off enough to get her to say yes to an upcoming I Do.

Gavin, the other Donnigan heartthrob, had a body Sadie truly envied. Had she not met Gear, and had Gavin not already hooked up with someone on a more permanent basis, she'd have tried him on for size. Man, could that guy run like a gazelle. She coveted his workouts.

"And then there is Theo, the youngest of the bunch," she said out loud.

"Is this where you do that weird dialoging—"

"A gem in the rough. A young man about to embark on a life-changing journey in the United States Marine Corps. A man with a hankering for an older woman, a seductress to show him the ways of love."

Theo blushed. "Sadie."

"But alas, Sadie is already taken by a man, the envy of all men."

"Here we go."

"A devil in disguise, who worships the ground she walks on. And poor, poor Theo can only watch from afar."

He stared at her. "Did you work on that all night or what?"

"No." She grinned. "Totally spontaneous. Did you like it?"

"Are you on drugs?"

She laughed, in a terrific mood despite her confusion about Gear. "Dude, the sun is shining. It's getting close to Halloween, and I got some action. More than once, even. Life is good."

Theo grinned with her. "Lucky you."

"Don't worry. Someday puberty will catch up with you, and you'll figure out how all your equipment works."

"This is why Elliot refused to work with you in here."

"Exactly. He's scared. Not you, Theo. You're much braver than he is. Braver than Landon was, too. You should have seen how my cousin terrified him when they were dating."

Theo leaned in. "Tell me more."

She filled him in on a few instances she'd witnessed when Ava and Landon had started dating, and he laughed, filing away the information as only a younger brother could.

They began serving cider not two minutes after the festival started. The day progressed from there. Sadie dealt with chattering children, adults annoyed at the long lines, and other people just happy to be alive. She felt it her duty to add to the festive air and got her face painted at the booth next door in exchange for free cookies and drinks.

Now she wore a skull on half of her face, and it was majorly creepy with her hair pulled back into a chaotic ponytail, with fake spiders and cobwebs hanging off her hair.

"That is so unhygienic. I get one spider in my cider, and I'm suing."

She recognized the deep grumble and felt herself blossoming into a smiling fool. She took a moment to compose herself, forcing a sneer. When she glanced up at her latest customer, she saw Gear wearing a cowboy hat and a bandana tied around his neck, a pair of dark glasses covering his gorgeous hazel eyes.

"Sue me, and I'll strike back. I'm known to have a lethal one-two combination." She fake punched him.

He laughed and yanked the man behind him so that they stood abreast. "Sadie, this is my baby brother, Thorvald. Thorvald, this is Sadie."

His brother sighed. He looked enough like Gear around the eyes to proclaim them related. "It's Thor. Hi, Sadie, nice to meet you." He held out a hand, larger than hers but more refined than Gear's. She shook it, noticing that he didn't have Gear's rough knuckles or calluses either.

"Hi. This is Theo, my partner today." She glanced at Theo, who nodded at them and took care of the next customer in line. "So, you two slumming?"

Gear chuckled. "Why do you think we came here first? Love the face, by the way. It's so you. So very... deathlike."

"Well, the cowboy getup ain't you." Before he could ask, she fetched cider for him and his brother and handed him a festive prewrapped bag of cookies she'd put together that morning. "Come talk to me while I work." She nodded for them to join her in the tent.

The costume parade started, and the crowd in front of her cleared out fast, giving her some breathing room.

"I'm going to get more supplies while I can," Theo said.

"Good idea."

He grabbed the store tricycle, which had a large basket in the back, and rode off to Sofa's, a short distance away.

"So," she said to the men guzzling their hot drinks, "how's it going?"

Thor answered, "We got here half an hour ago. It took that long to find you. There are a lot of people here."

Gear chuckled. "My brother's a scientist. He's right now, no doubt, doing the math and trying to figure out how many people can actually fit in the square footage of the festival's area. For fun."

Thor grinned. "I'd tell you, but then I'd have to kill you. It's a lot, that's all I can say."

Sadie liked him on sight. Thor looked to be a few years younger than Gear. He had the same dark hair, but a rangy build, and stood a few inches shorter than his brother. Like Gear, he had hazel eyes, but his seemed softer, not as intense. She recognized in him a calm gentleness missing in Gear.

"You eyeing my brother for some reason?" Gear asked, his voice deep.

"Just wondering how you two can be related. He seems so smart, relaxed, and, well, nice."

Thor grinned. "Oh, I like her."

Gear broke open the bag of cookies and shoved one in Thor's mouth. "Shut up and eat." He turned to Sadie. "So I was thinking if you're not busy later, maybe we could hang out."

"Hmm."

"What? It's easy. Yes or no?"

"I'm thinking."

"Don't hurt yourself."

Thor choked on laughter.

Gear pounded him on the back.

"Jesus, Gear. Try not to kill your brother. Here, Thor. Have some water." She handed him a water bottle.

"Thanks," he rasped. "Ah. That cookie was awesome. Snickerdoodle, right? Orchid sometimes makes those."

"Who's Orchid?"

"Our mom," Thor and Gear said together.

"You call your mom by her first name?"

Gear nodded. "Yeah, Otis too. Our dad. Our parents are... How should I put this?"

"Crazy. And not just crazy in love," Thor added. "But, like, full-on wacko. But hey, it works for them, and we didn't turn out too badly." He eyed his brother. "Well, Iris and I are stable."

Gear pinched the bridge of his nose, pushing up his glasses. "Look, just ask her."

"Ask me what?" Sadie looked from Gear to Thor, waiting.

Thor cleared his throat. "Well, my brother was telling me how great your food was from that party. And these cookies are divine."

Gear snorted. "*Divine*. Can't take the professor out in public, can I?"

Thor ignored him. "Just amazing."

"Thanks." Sadie beamed. "One thing we do right at Sofa's—and that's bake."

"So I have a faculty party coming up, and some idiot put me in charge of handling the food. Do you think we could talk about you catering for us?"

She nodded. "Sure. I'll get you some quotes if you can tell me what you're looking for. Cookies and cupcakes, or appetizers, or a sit-down lunch, and for how many."

"Wait, cupcakes?" Gear took his glasses off, and she liked being able to see his eyes. "I haven't tried your cupcakes yet."

The ringing of a bike bell signaled Theo had returned. But Elliot stepped through the back instead.

"Elliot, did you bring any cupcakes?"

"As a matter of fact, I did." He grinned, looked over her guests, and raised a brow.

"Elliot, you know Gear. This is his brother, Thorv—"

"Just Thor. Nice to meet you." Thor held out a hand.

Elliot took it, and the pair blinked at each other before quickly pulling away.

She looked at Gear to see if he'd witnessed the weirdness, but he seemed too fixated on her breasts to notice.

She cleared her throat.

He glanced up without an iota of shame and gave her a wide grin. "I was looking for more spiders."

"Uh-huh. So Elliot, Thor might want to hire us to cater a party. You want to set him up with the deets?"

"Sure." Elliot's smile looked a little too forced, and she would have asked him what was wrong, but the sound of rushing voices drew her attention.

"Shit." Gear sighed. "Why today of all days?"

———

A dozen photographers and a few people with recorders rushed the tent. "Gear, can you tell us what brought you out here today?"

"Are you now selling food?"

"Can you put any truth to the rumor that Sahara is having B-Man's twins?"

"When will you come back to the show?"

"Do you consider this a major failure on your part, your inability to hold on to the company you started? B-Man told us it's official. You're no longer a member of the Motorcycle Madnezz team."

"Is this your mistress?" One of the female reporters smirked. As if to say, you can do so much better.

Gear could see Sadie's temper growing, her face turning red. He sensed his brother slipping out the back, as Gear had ordered him to do should they get sidelined by press. A good thing. Gear tried to keep his family out of the media as best he could. No sense in Thor getting targeted because he stood too close to Gear. Now if only he could do the same for Sadie and Elliot.

Before Gear could stop her, Sadie took a step forward. "None of you want to hear it, but the truth is that B-Man was plowing Sahara for months while tossing Gear's reputation down the toilet."

The crowd erupted into more questions and shutter clicks. Gear groaned. "Guys, gimme a break. I'm here talking to friends, trying to enjoy the Halloween Festival. Sofa's was nice enough to give me some cookies and cider. Try some. They're better than anything you'll eat here."

"So you're now part owner of Sofa's?" someone asked.

"The hell he is," Sadie argued. "You people are not only stupid, you're sad. You're also standing in the way of my paying customers." She turned to the woman who'd asked the mistress question. "And lady, who the hell uses the term *mistress* anymore? How old are you, anyway?"

A few of the other reporters snickered. The woman didn't look amused. At all.

"So you admit you're sleeping together?"

"Do you admit you're about as clever as a clapping toy monkey? I'm selling cookies. And cupcakes. Oh, and spiced cider. Chick, you have no idea who you're dealing with. Gear, schmere. Today is about Halloween and Sofa's Spookville."

A few locals seemed to recognize the name.

"We put on a spread every Halloween."

Had Gear been worried Sadie wouldn't be able to hold her own? Man, was he wrong.

He took a step back, and everyone focused on him again. *Hell.* "Look, I'm interrupting business. You can bug the shit out of me out there as well as you can in here." He left the tent.

Most of the crowd went with him. Unfortunately, a few of the more aggressive types stayed near Sadie. Gear refused to answer anything more than the bare minimum, legally under a gag order, which sucked so much ass. He told them he'd left the show, had nothing to do with Sofa's with the exception of enjoying their food, and that Sahara and B-Man deserved each other. Which set off more questions.

And that's when all hell broke loose.

He gaped as two of the reporters in front of Sadie's tent stood drenched in water. A few ice cubes littered the ground near them. Make that drenched in *ice* water.

"How dare you?" the mistress questioner yelled. "You assaulted us!"

"With water? Give me a break. Hey, I told you to move."

"Three times," Elliot added.

Sadie continued, "We have to keep the milk cold, you know? And that ice was melting. We can't serve bad milk to customers, or we'll get in trouble. We normally dump the water where you're standing. It's not my fault you two refused to get out of the way."

"You throw water where customers would be standing, you stupid bitch?" the nasty female reporter screamed.

"Lady, there are kids around." Sadie frowned. "Keep it clean, would ya?" She smiled and waved at a group of people gaping at the spectacle nearby while the reporters around Gear started focusing on the real story—bitchy Marsha Concannon getting the tables turned on her.

Sadie waved at the crowd. "Who wants bat cookies? Devil's food cupcakes? Ooo, who wants to see a real witch? She's right here!"

Gear couldn't help chuckling as he walked quickly away, forcing the others to walk with him or lose a shot of him. He made it to his bike, confident Thor would find another way home. Then he hightailed it back to his place, wondering how the press would spin things.

That evening at home, he found out.

———◦◦◦———

Thor sat next to him, both of them basking outside in Gear's in-ground hot tub. Sadie had supposedly been too busy to meet that night. Gear still thought he scared her. But after seeing the hatchet job the news had done, he worried he might have scared her away for good.

"Oh hell."

Thor turned up the volume on the tablet that he refused to leave inside. He had the thing propped up on a lap table right next to the tub. "This isn't good."

The woman Sadie had iced—Marsha Concannon, a real asshole, in Gear's opinion—was ripping Sadie a new one. "Gear's angry new mistress—I'm sorry, his angry *friend*—got violent today when approached about their relationship. She also had some very unflattering things to say about B-Man and Sahara. I'm sensing some jealousy issues." Marsha tittered. "But then, who wouldn't?" They flashed a picture of Sahara at her best, side by side with Sadie's painted face, cobwebbed hair, and angry snarl.

"That has to hurt," Thor noted. "I feel for you. But hey, if you want to see where this goes with her, she'll have to get used to stuff like this."

"Why? I'm leaving the spotlight, Bro. No more TV. I'm done with all that."

"You wish. It's going to take time to wind down, no matter how much you want to sweep it all away." Thor turned off his tablet and slunk back into the tub. "Ah. Man, this feels good."

"It would have felt better if I'd been sharing it with Sadie," Gear muttered.

"Too bad." Thor sighed. "Her brother seemed nice."

"Who, Elliot? He's cool. Funny. And he makes great cider."

"He's a cook?"

"He owns Sofa's with Sadie and her sister. I guess he's a cook. I mean, he bakes, but he also makes food, like catering and shit. Why?" He saw his brother's flush, and he didn't think it was from the heat. "Oh, hell no. You can't be sniffing after Elliot. You'll make things worse and screw it up for me with Sadie."

Thor gave a harsh laugh. "Seriously? You think *I'll* be the one screwing up your supposed relationship? And just what is that, anyway? Because the last I knew, you were off women forever. Then you followed that with a few choice names for Sahara. Followed by even more choice names for Brian. Though he really is an ass. I never liked him."

Gear grunted.

"Well?"

Gear chose to change the subject, because he didn't know the answer to Thor's question. "Brian wasn't lying when he told them it's official. Though I should have been the one setting everyone straight." He sighed. "I saw my lawyer again a few days ago. We finally came to a settlement the network accepted. I can't talk about what happened—"

"What? That's ridiculous!"

"I'm out all the way. I have no rights to Motorcycle Madnezz. But the bike and tools I brought to the show come home with me. And I still retain credit on the bikes I did while on the show, so I can have that to fall back on when it comes to prior work cred."

"That's it?"

"That and they bought out my shares in the company. It's still not much, because they squeezed me out of the bonus shares I thought were mine, but fuck it. It's done. Over. And anything that happens from here on out is no longer under their control. I can set up shop, work for someone else, leave the business altogether. It's my choice. I'm done with fucking TV. No more appearances."

He still didn't know what to do with himself. The past two months had been agony, going into the shop to finish orders, working alongside guys who'd once been his friends. Only Smoke and Chains still talked to him. But the bitterness of all he'd endured stung.

Did he have it in him to start fresh with a new garage, new bikes? Should he do what he loved best and focus on the bikes alone, which would mean working for someone else? He'd been approached by a few custom places looking for a designer. Problem was he'd be losing control by working for a boss. He really didn't want to do that.

"You need to find a new place to work. Your own,"

Thor said as if reading his mind. "You can't work for anyone else. You're an asshole."

"Hey."

"Truth hurts. You're just like Otis. You need to create, but it has to be your *own* thing, your *own* way. Why not use your current notoriety"—at Gear's glare, he amended—"fame, and get a small place? Do everything your way. Iris will help you with a new brand. Screw Motorcycle Madnezz. Do something crazy. Like Cycle Junkies."

"Oh, because *that* name has never been used." Gear snorted.

"Or Motorcycle Gods. Bikes We Likes."

"Just stop."

"Or how about Manly Men and the Power Tools That Love Them?"

Gear had to chuckle at that one. "Okay, I get it. You think I should hop right back on the horse."

"I would have said *bike* to make it a proper analogy, but yeah. You're gun-shy now, because you got majorly burned. But you have your health. You have me and Iris. Mom and Dad too."

"And…? Sweeten the pot a little, Bro."

Thor splashed him. "Well, you might have Sadie too. That's if she hasn't seen tonight's entertainment news feeds. And if you're even in a relationship, because you swore you'd never have one again."

Gear sighed. "She's cool. I really like her. I didn't want to. Didn't plan on her. But she really rocked the Xena outfit. She likes beer and burgers. She says what she's thinking, and she's not all that impressed that I was on TV. That's kind of nice."

"There is that. You haven't had to work for a woman in a long time. Especially not since the show aired."

"Fame sucks. Trust me. I didn't want it from day one. Brian talked me into it. And stupid me, I listened."

"Okay, if the pity party is starting again, I'm done." Thor walked out of the tub and wrapped up in his robe. "I need to head out anyway. A bunch of us are geeking out over some old-school D&D."

"If only you meant Dances & Dolls." A popular strip club downtown.

"Plebeian."

"Huh?"

"Insulting you is pointless when you start feeling sorry for yourself. I'll talk to you later. I have a date." Thor darted back into the house.

"With a board game and nerds," Gear mumbled. Damn it. He did feel sorry for himself. He needed to go out. To think about something else. To see Sadie.

Gear groaned and rested his head back, staring at the starlit sky. He had the perfect backdrop for seduction. And no Sadie. He could call any of over a dozen women to join him for an easy fuck. But none of that mattered. He wanted Xena.

His warrior princess with her trash talk, her right hook, and her ice water–tossing, obnoxious self.

He grinned, remembering Marsha's shock. That grin faded when he considered Marsha's revenge. *Shit*. What if Sofa's suffered because of that post? He jumped out of the hot tub, turned off the jets, and put the cover back on. Then he hurried inside and, after drying off, called Sadie.

"What?" she snarled on the second ring.

"Ah, hi."

"Oh. Hi, Gear."

He frowned. "You sound tired. Everything okay?"

"You obviously haven't seen Facebook or YouTube lately. Congrats. You're viral."

He cringed. "I am so sorry. I didn't think they'd find me. They must have caught on to the Camry."

"Ya think?"

He felt awful. So of course he went on the attack. "Who the hell told you to throw ice water at those reporters?"

"She was a bitch. She deserved it."

"Well, yeah, but—"

"And you should stop being such a pussy and defend yourself."

"What?" *Pussy?* "I have," he growled. "But no one listened."

"Probably because every word out of your mouth is insulting to one faction or another. Well, I told the truth, defended your sorry ass, and I'm not sorry."

"That's two sorrys." Great. Now he sounded like Thor.

"You know what? I'm going to drink, wolf down some pizza, and try to forget the verbal smackdown my brother already gave me. I can do without your shit too." She hung up.

He swore and got dressed, then took his quieter bike, the one without the monster pipes, over to Sadie's. No way in hell they'd end the conversation like that. It took him a good forty-five minutes to get to her place. Traffic in Seattle sucked worse every day, but he loved the city. His family lived nearby, and he'd made business contacts here—that probably wouldn't last. But still.

Seattle, home to the Mariners, the Seahawks, and a damn good cup of coffee. It was home.

And the traffic still sucked ass.

He was grumbling to himself as he drove to Sadie's apartment building. He parked down the street, hoping no one messed with the bike. It wasn't his bling bike, more like a crotch rocket, but it blended and got the job done. He carried his helmet with him as he walked to her door, then realized he needed a key to get in the building. *Shit*.

A man exited, recognized him, and asked for an autograph, holding out an *Entertainment Weekly* magazine. Gear flushed. Who was he to sign anything? Still, he signed the thing, thanked the guy for watching, and felt good when the dude expressed sympathy for being screwed over. So one guy believed him. Then he was nice enough to open the door.

Gear hurriedly slipped through and soon found himself knocking on Sadie's door. No way he'd call and give her a chance to ignore him again.

"Hold on, Elliot," she yelled, opened the door, then tried to close it on him.

He pushed his way through and leaned back against it. "Now, we can talk."

She glared. Was it wrong that he grew hard looking at all that fierce, feminine fury?

"You."

He swallowed. "Me."

"You did this."

He kept quiet.

"I—You—Oh." She stormed out of the entryway and back down the hall to her open kitchen and living area. While she paced, he took in more details. She liked blue, because he remembered pale blue on her bedroom walls.

A neutral gray coated the living room, broken up by blue pillows, paintings, and a throw over the ugly-as-hell couch. Her kitchen was white. And no longer spotless. A giant pizza box, half empty, and a six-pack of beer with two missing sat on the counter. He saw a bag of chips and salsa, some Jujyfruits candy, and olives nearby.

"Are you pregnant?"

She stopped and stared. "*What?*"

"Olives and candy and chips? That's weird."

"That's comfort food." She flounced down on the couch, tapping her foot. "I'm so pissed right now."

"At me?"

"At me." She swore. "I have a temper, and as Elliot so kindly pointed out to me, this is the second time I've put us under the gun of a potential lawsuit. Though I don't see how dumping our ice water at the park is hurting anybody."

He felt for her. She looked miserable.

Sadie wore her hair down. Her cheeks were flushed, her pajamas barely hiding her braless rack and long, toned legs. He sat down next to her before she could see his erection and suspect him of coming over for sex. *Which I did not*, he reminded his cock.

"Look, Sadie, Elliot should remember that no one saw you punch Sahara but me. So you're really down to just one lawsuit."

"Thanks." She blew out a breath. "I didn't mean to go off on those cretins. But I can't stand when the little guy gets stepped on." She gave him a once-over. "Though you're not exactly little."

"You hate injustice."

"Exactly." She grabbed an open beer in front of her

and downed some. "Want a beer? There's more on the counter."

"Thanks." He helped himself to one and kicked back with her. "I'm really sorry about all this."

She sighed. "It's not your fault. I mean, it is for getting into TV and all, but you can't help those vultures going after you. I guess it could be worse. They could be camped out on my doorstep."

"Don't even think it." He shuddered. "It started out slow, you know. The whole fame–infamy thing. We had a show about building custom bikes. I was all about making the motorcycles. I left Brian and Sahara to all that other bullshit. The acting bits. The unnecessary drama." He drank some of his beer. "I think you'd like the shop the way it started. Some of the guys are okay. Or *were* okay. Who the hell knows what they think anymore?"

He would miss ragging on Smoke. Hearing about Chains's latest foray into online dating. The guys were huge and dense when it came to women. But genuine and serious about bikes. Then again, maybe he'd been wrong about them too.

"It's weird. We've been on for three years. On my way inside your place, some guy asked for my autograph." He shook his head. "Me. Who the fuck am I? I just build bikes. Big deal. It's not brain surgery."

"Or rocket science," she agreed a little too readily.

He turned to argue, saw her smirk, and relaxed. "So I'm forgiven?"

"I was never really mad at you. Sorry. You were an easy target."

"I don't know about easy."

"Trust me. You're easy." She drank again. "I saw the hard-on you're trying to hide. You put the *e* in easy."

He groaned and held the bottle to his forehead to cool off. "It's your fault for not wearing a bra. Seriously, I only came over to apologize. I swear I'm not here for sex."

"Even if I want some?"

What did a guy say to that? *No, because I want you to see me as more than a sex toy? Or hell yes, because I'm not right unless I'm with you. Inside you. Together.*

So he did what men always did when unsure of the answer. He drank beer and refused to respond.

Chapter 9

HOW HAD SHE MISSED HER OPPORTUNITY? SHE'D HAD a sexy, repentant Gear all to herself, and Sadie had fallen asleep on him. At nine on a Saturday night.

I am so lame.

She stared up at her bedroom ceiling, Gear breathing quietly beside her on her bed. To her consternation, she still wore her clothes. A peek at him showed him fully dressed, minus his boots. They'd cuddled under her blankets together.

Sadie closed her eyes and turned, pretending she was still asleep.

He hugged her tight, murmured her name, and sighed.

And *bam*, her ability to withstand the guy sank to an all-time low.

She liked Gear. A lot. More than was healthy. For all her demands that they remain casual, she had feelings for the guy. And that was plain stupid. They'd really just met. And if that picture of her looking like something out of *The Exorcist* next to the gorgeous Sahara had taught her anything, it was that Sadie was so far out of Gear's league, it was ludicrous.

She burrowed closer to him, melting when he held her protectively, keeping the world out while keeping her warm.

She tried hard to forget her brother cursing her out. Elliot's rebuke had stung. Mostly because she knew he was right. Acting out, like a five-year-old having a temper tantrum, did no one any good. Besides, that nasty reporter had had the last laugh, making Sadie look like a total monster while Sahara once again came out smelling like a rose.

I hope Marcia, Marcia, Marcia gets a cold from that ice water, she thought nastily. Then she felt guilty for bringing *The Brady Bunch* into her drama.

Gear stirred, and she ran her hand over his chest, stroking lightly. He was so much more than a personality on TV. So what the hell was he doing with her?

"I know you're up," he said, his voice rumbly.

Busted.

"Come on. I want to take you somewhere. Let me clean up real quick." He moved fast when he wanted to. Darting out of bed, he shut himself in her bathroom and emerged moments later looking fresh and clean, though that shadow of a beard was sexy hot. "Your turn."

"Hnnng." Which meant *I'm not a morning person, even if I am awake*.

"Get up," he barked.

She grudgingly rose, closed herself in the bathroom, then emerged like a real person. Mostly.

"Put some clean clothes on," he nagged. "And by all that's holy, wear a bra. It's not cool for a guy to bust a nut while on a bike."

"What are you talking about?" *He thinks I'm sexy. Of course I am. Yes, I am.*

She hated when her legendary confidence took a nosedive. But man, that picture of her next to Sahara had sure done the trick.

"I'll make you some coffee." He left her dithering in the bedroom.

Not sure what the hell he had up his sleeve, she changed into clean jeans, a sweatshirt, clean underclothes—including a bra—and her Halloween socks. They had alternating neon-green and orange stripes, went from her calf to her toes, and hugged each toe individually.

He stared at them when she walked in, his hands on the open cabinet doors as he searched for coffee. "What is on your feet?"

"Do you like my witchy toe socks? Aren't they sexy?"

"Er, ah, sure." He turned back to the cabinet. "Where's the coffee?"

"What's going on?"

"Well, I'd like to make up for yesterday. I know you said it's not my fault, and I agree. But how about we take off for a while today, just you and me?" He frowned. "Oh, you probably have to work, don't you? Sorry. I'm keeping you from the shop, huh?"

"Actually, no. Elliot told me to stay home today. He's hoping the backlash from my ice fit will disappear if no one sees me." She gave him a real grin. "So at least I have that going for me."

"Great." He smiled at her.

Sadie couldn't help it. She had to kiss him. She walked up to him and tried to pull him closer, but he held back. "What?"

"Did you brush your teeth?"

She blinked. "Seriously?"

He waited.

"Yes, I brushed my teeth. I'm not an animal."

He dragged her close and kissed the breath out of her. Great. Now she felt all hot and bothered, and he wanted to leave the house. He pulled her with him toward the front door and stopped.

"Shoot. I only have one helmet."

"Okay, I'm not sure what's going on, but if you think I'm getting on a motorcycle in fifty-five-degree weather, you're nuts."

"Oh." He seemed disappointed. "So we'll take your car."

"My car?"

"Yeah. Come on. I have a surprise for you."

"One that involves donuts?"

"How do you stay so fit eating crap?"

"It's a gift. Like my mouth." She meant her attitude. He seemed to take her words to mean something else, because he fixated on her lips and gave a hungry smile.

"Yeah, a real gift."

She chuckled. "Come on. Donuts first. Sex after."

"If you insist."

An hour later, they sat parked in a field in the Issaquah Valley.

"What is this?" she asked as she munched on a Bavarian cream donut.

"Hey, that was mine."

"You already had three of them." Where did the guy put it all? "But I'll share if you give me some coffee."

"Fine." He sighed. "Have you noticed your habit of taking my food?"

"Problem?" She glared. If he thought he could take the coffee back, he was insane.

"Keep it." He tried to hide it, but she saw his grin. "So this is what I wanted to show you."

"It's gorgeous out here." Issaquah lay about twenty

minutes east of Seattle and had some of the most beautiful views of the Pacific Northwest. Sadie had gone hiking with Rose years ago up to Poo Poo Point. Great outlook of Issaquah surrounded by lush ferns and large trees, just on the shoulder of West Tiger Mountain.

But he hadn't taken them to a mountain. The clearing had acres of space, with a view of Mount Rainier and the Issaquah Alps if she stood just right.

"This is where we hold Renaissance Daze. My parents run a kind of steampunk renaissance fair every summer. It's a mix of metal and medieval."

"Hold on. I know that fair. I mean, I never went, but it's become *the thing* to do during the summer."

"Yeah. My parents bought the land over thirty years ago. I never asked my dad how they financed it, because I don't want to know. I told you my dad was a biker. Mom a hippie. I think between the two of them, they had drug or gun money. But whatever. They bought the land, and they do great stuff with it every year. It's actually pretty fun, unless you have to work for Otis. Then it sucks."

She laughed and got out of the car. Gear had insisted on driving, and since she'd wanted to eat more than argue, she'd let him. She walked over the field, waiting for him to join her. "What's that?" she asked, pointing to a structure some distance away.

"The castle."

"Really?" This she had to see.

"Well, not a real castle. But it's a pretty good scaled-down version of one. They hold weddings and special events there starting in the spring. They just closed the place down a few weeks ago for the season, so it's still usable. Want to see inside?"

"Yeah."

He took her over to it. After punching in a key code for the door, they entered the mock castle in all its stone glory.

"This is amazing."

"It is cool." Gear smiled. "The interior is real river rock, but as you move through the place, it turns into hardwood floors and drywall. It's really more of an upscale house. My family lives in it while the summer's on. Well, Otis, Orchid, and Iris do. Professor Thor has his own work at the university, and I do—did—my thing."

"This is so awesome." She walked through the ground level, into a cozy living area, dining area, and gigantic kitchen, where she imagined they cooked for the masses. Up the stairs, bedrooms lined a long hall, which looked over the downstairs. The hallway was shaped like an I, long on one end and shorter on the sides, where the bathrooms were, apparently.

Each space had a different color theme, but all the rooms appeared well-appointed, comfortable, and upscale. The furniture seemed handcrafted, yet sleek and almost modern, which shouldn't have fit the homey atmosphere but did. Sadie was particularly taken with the blue room, done in bold navy, accented with a sky blue that oddly worked.

"My mom decorated. That's why it's weird." He shrugged.

Sadie felt the chill in the air, but it felt warmer than outside. "So…what now?"

"I don't know." He stuffed his hands in his pockets. "I just wanted to show you the place. Sometimes I come here to get away from it all, you know?"

She nodded. "You had a hard time adjusting to the show, didn't you? I mean, you told me you didn't like the TV part, but you weren't kidding. So why did you do it?"

He sighed. "I don't know. I guess I just wanted to make more bikes, and the show gave us the money to do that. Plus Brian thought it was a good idea, and Sahara..."

A surge of jealousy rushed through Sadie at thoughts of Gear's ex. "Why her?" she blurted. "What did you see in her?"

"Besides the obvious, you mean?" he said wryly. "Look, I'm a guy. I can admit I was blinded by tits and ass. But she wasn't always such a witch. At the beginning, she acted like she cared, and I think maybe she did. I wasn't a prince. I take my share of blame for things not working out."

"Yeah?" Sadie sat on the bed, relaxing into the firm yet soft-topped mattress. The cream-colored comforter would look right at home in her bedroom. "What did you do that was so bad?"

"I worked. A lot. She spent time with Brian while I fell deeper in love with my bikes." He sighed and joined her on the bed, but she didn't get the sense he was setting her up for sex. Gear was talking to her, so she listened. "I should have seen that she and I wanted different things. But by that time the show was getting popular. Everyone wanted to see us 'in love.' Good old Brian was standing by, the charming Romeo with a different chick on his arm every episode."

"Man, I really missed out by not watching."

He laughed, his expression easing. "Nah. You ask me, the best parts were our bike reveals. When the audience got to see what the guys worked so hard on. Brian rarely did much mechanical work. His talents were all in building the business, number crunching, and playing a part. I'm curious to see who they get to replace me. Or maybe they'll just upgrade one of the guys in the shop to lead mechanic. I don't know."

He seemed to be getting down again, and Sadie didn't want to let him. He'd shared himself, and she appreciated that. They felt like real friends here. Him confessing things, showing her a place that meant something to him. She felt like she should return the favor.

"You want to know something about me? Something deep?"

He nodded, his gaze focused on her. And not on just her body. On Sadie.

"When I was ten, my mom died. It was really hard. She was my world, and then she was gone. Cancer." Sadie shrugged. The pain had faded, now just a dull ache. But she still missed her mother. "Dad did his best to keep us on the straight and narrow. I'm a lot like him, actually."

"Yeah?" Gear kicked off his boots and propped himself back on the bed. He rested his hands behind his head and watched her.

Sadie didn't want him to see her while she shared, so she lay next to him, contemplating the crown molding around the ceiling. "Rose looks exactly like Mom. Pretty, petite. She even acts like Mom, all gracious and nice." Sadie grimaced. "I'm like Dad. Big and mouthy."

"I like mouthy."

She heard Gear's grin and smiled. "Somehow I'm not surprised. Anyhow, losing Mom hit me a lot harder than it seemed to hit Elliot and Rose. I kind of shut down. Oh, not with my family. But with anyone else. It was hard for me to let people in. Years went by. I dated. I'm no nun."

"You got that right."

She slugged him but appreciated him keeping the mood light. "I guess I just never fell in love. Then I met Adrian. I was twenty-six. He was a few years older. Handsome, funny. He got me. A lot of guys don't. I'm too intimidating, or so my cousin says. She's a shrink. She'd know."

"Ah. Go on."

"Well, Adrian was a great guy. We were tight. I mean, we moved in together. He was an instructor at UW. When we got serious, he started wanting me to be someone I'm not. Then it turned out he wanted me to be more like the chick he really wanted. But she was married."

"What an ass."

"Yeah. Turns out he didn't want to wait for her to get divorced, so he slept with her. Right under my nose. That really hurt. I mean, we were together for four years. I couldn't believe I didn't see it. What made it worse was that Annette was a friend of mine. And she didn't care about me either."

"What dicks."

"Her too?"

"It's not a gender-specific insult. You can be a chick and be a dick."

"Oh, okay then." She wanted to laugh, which was odd, because thinking about Adrian had never induced more than tears or anger. She turned to see Gear propped up on his elbow, watching her.

"How did you find out they were cheating?"

"I walked in on them having sex at her place. I'd come over to talk, and her door was unlocked. I think she wanted me to find out, though she never said so.

"I kicked him in the balls, then refused to listen to her when she broke down crying, *so sorry* about it all. I left, called her husband, and told him everything. I'm not sorry about that either." Just thinking about what they'd done made her want to kick Adrian in the nuts all over again.

"Hurts, doesn't it? Two months ago, I came home early one day to apologize for something I'd done. I still can't remember what we'd fought about. Probably me not being home enough. But I had to do all the stuff she wanted me to for the show in addition to building the bikes. Anyway, I get home to hear them going at it. I walk in, they're humping in my house. In my bed."

"Wait, the house you live in now?"

"Yep. It sucked. I had to get out of there. I was so angry, I knew I'd kill him if I stuck around. I mean, like really kill him. Brian was my friend way before I'd ever met Sahara. I was angry, but more at him, if that makes sense."

"It does." Though she'd been devastated by Adrian, since Annette had been a friend, but not a super-close one.

"I spent some time by myself, not even with my family. A week went by, and I thought about my future. I went back to work. Then he and Sahara tracked me down. I'd been trying to work through shit by fixing my latest project, and they wouldn't let me be. I lost it. I mean, *lost it*."

"Was that the punch on TV?"

"Yeah. It happened a while ago, but we shoot the show months in advance. I only stopped hitting him because people pulled me off him. Afterward, I realized he'd purposefully sought me out while the cameras were rolling, after he and Sahara had made up a story about me being the bad guy." He paused. "I learned he'd been doing her for months before I found out. But like I said, she and I had pretty much called it quits a while ago. Hadn't seen her naked or had sex with her since, ah…" He thought about it. "Probably back in late spring. I don't remember, to tell you the truth."

She watched him watching her. "We're a pair, aren't we?"

He toyed with a strand of hair over her shoulder. "Yeah, we are." He gave her a slow smile. "I would have liked to have seen you kick that fucker in the balls."

She laughed. "I wish I could have been there when you punched that asshole in the face."

He nodded, his expression growing serious. "I'd never cheat on someone I care about. It's wrong. For me, at least. I'm not into open relationships. Or closed ones where only one person is fucking around. If you can't be loyal with someone, bail on the relationship."

She leaned up to face him. "Exactly." She bit her lip. None of this with Gear felt casual anymore. If it ever had. "Do you think Sahara's better in bed than me? I mean, she's prettier. Probably nicer."

He scowled. "First of all, she's not nice. She's pretty, but that's all she is. You're ten times the woman she is. And you rock my world in bed."

"Oh. Good." Sadie didn't know what else to say to that.

"What about me? Am I better in the sack than

Adrian? And what kind of a name is Adrian, anyway? It's a pussy name."

She grinned. "You're right. And you're ten times the man pussy-boy was."

"Good. Great. Now that we got that cleared up, want to get up and go home? Maybe hang out or something?"

She had all day free for once, and Gear all to herself.

"I, ah, I didn't bring you here for a fuck or anything." His cheeks turned red. "I just wanted to share this with you. That's all."

He started to rise, and she pushed him back down.

"Hold on, hero. What if *I* want *you*? What if I need some reassurance that I'm woman enough for you?" *Oh God. Did I really say that out loud?* "I mean, you must have a ton of chicks in your little black book that you could call for a good time. Why me?"

"Xena, if you have to ask, I must not be doing it right. Here. Feel this." He took her hand between them and pressed it against his groin. "I'm always like this with you. But mostly, it's from watching you kick ass. And eating your cookies. And hearing you make fun of your brother, because you're really good at that."

She grinned.

"Yeah, I have a thing about your smart mouth."

"I have a thing about yours too," she murmured and straddled him, staring down at his bright eyes. "You sure do know what you're doing when it comes to making me feel good." She leaned down to kiss him.

Unlike their previous kisses, this one felt different. He kissed her with more feeling and meaning, but she didn't know what exactly he meant. Or when he pulled back, why he looked at her that way.

"What?"

He stroked her cheeks, then her lips. She opened her mouth and nipped his thumb.

His eyes grew darker. His hand trailed over her throat and stayed there. He tightened his grip, not hard or threatening, but firm. In control. He tugged her down toward him, and she went willingly.

Then, before she could blink, he flipped them so that her back was to the bed, and he loomed over her. Gear threaded his hands in her hair and held her still. "You're beautiful, Sadie. No, don't look away. Look at me."

She watched him undress her piece by piece, until she lay naked while he remained fully clothed.

He caressed her everywhere while avoiding that needy spot between her legs. "I have one condom on me. It's in my back pocket." He kissed her breasts, lingering over her taut nipples while he plumped her sensitive flesh. "And I don't want to use it."

She arched up into him as he sucked her closer to orgasm. "Wh-what?"

"I want to come inside you. No condom. But I don't know that it's safe. Or smart." He groaned. "I just know I want you. Forget I said anything."

Before she could respond, he kissed her. He moved down her body slowly, his mouth temptation itself. Gear knew how to kiss. He used his whole mouth, and he knew just where to put it. Over her nipples, her belly, on the sensitive sides of her ribs. He dragged his lips over the inside of her thighs while rubbing his fingers against her labia, spreading her arousal.

He sighed. "I love how wet you get for me. Love eating you, Sadie." He put his mouth where his words were, and he loved her into an orgasm that flowed through her hard and fast, like a tidal wave of pleasure that finally ebbed.

She caught her breath as he rose and stripped nude. The condom went on without her prodding, but now that he'd planted the seed, so to speak, she couldn't stop thinking about him being inside her, skin to skin.

He lowered himself to her, and she put a hand to his chest to stop him.

"Wait."

He paused, his gaze intense, his body rock hard.

"I want to touch you. To make you feel the way you make me feel."

"I don't think I can wait. Not this time." He watched her while he moved between her legs, and she dragged her hand over his chest, pinching his nipples.

He liked that as much as she did, because he nudged her sex, getting himself all slick, then thrust deep, moaning her name as he moved. "Fuck. You feel so good, Sadie."

He wasn't having sex with a faceless woman. When Gear joined her, he joined *her*. Sadie Liberato. She got him this way, frantic to couple with her. To be one, inside her.

Gear stared into her eyes as he took her, and their passion burned hotter, the connection stronger, as he neared his end. "Love fucking you. Need you tight around me. Fuck," he rasped as he stroked. He felt so thick inside her, leaving not one part of her untouched as he delved deep.

His breathing grew choppy, his eyes wild as he neared his end.

"Come, baby," Sadie urged, and wrapped her ankles around his back. That put her clit in contact with his pelvis, and his every thrust increased her arousal.

Gear grew rougher, and his powerful body owned every part of her. Mind, body…and heart.

"In me," she whispered, needing to see him surrender.

He groaned and gave one last push, then stilled while his body jerked inside her.

She held him tight, this man who, for this time at least, belonged to her. While he gave her all he had, she took what she could. And she knew it wasn't enough.

―⁓―

They slept for a short time after that, a nap much needed and surprisingly comfortable on top of the comforter, but under a warm, fuzzy blanket.

When Sadie next woke, she saw the sun shining into the room, and Gear sliding his fingers through her hair.

"Hey, Sleeping Beauty."

She cracked her jaw on a yawn, and Gear grinned. She didn't think she'd ever seen him so relaxed. Even in the short duration of their association, he'd mostly seemed guarded. Not so now.

"Man, great sex is blinding. Who knew?" she teased and stretched.

The blanket rode down, exposing her breasts.

"Mmm. Brunch." He feasted, and her arousal returned as if it had never left.

"I'm recharged," she purred and wrapped her hands around his shoulders. "Coffee, donuts, and sex. My life is complete."

"No. Not just sex," he corrected. "Sex with me. Say it."

"Possessive, are we?"

He tightened his hold on her hair, and the bite of pain produced a swell of pleasure. "Say it."

"Sex with you, Gear Blackstone."

He moved closer to her, and she felt him hard and insistent against her hip. "My condom is gone. I'm naked, Sadie. All over." He ground over her skin, his cock hot, hard.

"You're a needy guy, aren't you?" She kissed him, wanting more.

The wake-up kiss became something else. A prelude to a fast, hot interlude.

And she wanted it. Wanted him.

"In me."

"But, the condom…"

"In me," she urged, and he didn't need any more prodding.

Gear slid inside her, and the sensation was incredible.

"*Oh fuck*. You feel so good. So fuckin' good." He moved faster, his body brushing hers in all the right places. She gripped his tight ass, and he flexed, moaning.

"Oh, oh yeah." Ground into an orgasm, Sadie cried out, unable to process more than the ecstasy of Gear inside her.

He thrust, his body a powerhouse, until he hurriedly jerked out of her and came all over her belly. "God. Yeah." He continued to spend, and the warmth that could have been inside her but wasn't should have freaked her out.

The timing wasn't right for a baby at this point in her cycle. But what woman with a brain relied on *almosts* and *maybes* when it came to possibly getting pregnant?

He lay over her, panting, and the warmth of his breath fluttered over her, a gentle caress while he fit against her like that last puzzle piece that had always been missing.

"You were inside me." She stroked his back, then his arm, staring at his tattoos. "I love this. All the colors, the flowers and skulls. The motorcycles." She smiled, dreamy *for him*. The way he touched her, made her feel. Like she mattered so much. *Gear, I think I'm falling in lo—*

"Hey there," a deep voice called from somewhere in the house. "Anybody home?"

Gear and Sadie froze.

"Home invasion?" she whispered.

"Worse. My dad."

They hurried to dress and clean up. Gear sacrificed his underwear to clean up her belly and stuffed it in his jacket pocket. She finger-combed her hair and hoped she didn't look as if she'd just been royally fucked.

When she realized what she'd wanted to say to him, she wanted to sink through the floor. But that would have to wait.

A glance over her shoulder showed evidence of their time together.

"Gear, the bed."

They rushed to straighten out the comforter, but she had a feeling it would need to be washed. The blanket too.

"Drop the blanket under the bed. We'll take it with us when we go." He nudged it under the bed, then put an arm around her shoulders and dragged her to the window.

Loud steps could be heard coming up the stairs.

In a louder voice, Gear said, "And there you can see the imprint where we put the crowd. The stands go there." He pointed at the field. "Villager tents go all around and are populated by all sorts of trinket stands."

"Very cool." What the hell was he pointing at? She didn't see anything.

"Hey, now. What's this?"

Gear and Sadie turned to confront a mammoth of a man. Even taller than Gear, the older gentleman—a term she used loosely—by the doorframe had to stand at least six and a half feet tall. He had dark hair threaded with gray pulled back into a ponytail, dark eyes, and he wore Gear's face. Except his eyes looked meaner, his face a study of hard knocks and lessons learned. She wouldn't want to meet this guy in a dark alley. Or a lit one either.

When he saw Gear, he smiled, love for his oldest clear. "Hey, boy. Who's your friend?"

"Otis, meet Sadie. Sadie, my dad, Otis."

She held out a hand but couldn't move to meet him because Gear refused to let her go.

Otis noticed and grinned wider. He stepped close and shook her hand. "Nice to meet you. Why don't you two come on down and get something to eat? Your mother brought a picnic, Harrison. Enough to feed at least three of me."

Gear groaned.

"Harrison?" Sadie frowned.

Otis laughed. "Harrison M. Blackstone, my boy. Or as you know him, Gear."

"Harrison." Sadie stared up at Gear, watching his cheeks turn pink. "Oh man. You must really hate that I know that."

"I do. Like you can't believe." He glared at his father. "Thanks a lot, Otis."

"Anytime, boy. Anytime. Now, how about something to eat while you introduce your mother to your friend."

"Yeah, *Harrison*. Let's go." Sadie practically skipped out of the room, but not fast enough to miss Otis saying, "And don't worry. We're here to grab all the linens to be laundered one final time. Just make sure your mother doesn't find out what you were up to, or you'll never hear the end of it."

"Dad, shut up."

Otis just laughed.

Chapter 10

Sadie couldn't stop staring at Gear's parents. She could totally see their looks in their son, but they were each fascinating on their own.

Otis owned his big-bad-biker cred. He'd supposedly been out of the rough life for years, since just before his kids had been born. But that toughness had never left his features. He had a wariness to him that told her he'd seen a lot in his life.

Black hair just starting to go gray, and that same dark shadow of a beard that graced Gear's face. He had a diamond stud in one ear, his hair long enough to put back. Yet he didn't appear feminine or trying too hard to look sexy and mean. He just did.

"You stare any harder and your eyes will dry out." Gear didn't sound pleased.

Otis—he'd told her to call him that—laughed. "She's obviously trying to see where you get your good looks from."

"Yeah, that's gotta be it." Gear rolled his eyes. "Yo, Orchid. What are you guys doing here?"

His mother, on the other hand, looked like an earth goddess. She wore a flowy, floral dress over purple tights tucked into black canvas—not leather—boots. Her long red hair waved over her shoulders, the loose curls strewn with lighter blond, nearly white strands.

Her hazel eyes sparkled, mirth and patience twined as she looked from her son to Sadie.

"We're here for our annual cleanup, Harrison. You know that."

He'd stopped grimacing after about the tenth time his parents called him that, no longer glancing over at her to see Sadie's smirk. She loved his names. Gear fit him, but oddly, Harrison did too. Not a stuffy name for a stuffy guy, but a grand name that fit the responsible, funny, tender man she'd come to know.

"I thought you guys did that at the beginning of November."

Otis shrugged and sat down across from Sadie at the overlarge kitchen island. Covered in a white-and-gray marble top, the island had a gas stove, prep sink, and plenty of space, much of it now occupied by bags of food. Orchid continued to pull out containers of potato salad, baked beans, salad, watermelon...

"You really did pack a picnic." Sadie stared. "It feels like summer in here."

"Even though it's October." Gear groaned. "This isn't some kind of weird pagan ritual where you and Otis do weird things in the moonlight and call out to the spirits of yesterday, is it?"

Orchid frowned while Otis smothered a grin.

"No. We did that on the summer solstice, and there was nothing strange about your father and I making sweet love on that bed of—"

"And I'm happy with that answer." Gear cut her off. To his father, he said, "Not sure if you heard, but I'm totally out of Motorcycle Madnezz now."

"Good." Otis grunted. His gaze shifted back to Sadie,

and she felt it like an anvil on her shoulders. "So I saw an interesting video yesterday."

"Were people naked in it, or was it a different kind of movie?" she had to ask.

Orchid laughed. Gear groaned.

Otis snorted. "Well, I watched one of them too, but that was later. This one was of an angry woman tossing cold water all over Marsha Concannon." Otis gave a wolflike grin. "Very nice."

"She was a nasty piece of work. Kept asking stupid questions and wouldn't leave when I told her to." She spared Gear a glance, noticing his attention on the food his mother pushed toward him. Before he could reach for what looked like half a roast beef sandwich, she nabbed it, took a bite, then remembered to chew and swallow before talking again. "And mind you, I was nice. I asked her a few times to move her skanky ass…er, butt. Then I threw out our bad water. The ice was melting, and we use it to keep our milk cold. It has to be fresh to serve to the kids, you know."

Otis nodded. "Makes sense."

Orchid's eyes widened. "You threw ice water over a reporter? And they caught it on film?"

"Nine other networks aired it. At Concannon's expense, I'm sure," Gear said and snatched the other half of the sandwich before Sadie could.

"Orchid, this is really good," Sadie said. "What's on it?"

"Roast beef, lettuce, tomato, my famous garlic aioli, and some fresh beets marinated in a vinaigrette."

"Oh, the beets. That's where I'm getting all this fabulous taste."

Orchid smiled. "I make all our food from scratch. We're farm-to-table people."

"You have a farm?"

"More like an expansive greenhouse," Gear explained. "Orchid cans a lot of the stuff she plants outdoors. Then they continue to have food all year long from the greenhouse. Fruits and veggies you can't get in the cold."

"What about meat?"

"Ah, a girl after my own heart," Otis said. "Orchid's a vegetarian."

"Pescetarian," she corrected. "Meaning I eat eggs and dairy, as well as fish, in addition to fruits and vegetables. But no meat."

"So no chicken or turkey?" How did the woman handle Thanksgivings?

"Nope."

"Growing up was harsh," Gear said. "Orchid used to make us eat a lot of fish."

"Gives you a good dose of omega-3 fatty acids." Orchid nodded. "You should be thanking me."

"*He* never had to eat it." Gear shot a thumb toward his father.

"Of course not," Otis scoffed. "I'm the man of the house. I eat red meat."

"He eats meat when he buys it from the butcher," Orchid corrected. She winked at her husband. "But with that big body, he needs more than fish and vegetables can give him."

"You got that right." Otis accepted the sandwich his wife pushed his way. "Thanks, baby."

To anyone not knowing Otis and Orchid to be Gear's

parents, the pair seemed much like his older contemporaries. Sadie liked them. They seemed right at home being themselves.

"You guys are why Gear—I'm sorry, *Harrison*—is so normal. Well, maybe I should say *down to earth*."

Otis grinned. "Yep. No way a kid of mine is going to get a big head over a stupid TV show."

"He doesn't mean it like that," Orchid quickly said to Gear. "You know what he means, honey."

To Sadie's surprise, Gear glared at his father, and not in a fake-annoyed kind of way either. He seemed genuinely irritated.

Uh-oh. Some family tension.

"You're still pissed we never put Chrome on the show? Seriously? He'd just gotten out of prison for drug running. Come on, Otis. Get real. I barely managed to survive three years of that show. If Chrome had gotten too popular, you know he'd have gotten busted for something sooner than he did."

"Well, you got that part right. Motherfucker couldn't handle his pills, but the money from the show might have helped him stay cleaner longer."

Gear shot his father a look.

Otis glared back.

"Wow," Sadie drawled to defuse the tension. "And I thought I was the only one who used big, bad words around non-family."

At that, Otis blinked. "Huh?"

"Your use of *motherfucker*. Inspiring."

Gear coughed.

"Is that what the M. in Harrison M. Blackstone stands for?"

Gear glared. "Never mind that."

Oh, a mystery. She grinned, wanting to know more.

"I apologize for my husband." Orchid sighed. "He's barely housebroken, even after all these years."

"That's why you love me," Otis told her. "So how did you two meet, anyway? You a *Madnezz* groupie? Trying to jump on my boy when he's barely over Sahara?"

"Barely over?" Gear huffed. "Try glad to be rid of. It's taken me a good five months to get rid of her."

"I told you," Orchid said to her husband.

"Well, how was I to know? She was a looker and about the only woman I knew who could pull you away from a bike." He shot Sadie a once-over.

"I know. I'm a hag. Sahara's much hotter. Blah-blah."

Otis grinned. "Lot of piss and vinegar in this one. So you're bangin' my boy."

"*Dad.*"

"Takes a lot to get him to call me that." Otis chuckled. "You pregnant?"

Sadie liked this guy. He was just her speed. Obnoxious and funny. "Yep. With a pack of wild ones. We think twins. I'm the luckiest girl around. Harrison's gonna marry me, no prenup or anything. We're going to sell this place when you die, then put up condos for rich white people to buy while tearing up the land. We might even start a cattle farm over yonder." She nodded to the window behind her.

His parents stared at her, openmouthed.

Gear gave a fake gasp. "Jesus, Sadie. I thought we agreed not to tell them that yet."

Otis started laughing. Orchid soon joined him, but

Sadie thought the release might be because none of it was true, not just that she'd been funny.

Gear looked oddly satisfied. "Twins, huh? You sure they're mine?"

"Well, they aren't Brian's. He's got a small dick." She paused. "Or so Sahara said."

Otis came around the island and pulled her into a bear hug. "I like you, Sadie No Last Name. Now tell me how you met my son."

"And don't leave anything out," Orchid ordered, smiling at her. She pushed more food at them, and his parents sat with rapt fascination as Sadie explained meeting Gear at the Halloween party. Leaving out that small tidbit about having sex with him, she basically filled them in on everything. Including that punch.

Otis slapped her on the back, and she would have stumbled had Gear not caught her.

"Otis."

He flushed. "Oh, sorry, Sadie. Thought I'd just tapped you."

"No problem." The man was a monster.

"You know, violence is never the answer," Orchid said quietly.

The three of them turned to stare at her.

"But in Sahara's case, it was justified," Orchid added. "I never trusted that girl."

"She wears real fur," Otis explained. "And she's a bitch. Pretty, but nasty."

"No kidding." Sadie made a grab for the apple pie sitting near her plate. "Oh my gosh. Orchid, you can really cook."

Gear smiled. "Like Sadie told you, she and Elliot run Sofa's."

"Don't forget Rose."

Gear nodded. "Sorry. Her sister Rose too."

"Wait. Sofa's?" his father said. His brows rose. "As in, Sofa's Spookville?"

"I told you people know us for that," she said to Gear. "Yeah. This year Gear helped us decorate."

"Oh, we'll have to swing by. I love that haunted house. I used to have a dollhouse like that as a girl." Orchid smiled. "Well, it wasn't haunted. But it was fun to play with."

"It's actually Rose's old house. But the monster dolls are mine," Sadie said. "Anytime you guys plan to swing by, let me know and I'll set aside some cookies for you."

"How about cinnamon buns? Those are my favorite," Otis said.

"Yep. Can do."

"So you and Harrison," Orchid said. "You're dating?"

"She's pregnant, honey. You heard her," Otis corrected. Then he turned a serious gaze Gear's way. "You be good to her. I like this one. And she looks sturdy enough to carry a new generation of Blackstones."

"Otis, seriously."

"Um, you know we were kidding about babies, right?" Sadie didn't like the look the pair shared. "We've known each other all of a week."

"Eight days, really," Gear said. At her look, he held up his hands. "What? It's true. We met last Saturday at the party. Today is Sunday. That's eight days."

"Counting them, are we?"

"I, ah…" Gear blushed.

She stared, fascinated.

So did his parents.

He cleared his throat. "Well, Otis, Orchid. We have to be going. Sadie has to get back to work later." He gripped her by the hand to stop her from correcting him. "And I need to get back too. Got a few things to do before I figure out where to go from here."

Otis frowned. "You're not going to work for Sanders, are you?"

"I don't think so."

"Sanders?" Sadie asked.

"A competitor and old friend of mine," Gear explained. "He has a custom shop in Tacoma. Big name in the motorcycle world."

She shook her head. "You can't work for anyone else."

"Why not?" He frowned at her.

She snorted. "Duh. Because you're too controlling. You have your own way of doing things. So do your own thing, this time with no partners. That way if it screws up, you only have yourself to blame."

Otis nodded. "What she said."

Gear clenched his jaw. "I'm considering all my options."

Sadie shrugged, thinking him an idiot if he discounted his personality quirks in the face of a new job. "Whatever. But you're an idiot if you try making *Motorcycle Madnezz, Part Two*."

"Thanks so much."

"If I wasn't already taken, I'd marry you," Otis said to her. He surprised her by latching on to her bicep and squeezing. "Check it out, Orchid. The girl is stacked. She's got muscle."

"I work for a living," Sadie joked, trying to tug her arm free.

Gear wrenched her from his father. "Okay, now

that you're manhandling my girlfriend, we really need to go."

Otis and Orchid looked giddy. "Fine, fine." Otis coughed. "But make sure we see you both at the Halloween party. It's at the house this year, in Ballard." He leaned closer to Sadie and whispered, "And I'll tell you what that *M* in his name stands for."

"Oh, it's a date." Sadie beamed.

"Sure. Okay." Gear dragged her toward the exit. "See you then."

"Bye, Sadie," Orchid called out, waving. "Nice to meet you."

"Later, girl," Otis added.

"Bye," she said as the door closed behind her. "Geez, Harrison. Quit dragging me around. Something else you and your dad have in common. Manhandling women," she teased. Then she noted the tension in his frame. "What's wrong?"

He stopped, in full view of the house. "You're coming with me to the party, right?"

"Sure. Why wouldn't I?"

He relaxed. "I don't know. They didn't scare you away?"

She stared at him for a moment, then laughed. "Seriously? Your dad is awesome. And your mom is so pretty and handy in the kitchen. She's like Rose, only earthier. I liked them." A lot.

He smiled, an expression of joy that made his face shine with true beauty. "Yeah? They're usually an acquired taste." He paused. "Sahara couldn't stand them."

Sadie shrugged and did her best not to gape at the wonder that was Gear. "When you meet my dad, you'll see yours is a treat by comparison." Wait. Meet her father? Sadie didn't take guys home to meet the family. Yet she wanted to see her father and Gear together.

Gear hugged her, then grabbed her by the hand and started walking with her back across the field.

Then what he'd said earlier came back to her. She stopped, pulling him to a halt. "Your girlfriend?"

———

Gear had wondered when she'd reference his slip of the tongue. It hadn't been intentional to call her that. But the moment the word had come out, he'd realized the truth of it. Sadie wasn't casual to him. She was someone he wanted in his life. As what, he wasn't yet sure. But he knew for a fact she meant something. He wanted to be around her when not with her. He cared about her feelings and opinions. And it had mattered—more than he wanted to believe—that his parents like her.

"Sorry. I meant to say *friend*, but it came out *girl-friend*. But you're a girl who's a friend, so I wasn't wrong, was I?"

The panic on her face would have been laughable if he hadn't felt the same, worried he'd screwed up a good thing by going too fast.

"Um, no. I guess not." She cleared her throat. "No biggie."

But it was. He held her hand as they walked back to the car. "I was lying about having something to do today. But are you busy?"

"For once, no." She blew out a breath.

They entered the car and sat there for a minute. Then she turned to him, her expression serious. He was going to have to apologize for the girlfriend slip. For arguing with her, maybe even for having sex with her before his parents had arrived, putting her on the spot, unintentional though it had been.

"Sadie, I—"

Before he could apologize, she held out her hand. "Keys."

He stared at her. "Huh?"

"I want my keys. Letting you drive on the way made sense, because I was hungry and didn't know where we were going. But it's my car. I drive."

Relieved she didn't want to roast him over hot coals for making more of their relationship than she wanted, he handed over the keys and switched seats with her. "Cool. Your car, you drive. So what's next?"

"Next?" She drove them away from the field toward home. "Next we go back to town. I need to hit the gym. Sex with you was great, but I need a run." She paused. "You want to come with me?" *Why invite him to something personal to you, dummy? You already had sex with the guy. Time to cut bait and move on.*

"The gym?" He studied her. She could feel his gaze on her like a brand. "Sure. I could go for a workout that doesn't involve your pussy. Not that I'd prefer it though."

"*Gear.*"

He laughed. "Blushing, Sadie? Ha. But I'm serious. I'd rather work out with you, but I'll take the gym. Besides, I need a new place to go." He paused. "So do I pretend I don't know you there or what? You know, to keep any possible press away."

She didn't like the idea of faking anything, but she

hated the thought of more microphones shoved in her face. Of possibly seeing herself on TV, all sweaty and tired next to a picture of Sahara in a fake tan and bikini. "We are *acquaintances* at Jameson's Gym. Nothing more. And it's not because of you, it's—"

"I get it." In a quieter voice, he added, "I really don't want you affected by the shit going on around me. If I can shield you from that, I will."

She bit her lip. The notion of him wanting to protect her was her Achilles' heel when it came to Gear. "I can protect myself."

"I know." He reached for her hand and squeezed it, and didn't let go. "But you shouldn't have to." He tugged her hand to his lap and kept their hands joined. "Besides, if my father finds out I didn't watch out for his new favorite chick, he'll pound me into tomorrow."

She glanced at him. "Would he really hit you?"

"Would and did. When I told him I was doing the TV show, we had a knockout fight."

She gaped. "Seriously? Like, you really hit each other?"

"It's out of love. And he didn't beat me too badly." Gear shrugged. "It's honestly more like wrestling, with a few body blows thrown in for good measure. Love taps, according to Otis." He chuckled. "My family is a little different than yours. And my relationship with Otis is…challenging. I love my dad, but he's a brawler, and proud of it. Me, he tosses around, because he knows I can take it and he's careful not to do too much damage. Plus I hit back. I could give a shit he's twenty-plus years older. But he doesn't do it all that much anymore. Well, not usually. He used to try the same with Thor a long time ago, but Thor's more like Mom."

"What about your sister?"

"No way. My dad has never and will never hurt a woman. Or a kid. A guy? Sure. His son? Only out of love." Gear rubbed his chin. "Bastard knocked me sideways the last time he thought I was ruining my life." Gear sighed. "Turned out he was right."

"Bullshit."

Gear turned in his seat to face her, keeping his hand locked around hers. "What?"

"You didn't ruin anything. We are who we are by the choices we make. So you got screwed over by your friends. You learned. Now you'll be more cautious in the future. And if you're not, you're a moron."

"Thanks. That means a lot coming from you," he said drily.

"What does *that* mean?"

He kissed the back of her hand, startling her. Heat built from that tiny caress. "It means you let some bozo from many years ago make you cautious. But hey, his loss, my gain."

"Huh?"

"Adrian. You remember. Huge douche? Cheated on you?"

"I know who he is, *Harrison*."

He sighed. "I hate that name."

She wanted to be angrier about him judging her, but his disgust made her laugh instead. "Anyone ever call you Harry?"

"Once. Then they died."

"Uh-huh. So, your point?"

"Adrian of the tiny dick hurt you, so you hide yourself behind your tough-chick persona. Though it's not really a persona; it's you. You're tough, but you're sweet. It takes a man like me to see that."

"Like you? What kind of man are you?" Damn him for seeing through her.

He stroked her hand with his thumb, and she had thoughts about pulling over and riding him until they both came. So wrong to be so infatuated and obsessed with the man's body. Hell. With Gear, the man.

"I'm a regular guy who loves motorcycles, my family, and having a good time. I want a life without drama. Friends I can rely on, and a steady diet of orgasms, beer, and pizza in my life."

"Hmm. That's a pretty good list."

"I know." He smiled and kissed her hand again.

"Screw it." She pulled off the road and parked behind a bunch of trees, shielded from the road.

"Sadie?"

Before she thought too hard about what she planned to do, she unbuckled her seat belt. "Get in the back. I have something to say to you, and I need to look at you, face-to-face, when I do."

He met her in the backseat, wary. "I—"

God, he was hot. His frown, that dark stubble on his face, those blazing eyes… She leaned close and kissed him.

In the seconds it took him to unfreeze, she'd unfastened his jeans, pulled down his zipper, and taken him out.

"What the fuck—" He groaned as she leaned down and took him in her mouth. While sucking him off, she awkwardly shimmied out of her shoes, jeans, and panties.

Once free of restriction, she straddled him, taking him inside her in one swift, downward plunge.

"Christ, car sex." He stared into her eyes as he guided her faster, up and down over his long, fat cock. "You're gorgeous. So fuckin' hot."

He yanked her close by her hair and kissed her, nipping her lip.

The shock of pain triggered the wildness inside her that needed an outlet. She came hard, squeezing him, as he filled her the way no one ever had.

"Gonna come," he warned and started to push her up off him.

But she tightened her grip and eased back down. "No. Inside me."

"But—"

"In me," she said breathlessly and kissed him again.

He moaned, dragged her over him, grinding inside her, and then pumped once more and climaxed.

His tortured expression eased as she drained him of his seed.

She felt so much satisfaction in taking his control. Like she mattered on a level far deeper than the physical.

"Sadie." He sighed, then kissed her, now stroking her hips as he started to soften inside her. "So…"

"So," she repeated, and ran her hands through his hair.

He closed his eyes and leaned in to her, setting his forehead against hers. After a moment, he pulled back and stared into her eyes.

"So…?" she prodded gently, feeling at peace with the world as she hadn't in…well, forever.

"Twins are a possibility, huh?"

She froze. Babies? "Um, I, well…" She flushed. "Not in my family." She sounded hoarse, the gravity of what they'd done shocking her to silence.

But Gear wouldn't have it. He kissed her, melting her fears into meaningless nothings.

He trailed his mouth behind her ear and teased with tiny kisses.

And reality returned, if just for a moment. "Not the right time of the month," she said. "Should be...ah, yeah." His fingers found her clit, and he played with her, rousing her lust once more, this time tempered with deeper affection for the man she didn't want to be without. "You're really good at sex."

He chuckled, still inside her. "Yeah, I am. But you make it so much better." He kissed his way to her mouth. "Safe, huh? Enough for a second go?"

No. She shouldn't chance it. "Probably not."

"You're right." He urged her to rock faster over him while continuing to rub her clit. "We shouldn't do this."

"No," she moaned, clenching his neck as she plastered her mouth to his and sucked his breath away.

They didn't stop until they'd both come again. And no matter how much Sadie knew she'd made a mistake—twice—she couldn't bring herself to regret one second of her time with a man she'd started to fall hard for.

"I'm an idiot."

He groaned and hugged her tight. "That makes two of us." After some time, he asked, making no move to separate from her, "Do we still need to go to the gym? I mean, we just worked out."

She smiled and kissed his chest. "Yeah. No getting out of gym night. Don't worry. You'll like it. You'll see."

"Only with you, Xena." He kissed the top of her head.

Oh yeah. She was toast.

Chapter 11

"I said I'm sorry," Elliot apologized for the fourth time that afternoon.

Though it had been a few days since the water incident at the festival, Elliot hadn't calmed down enough to talk to Sadie like a real person until that afternoon.

"Oh? Could you be more specific?" she asked, her voice like ice. Hmm, ice. Maybe they should add some abominable snowman cupcakes to the menu. *Frozen* continued to be popular costume inspiration, for the kids at least, according to the stores carrying so many Elsa and Anna dresses.

Elliot groaned. "Look. I had a legitimate reason to be upset. If we get sued, we're screwed. But you're right. I shouldn't have cursed you out like that."

"Yeah, like *that* bothered me."

"Okay. I know. It was the not talking to you for two days. Immature, and I apologize. *Again*."

"But then, you are my little brother. I should have anticipated you'd act like a baby about it."

Elliot ground his teeth. "I'm. Sorry."

"Do you mean it?"

His sputtering turned to wild laughter. "God, you're annoying. No wonder you and the motorcycle god get along so well."

She smirked. She and Gear spent every day together in some way. Though their relationship was new, if she could even call it a relationship, she loved every second of it. She was never bored with Gear around. Even when he annoyed her, because he had a thing about taking control of *her* TV remote at *her* apartment, he amused her.

"So are you guys an item now or what?"

She shrugged. She'd gone to the clinic to get on birth control on Monday. And though she should be more nervous about what she'd done with Gear, it felt *right*. Even now, she had no regrets. Weird, but there it was.

"We are what we are, Elliot. Why do you need to label it?"

He sighed. "You are so in denial. But God forbid I say how glad I am you have a boyfriend I like. Fine. We'll call him your fun buddy. How's that?"

"Easier to swallow than fuck buddy, I guess." She waited for Elliot to jump on *swallow*.

He cleared his throat. "Not touching that one at all. Because the thought makes me ill. Seriously, violently sick."

"Thanks, Bro." Sadie grinned. "Now tell me how thankful you are that I'm a crazy woman who attacks reporters." He looked like he'd swallowed a lemon, and she laughed. "We've been packed since Sunday, haven't we?"

"Oh fine. All right. Yes. Ever since you threw water on that woman, customers have been coming by in droves to see you in action. And even when you're not out front, we're selling like hotcakes. Hell, maybe we should add those to the menu." He grinned at her laughter. "We also had a call from two local stations to do an interview on the store and you."

"No interviews."

"Which is what I thought you'd say. But they're settling for doing a piece on Spookville and asking the locals what they think of it instead. Great PR, you know."

"Yes, I do."

He huffed. "Yeah, well, your attention got *The Stranger* involved too. They're putting us in their piece about the best-kept foodie secrets in Seattle. I didn't think we were that much of a secret, but one of their people knows someone at the Food Network, and now the Food Network wants to include us in their Best Places to Eat for Halloween segment." He watched her. "It's not reality TV, like Gear's show. But it's an amazing opportunity."

"Hell yeah. The Food Network?" She saw how much he wanted her to agree to it. "So long as you or Rose handle the TV part, I'm in. Now what you're really thinking is, 'Thanks for getting us so much publicity, Sadie. You're amazing and awesome. And I'm a jerky loser for doubting you.'"

"Yes," he said wryly. "That's exactly what I'm not thinking."

She grinned. "Hey, whatever happened with Gear's brother? That catering gig? Did he call you?"

Elliot's shark-like grin alerted her to trouble.

"What happened?"

"Nothing."

"Give. What are you hiding?"

"Not a thing. Thor booked us for November 4th. A gathering of maybe fifty people. Sandwiches and hors d'oeuvres. Some easy desserts. If all goes well, we might have an in with the university for some other gigs."

"Wow. And all because I threw water on a skank. I rock."

"Yes, because it's all about you, Sadie."

As they continued to work, Elliot filled her in on some gossip about members at the gym who'd been getting into trouble. "What's going on with your boy toy working out at Jameson's? Someone said they spotted Gear Blackstone at the gym Sunday night. And again yesterday."

"He switched gyms, I guess." She'd arrived just before him and watched him interact with fans. He was gracious, not too flirty or friendly, and most of the folks at Jameson's left him alone. Apparently they were just biding their time.

"Well, a lot of women, and a few men, are ecstatic to think they have a shot with him. You know Megan and Michelle."

"No."

"That's because you go to work out." He sounded disgusted. "How can you pass up the opportunity for good gossip? That place is a gold mine."

"Uh-huh."

"Anyway, from what I heard, Gear was alone." When she said nothing, he continued, "He didn't give any do-me vibes. When Frank hit on him, he was polite but not interested." When she still said nothing, he crossed to her and gave her his pleading eyes. "Please, please, tell me what's going on."

"Nothing. He's working out at Jameson's now, and we're acting like distant acquaintances. I don't want reporters hounding me over him." She glared at Elliot. "So keep those flapping lips shut."

"Really? Flapping lips?"

"Really." She tried not to laugh at his pique. "Oh, you know what I mean. Gear's our friend. You can talk to him. I just don't want any more attention from those television piranhas."

Elliot moved back to the lemon tarts he'd been making. "Fair enough." She didn't trust his tone. "So Dad called."

"And?"

"He's back from his trip to Florence."

"And? Still waiting for the other shoe to drop."

"And he wants you to bring Gear by for dinner Saturday night." Elliot's wide smile didn't help. "Rose and Joe will be there. I will too, solo, of course, since I'm single. But he said to make sure you and your new *boyfriend* came."

"Oh man."

"Oh yeah. Dad wants to meet the man who's charmed our dear sister."

"How would he know I've been charmed?"

"I told him."

"You ass."

"You're welcome." Elliot shrugged. "Come on. You know you might as well get it over with. He vets all our significant others. Probably why Jason and I didn't work out. Dad hated him."

"Dad hates all your boyfriends because none of them stand up to you."

"And they're scared of him."

She looked at him. "Normal people are scared of him. I'm scared of him."

"Oh stop."

Their father was a genius accountant, numbers man, and overall business guru. And he had a lot of friends in some not-so-nice places. He also did a lot of work with people overseas. Yet he'd been adamant, years ago when Sadie had asked, that he was not tied in any way, shape, or form to the mob. He'd laughed at the notion, but Sadie still secretly wondered.

"He's an accountant who doesn't take crap from anyone," Elliot reminded her. "Not a secret mob boss. You watch too much TV. And speaking of which… *Motorcycle Madnezz*'s new season starts next month. I heard they're filming now."

"Yeah?" Gear hadn't mentioned it. "Do you know who they got to replace Gear?"

Elliot frowned. "I don't know. I've been so busy trying to organize events with Rose that I'm kind of on the outs about my favorite show."

"Want me to ask him?" Gear hadn't said much about his work lately. She had a feeling he was still having a tough time trying to decide what to do about his life.

Since Sadie was far from perfect in regard to her career, she hadn't tried to tell him what to do after that instance with his parents. Not that he'd asked. Hmm. They should probably talk about that.

Since spending Sunday together, they'd seen each other Monday and Tuesday. But she wondered if being around him too much had started to annoy him. She hadn't heard from him since he'd texted her a good morning.

Maybe they'd be smarter to give each other some space?

Rose entered the back, stroking her belly. Sadie studied her sister's small bump. "What're the little guys up to today?"

Rose smiled, a little mother already. "Feel."

Sadie washed her hands, then came over to feel Rose's tummy. "Are they sleeping?"

"One of them is awake." Rose and Joe refused to find out the sex of the babies, which Sadie thought just stupid.

"How can you prepare for the bundles of joy without getting stuff first? I mean, do I get you two pink onesies or two blue stuffed bears?"

"No, no, Sadie. You get orange or yellow or brown. Gender-neutral colors," Elliot informed her, then rolled his eyes. "I know, a load of crap. Jesus, Rose. Just tell us."

"We don't know, and we won't find out for another three months," Rose said primly.

A tiny foot kicked her hand, and Sadie gasped. "He kicked me. Oh, do it again, Sadie junior."

"Sadie for a boy?" Elliot asked, a dopey grin on his face. He, like Sadie, was as excited as Rose about the babies.

"Sadie is a name to end all names. Girl, boy, dog, cat. It's perfect."

"You keep thinking that." Elliot laughed. "Personally, I'm thinking we can have an Elliot Joseph, for me and Joe, or a Sadie Marina for you and Mom."

Rose smiled, a maternal glow radiating from her. "If it's a girl, Marina will be somewhere in her name. Joe already agreed." She patted Sadie's hand. "The babies like you."

"Duh. I'm their favorite aunt." Sadie smiled and pulled her hand back.

Elliot murmured, "Only aunt. Lucky for them they have a stellar uncle."

"Oh, I meant to tell you." Rose made a sad face. "Joe

and I can't come to dinner Saturday. His brother is in town, and we're supposed to see him." She frowned. "I don't like him."

"You don't need the stress. Don't go," Sadie ordered.

"I need to be there for Joe. And I'm bummed I'm going to miss Dad grilling Gear." Rose sighed. "That was going to be the high point of the night."

"I'm sure." Sadie ignored Elliot's smirk. "I don't even know if Gear can go. He might be busy."

"He's not. I already asked him, and he said he'll be there." That was Elliot. Mr. Helpful. "Gee, what fun we'll have. I'll fill you in, Rose. Don't worry."

She brightened. "Great. Oh, and Ava is here wanting to see you, Sadie. I told her to come on back when she's done talking to Theo." Rose left them to help Theo man the counter.

Sadie held back a groan. She'd been avoiding her cousin, especially around Elliot, because she didn't want the third degree about Gear and who he was to her, since she wasn't sure she wanted to know. Everything about the man appealed to her. If anyone could get her to admit out loud what she feared feeling, it would be Dr. Ava Rosenthal. Her nosy cousin.

Why was hiding from one's feelings so wrong, anyway?

Ava strolled in, laughing at something the bruiser beside her said. Good. With Landon, her fiancé, with her, Ava would be less inclined to pry into Sadie's love life.

"I see Theo's still holding up," Landon said, his deep voice filling the large room.

Elliot sighed. Sadie understood the sound. Landon was six feet, four inches of pure man. An ex-Marine with a body made for warfare—especially the kind kinky folks might get up to in bed. She wondered how Ava kept up with the guy and had to give props to her mild-mannered cousin. Theo's older brother had a kind of take-charge aura to him. She could totally envision Landon wearing a Marine Corps uniform.

So unlike Gear and his laid-back attitude. Yet her *fun buddy* had that same kind of domineering, masculine presence. Personally, she thought him better looking than Ava's hunky blond.

"Theo's great," Sadie said, defending her employee. "He works hard and has a real attitude." She smiled. "My kind of kid."

Landon laughed. "Figures. You know he ships out December 1st. I wanted to do something special for him. Thinking about hiring someone to cater a party for us. Know anyone I can ask?"

Elliot watched him, a smirk on his face. "I'll do it for free, Landon. I'm sure you and I can come to some kind of…arrangement," he purred.

Ava did her best to hide a smile.

Landon turned pink and frowned. "If I say fuck off, you'll somehow turn that into innuendo, right?"

"You betcha."

"Asshole."

"Now that word I can totally work with. You see, I—"

"Shut it, Casanova," Sadie cut in before Elliot grossed everyone out with his sexual experiences. Some things a sister did *not* need to know about her brother.

Landon chuckled. "You guys crack me up. Later, slackers." To Ava, he said, "Bye, baby. See you at home." He kissed her, and she waved at him when he left, then sagged against the wall.

Ava fanned herself. "He just keeps getting better."

Sadie used to get envious seeing her cousin so in love. But now she didn't feel that same tug of want, because Gear seemed to fill that void in her. Not love, she thought in a rush, but affection. Acceptance. Belonging—something she'd never really had with any man who wasn't a relation.

After chitchatting with Elliot, Ava slowly approached. The tricky psychologist might as well have been wearing blinking yellow lights.

Caution. Caution.

"I'm not talking to you," Sadie said, remaining firm. *Show no weakness, or she'll eat you alive.*

Elliot kneaded dough and watched them, making Sadie feel like the star of her own doomed reality show.

Ava gave her a patient smile—ironically the same one she used for her actual *patients*. "I hear you have a boyfriend."

"He's a man who's a friend. So yeah, I guess you could call him that."

"Oh?" Ava just stared at her with that clinical expression Sadie despised—because it made her spill her guts in seconds. "That's not what I heard. You met his parents. You're sleeping with him. And he's meeting Uncle Tony on Saturday."

"I…well. Maybe. Gear is, ah—"

Ava's eyes twinkled. "Gear Blackstone, the famous ex-member of *Motorcycle Madnezz*, is dating my cousin. I really need to hear all about this. From you this time, not Elliot."

"Elliot." Sadie glared at her brother.

"What? She asked how you were doing. I told her

what I knew." He smiled, his eyes mean. "*All* I knew. Now go on, take a break. I got this."

"But we're busy. I—"

Ava pulled her away. "Wash your hands. Grab us some salads, and I'll meet you out front. Oh, and I already paid Theo for the food."

"What?" Elliot scowled. "You're family. You don't pay."

"It makes Theo feel good, like he's doing his job. If I just take the food, it doesn't count."

Elliot blinked. "That makes no sense."

"Welcome to my world," Sadie muttered, dragging her feet. There was no putting off her cousin. Ava would wait to talk to her, maybe even ask Sadie's dad how Sadie was *really* doing. She'd done that the last time Sadie had dated a real loser, one who'd lasted more than two dinners and a movie. Her father had then felt the need to meddle in her life, hanging around, wanting to have father-daughter time. To talk about…stuff.

Sadie shivered. It had been a nightmare.

"Fine. But leave my dad out of it."

Ava frowned. "I love Uncle Tony."

"Love him without me near. I can use less daddy time with that barracuda."

"Sadie."

"Please. You've met him. Am I wrong?"

"Well, no." Ava smiled. "I'll meet you out front."

A salad and an apple juice later, Sadie felt pleasantly full. "Okay, ask."

"What's the situation with you and Gear? Elliot and Rose really like him."

"He's a great guy." Sadie fiddled with her straw. "We

might be dating." *He called me his girlfriend but took it back. Yet we have sex almost daily, and he's constantly giving me orgasms. He kisses the top of my head and cuddles me, and I have to work hard to suppress lovey-dovey feelings. Oh, and I have a total dad crush on his old man.*

"Uh-huh." Somehow Ava didn't sound convinced.

"Great. So that's that."

"What's wrong?"

"What?"

"You seem nervous."

Sadie stilled her tapping toes. "I'm not. I just hate getting grilled about the men in my life."

"You have no men in your life." Ava studied her, her green gaze piercing. "But Elliot seems to think you have one now." She paused. "On a scale of one to ten, what is he?"

They'd had this discussion before. "A nine." Lie. More like an eleven.

Ava raised a brow. "Tell me three things you like about him. Go."

"He's hot. Fun. And a little mean."

"A little?"

"Well, he's kind of obnoxious." Sadie grinned, remembering his hissy when he'd found her cheating at sex monopoly. She'd ended up paying rent on her back several times. "And coarse. He's a guy's guy."

"And you love him."

She nodded before she could stop herself, then froze.

"Sucker." Ava laughed. "Oh, relax. You know I won't say anything. Doctor-patient confidentiality."

"You're *not* my doctor."

"Too bad, because I'd be rolling in money if I were. You need therapy like a fish needs water."

"Funny."

Ava smiled. "I want to meet this guy."

"We're not that close."

"Oh?"

"It's all happened so fast."

"Sometimes it does. Doesn't mean what you feel isn't real."

"I can't love him. Can I?" Sadie nibbled at her fingernail, realized what she'd done, and put her hands flat on the table. Only her father and Ava could get to her like this. "Look, I met his parents. He called me his girlfriend, then retracted it. He and I are just having fun. He broke off with a woman he was engaged to not long ago. One a lot prettier than me."

"What does pretty have to do with it?"

Everything—according to Adrian. She bit her lip. She and her cousin had gone rounds about Sadie's hang-ups regarding the Douche.

"Have you seen *Motorcycle Madnezz*?" she asked Ava.

"Landon made me watch it once. I liked Gear. And Smoke. He was intriguing."

"Well, I never watched the show until right before Gear left. But I can tell you that in real life, Gear's a regular guy. Says it like it is. No pretense."

"Good. You need real. Is he nice to you?"

"Yeah." Sadie contained a blush, remembering how nice he'd been the previous night.

"Do you feel like he respects you?"

"Yep. Look, Ava. He and I are good. In the words of Landon Donnigan, 'Don't shrink me.'"

Ava cringed. "I really hate that expression."

"I know." Sadie laughed, feeling better. "Now forget I said anything about Gear and tell me about you. How are you and Love Buns doing? Are they having another self-defense class at the gym? I need one. I want to learn how to karate chop a guy in the throat."

"I'll talk to him about it." Ava's tone didn't sound promising. "He's been busy at work, and his brother has been so into his girlfriend he's not thinking about much else lately."

"Too bad."

"What?"

"For me. I really want to do some butt kicking." She leaned close. "Did you know I punched Sahara Blankenship, from *Motorcycle Madnezz*, in the face?"

Ava's eyes widened. "You *did not*. That was you?"

"Yep." She told her cousin how it had happened, and Ava grew incensed on her behalf. *Yeah*, Sadie thought. *You gotta love family.*

"Gear saw you do this?"

Sadie nodded.

Ava smiled. "I bet he loved that."

"He did. But for the record, there were no witnesses. You get me?"

Ava twisted an invisible key over her lips. "Right." She paused. "So you're bringing him to dinner Saturday night?"

"Maybe."

"Hmm. I'll try to be there. You know Uncle Tony wants another look at Landon. Maybe if we're there, he won't give Gear such a hard time."

"Oh, hey. That's nice. No wonder you're my favorite cousin."

"You mean your only cousin."

"Yep. What I said."

Ava left a short time later, and Theo cornered Sadie before she could join her brother in the back once more.

"Look, if they're on you guys about a surprise party, I don't want to be a bother."

"What bother? Landon wants to pay us. I mean, he would if we were having a party. Which we're not." Talk about loose lips. She could have smacked herself.

"Okay, then I'll give you a list of what to make." Theo didn't pause before adding, "Elliot's tiny corn dogs and mini quiches need to be there. The shrimp ones, not your cheesy things."

"What?"

"No offense, but his are better."

"You little punk." She narrowed her eyes on him, but he looked over her shoulder and smiled, ignoring her.

What else is new?

"Hey, Gear. What's up?"

Her heart raced at mention of the man's name. *And you love him*, Ava had said. Sadie was doomed. She'd fallen in love with Gear Blackstone. God. How lame could she be to fall for a guy because he liked her? She turned around with a big smile on her face and forced herself to feel it.

"Harrison." She had to laugh at his sour expression.

Theo frowned. "Harrison?"

"Inside joke." Gear walked around the counter and dragged her by the arm into the back.

Chapter 12

SADIE SNARLED TO COVER THE SHEER PLEASURE OF being with her lover again. "Hey, get off."

"Call me Harrison again and I'll make it impossible for you to sit for a month."

"Now that's what I call a man's man," Elliot said, his eyes gleaming with mirth as he worked on dough for his homemade baguettes. "I too have dated a man's man and found it difficult to sit for a month. Only the most dedicated of lovers can—"

"Shut up," she and Gear said at the same time.

Next to Elliot, Rose laughed. "You're right, Elliot. They are cute together." She waved at Gear and left for the front of the shop.

Elliot smirked. "Sorry, but you two are so easy." He shoved his dough into the proofing oven, then went to wash his hands.

Gear let go of Sadie's arm, only to grab her hand. He squeezed.

She looked at him, saw him seeming not quite right, and squeezed back. "You okay? Elliot was just teasing."

"Yeah, I'm good." He kissed her, totally disregarding Elliot's presence.

"Oh wow. I'm out. Enjoy your privacy, but promise not to be naughty on my prep table. I haven't cleaned all the flour off it yet."

"Elliot," Sadie said when she could breathe again.

But her brother had already gone.

She watched Gear, saw his worry, and stroked his shoulders. "What's wrong?"

He sighed, pulled himself away, and started pacing.

"Gear?"

"I ran into Sahara and Brian today downtown near the ferry. Oh, and their camera crew," he growled. "What a couple of fucknuts."

"Yeah."

"Do you know they had the audacity to replace me with Finn O'Hara?"

"Um, who is Finn O'Hara?"

"The most dishonest, thieving asshole on the face of the planet. He steals ideas, can't fix shit, and is a general dickhead twenty-four seven. Just because."

"You're a dickhead too."

"Yeah, but I'm good at it," he snarled and kept pacing.

She wanted to laugh, but she could see he'd been hurt by his replacement. "Gear, you're off the show."

"I know that."

"And you know they can never replace you. You were too good at what you did." That seemed to mollify him.

"Well, that's true."

"So really, it's a good thing they brought in a loser. He'll just make you look that much better by comparison, right?"

Gear sighed and stopped pacing. "I guess. It's just... Sadie, I worked so hard to make Madnezz the place to be when it comes to building bikes. He's going to ruin everything I busted my ass to create."

She crossed to him and gave him the hug he needed.

"I'm sorry." No platitudes, no trying to convince him he was better off away from the show. That he could rebuild, better, somewhere else. He hurt, and he needed to own that hurt.

They stood together for a few moments, then he did that thing that totally ruined her, the thing that made her realize her feelings for the big doofus were so full of love she was like a fat red valentine waiting to be popped by Cupid's arrow. He kissed the top of her head and sighed her name.

"You make me feel good, you know that?"

She warmed. "I'm good at sex. I know this."

He pulled back, his expression sober. "No. I'm serious. When I'm with you, I feel good. Great. Like I'm doing what I should be doing, no matter what that is."

She blushed. "Um, good. That's nice."

He frowned for a moment before his lips quirked in a smile. "You're so cute when you turn pink."

"Shut up."

"Yeah, so damn pretty with your hair up in a frizzy ponytail and flour on your nose." He kissed said nose, then kissed her lips.

Before the flames of desire built too high, he doused her ardor by mentioning, of all things, her father. "Elliot told me I have to go to dinner this weekend to get scoped out by your dad. Any hint of what to expect?"

"Elliot's a dick."

Gear chuckled. "Will your dad like me as much as my parents love you?"

Sadie stared at him. "What?"

"My dad wants to adopt you. He said you're a better man than I'll ever be. And no, that's not an affront to you being in any way manly. He also said you're fine as shit. Mom agreed."

"*What?*"

"My dad calling you a better man than me is his way of saying he approves of you. Don't ask; it makes no sense. It just is."

"Ah, good. I think."

"Mom liked the way I looked at you."

She saw the intense way he watched her right now. "Like you are now?"

"Huh?"

"You're looking at me funny right now. I can't tell if you want to beat me or fuck me."

"*Sadie.*" He let out a loud sigh. "That mouth. Your brother and sister could walk in at any minute."

"So no on beating or no on fucking?"

"You got a closet?"

She laughed. "Kidding."

"I wasn't."

She grinned, feeling lighter than she had a right to. "Dinner's on Saturday. My dad's a pill. But he'll love you. You're a man's man, like Elliot said."

"Great. I have no idea what that means."

"It just means that as long as you're nice to me, he'll like you."

He snorted. "Like you'd let me be anything but nice. I have a feeling if I tried being a real shit, you'd deck me."

"Maybe."

"I've seen you move." He cradled her fist in his giant hand. "I'm afraid."

"Good." She smiled, then looked at him with wariness. "Are you okay?"

"I am when I'm with you." He smiled. Before she could ask what that meant exactly, he kissed her breathless, then swatted her ass and stepped back. "I'm going to be busy with work for the next few days, so I might not see you. But I'll be at the gym Friday night. And definitely at dinner with you for Saturday, okay? I'll pick you up at five."

She knew they needed distance. But still, she didn't like not spending time with him. "Sounds good. We're not tied at the hip, you know," she said, more for herself than him. "You don't have to check in with me if you have stuff to do."

"Yeah." He just smiled at her frown. "Later, Xena."

"Satan," she said to be snippy.

His laughter followed him out of the room. And she already missed him.

Gear spent Thursday at home, running numbers with Thor—between Thor's classes—on starting his own garage. Though he'd had the past two months to really think about making it happen, Gear had spent his time at the Madnezz garage as usual, putting off the inevitable.

Thor had tried to nudge his older brother in the right direction, but like Otis, Gear could be unmovable. Irrational. A giant moron.

But Gear could no longer afford to wait. Thor knew his brother. Gear did his best when fully occupied. Give the guy too much time, and he'd get into trouble. With his fists, a girl, a bad business decision...

How Gear couldn't see his own patterns, Thor didn't know. But talking with the gearhead—no pun intended—never helped. Orchid understood and had agreed with Thor when he'd discussed it with her. But Gear could be so stubborn.

With his brother's shares in the business now sold, a tidy profit sat in the bank, waiting to be tapped. No time like the present…if big brother would stop acting so damn scattered.

"With the right location and the right expectations," Thor was saying to the man pacing like a tiger in a zoo, "you won't have a problem making this work. So have you figured out what you're going to wear to the Halloween party? Please tell me you'll finally wear the Spartacus costume. You have no idea how I'm dying to say Spartac-ass again." He *loved* that line. Couldn't wait to use it in public, but Gear wasn't helping.

No, Gear was staring into space as he paced, and Thor imagined his brother breaking into a sweat at the thought of starting all over. Not that Gear would be doing that, but he didn't see his business as a lateral move. No, he only saw that he'd failed.

Thor really wished Gear would get it in gear. He laughed. *I'm the king of bad puns today*.

His brother finally stopped pacing. "What are you laughing at?"

"Never mind. So, the party. Is Sadie coming?"

"I guess. Otis invited her."

"I know." Thor knew he wore that *I know something you don't* smile he'd used as a child, the one that normally preceded Gear getting his ass handed to him by their father.

"I'll bite. What do you know?"

"First, tell me what you plan to do about the business."

"I don't know. Now what did Otis say?"

"Gear, focus." Thor narrowed his eyes, aggravated by his brother's deliberate avoidance. "Do you or don't you want your own garage?"

"I do. But—"

"You're afraid you'll fail again."

"Fuck you." Once more, Gear paced—a terrible tell that anyone who knew him would understand. He was afraid. As much as Thor sympathized, Gear didn't do well with gentle compassion. No, his dipshit brother needed a swift kick in the ass.

"You failed. We all know it," Thor said, rubbing it in. "But that's *good*. Failure means you tried. Something didn't work—"

"Yeah, my relationship with Sahara. My friendship with Brian."

"And you learned from it. From failure comes the inspiration for new ideas, new challenges. So what's next?"

Gear threw up his hands. "I don't know. All I really care about is Sadie, and I'm pretty sure she's still up in the air about us."

Ah, the heart of the matter. Sadie Liberato. Thor had liked her when he'd met her. He'd liked her even more after hearing how she'd decked Sahara. And according to his mother, the woman had unknowingly wrapped Gear around her not-so-little finger.

"I thought we were talking about work?"

"I mean, she's sexy. She's annoying. Funny." Gear ran his hands through his hair. Fascinating. He'd never acted so messed up about Sahara. "It's like we're the same. She doesn't care what I do or did. She just likes me." He turned to Thor, looking out of control. "So how the fuck do I get her to see that I'm serious about her? She's not just an easy lay." Gear barked a laugh. "Nothing easy about her, that pain in my ass."

Thor bit back a smile. "What did she say when you talked to her about starting your own business?"

"She mouthed off at lunch with Mom and Dad about how I should be my own boss. Other than that, I didn't talk to her about it, really. Just how I'm pissed they're using O'Hara, that putz, to ruin the business I made." Gear swore for a while, then tapered off. "You think she'd have some good ideas about work?"

"She's smart, right?"

"Yeah."

"Focused?"

Gear frowned. "I don't know. She's happy in her job."

"So she has a unique perspective for you. She's satisfied with work. That's what you want to be. How you *used* to be." If it took Sadie to get Gear's head out of his ass, Thor would use her. "Go talk to her. See if she agrees with the rest of us. That you need to stop wishing for what was and start your own future today."

"Hmm. Maybe you're right. But I can't see her until Friday night. I think she wants some space, but she's too weirded out by us to tell me." Gear looked like he wanted to say something else, but he stopped himself.

"What?"

"Nothing." Gear kicked at his shoe. "You ever think of having kids?"

Whoa. Talk about totally out of left field. "Um, maybe."

"I want some. Kids, I mean."

"You do?"

"Yeah. I always thought I'd have 'em. I mean, I'm

not pining to be a dad or anything. But I always saw myself with a wife and kids. I'm thirty-three. Not that young anymore."

"But not old, either."

"I never wanted them with Sahara." He met Thor's gaze, his intense with an emotion Thor couldn't place. "She was gorgeous and driven, and frankly, too far above me. At least, she thought so. I just wanted to build bikes, to make something I could be proud of. Like how Dad built the fair and had us working it growing up."

"I thought you hated that."

"I did, but part of me didn't. It was all of us, our fucked-up family, making it work." Gear laughed. "Otis is a jackass, but he's good at putting shit together."

"You're a lot like him."

"Thanks."

Realizing how that sounded, Thor tried to explain, but Gear waved away his apology. "No, you're right. Thing is, Otis knows why it all works. Why he and Orchid, who couldn't be more different, are so right together."

"Magic."

Gear nodded. "It makes no sense, but it's right. I didn't have that with Sahara. Never even thought about it."

Thor understood. "But you're thinking about it now. With Sadie. A woman you really just met."

Gear sighed. "It's stupid. I've been trying to convince myself that it's just that I've finally found a nice chick. The sex is off the charts. Must be chemistry making me nuts about her."

"Well, that and she swears like a sailor and bakes killer cookies," Thor offered.

Gear gave him a weak grin.

Oh my God. He's in love.

"I think about her a lot. Like, all the time. And it matters to me if she likes my ideas or not."

"So ask her what she thinks about your future, but don't make decisions based on that," Thor said quickly. What if Sadie Liberato turned out to be worse than Sahara? A far-fetched likelihood, but possible nonetheless. "Trust your gut, Gear. Not your dick, your brain, or your heart. Your gut."

"Not very scientific, professor."

Thor grimaced. "No, but it's a known fact you have instincts like Dad. Do what feels right."

"Yeah?" Before Thor knew it, Gear had him in a headlock. "Because this feels right to me, Thorvald."

"I hate you," he choked out while Gear laughed and ruffled his hair.

"I love you too. How about we split a pizza and talk about something else?"

"Pizza again?"

"Fine. Burgers it is."

Thor made a face. "I'll have a salad...as soon as you let go of my neck."

Gear laughed, and Thor knew the idiot would call on Sadie soon enough.

Which reminded him. Time to call her sexy brother back and check on the catering for the university party. It wouldn't hurt to feel Elliot out...so to speak.

Friday afternoon, Gear stood in the Motorcycle Madnezz garage, feeling down but not out. He hadn't been to the garage in a month. The office had been cleared of all his crap save the box he now carried. He'd forgotten about it until Smoke called and reminded him about that last bit of odds and ends.

The open bay had several stations, each belonging to a member of the team. He saw eight in all and realized they'd hired some new guys he didn't recognize. Too many people for the scope of what they'd been doing. Or what *Gear* had been doing.

The tools looked a little too organized. How the hell could a guy work when he had to dig through three drawers to find a torque wrench? The sexy posters had also been taken down. No more *Sports Illustrated* models to look at. Now they had framed motivational posters and pics of big bikes. Oh hell. Had they accepted that Honda sponsorship he'd been against? Not that he hated Honda, but the point of the shop was to build Motorcycle Madnezz bikes. Not Hondas or BMWs or Harleys.

A poster there for a Honda Africa Twin CRF1000L, and next to it, a Gold Wing F6B—a touring bike rich assholes bought to travel between five-star hotels. What the hell? Next they'd be showcasing Harley Road Kings, which no self-respecting hard-core biker would ever ride. They were too comfortable and too classy for Otis, for sure.

The place was undergoing a remodel. They'd changed the MM colors from black and gold to green and red. Sahara's choice, no doubt. She'd tried to change them a while back, but they'd felt too Christmassy to him. Still did.

He snorted. A bad decision he had no part in making or living with.

Speaking of which, he needed to talk to Sadie soon. Damn it. He missed her. Though she'd acted as if it was perfectly fine with her not to see him until tonight at the gym or even tomorrow evening for dinner, he refused to wait. Like Thor had said, Sadie had some cool insights when it came to work. She seemed to genuinely love her job and thrived on being low-key. Low-drama. What he wanted his middle name to be.

"Well, well. It's Friday the 13th, and look who walked in. How appropriate." Sahara's bitchy tone made the hair on the back of his neck stand on end.

"Yo, Sahara." He nodded, trying to remain professional. Detached. He'd spotted the new cameras mounted near the ceilings. Saw the camera guys staying back, out of the way as Sahara sauntered toward him. She wore tight jeans and a clingy pink shirt that showed off her ample cleavage. Her hair had been pulled back, and silver earrings dangled from each ear.

Yeah, she looked fuckable. But she had nothing on Sadie, who wore her sensuality so naturally. He felt nothing but disgust with himself for wasting three perfectly good years of his life on Sahara, who was little more than a user.

"Like what you see?" she asked, her voice low, seductive…but loud enough to carry to the cameras.

"Nah. Been there, done that."

She glared.

Near them, a few of the mechanics who'd come closer to greet Gear snickered.

"Fuck off," she said to them.

He noticed Smoke leaning back against his workbench, arms crossed over his broad chest, his face

mostly hidden by that ball cap he almost never took off.
"Yo, Gear."

"Smoke."

"What's up, man?"

They ignored Sahara as if she wasn't there. Gear saw
Smoke's subtle grin, knew the guy couldn't stand her
and probably did it on purpose.

"Not much. Just came to get the last of my stuff."
Gear nodded to the box under his arm.

"So word has it you're gonna open your own shop."

The silence in the place was telling. Everyone—
including Gear—wanted to know what he'd be doing
with himself in the future.

"Maybe." He refused to commit on air, giving
Madnezz any more ratings than they deserved.

"Well, if you do, let me know. If I work for this cant
anymore, I'm gonna lose my shit."

Gear blinked. "This *cant*?"

"If I use the c-word I mean, the censors will cut the
segment. You hear me though, don't you, Gear?"

Gear started laughing. "*Cant*. Oh man. Yeah, I feel
you."

Sahara started screaming for Brian, Torch, and a few
of her favorite dickheads in back.

Gear shook his head and walked toward the exit. "I'll
call you, Smoke."

"Good. Do that."

Before he got to the door, someone wrenched the
box out of his arms and shoved him face-first against
the wall.

Gear spun and automatically engaged. A fist to his
assailant's belly, and Brian bent over with a *whoosh*.

"Not cool, siccing Brian on him, Sahara," Smoke said in the trademark smoky voice that had garnered him the nickname. "Torch, man, *get off*."

Gear heard a scuffle. Saw more men involved as three of the new guys came to Brian's defense, circling Gear.

"Kick his ass," Brian yelled, still holding his belly. The pussy.

Gear had been waiting to expend his anger for so long. Despite knowing this free-for-all would likely net *Madnezz* its highest ratings to date, the opportunity to get back at Brian and Brian's loyal followers was too good to pass up.

Going with Sadie's defense, Gear let himself be hit, just once, then let them have it. And God, it felt *good*.

Chapter 13

Sadie opened the door to Gear, having expected him to stop by. They needed to talk about dinner at her dad's tomorrow, and she wanted to prepare him.

But she hadn't anticipated the bruised giant standing on her doorstep. "What the hell happened to you?" She stepped back to let him inside.

He didn't limp or seem too injured to move with his usual smooth stride. But he had a split lip and a bruise on his cheek. Other than that, he looked like her Gear. To be honest, the bruises enhanced his tough-guy appeal, which, sadly, turned her on.

"Went to the garage today," he said in a low voice. "Picked up the rest of my stuff. It's all broken now." He sighed. "Got anything to drink?"

"How about some hot cider?"

"With whiskey?"

"I don't have any of the hard stuff. But I could spit in it to make it a tough-guy drink if you like."

He smiled, then winced. "Very funny. The cider will do, thanks."

"Sure." She put some on the stove to warm up, wanting a glass herself. "So did you win? Because from your face, I can't tell."

"I kicked some ass, got one of my guys fired, and probably sent *Madnezz* ratings into the stratosphere. So though I technically won, I'm a loser."

"I don't sleep with losers."

"Again, I technically *won*." He leaned against the counter and smiled at her, pulling his hurt lip. He looked her over, his grin widening.

"What?"

"I like the look." He nodded to her hair, which she'd thrown up into a clip, leaving the dark-brown stuff to trickle down the back of her neck. The way she wore it softened her face, and she'd wanted to look her best for Gear. Which in turn pissed her off and amused her. Sadie was Sadie. No amount of makeup would put her in the same class as slutty Sahara.

"No bra?"

"I thought it would save time later. No underwear either," she said, sounding chipper.

He chuckled. "I had a shitty afternoon, but two seconds with you and I'm happy. Weird."

She nodded. "Totally weird." She poured them both some cider, than added the molasses-and-cream cupcakes she'd brought home for him. Working at Sofa's was both good and bad. Good, because she got to take home a lot of their creations, sampling new ideas to see what worked and didn't. Bad, because if she didn't constantly work out, she'd weigh a bazillion pounds.

Not that Sadie cared so much about her looks, but twenty pounds over her fighting weight turned her into a slug and made it difficult to sleep. And Sadie prized her ability to sleep anywhere, in any condition.

She led him to sit with her at her dining table just off the kitchen. "So give me the details."

He sat without protest and sipped from his mug. "That is damn good. Tell Elliot he's a master."

"He knows he's good. Adding to his colossal ego gives me nothing but headaches when he starts bragging." She nudged him to eat a cupcake. "Tell me if you like it."

"What's in it?"

"Imagine a soft Mary Jane rolled around cream and touched with caramel."

He nodded, looking hungrily at the treat. "So like Bit-O-Honey and Cow Tales?"

"No, I said Mary Jane." She looked down her nose at him. "Quit acting like you know your Halloween candy to impress me and take a bite."

He did and moaned, and his food-gasm was as sexy to watch as Gear shirtless. *Yum*.

"Can I have yours too?" he asked as he licked his fingers.

She blinked. "Did you even chew? It's like watching a dog gobble down a treat."

"Gimme."

She slid the cupcake his way and watched him down it with pleasure. Sadie had always liked watching people eat her creations, but seeing Gear enjoy them made it even more satisfying.

"Last bite's for you." He held out a small piece. "And trust me, I'm not really wanting to share. Hurry before I change my mind."

She ate it off his fingers, licking one clean of the creamy frosting.

His gaze darkened, but he merely wiped his hands on a napkin.

"It's good," she agreed.

"It's delicious. But you need better decorations. That's too plain to add to Sofa's Halloween treats."

"I'm going to make spiders out of them. Or big ghosts with lots of cream cheese frosting."

"Nice."

Sadie sat sipping her cider, waiting for Gear to talk. They watched each other in silence, each beginning to smile more, until they both started laughing.

"I like our staring contests," he teased. "But I won that one."

"Like hell you did."

"You blinked."

"I did not."

"Yep, you did."

"So is this your way of avoiding talking about the fight?"

He groaned. "No. But it's more fun staring at your face than taking a fist to mine."

"Man. Who'd you let hit you?"

He laughed. "I totally did. I took a page from your book. If it was self-defense, they can't come after me later. Except it turned into an all-comers brawl. I went to pick up the box Smoke told me about. I had a few things left I wanted. A cup Iris gave me, some papers of my brother's he wanted back. Nothing major. Stuff I could have let go, to be honest."

"But you wanted to see the shop," she said for him.

He nodded, his look one of grim satisfaction. "It looks terrible. All the girlie posters are down. They have *Honda* posters up. That's sell-out material right there."

"Huh?"

"We're—*we were*—a real shop, crafting our own bikes. You don't put up factory pictures in your own house unless you're specializing in rebuilds, which we didn't. That's bullshit. They should have had pictures of our old bikes up, the great stuff we've done." He shook his head and said slowly, as if the idea had just dawned, "Except they won't, because I helped build them." He chuckled. "Classic."

"So what else happened?"

"They changed the colors to red and green."

She frowned. "Those are Christmas colors."

"Yep." He clinked his mug against hers and took a long swig of cider. "Sahara's great with fashion, terrible with bikes."

Sadie didn't want to ask but couldn't help herself. "So how was Her Bitchiness?"

He grimaced. "She walked out wearing tight jeans and a low-cut shirt that had to be hurting her boobs it was so tight."

"So trampy." Sadie wanted to punch the snotty blond again. "Bet she flirted with you, huh?"

"Yeah. It was gross." He shook his head. "I can't believe I ever dated her, let alone got engaged. If I ever do something that stupid again with a user like that, deck me."

Her mood brightened. "I'm happy to hit you any time, Gear. Just for fun, even."

He stroked her cheek. "Aw, so sweet." They grinned at each other. "A funny thing happened just before the fight. Smoke asked if I'm setting up my own shop, because he wants a job. I get the feeling he hates it there."

"Really?"

"Well, Smoke called Sahara a cant. Because he said if he'd called her that *other* c-word, he'd have been censored. Needless to say, she didn't find that too amusing."

Sadie grinned. She liked this Smoke guy. "A *cant*?

That's awesome. I love it. And I really hate the c-word, by the way. But she is *soooo* it."

"I know. Anyhow, everyone jumped in the fight. Even a few of the camera guys. I could hear the director in the background telling us to keep rolling, like we were faking. I don't know. Maybe some of them were. Not me. I took Brian down hard. He tried using his poseur mechanics to drill me, but after I went through three of them, I nailed Brian. Now his face looks like I steamrolled over it, and I hit him hard enough in the gut to leave a mark."

"My hero," Sadie said drily. "Might I remind you that you can be charged with aggravated assault?" At his raised brow, she said, "Hey. I watch *Law & Order* reruns."

He rolled his eyes. "Yeah, okay, DA McCoy. Bottom line is no charges will be filed if I don't file them first. Soon as I left, I got a call from the network lawyers. Dicks," he muttered. "Sahara was shrieking like a banshee through it all. Smoke did good, punching the lights out of Torch—who I think is also screwing Sahara, though I can't be sure. Chains just watched from the sidelines, laughing and kicking back anyone who tried to run from the fight." He smiled. "It was kind of awesome."

"I'll bet. You know, you guys have the best names. Gear, Smoke, Chains, Torch. Is there a Wheels? A Handle? Oh, I know, how about a Kickstand?"

"You're hilarious." Gear glared. "We're men, damn it. We can't go around being cool if we're telling Larry and Francis to pass the wrench, please."

She chuckled and rested her chin on her hand, elbow on the table, actually envious of his altercations. "You're so lucky. The closest I ever got to a brawl was last year on Black Friday, shopping in a Victoria's Secret. I didn't even want anything. I just went with Ava to spice up her life. So much I could tell you about my cousin, but I'll save it for a rainy day. There was a sale on thongs, and it turned shockingly ugly. I mean, twenty bucks for dental floss that gets stuck up your ass, and these women were fighting over them."

He chuckled. "Bet you won."

"Bet I did." She paused. "Unfortunately, one of the security guards got a little too grabby breaking us up. After I belted him, Ava had to drag me away, promising she'd get me counseling for my anger issues—which I don't have, by the way."

"Yeah. Right."

She glared at him. "Hey, I didn't go to my old job and start bashing heads. Shopping is a whole other animal."

"If you say so." He rubbed the back of his neck. "Smoke got canned. A few other guys quit on the spot. Good guys. But I'm not opening up a shop to employ people."

She just sat and waited, knowing he needed to talk it out.

Gear sighed. "This should be a simple answer, you know? Start a new shop. Get back to doing what you love. Build bikes. But I started that before, and it all got fucked up."

She nodded.

"You bake."

"And cook and prepare food. All that."

"Right. Whatever."

"Not whatever."

He sighed. "My point is that you're doing what you love. And you get paid to do it. So what's your advice, because you seem happy?"

Sadie shrugged. "I made a deal with myself a long time ago not to get bent about money. I have enough. This apartment isn't huge, but it's home. To be honest, I can afford it because my dad bought the building, but he doesn't let me skate on rent."

"He bought the building?" Gear's eyes widened.

"Not the point. Money isn't a huge motivator for me." *Frankly, I'm not sure what is.* "Gear, I'm a pretty boring person. I don't have many expensive habits. I like movies and TV. I have a thing for a chocolate shop in Queen Anne that has the best white chocolate raspberry truffles." She licked her lips, saw him fixate there, and felt a moment of satisfaction that she could distract him. "Lingerie, a nice soap or candle, and I'm happy. Simple pleasures. But I'm also not looking to advance, which makes me the bad seed in my family."

"How's that?"

"My father is a money man. He's a bigwig accountant who flies around the world, at his clients' expense, to fix their books. Not fix them, as in illegally. But settling up their accounts and looking for flaws in accounting. He's legal," she emphasized, still hoping that was true. "Anyhow, he makes a lot of money, and he's constantly disappointed I'm not trying to climb the next rung in the corporate ladder in my quest for success. But I don't measure success by dollars. I like baking."

"And cooking and preparing," he said, his gaze intent.

"Yeah, that. I love working with family, making Sofa's into something. I turned down chances to be interviewed after that mess with the reporter. And aside from a small raise if the business does better, I'm good with my life. Well, my material things. I don't need a bigger car, a bigger house, or a hot tub. Though if you gave me 24-7 access to yours, we could be best friends forever." She winked. "I do like soaking in my own tub. It's the little luxuries for me. Knowing I have a roof over my head, that I love my job, that I have sex with a tough guy when I want." She teased, saw him nod, and felt warm that the statement was true.

"That's what I want, except the part about the tough guy. Make mine a tough woman, and I'm there." Gear smiled.

"Yeah, but my needs aren't yours. You like making bikes, right? And you like selling them."

He nodded.

"So do it. But do it for you. Not to give some dope a job. Not to outsell Sahara and Brian. But because you're happy. An old friend of mine once told me that doing what you love for money can take the joy out of it. Since I've never pushed myself that hard—I admit, I'm kind of like a sloth or a cat when it comes to being slow and enjoying my downtime—I haven't hit too many challenges I haven't overcome." Which, come to think of it, put her relationship with Gear in an all-new light.

"What's that look?" he asked.

"You. You're my biggest challenge. Huh."

"Is that a good huh or a bad huh?"

"Not sure yet."

"It'll be good. Trust me."

"I do." Mostly. But he hadn't been tested yet. He hadn't gotten tired of her and compared her to the latest bimbos wanting a piece of him. Like the groupies from the gym, or any of the millions of viewers who had a thing for Gear Blackstone. The thought of rough times coming worried her, but no sense in crossing that bridge until she came to it.

"Nah, you don't really trust me, deep down." He didn't sound bothered by the fact.

"You think I don't trust you, and you don't care?"

"I figure it'll take time to prove it to you. I got plenty of that."

She didn't believe him. "Sure. Keep thinking that. You're already itching to do something with yourself. Me? I'd have taken the time off to go sightseeing."

"Where?"

She shrugged. "Hawaii is nice. I visited once as a kid. Great holiday. Or Vancouver. I love Canada. They're so polite up there; it's like another planet."

He grinned. "To you it would be."

She flipped him off. "But this isn't about me, Harrison. This is about you. What do you want to do?"

"Besides you?"

"Gear."

He groaned. "I don't know. I mean, I do. I want to build bikes and be excited each day to wake up and go to work. I want to be satisfied by my life. Like you're satisfied."

But she wasn't. Not entirely. Because when Gear left to go home, she'd be lonely. And when they didn't spend time together, she missed him. Somehow, he'd become a weakness she hadn't known she'd had. The thought of coming home to him every day, of sharing her time and body and making a future with him, had become an intangible dream.

Hell.

"Sadie, I think I'm going to start a new shop. Small. Just me as the owner, the decision maker. Then maybe I'll bring Smoke on. But that's it."

"You sure?"

"Well, Chains is cool. And he's a master at Photoshop rendering. He's also got a contemporary aesthetic that I like."

She blinked. "Who are you? And what have you done with my gritty boyfriend?" *Whoops*. The b-word had slipped out.

But he only grinned. "What you've failed to realize is I really *am* the motorcycle god Elliot calls me when he thinks I can't hear him. I know bikes. I know design. I'm just not as good with people."

"Well, you know me. I'm good people," she said, defending him.

His smile broadened. "Yeah, you are." He stood and pulled her with him from the table. "You're the best people, Sadie." He nuzzled her neck, then kissed her. "The absolute best."

She couldn't trust the emotion shining in his eyes and chalked it up to pent-up lust. "So, ah, you want to go to the bedroom?"

"Why? I have all I want right here."

She swallowed. "Okay." Sure, if he wanted to bend her over the table and get their freak on, she was ready. Just thinking about it got her nice and wet.

Instead, they spent the next two hours playing a stupid card game while he cheated his way to victory. Or so she claimed while he beat the pants off her by getting all the good cards.

To her surprise, he left with a kiss that melted her bones, as well as a promise to come early to pick her up the next day.

"Huh." She closed the door behind him, wondering if no sex was a good or bad thing. He'd been erect most of the night. He really did rock a pair of jeans with that impressive package. And he'd dropped the jacket, wearing a T-shirt that showed off his amazing torso and the tats she wanted to sigh and stare at all night. Something about a muscular man with a sleeve of tattoos really got her going.

Then she realized she hadn't told him anything about her father aside from him owning her building. Oh well. She could text him, could call him. But then, she hadn't had any prior warning about his folks. Time to see what Gear was really made of.

The thought made her smile.

Handsome tough guy Gear Blackstone versus Big Tony Liberato, accountant extraordinaire. The match of the decade—she couldn't wait.

—✺—

Gear didn't know what to expect from Sadie's dad. But the fact he was nervous about meeting the guy told him all he needed to know about his feelings for Sadie. They'd gone from admiration to affection to something much deeper, more serious, and all-consuming.

He'd asked Elliot for a few tips since Sadie refused to help him out when he'd asked that morning. The witch.

Hey, you never told me Otis would be there after we had sex. *You're on your own, Harrison,* she'd texted. *And I still want to know what the M stands for.*

He smothered a laugh. Sadie could be such a pain. He wondered what it would take to get her to move in with him. *And I'm already thinking about her moving in when I haven't brought her home yet?* Yeah, he had it bad.

But now, with him officially off the show, he thought the press had backed off enough to bring her by and let her see his place. Maybe tonight, if he didn't alienate her father and family by acting like a dick.

He glanced down at his black jeans and brown sweater, safe clothes to wear to a meet-the-parent dinner, or so Iris had said. His sister still wanted to meet Sadie, but Gear was doing his best to keep them apart. Bad enough Sadie had had to meet Orchid with no warning. He wanted to convince her to take a chance on him before Iris and her positivity scared her away. Too much Orchid and Iris, and he feared Sadie might bolt. He had enough working against him with his gorgeous but nasty ex.

He didn't like Sadie comparing herself to Sahara in any way. That one time she'd mentioned not being enough of a woman to manage him? Laughable. She owned his ass and had no idea. A smart move to keep it that way, no doubt.

He parked his SUV, a concession to Seattle's often-crappy weather when riding a bike wasn't comfortable, and had just gotten out to get Sadie when she exited her apartment building. She wore a knee-length skirt, leather boots that ended below her knees, and a formfitting dark-blue sweater under her gray coat. Her hair was down, her lashes seemed thicker, her lips a deep red.

He gaped as she neared, walking with a sexy swagger

that had him aroused from her first step. "You're wearing *makeup*? A *skirt*? Tell me you're wearing panties, or this evening is over. We'll be going back in your apartment and not leaving for hours."

She smirked. "A matching bra and panty set. White lace, since I'm so innocent and virginal."

He choked on laughter. And desire. "Damn, Xena. Just…damn." He opened the door for her and closed it once she'd sat.

Inside the SUV, he studied her before starting the car. "What's up with the outfit? Is it for me or your old man?"

"*Please* make sure to call him that. He'll love it."

He snorted. They drove in silence toward her dad's house in Queen Anne. Apparently Mr. Liberato lived in a posh house with a view of the city. According to Elliot, the guy had expensive tastes. To look at him was to know he could buy and sell you several times over. Tony Liberato loved his family only slightly more than making money but would do anything for his kids. Joe, Rose's husband, had practically had to sign a blood oath that he'd treat Rose right before Tony had given his okay for their marriage. And that was after two years of dating.

Okay then. No pressure to impress the guy, considering Gear was sporting bruises, had just been fired from his last gig, and recently dumped his ex in a public spectacle that had yet to fade from prime time. Oh, and he'd only met Sadie two weeks ago. Not that he was planning to ask her to marry him yet. Because if he was thinking about it, she'd say no.

Any sane, normal person would reject an offer like that. Hell, any normal person would think twice about being with a guy who fell for a girl that quickly. He also knew if she'd give him a hint of a *yes*, he'd buy her a ring tomorrow. As big as she wanted. He glanced at her, thinking she looked as pretty in profile as she did full-on.

She raised a brow, blew him a kiss, then turned on the radio. Some nice techno off a satellite channel. "Nervous? Don't be. He'll hate you on sight."

"You're not helping."

She chuckled. "I'm kidding. Dad's a good guy. He'll love you."

"It matters to you what he thinks?"

She nodded. "He's my dad. He's annoying when he tries telling me how to live my life, or when he tries to be my friend and hang out. Ugh. But yeah, I love him. I care what he thinks." She held his hand. "Don't be scared, Harrison. I'll protect you."

"Screw you."

She laughed.

Oh man. I love her like crazy.

I am so fucked.

Half an hour later, Gear found himself cornered by her father in the guy's massive living room. It had wall-to-wall bookcases on one side, crammed with actual books. Not just knickknacks, but stuff the guy had actually read. Treatises on historical battles, nonfiction accounts of economic policies that had raised and destroyed civilizations, and a host of biographies of famous people. No fiction for this guy who didn't seem to possess a sense of humor.

Gear would bet money that Big Tony had ties to

organized crime. At least, from a few of the things the guy had said, it seemed he wanted Gear to believe that. He also looked like a Mafia thug, tall and bulked up. Where Sadie got her height, no doubt. Tony had dark eyes, short, perfectly styled hair, and olive skin tanned from a recent trip to Italy. He reminded Gear of Otis, oddly enough, with the ready stance of a man who probably knew how to use his fists.

He'd sized up Gear from their handshake, and Gear had the notion he'd failed without realizing he'd taken the test.

In the kitchen, where Tony's personal chef had prepared a feast of lasagna, salad, broccoli casserole, and a few other appetizers Elliot was salivating over, Sadie, her cousin, Ava, and Ava's fiancé, Landon, chatted and laughed, oblivious to the brutal inquisition about to take place a few steps away.

"So." Tony had a deep baritone, rich and clear and demanding notice.

Gear waited.

"A reality TV star?" Tony sounded amused.

Patronizing bastard. "Nope. I build motorcycles."

"Ah." The guy stared, saying nothing. Over his shoulder, Gear saw Sadie looking concerned. Then she noticed him watching her and flashed him a smile and a thumbs-up.

More like thumbs-down as this imagined Roman emperor ordered his death in the sandy arena.

"Ever watched *Gladiator*?" Gear asked.

The big man started. "What? Why, yes, I think I have."

"Huh." Gear said nothing more, just smiled.

Tony's eyes narrowed.

Great. Now he'd started a nonverbal war with Sadie's dad.

"How did you meet my daughter? Elliot mentioned a party a few weeks ago."

"Yep. Your daughter clocked my ex. Right in the face."

Tony said nothing.

"It was beautiful." Gear grinned.

"So you like watching women fight over you?"

"I love watching a bully get her ass handed to her, yeah." Gear forced himself to be calm. "My ex hit Sadie, and Sadie defended herself. She's a strong ch—woman." Not chick. Woman. "Doesn't need a man to rescue her."

Tony nodded. "Her mother and I raised her right."

"I'd say so."

They watched each other. Gear had the hysterical idea to whistle, as if signaling the prelude to a Western gunfight. If he thought about it hard enough, he could envision tumbleweed passing through the living room, especially standing on that sandy plain where the emperor had ordered him disemboweled.

"It's time to eat, Dad. Leave Gear alone," Elliot called out.

Tony grunted and turned on the heel of his five-hundred-dollar shoes. Gear recognized them because Sahara had once tried to get him to buy a pair for a formal event. As if.

They all sat at a large dining table overlooking Lake Union. Gorgeous with the lights at night and the full moon out.

Tony, of course, sat at the head of the table. On his right sat Ava and Landon. On his left, Sadie, Gear, and Elliot.

"Giving you a hard time, eh?" Elliot murmured as Tony turned to Ava with a smile. The joy turned his features from hard to handsome, and Gear could see where Sadie got her looks. For all that she wasn't as classically attractive as her siblings, she had an inner beauty and an inner fierceness she'd definitely inherited from her father.

"You could say that." Gear frowned at Elliot's grin. "Not funny, dude."

"Oh, it is. You should have seen how he made my ex cry. You're holding up okay. Don't chicken out now."

Gear snorted. "Please. I've never walked away from a fight worth winning."

"What's that?" Tony asked, his voice modulated, pleasant. But the look he shot Gear was anything but cordial.

Gear smiled through his teeth. "Oh, nothing, Mr. Liberato. Just talking to Elliot."

"Call him Tony," Sadie said, then elbowed her dad. "Right, Dad?"

"Sure." He shot Gear a death glare. "I'm happy to be on informal terms with my daughter's latest defiler."

Ava choked on her water, and Landon coughed to cover what sounded like a laugh. Gear had gotten no more than a quick intro to Ava's dude, but at least Landon seemed to have a sense of humor.

Sadie groaned. "Give it a rest, Dad. I'm not a virgin and haven't been for many years."

Gear would have said "*You got that right*," but Elliot beat him to it. Plus, he didn't quite have the stones to say that to his girlfriend's father.

"Man. And I thought my parents were bad," he murmured to her.

But Tony had heard. He raised his brows the way Sadie did, with an arrogance that fit him. "You met his parents?"

"Yep," Gear said before Sadie could answer. "Right after she'd told them about marrying me for my money and being pregnant with twins, we all shared an amazing picnic together in a castle overlooking the mountains. It was magical." He dug into his salad with gusto. "Man, this is good dressing. I'll have to get the recipe for my mom." He glanced up and saw everyone staring at him. Some in horror, some in awe. And Sadie with a mix of the two. "What? Was it something I said?"

Chapter 14

SADIE HAD KNOWN HER FATHER WOULD VERBALLY knock Gear around a little. He'd done it to all of his children's—and even his niece's—significant others. Joe had weathered the storm. Jason, Elliot's ex, sure hadn't. Ava's Landon had passed muster. Mostly. But she knew her dad hadn't let Landon completely off the hook yet. Marrying into the family came with a price.

But even for her father, Gear seemed to be on another level of "fuck with" entirely.

Her dad turned to her, sounding way too calm, considering the anger in his eyes. "You're pregnant and married to this…man?"

She wanted to kick Gear. Great. Now she was in the hot seat. "No, of course not. I was messing with his parents because they were asking me a lot of questions, kind of like what you're doing to Gear."

"Standard parental behavior, particularly from a male authority figure in the family," *Dr*. Ava said.

Elliot groaned.

"Uncle Tony is asserting his rights as your father to protect you. And Gear, an unknown, must prove his mettle to show he deserves you."

Tony smiled. "Yes, exactly. Because from where I'm sitting, I'm not seeing much to recommend him."

Before Gear or Sadie could speak, Tony ticked off on his fingers. "He's got no job. He's a social media nightmare. He just had a fight recently; look at his face. He's a thug with no education—"

"Now hold on there," Gear said, no doubt swallowing down the *old man* he'd considered tacking on. "First, I'm self-employed. I'm also financially responsible, with a savings account, even. And hey, I know how to write checks too."

"Gear," Sadie cautioned and gripped his leg under the table.

Her father saw the motion and frowned, looking like a well-dressed grim reaper.

"Hey, I have a right to defend myself. He's got legit concerns, so I'm answering them. Second, I did get in a fight, not my fault. I won, in case you were wondering." He forced a smile. "You'll probably see footage of it tomorrow, or whenever they air the stupid episode."

Elliot leaned closer. "This is gold. So what else happened? Did B-Man break up with Sahara yet? Because that's where I see the show heading."

"Elliot," Sadie snapped.

Gear continued. "My ex–business partner, the guy who went behind my back to steal my show and my fiancée—good riddance to her—tried to sucker punch me. Well, Blackstones aren't meant to take a beating. So I showed him, and his weak posse, how to fight for real." To Sadie, he said, "They got nothing on you, Xena."

Her father frowned but didn't speak. That was a good sign. Sadie held her breath.

"Third, I graduated from high school and have an associate's degree in business. I also have a genius brother with an IQ higher than anyone at this table. And he's my financial consultant. Plus my parents taught me all sorts of stuff that's worth a hell of a lot more than a piece of paper with BS on it."

Of course Gear couldn't let it be. The *BS* obviously stood for *bullshit*.

Her father read between the lines as well as she did. He clenched his jaw as he regarded Gear.

She squeezed Gear's leg, and he put a hand over hers and eased her grip, so that he was now holding her hand.

"But I think the real question is, what am I doing with your daughter?"

"See, Dad?" Elliot spoke up. "He's not as dumb as he looks."

Landon guffawed, and Ava bit back a grin.

Sadie would reward Elliot later for adding some levity to this lovely family gathering. Did her father really have to put on this dog-and-pony show every time she brought someone home? Although, to be fair, she hadn't brought anyone home since Adrian. And Tony hadn't liked him at all.

"Elliot." Her father glared, but Sadie thought she'd spotted a glimmer of amusement on his face. "Well? What are you doing with Sadie?"

"I'm not knocking her up."

Sadie covered her face and groaned.

"That was said to annoy my parents. Your daughter and I are enjoying each other's company. She's smart, funny, obnoxious—"

"Hey." He'd been doing so well.

"And throws a mean right hook. I appreciate that in a woman. Plus, she makes the most delicious molasses cupcakes you've ever tasted."

Elliot brightened. "Oh, so they turned out okay? Awesome."

She nodded. "He ate them both in, like, two seconds. I barely had a taste—well, after the two I ate at the shop." More like three. She really needed to hit the gym. "They're even better after a few hours."

Ava frowned. "I notice you didn't bring any for us."

Landon crossed his arms over his chest. "Yeah. We manly types burn off a lot of calories. You might have brought us some cupcakes, cupcake." A look from Tony had Landon rolling his eyes. "I'm just sayin'…" he mumbled.

Her dad turned back to Gear, his gaze intense. "So in essence, you're hot for my daughter's…sweets?"

Gear opened and closed his mouth. "Um, I guess. Is that a euphemism? Or are we really talking baked goods? God's honest truth, I'm hot for both. So yeah."

Tony rubbed his temple. "I think I have a headache."

"You know what's good for that?" Gear asked. "Pressure points here." He showed them by pressing his thumbs in the under-arches of his brows. "And if it's sinus related, here." He pushed on his cheeks on either side of his nose. "You can also use peppermint oil on your skin, or oil of lavender in a warm bath."

Sadie stared at him.

He shrugged. "Sorry. My mother's studying naturopathy in addition to running the fair. But it really works," he told Sadie.

"Fair?" Her father's resistance was weakening. She heard the interest he couldn't hide.

"Gear's parents run Renaissance Daze, that medieval fair in the summer that's gotten so popular."

"Oh." Ava smiled. "We went to that this past summer. It was a hoot."

"A hoot," Landon deadpanned. "*Ow*. Stop kicking me, woman. Yeah, it was fun." Landon glanced at Ava with the look of a man in love. "She made me go, and I was glad I did. The turkey legs and corn on the cob were amazing."

Gear smiled. "That was my idea. The buttered husks of corn are popular at the county fair, and they sold out the ass." At her father's look, he coughed. "Er, they sold well."

Tony nodded. Sadie thought her father had begun to thaw toward Gear, who appeared less sophisticated than Sadie's usual type, she guessed. Not that she had a type.

"Do you work with your parents then?" Of course her father would approve of that. "Learning the family business? Making them proud?"

She stuck her tongue out at him, saw her father's smirk, and knew he'd baited her deliberately.

"I did as a kid. Learned how to work hard from Otis."

Tony frowned. "Otis?"

"My dad."

"You call him by his first name?"

"If I called him some of the other names he's earned, he'd kick my ass," Gear said, blunt yet honest.

"He would." Sadie nodded. "Otis is huge."

Her father seemed fascinated. "So you won't work with your father?"

"No way. He's in charge, and that's cool. But I'm in charge of my business. We butted heads too much when I was younger. I need to be my own boss, or so I've been told." He squeezed Sadie's hand, and she flushed, feeling warm all over.

Across the table, Ava gave her a subtle nod, as if to say things were going well.

Her father watched them. "I tried to get Sadie to come work with me out of college, but she has no drive."

"Sure she does," Gear said. "It's just not financial."

"It's not managerial either," Elliot added. "She likes not being the boss."

"'Well, the world needs ditchdiggers, too,'" Gear said.

Landon laughed. "*Caddyshack*. Spot on, man."

"What?" Tony asked.

Sadie grinned. "Come on, Dad. You know you love that movie."

"Well, maybe I do. But I'd like it if you weren't such a ditchdigger and more a business owner."

"Um, hello? I co-own the place with Elliot and Rose."

"Yes, but they do all the work. You just help out." A familiar argument they'd had forever.

"That's bull. She carries her weight," Gear argued. "For the record, your daughter is one of the best people I've ever met. She's loyal, hardworking—"

"Seriously?" Elliot said.

"—and amazing in the kitchen."

"He means making confections, Dad. We haven't done it in the kitchen yet," Sadie said, just to be nasty.

"For God's sake, Sadie. I work there!" Elliot exclaimed, clearly enjoying himself.

"Oh man. This is so much better on the other end," Landon said to Ava. "Now I see why Joe was so thankful when I showed up for family dinner."

Sadie glared at them and said to her dad, "I really

don't appreciate this dinner turning into a witch-hunt. Can't you just appreciate my job and my boyfriend and let it go already?"

"I'm sorry. Your boyfriend?" Tony asked, apparently not believing them to be a couple.

"You're damn right." Gear pulled their clasped hands out from under the table and placed them on top, clearly visible. "And if you don't like it, you can go to—"

"Get yourself a new attitude," Sadie interrupted, and just in time. Her father would stand for confrontation, an argument, a discussion. But not disrespect. Granted, he'd started it. But in his eyes, Gear was the interloper, the one who had to prove himself. Not Tony.

Gear stared down her father, and it was a glorious sight to behold. Inside, she composed ballads about her brave and stalwart boyfriend. *Jesus, I called him that. Out loud. In front of everyone.*

"So, guns at dawn?" Gear asked.

Her father cracked a smile. "Don't push it, Blackstone." He turned back to his meal. "So Landon, Ava tells me you just got promoted. Is that right?"

Sadie relaxed. Dinner hadn't ended yet, or gone as easily as she'd hoped, but she thought they'd weathered the storm.

In the SUV on the way home, she turned to Gear, pleased they'd made it.

"Your dad hates me," he groused.

She swallowed. "No. He's just an ass when you're new."

"I gotta say I wasn't too pleased with him either."

She started to get nervous. Gear wasn't laughing off

the dinner. "He was rude, but you held your own. I think he respected you."

He grumbled, "My parents were a lot nicer to you than he was to me."

"Well, I'm amazing."

"And I'm not?"

She'd thought he might be teasing, but Gear seemed genuinely upset.

"Hey. Where are you going?"

"I'm taking you to my place. You've never been, and frankly, I need to be back in my own territory."

She'd been so concerned about how her father would take Gear that she hadn't thought about how Gear would react to her dad. That Big Tony might have pushed him away before she was ready to watch him leave.

She had no illusions that at some point, Gear would find someone better. Sadie knew she was awesome, but men seldom remembered that after time spent with her. Still, she hadn't thought their new relationship, such as it was, would end so soon.

She sat back in her seat and turned on the radio, needing something to fill the ugly silence.

She roused herself from the blurred view of the city and noted they'd crept into West Seattle. The Craftsman-style house they pulled up to was beautiful. Prettier than she would have thought for Gear. He pulled into a tiny driveway and parked.

They sat in silence.

"Sorry for being a dick. Your dad pissed me off."

She shrugged, wanting to cry and feeling angry at the pathetic emotion.

"Come on."

She followed him out of the SUV into the house and couldn't help comparing it to hers. It was bigger, nicer, more expensive, and looked like something out of a home-and-garden magazine. Hardwoods, cream-colored walls decorated with vintage photos of motorcycles and landscapes, a killer sound system and big-screen TV, and a fireplace drew the eye. She drooled over his kitchen with its granite countertops, white oak cabinets, and glass-tiled backsplash. And the appliances. Gear had a double oven, a six-burner gas-top range, and a prep sink.

"Do you even cook?" she asked as they passed through the kitchen.

"Sometimes."

"So this was all Sahara's doing?" Now she really hated the skank.

"Not all. Most of it was mine and Iris's. Oh, and Orchid's too."

She followed him up the stairs past the media room—her media room consisted of her ugly couch and a TV—to what appeared to be his bedroom. Gray dominated his walls, the huge bed littered with pillows and strewn blankets. He favored dark mahogany furniture, and she wanted to hate the sense of style—just in case it had been Sahara's—but couldn't.

He followed her gaze to the bed and grimaced. "Don't worry. I chucked the other bed the minute I found them fucking on it. This one has only ever had me in it."

"No one else?"

He angrily yanked his sweater off, then his boots and socks. "Nope. Too busy being a deviant and illiterate thug to screw half the population. Sorry."

"Gear, stop." She planted her hands on her hips. "No, no. Keep undressing. Just stop with the attitude."

To her relief, he stripped down to his boxer briefs, and *hel-lo womanhood*, he looked amazing. A veritable twelve-pack with the most amazing obliques.

"I'm not good enough for you, is that it?"

"Are you high? Of course you're good enough." Not wanting him to be the only one getting naked, she tossed off her boots and socks, stepped out of her skirt, and threw her jacket over a nearby chair, then did the same with her shirt. "Happy now?"

"No," he growled and shoved her back onto his bed. She couldn't help noticing how aroused he'd become.

And now, so was she.

"What the hell do you want?" she asked him.

"The truth. So you don't think I'm not good enough for you?"

"Wait. I don't think you're not...?" That meant he was good enough, right? "Yes, yes, you're fine. You're great. I never said you weren't. What are you, crazy? You're the one with the expensive house and TV show and fiancée with fake boobs and hair. You know, the one I can't possibly compete with."

"*Ex*-fiancée." He loomed over her, staring from her lace bra to her lace panties. "The hair wasn't fake, by the way."

"I feel so much better now, thanks," she sneered. "Maybe it's *you* who's too good for *me*."

He gave an angry laugh. "You're high. I just think it's funny that I'm good enough to fuck, but not good enough to marry or have kids with."

"What the hell are you talking about?" What exactly had her father said to him that she hadn't overheard?

"It's all a big joke that we're dating. That I'm calling you my girlfriend. I'm no professor like Adrian was."

"Why bring Adrian up at all?" Was he drunk? He'd only had a beer at dinner. But maybe she'd missed him tucking away a few others?

"Or a fancy accountant like your dad." He slid his fingers in the waistband of his underwear, the head of his cock peeking out with each pass.

"So what?"

"So if I asked you to marry me and have kids with me, you'd say no. Because I'm just a grease monkey with no education."

She gave an angry laugh and leaned back on her elbows on the bed, glaring up at him. "Fuck you. You have more of an education than I do. I graduated high school and got my certificate from culinary school. Then I majored in real life." She looked at him with disappointment. "If I asked you to marry me, you'd tell me no. Be honest. I'm not half as pretty as your ex and not nearly as wealthy."

"Fuck that. You're hot, and you know it. Did you ever think I don't care about money either? That I got carried away with my bikes and the show? That maybe if you did ask me, I'd say yes?" he hissed and came down on top of her.

Oh my God, he was sexy as hell in his rage. "Yeah? Well, maybe I'd say yes if I was asked, too."

"I'd knock you up first, because that's how us low-brow monkeys do it," he said, breathing hard, getting as worked up as she was. He yanked down his underwear, and she felt his cock spring against her belly.

"Go for it, big guy," she dared, wanting nothing more

than to be with Gear forever. A dream she'd never have. But so angry with that denial, she reached for insanity and yanked him down to her.

He fell on her like a starving man, kissing her, nipping at her, giving it to her as rough as she gave it back. He teethed her through her bra, swearing when he couldn't tear it off fast enough. Then his mouth was there, sucking her nipples and laving them with attention.

"Damn it. More," she demanded.

He groaned, sucked harder, and had her arching off the bed into his hot, wet mouth.

Gear ground against her belly, his cock hard, thick, and more than ready to enter her. But her panties were in the way.

He literally *ripped them off*. She'd never had a man tear her underwear off, and the wildness of his excitement fed hers.

Before she could say a thing, he nudged her thighs wide and thrust.

She cried his name as he fucked her with a raw need he couldn't disguise with words. He pounded into her, and she took every single inch.

She whispered naughty things in his ear, things she wanted him to do to her. Things she wanted to do to him. He groaned and strained, his body rubbing against hers in all the best places while he stretched her tight sex.

He kissed her, penetrating her mouth with his tongue. Then he slipped his lips to her cheek, her neck, and moaned her name as he catapulted her into an orgasm that ripped her apart.

She took him right along with her, because Gear

swore as he came inside her, the rush like nothing she'd ever felt.

Gear and Sadie, together, floating in pleasure she couldn't deny.

After some time, he kissed his way from her neck to her face. But when he pulled his head back to look down at her, she saw that his attitude hadn't softened. Nor had his cock all the way, still stuffed inside her.

"You think I can be a real uneducated asshole, huh?"

She groaned. "That was my dad, dumb-ass."

His mean grin made her shiver. "Yeah? Well, I'm a demon in the sack, baby. And it's time you found out just what that means." He paused and rotated his pelvis, letting her feel him deeper. "Oh, and I'm not wearing a condom for any of it. You said the timing wasn't right, remember? We'll just have to deal."

Her heart raced, her desire for a baby, for Gear, too much to handle just then. But she could work with sex.

"Yeah. We'll have to deal," she agreed, glaring up at him. "So you'd better think twice before bailing on me."

He laughed, a harsh sound that soothed the ache in her soul. "Nuh-uh. It's too late for *you*, Xena. Because I've already decided to keep what I want. And what I want is you."

He kissed her again, and their angry sex turned more passionate, more intense. Then Sadie was feeling nothing but orgasmic, dying that little death all over again.

"You really are the devil," she panted sometime later, after her third orgasm.

"And I'm just getting started."

Chapter 15

GEAR GROANED, HANGING HIS HEAD OVER A STEAMING cup of coffee.

A week after he'd lost his mind with Sadie, and after the absolute best sex of his life, he contemplated the mess he'd made. Or hadn't made.

What kind of an unmarried, uncommitted idiot wanted to get a woman pregnant? That was no way to make a relationship work. He didn't want to trap Sadie with a baby. But damn, he wanted to practice making one with her all the time. And hey, if in the meantime she had a kid, even better.

He groaned again. "What am I thinking?"

For a week, they'd been spending nights at his or her place. He worked out at the gym while trying to figure out how to deal with the future. He'd been checking out places to build his new empire, small though it might be.

Sadie continued to work at Sofa's, constantly bringing him new treats to try. Nothing had come close to those molasses cupcakes, and he'd asked if she'd been trying to kill him with the amount of sugar in her homemade candy-corn cookies.

They felt like a couple. They talked, laughed, and bounced ideas off each other about their respective jobs. But they hadn't discussed their insanity last weekend, fucking without protection. And it hadn't all been *fucking* either. They'd made love for hours. The sensual hedonist that was his girlfriend had fried his circuits. She'd actually tired him out after their marathon weekend. Though ever since, by unspoken agreement, he wore condoms.

Sadie was so Sadie, acting all tough, as if what they'd done didn't scare her. He could see she was as freaked out as he was about their actions. He wished he didn't know why he'd been so angry.

Her father's opinion meant something to Sadie, and knowing her father thought him not good enough for his daughter had scared the crap out of Gear. He worried that Sadie might take Tony's opinion to heart and kick him to the curb.

He couldn't lose her. Sadie was amazing. Loyal, sexy, tough, funny. He loved everything about her. Even the way she stole his food and made fun of his name. She'd started calling him Gear Shaft after overhearing him talk to Chains the other day. God knew how she'd torment him if she ever found out what the *M* in Harrison M. Blackstone revealed.

Some part of him wanted to watch her find out. To see her glee and have all her attention as she picked on him, then soothed his wounded ego with kisses and brownies. The woman fed more than his appetite for sweets. She fed that need inside him for someone special who'd understand him. Complete him.

"I'm a Hallmark card. Fuck me." He drank his coffee, both pleased and worried that she'd insisted on staying home last night, wanting some space.

Damn it, he wanted to wake up with her. She'd left a few things behind the last time she'd stayed the night. Some dirty socks, a hair band, but still. Proof she'd been here, with him. He'd hidden the band in his nightstand and tossed the socks in his hamper with his clothes. As if they belonged there, always.

Tired of feeling dopey and out of sorts, he dressed and met Thor in an industrial area he'd been scouting for where to set up shop.

"I like it." Thor glanced around the building. "It's been used as a garage before, so you're probably set on the zoning and permits. The lease isn't so bad, and the location is ideal. It's like grunge central down here."

In an area of the city that was up and coming, but mostly limited to car shops, an outdoor foot court, and some trendy industrial-type clothing stores, Gear thought he'd found his new site. Hip car chic, he'd overheard the neighbor say when recommending the place.

"Yeah, the last owners owned a garage, and they're willing to kick in some of the old equipment if we want it." Gear had kept some of what he'd had at Madnezz, but not much. "The more expensive items like a motorcycle lift, tire changer, air hydraulic repair press, those are nothing next to the cost to build a separate area for paint. Especially with proper ventilation, insurance…" He mentally ticked off item after item. After his experience with Motorcycle Madnezz, he knew he'd been looking at over fifty grand, easy, to get started. But he wanted to do it right, if on a small scale.

And he needed clients for that. Right now, he could work on orders in his personal garage, but only small jobs. He needed to set up shop, and his hunger to do so felt good.

"Are you going to take it?" Thor asked.

"I think so." Gear nodded, the pressure that weighed him down easing as he made his decision. "It feels right."

Thor clapped him on the back. "I'll go get the agent back in here to sign some papers."

An hour and a half later, after Thor had thoroughly looked over the documents, Professor Brain had declared them fit for signing, with no hidden addenda to screw Gear over, and Gear signed his name and accepted the keys.

"Wow." Thor grinned. "That was fast. It's yours. Right now."

Gear blew out a breath. "Yep. All mine. And the first thing I need to do is—" He struck the notion of *call Sadie and let her know* when Thor said, "Buy your brother some lunch, because he really is almighty and powerfully hungry."

"Yeah, that." Gear smiled and walked his brother down the block to the food court. Over a dozen food trucks encompassed the small square, with picnic tables and even an overhead canopy to protect from Seattle's wet weather.

After ordering some fish tacos, they settled down to an overcast afternoon.

"I'm thinking about joining that gym you're going to," Thor said out of the blue.

Gear just stared at him. "Why?"

"I think I should make group fitness a part of my daily activity."

"Ah, okay."

"What is it? Jameson's Gym, right? In Green Lake? It's a little out of the way for you, isn't it?"

"Sadie goes there." Gear shrugged. "I'm cool with it."

Thor gave him a knowing look.

"What?"

"Where do you see this thing with Sadie going? You talked about having children, Gear. You've never, *ever* expressed a desire to have a family in your thirty-three years."

"Well, not to you."

Thor just looked at him.

He groaned. "I'm really, really into Sadie. It's so bizarre, but I feel like I've known her forever. I don't like being without her. And I have a bad feeling I'm more into her than she's into me."

"Does she know how you feel?"

"Are you nuts? I just met the girl. I don't want to be that guy who comes on too strong and freaks her out. The creepy one she tells all her friends about."

"Sadie doesn't have any friends."

"How do you know?"

"Elliot and I talked about you two, as well as the catering job he's doing for the university. He thinks you're good for her, that you'll get her to at least be a little bit more social. Though honestly, you two are a bit too much alike."

"Too much?"

"Well, you spend as much time with me as you do your garage heathens. Like Sadie, you're all about work."

"Heathens?" Gear chuckled. "Anyway, that's over with. Now I just have you, my lucky little brother." He slapped his brother on the back and had to smile at the audible *oomph* he heard. "Okay, so we don't have a lot in the way of friends. We both love our families." He frowned, thinking about Sadie's pain-in-the-ass father.

"Otis and Orchid like her a lot."

"Yeah, well, that might be where Sadie and I differ.

Her dad hates me." He gave Thor the rundown on his one and only Liberato family dinner.

"That's harsh."

"Then why are you smiling?"

Thor laughed. "Because I can see it, you sitting there, trying to make a good impression. Her big, bad dad having it in for you no matter what you did or said." Thor laughed again. "Did he really use the word *defiler* in a sentence? I have to meet this guy."

"Yes." Gear deflated. "It's bad enough her dad doesn't like me. She thinks I'm just okay. We have great sex."

"TMI, dude."

"But nothing I do impresses her. She's not a fan of the show. She doesn't care about money."

"Which is actually good for you, because once you get the shop up and running, you won't have much."

Gear scowled. "Not helping. Shit. There's got to be something I can do, something I have, that will show her how much I like her."

"Maybe that's your problem. You 'like' her. I bet if you told her how cute and 'likeable' she is, she'd be all aflutter."

"Ass."

"Seems to me like you love her. Say it."

"I will when I'm ready." Nerves made him feel like he'd eaten something sour.

Thor shook his head. "Accept your emotions. Being in tune with yourself doesn't make you gay."

"I never said it did." Where the hell had *that* come from?

"I know, but you and Otis are always trying to

out-macho each other. God forbid you be less manly and more compassionate."

"Do you have a point to any of this?"

"Not really. I just like criticizing you." Thor gave him a wide smile. "Actually, I think you should chill out. Take your time and let this good thing you have going with her flourish into a long-term relationship. For some reason, you seem panicked that you like her more than she likes you and that somehow that's a disaster after... How long have you been dating? Three whole weeks?"

"Feels longer than that," Gear muttered. "Look, I can't help it. She makes me nutty."

"But in a good way, I think." Thor shrugged. "It's been a while since my last serious relationship, but I can tell you that shared core values and an ability to communicate are what make it work. Even when Evelyn and I broke up, we talked it through, and we're still good friends today because of it."

His brother's sexuality confused the hell out of Gear, because Gear had only ever been into women. Yet, Thor's ease with himself and who he wanted to be had always been more important than anything else about him. Truthfully, Thor seemed a lot healthier emotionally than Gear had ever been. *I am* so *not telling him that, or I'll never hear the end of it.*

"You're weird, but I love you." Gear shook his head. "It's unnatural for a guy to be so mature and comfortable in relationships at your age."

"Um, Grandpa, I'm only four years younger than you." Thor huffed. "Though I sometimes think I live in dog years. I'm actually more like two hundred and three."

"Hey, math whiz, ease up on the thinking and just

eat, would you? You're making my head hurt." *It's bad enough I can't stop thinking about screwing up with Sadie*. Under his breath, Gear reminded himself to be cool and take it day by day.

"Yep. Talking to yourself. That's the beginning of the end for sure." Thor shook his head. "Next round of tacos is on me, Bro."

Sad when a guy's little brother made the most sense.

After Thor left to head back to school, Gear made a few phone calls. The first was to Smoke.

"You still want a job?" he asked the taciturn mechanic.

"Yep."

That was Smoke. He spoke when he had something to say, not a fan of idle chitchat.

"I'm opening up a shop. Small. Two-, maybe three-man operation. I need help setting everything up. You in?"

"Pay the same?"

"Probably less until we're on our feet. I'd give it six months."

"I give it three. I got messages for you from four of our old clients wanting new bikes. Not the new Motorcycle Madnezz bikes. Yours."

Gear had a few warm fuzzies from knowing he was still in demand. "Cool. Text me the numbers."

"Done."

"So if I was to add another guy, what do you think of Chains?"

"You mean Francis?" Smoke taunted.

Gear heard some swearing in the background. "Oh, is he there?"

"No. I like talking about him because he's so much fun to be around."

"*Asshole*." That was Chains, all right. More inventive cursing behind Smoke, then Smoke's raspy laugh.

"He's okay, I guess. I mean, he's a pussy in a fight. But he's useful in the shop."

"Right." Gear did the math. "I'm thinking you and I start up. We bring Chains in on a contractual basis for certain designs. Then, once we have enough cash flow, maybe we do full time. You get that, Chains?" he asked, knowing Smoke would have put him on speaker for his buddy to overhear.

"Yeah," Chains answered.

Smoke rumbled, "Not gonna take that long to be rolling in orders, unless your new shop is something Sahara would like."

"No way." Gear knew what Smoke was talking about. Madnezz had started out small and thrived. Then Sahara—and Brian—had taken them big at the behest of the studio. He'd never liked so many people around, getting in his space, around his things. "And we'll have one boss—me."

"Works for me."

"I'm good," Chains added.

"Then we're done. I'll call you next week to kick things in motion."

"Right." Smoke hung up before Gear could.

With his employees in place, a shop to fill, and plans to be made, Gear cycled through his list of contacts, wondering about putting out a heads-up about his new business. But Iris had taken him through his first launch. He should probably use her again. Not just because it made sense, business-wise, but because if he didn't, she'd pout and grow generally unbearable, forcing him to grovel, apologize, and act sorry for not thinking of her.

He called and left her a message.

Feeling better about life, he sent Sadie a text, because he couldn't stop himself.

She answered back right away with congratulations for getting his head out of his ass, finally.

Gear laughed. "Oh yeah. I'm definitely gonna marry that one."

———⁓———

Sadie put her phone back in her pocket, smiling. Gear seemed in good spirits. About time he made up his mind to start again. She knew better than most that indecision could be a killer. Back when she'd been attending a community college to get her culinary arts certificate, she'd worked while studying and taken two years to get her one-year certificate.

But she'd done it on her own and was proud of the fact. Then came the question of what to do with her skills. She'd wasted the next three years working in diners and small restaurants, and eventually found herself in a bakery. Three years spent wavering about cooking choices and not going forward.

Then she'd found a love of baking, something she'd always had, really, and taken it to the next level. She'd attended classes at South Seattle to specialize as a pastry chef, then found herself not liking the extreme attention to detail. She'd hated not being able to fudge with recipes, everything so exacting. Another year spent meditating on what she wanted to do. Then, by chance, she'd found a career at an up-and-coming restaurant downtown. She'd been lauded for her desserts, because they tasted delicious and were comforting. Not designer, but filling and soft on the palate.

Fast-forward to Adrian convincing her she could do better, which she hadn't. Thank God Elliot had decided to buy Sofa's. Because she'd finally found her niche. She hadn't made millions and probably never would. But she loved her job. It had only taken her seven years to find her happy place.

With any luck, Gear wouldn't take that long.

"Ahem."

"Sorry." Sadie flushed, not usually prone to wool-gathering. The shop wasn't too busy, with the afternoon rush having just ended. So though the store was full, the counter only had the one woman waiting to order.

"I'm in the mood for something light and sweet. What do you recommend?"

"Hmm. Are you fruity? Fluffy? Prefer chocolate to vanilla cream? Or both?"

The woman looked to be about Sadie's age. She smiled, and something about her struck Sadie as familiar. "I like fluffy and creamy, and chocolate's always a plus. Oh, and put a latte on my order too."

"Size and flavor?"

"A small vanilla latte."

Sadie marked it down. "How about a cream puff? They're medium-sized and not too heavy. I don't like to use dense cream in them."

"You made them?" The woman gave her a suspicious look Sadie didn't understand.

"Yes," she said slowly, wondering if she'd some-how offended the woman without realizing. "You're not a fan of Marsha Concannon or Sahara Blankenship, are you?"

The woman blinked. "Ah, no. Should I be?"

"Nah. So what'll it be?" After the lady ordered, Sadie said, "I'll bring it out to you."

"Thanks." The woman found a seat where she could study Sadie. And study she did.

Once the woman's order had been taken care of, Sadie took it to her, then sat at the table. "All right. Who are you and what do you want? Hey, you're not a reporter, are you?"

"What if I am?"

"Then you can talk to Elliot. Are you with the Food Network?"

"No. I did want to talk to you, though."

"Look, lady. I don't do interviews. I'm not famous, don't want to be famous, and have a full life based on donuts, cupcakes, and cookies. So if you want to know about Gear Blackstone, go talk to him." Sadie wanted to clock the woman in her perky face, but she managed to restrain herself and stood.

"Wait."

Sadie paused. "You have two seconds to make my day."

"Very Clint Eastwood of you."

That the woman knew the actor made her rise in Sadie's estimation. "One, two... And I'm done."

"I'm Iris."

Sadie knew that name.

"Iris Blackstone."

Sadie sat back down, studying her. "Oh yeah. It's your eyes. I knew you looked familiar." Sadie smiled. "Hi. I'm Sadie."

"I figured that out."

"So what's with the stare-a-thon?"

"You are *just* like my brother."

"Thanks?"

Iris laughed. "Yep. No wonder you two get along so well." Iris studied Sadie as she sipped her coffee. "I wanted to meet you, but for some reason Harry has been keeping me away from you."

"*Harry?*" Sadie's grin threatened to split her head in two. "He said only one person called him that, and he killed the guy." Or words to that effect.

"He lied. I'm the only one who sometimes calls him that." Iris smiled. "He hates it."

"Yeah. He hates when I call him Harrison, too." After a pause, Sadie decided to go easy on the woman. "What do you want to know?"

"Not much. I wanted to get a look at you. I've heard from my parents and seen you on the internet. But aside from a brief glimpse of your skeleton face while you threw water on that idiot reporter, I couldn't tell much about you."

"Not much to tell. I'm pretty much this." Sadie pointed at herself, hoping she wasn't disappointing Iris. Normally she'd tell a nosy body to pound sand, but this was Gear's younger sister.

They didn't look all that much alike. Thor and Gear looked more similar than Iris and Gear. But the shape and color of the eyes was the same. Iris was tall and lithe, with straight dark hair, more brown than black, and a crooked smile that seemed charming. She was pretty, not cute, and had a weird vibe. A happy-happy, joy-joy aura of goodness and light. That part Sadie found annoying.

"So you bake, you hate reporters, and you're dating my brother."

Sadie felt uncomfortable. "Yes. Are we done?"

Iris smiled. "Not yet. So you like my brother?"

"I think we covered that."

"Did we?" Iris bit into her cream puff and moaned. "Oh my God. This is *amazing*."

"I know."

"Have you made Gear one of these? 'Cause if you do, he'll never leave your side, ever. These are to die for." Iris consumed the rest in one big bite.

"Glad you like it. They're my favorite, if you want the truth. Though it is the season for Halloween. You should try our pumpkin rolls."

"I'll get one to go." Iris sighed. "I'm in heaven. That was so good."

A customer headed to the front, so Sadie excused herself to wait on him. Several more entered, and once she finished tallying up orders, she saw Iris standing by, watching her.

"Seen enough?"

"You're not a fan of people, are you?"

Sadie gave her a grim smile. "No. And especially not when they take five minutes, holding up the line, trying to decide between a monster macaroon and a pumpkin bread man. I say get both. It's easy."

Iris grinned. "You can box me up two more cream puffs and a pumpkin roll to go."

"That I can do."

"My brother really likes you, you know." She paused. "More than he ever liked Sahara."

Sadie started but didn't otherwise respond, placing

the box on the counter. She didn't know if she should give the girl the food for free, as goodwill toward Gear's family, but Iris took the choice from her and slapped a ten on the counter.

"Keep the change."

Never one to argue over a tip, Sadie did. "Thanks." After a moment, she said, "I like your brother too."

"He likes you *a lot*. Don't break his heart, or I'll hex you."

"Oh?"

Iris frowned. "Well, it won't really be a hex. I'm not a witch or anything. And real witches are more into pagan stuff that's all about the earth and do no harm, but—"

"The point?" Sadie interrupted before Iris launched into information overload.

"Any bad karma you put out there will come right back on you. And treating Harry badly won't do you any good."

"How about telling your brother this? *He* should be nice to *me*."

"He isn't?"

Sadie groaned. "He's great. I just meant at some point, being the famous Gear Blackstone, he'll get douchy or nasty, act like God's gift to women, and we'll break up. And it'll be his fault."

"Wow. You really went all the way there, didn't you?"

Flustered because she hadn't meant to let herself out there like that, Sadie forced herself to sound calm. "Any other questions?"

"Are you coming to the Halloween party next week?"

"I don't know." She didn't remember an invitation to one.

"Otis said he invited you."

"Oh, at the house in Ballard?"

"That's the one." Iris nodded. "Good. If you need a costume, come see me. Fair of Dreams is my shop. We also supply all the costumes for Renaissance Daze, so we're more than happy to suit you up in medieval garb. Though from what I hear, you did Xena proud."

Sadie shrugged. "I liked the sword."

"Hmm. You know, I could totally outfit you as a female knight. If you like swords, you'd love a battle-ax or staff."

"Maybe." Sadie liked the idea.

"Okay. I'd better go. See you at Halloween, unless I see you on the news before then," Iris teased, and in a low voice added, "Try not to beat anyone else up, okay?"

"Funny. Just like your brother."

Iris beamed. "Bye, Sadie."

Sadie watched her go, feeling lost and nervous and excited. She was really in deep with Gear. He might not think so, but she had never been so wrapped around a guy before, not counting Adrian. And she knew better. After Adrian had ripped her heart out, she'd done her best to protect it. An easy feat since most men didn't interest her much past their expiration date. A few sexual encounters and they spoiled.

Not Gear.

Everything about him appealed to her. Except for one thing, and that had more to do with her own insecurities than him. With his fame—infamy—and good looks, he had no shortage of women wanting to sleep with him. Yet he'd settled on Sadie. She'd thought about the why of it a lot. He obviously appreciated the fact she liked him in spite of *Motorcycle Madnezz*. They had off-the-charts sexual chemistry. They seemed to like the same things.

But she had a feeling sooner or later he'd see the real Sadie. The boring woman who didn't care about pleasing anyone but her family and herself. What happened when he got even more famous from his new bike shop, and he wanted to go out to galas and TV thingies? He'd want her to dress up and accompany him, and then she'd be that sad, non-famous-actor wife who looked like she'd rather be anywhere than on the red carpet.

Wait. *Wife?* What the hell was that? She kept subconsciously inserting words like *wife*, *forever*, *marriage*, and *babies* into her thoughts about Gear.

And that right there. Babies. She'd had unsafe sex with Gear all last weekend. She might be pregnant even now. The birth control she'd started last week wouldn't take effect until this coming Monday. She wished she could say that she feared having Gear's baby. But the irrational half of her wanted it. Bad.

For his part, Gear hadn't brought up their earlier stupidity, nor had he said anything about his part in forgoing condoms. For a guy always keen on being safe, he'd been a lot less than safe with her. Why did that make her feel special?

Because I'm a dope, that's why.

Her phone buzzed, and she saw a text from Gear about hitting the gym that night.

A smile formed before she could think it away. She should say no, should put more space between them and ready herself for the inevitable when they'd break up after the newness of being together wore off.

Yet Sadie knew her relationship with Gear was unlike any she'd ever had. *Damn it*. She loved the jackass. What the heck was she going to do when it all went to shit?

She texted him back. See you there. Slacker.

He sent her back X's and O's, followed by a smiling cupcake emoji with hearts in its eyes.

Sadie sighed and went back to work, thinking about Gear for the rest of the day.

Chapter 16

THAT NIGHT AT THE GYM, GEAR SAW SADIE AND GAVE her a nod. She nodded back at him, super serious, and he crossed his eyes at her, causing her to smile. Then glare and shoot him the finger.

He chuckled. His smile left him when some big guy with muscles walked over to her to talk.

She said something, laughed, then nodded toward Gear.

Wondering what she'd told the guy and beyond pleased to have been included at some part in her conversation, Gear waited to be approached.

The big guy smiled and stuck out a hand. "Hey. I meant to say hello before, but our paths haven't crossed. I'm Mac Jameson, owner of Jameson's Gym."

Gear nodded and accepted the man's hand. Owner or not, if he put the moves on Sadie, Gear would end him. He wondered what Sadie would think if she knew how primal and possessive he'd grown about her.

He cleared his throat. "Hi. I'm Gear."

"Yeah, seen the show. It's not going to be anything without you." Mac grimaced. "All that talky crap. I just wanted the bikes."

Gear smiled. "Me too."

"Sorry. Didn't mean to talk shop. Just wanted to make sure the gym fits you. If anyone gives you a hassle while you're here, let me know. We have a few famous faces, but at the gym, we keep it low key. No autographs and fame bullshit. Just weights and working out."

Elliot waved from across the room.

Mac pinched the bridge of his nose. "And if you can help it, no relationship crap either. This is a gym, damn it."

Gear laughed. "Everyone knows Elliot, huh?"

Mac nodded. "I swear, I love the guy, but he's such a pain in the ass. And don't tell him I said that, because he'll turn that into a joke, and next thing I know, everyone will think he and I are dating again. Not that we ever were dating. I just mean that somehow these rumors keep getting started." Mac frowned. "Even my wife thinks it's funny. I don't get it."

Gear nodded. "You said nothing. Got it."

"I'll leave you to it, then." Mac walked away, greeting other people, showing Gear that the guy hadn't made the stop to impress, but because he treated everyone the same.

That made Gear like the place even more.

Sadie glanced in his direction, then away. And the night progressed.

After doing some dead weights, followed by a *very* short run on the treadmill—he hated running, one large point of contention with his jackrabbit girlfriend—he went to refill his water bottle.

Leaning against the wall next to the water fountain, a chipper redhead turned her attention to him.

"Oh hi." She was all breathy. *Sadie would have a field day with this one.*

"Hi." He filled his bottle, wishing the flow wasn't so damn slow-going.

"I'm April. I know you. Gear Blackstone, right?" She turned up the wattage on her already bright smile. "How do you like the gym?"

"I like it just fine." *When women are leaving me alone*.

During his time at the gym, he'd mostly been left alone. A few guys had told him how much they'd liked the show, and yes, he'd found a few phone numbers tucked under his towel now and then, but for the most part, people let him be.

This woman seemed to want something.

"I was just wondering if you wanted to go out sometime." She ran a fingernail over his sweaty arm.

He subtly pulled away, trying not to cause a scene in Sadie's home away from home. "Ah, no thanks."

"You sure?" She stepped closer, and he smelled perfume, not sweat. Then, to his shock, her hand grazed the front of his shorts before she cupped him, then quickly dropped her hand.

"*Whoa*." He stepped back and bumped into Elliot. "Damn it." He glared at the woman, but she just smiled and walked by him.

"My name is April. I'll leave my number at the front desk in case you're interested."

Gear and Elliot watched her leave.

"I think I was just fondled." Gear couldn't believe it. In all his time on the show, before and after even, he'd never been so boldly, er, handled.

"Wow. That's much more a Megan move." Elliot stared after her.

"Does she do this a lot?" Maybe she had mental issues.

"Not that I know of. I think you should talk to Mac about that."

"I don't know." He felt stupid for wanting to complain. If a guy had done it to a woman, no question she should say something. But he was twice April's size.

"If you don't, I will. That's not cool."

Gear frowned. "Actually, if *you* mention to Mac you saw it, that might be better than me saying something. With my luck, crazy April will sell her story to the tabloids, and I'll end up being the grabber."

"I guess in some ways, fame does suck." Elliot paused. "And speaking of suck…"

"I'll stop you right there."

Elliot laughed. "I was just going to say it sucks to be you."

"You got that right." Gear couldn't help chuckling with him.

"What's so funny?" Sadie asked as she approached. "And what the hell is April smirking about?"

Gear shook his head at Elliot, not wanting to cause a scene that might spiral out of control, not in Sadie's gym. Sure, he was now a member too, but this spot was sacred to her.

Elliot glanced from her to Gear, and Gear knew the fool would spill his guts.

"Don't—"

"April grabbed him."

Sadie frowned. "What?"

"She totally cock-grabbed your boyfriend. I saw the whole thing."

Expecting Sadie to give him the third degree about it, Gear readied to defend himself.

"I'll be right back." Sadie walked away.

"Huh?"

"Watch." Elliot smiled with glee.

Gear looked for Sadie and saw her narrowing in on April.

"We should—"

"Watch and learn, Gear. My sister is not one for subtlety. Take note."

"I've seen this play out before." He cringed, waiting for April to get her ass handed to her.

Sadie had a discreet conversation. The redhead turned wide eyes to him, then hurried away.

"What was that?"

"My scary sister in action." Elliot sounded satisfied. "You sure you know what you're doing dating her?"

Sadie returned with a smile.

"Well?" he asked.

"I told her if she touched my man again, I'd shove her head up her ass, right after I ripped out her fake nails one by one and shoved those down her throat."

"Your man, huh?" Gear wanted to rock back on his heels and crow in delight. "So we're not in the closet anymore?"

"Hey, man." Elliot huffed. "That's my people's line."

"Shut up, Elliot," he and Sadie said at the same time.

"Ugh. Young love. So disgusting." Elliot left them, grinning ear to ear.

Gear couldn't wait. He kissed her, right there in the gym for anyone to see. "Man, I love you." He hadn't meant to declare it like that. Hell, he hadn't meant to say it at all.

Sadie blinked up at him when he finished. "I...ah... I have to go treadmill."

O-kay. So she planned to pretend he hadn't said it.

Probably for the best. They could continue as they'd been, no problem. "Sure thing. I'm gonna hit the sauna. Meet you back at your place after?"

"Yeah." She practically ran away from him, and Gear wondered if the happiness he'd experienced just now would last. Or if he'd ruined them after all.

Sadie ran as if her life depended on it. He'd said he loved her. *Loved. Her.* A slip of the tongue? Yet he hadn't seemed fazed by the admission. Hell, maybe he said that to all his girlfriends.

Angered at the thought, she ran faster and gave herself a slight incline. *Damn, damn, damn.* That look April had shot her had told her the woman was up to no good. April had never much liked her, not that Sadie had done anything to cause the hostility. So okay, maybe she'd once ordered the woman off her machine. But then, she'd been waiting for her turn, and April had butted in line.

The rumors about Gear and Sadie being more than friends had apparently hit April, because the redhead had sneered at her before sidling up to the counter, her predatory gaze on Gear.

Hearing April had groped her boyfriend, Sadie had no choice but to declare intent to do the bitch serious harm. And come on, what self-respecting person groped a stranger, anyway?

If Gear didn't say something to Mac, she intended to. April had something really wrong knocking around in her brain.

Sadie started huffing and knew she'd get a good

workout, thanks to Gear. It didn't help that April was beautiful and knew it, or that she'd conquered practically half the gym in her haste to beat out Michelle for gym bunny of the decade. Sadie had lied to Elliot; she listened to gym gossip. How could she not, with as much time as she spent in the place?

Then again, she'd been spending a lot less time at Jameson's since hooking up with Gear.

"*Man, I love you*," he'd said.

Sadie ran faster, unable to escape those blasted words.

Half an hour later, she preceded Gear into her apartment.

"Good workout? I saw smoke coming from your feet. You're like a deer on that thing," Gear said with a smile.

She shrugged, doing her best to put the love comment out of her mind. "I'm going to shower." She paused, waiting for him to ask to join her. He didn't.

"Gotta check my messages." He pulled out his phone and starting scrolling through it.

"Whatever." *He loves me. Right.* She huffed and stripped on her way to the shower. Once inside, she let the hot water ease her aches. The one thing she could say about Gear: he was good at keeping her not bored.

She took extra time getting clean, giving Gear a chance to join her. She didn't like playing games and normally didn't. But that thing with April and then Gear confessing stupid emotions had hers in a tailspin.

When he failed to join her after twenty minutes, she was steamed enough to dry herself through evaporation.

She toweled off and stormed into her bedroom, only to see Gear lying in her bed, naked and on his side. And he seemed very happy to see her.

"Man, you took forever."

She coughed. "Um, I was dirty."

He smiled. "I showered at the gym while you were doing your marathon. Come get me dirty again."

"I don't know. You're probably still contaminated from where April handled you."

He held himself for her, his erection taking center stage. "Don't worry. I scrubbed down hard. See? I'm all clean."

"Yeah?" She dropped her towel and charged the bed, landing on top of him but careful not to damage his precious cock. "Just how clean are you?"

Without giving him a chance to say anything, she scooted down his body and took him in her mouth.

"Sadie, Christ."

She loved taking him out of his comfort zone. She destroyed him in bed, and the powerful play gave her back the confidence she'd lost earlier.

She bobbed over him, sliding her tongue over the spot just under his crown, knowing how crazed it got him.

"Oh fuck. Yeah, baby. Suck me." He arched up into her, his hand gripping her shoulder, the other stroking her hair. "I thought of something."

She continued to blow him, cupping his balls as she drew harder, sucking with a fierceness he seemed to crave.

"For Halloween, I'll go as a cleaning guy. You go as my Hoover."

She paused, and his deep chuckle affected her enough that she pulled back to stare at him.

His smile caught her right in the feels. *Hell*.

"What do you think? You have powerful suction.

And you're really good at getting me clean." Then he dragged her over him and kissed her, taking any thoughts she had left.

He fucked her mouth with his tongue. His hands were everywhere—over her back, her arms, then down to the small of her back, pulling her into him. He found her ass and rubbed, and the massage felt amazing. Sexual and therapeutic.

"You wet for me, baby?" he asked, nipping her earlobe. "You ready for me to get some satisfaction?"

She would have promised him her great-grandmother's famous sauce recipe if he'd asked. "Sure," she said breathlessly, on fire as his hands pushed her to sit up, cupping her breasts.

He played with her, letting her angle herself over him, taking him deep inside her. Finally.

She arched her back while he massaged her breasts, his fascination with her nipples a joy of its own. He sat up and pulled her down at the same time, then sucked from each breast while she rode him, no thought but an orgasm so close she could taste it.

After pulling away from her breasts so he could watch her, he shoved a hand between them, fingering her clit.

"Gear," she rasped, her entire body like a live wire.

"Yeah. You like that." He watched her with intensity, and at any other time she might have been embarrassed.

But Sadie's body had control of her, and she wanted nothing more than to come.

"Squeeze me. Get me off, Sadie." His breathing increased, his arousal growing with hers. "I want to feel you come around me. Let me see you," he crooned and pinched her, and she cried out, lost to everything but the sensations of pleasure coursing through her.

He groaned, pumped into her faster, then stilled while she trembled in his arms.

They sat entwined for some time, her legs on either side of him, his body still full inside her, slowly starting to soften.

He planted kisses on her chest, her shoulders, her chin. When he reached her lips, the caress felt different. Not sexy or soft, but so caring.

"Man, I would worship you all day every day if I didn't worry about my dick falling off."

Thank God. Gear was back. She grinned. "The romance. I just can't take it."

He chuckled, rubbing her back with those big, callused hands. "Sorry. That didn't come out right."

"Oh, I think it came out just fine." She laughed, pressed so tightly against him she didn't fear him falling out of her.

"That comment was so…Elliot-like." Gear sighed. "And now the mood is truly gone."

"Hey, I gave you what you wanted. I messed you up."

"You mean I messed you up," he corrected and hugged her when she would have left him. "Now we get to talk about exactly what that means."

"Huh?"

"Sadie, let's stop dancing around. We're not into games and bullshit, right? So let's get this settled. Two weeks ago, we had crazy car sex, and I came inside you." He closed his eyes, a huge smile of satisfaction on his face. Then he opened his eyes, the green-and-gold colors entrancing. "I knew the risk, and I wasn't sorry I took it. Being in you was better than anything I've ever had in my life."

She blushed.

"I can't regret it. I won't. You said we were safe, that the possibility of you being pregnant was probably not gonna happen."

"That's what I said. I wasn't lying."

"I didn't think you were. But you and I talk about stuff. And we never talked about that. Why not?"

"I don't know." *Because I'm a moron who wants your baby? Yeah, crazy girlfriend wouldn't mind getting knocked up by you because I love you? Maybe? I think?*

"We just had unprotected sex again." He kissed her throat, then her mouth. "And you're probably not that safe."

"Well, uh…" Should she tell him she was on birth control now?

"So you could get pregnant." He ran a hand through her hair. "That should be freaking me the fuck out. But it's not. Because it's you."

"Okay, now *I'm* freaking the fuck out." Her heart raced. "I'm not ready to be a mom yet."

"It's not like I'm lined up to be father of the year either," he said drily. "But burying my head in the sand and pretending those things can't happen when we fuck raw, well, that's just stupid."

"I know." She groaned. "I went on birth control right after that time in the car, okay? The next day, as a matter of fact. We should be good." She couldn't read his expression. Relief? Annoyance? Anger? "Well? What's that look?"

"I don't know. Probably relief."

That would make sense. Wait. *Probably?*

"It's not like I want to do things backward. For me, I always thought I'd be the opposite of my parents, who popped out three kids, then decided to get married. Orchid's a born-again hippie, and Otis plays by no rules but his own."

"Yet you turned out okay." She stroked his neck, feeling the taut muscles sloping to his shoulders. "Mostly."

He chuckled, and she realized they were having the conversation with him still embedded inside her. Talk about doing things backward. Having unsafe sex, *then* talking about protection.

"The thing is, why didn't we talk about this before? We came home from the castle and just spent the last two weeks having sex with condoms. I'm okay with that. You know I am. But why didn't we talk about it?"

This conversation made her uncomfortable. She squirmed to get free and Gear let her. "Be right back," she said as she raced to the bathroom to clean up.

Once clean, she donned a robe and returned to him. He was sitting at the edge of the bed wearing a pair of sweatpants. Nothing else. Glory be to tattooing.

"Like it, huh? You're always staring."

"That's because you covered your dick. Trust me. I'd stare at that instead of your arm if you bared it again."

He smiled and shook his head. "See? We talk about my dick. My tats. But not about something important like a baby."

Or the fact you said you love me. She *so* wanted to say that but had no intention of opening that can of worms so soon after the baby stuff.

"What do you want?"

"I want the truth about what you're feeling." He

patted the spot next to him, and she sat, soothed by his body heat. "The last thing I want to do is scare you off. That's why I didn't bring it up. That and I kept waiting for you to say something. You're nothing if not vocal about what you want and don't want."

"You say that as if that's a bad thing."

"Not at all. With you, I know where I stand." He paused, took her hand in his, and rested it on his thigh. "Sahara was needy. She wanted to be the center of attention all the time. At first when we were dating, I liked being with her. But it didn't take long to see she wanted fame more than me. She had an agenda, and I didn't care because I had my own too. I wanted to build bikes. The more elaborate, the shinier, the faster, the better. And she helped me get to that point.

"But she and I could never talk like this. I never wanted to think about a baby with her. Never forgot myself with her, to the extent I'd come inside her without protection."

"Oh?" Sadie wanted an Academy Award for Best Not Acting Like His Words Mean Everything in an Awkward Scene.

"To be honest, I was afraid if I said something about it, you'd bail. I mean, what kind of lame guy doesn't care about being safe? And then you'd realize I'm not a great bet in the romance department either."

She squeezed his fingers, staring at their joined hands. "You? Mr. I'm Afraid My Dick Might Fall Off?" They both had a nice laugh about that. "I don't know, Gear. You and I happened so fast. I've never felt this kind of connection before." She took a leap. "It's a little scary."

"No shit." He cleared his throat. "I mean, I'm happy

being around you. Even when you're bitchy, or you make me eat food you know isn't good enough to be in Sofa's, I eat it and feel like a king because you want me to have it."

She felt too warm, alarmed he might begin to comprehend her deep feelings. "I like to feed people."

"Yeah, but I'm not just people. I'm the guy banging Sadie Liberato—I'm king of the world." He laughed and pulled her into his arms for a kiss. "Look, Sadie, I'm not trying to talk this to death. God knows I'd rather have my teeth pulled than have some Lifetime moment."

"Amen."

"But I want us to be good. We're good, yeah?"

She stared into his eyes, feeling *so much* good her heart threatened to burst. "Um, yeah. We're good. Sorry I didn't tell you about being on the pill before. I just wanted it to be totally safe before we did it again without a condom."

"Did *it*? Making love, you mean?" he teased.

"Nah. Making love is for wimps. You and me, we're solid fuckers."

He slapped a hand over her mouth. "Sadie, that mouth. It's so dirty."

She nodded and licked his hand.

"Ew."

"That's what you get."

"Oh?" He rolled them both back on the bed. "I don't think so, you dirty girl. Now use that mouth for good."

"For good?" She chuckled, loving how fun Gear could be in bed.

"Yeah. Get me clean. You know, now, while I'm small and soft and able to fit all in your mouth."

She glanced at him lowering his pants and saw he'd lied. "Not that soft or small." Even flaccid, Gear was huge. "Though I have to admit, I've never heard a guy willingly call himself tiny." She gripped him, feeling his heartbeat in the rush of blood there.

"Never said tiny," he rasped. "And I'll do whatever I have to to keep you in line, woman. Now shut up and blow me."

"Ah, there's my Romeo with his love words." She grinned. "What do I get if I do?"

"You get an awesome costume for my folks' Halloween party. I'll take care of it."

"Hmm. That sounds like a good deal."

"And one more thing," he said on a moan. "You get a protein shake free of charge."

"Okay, no more food references from you. I can only stomach so much." Realizing her bad pun and knowing he'd heard it because he laughed, she shut him up fast with her lips and tongue.

Ha. Not so funny now, am I?

He had the last laugh when he considered turnabout fair play. And he multiplied his big win when he hugged her to sleep and kissed the top of her head, murmuring love words when he thought her asleep.

The big jerk. *Now what do I do about that?*

As she nodded off in dreamland, where they were the golden couple, in love and finding their happily ever after, and where it was safe, she admitted, "I love you too."

Chapter 17

GEAR DIDN'T KNOW WHAT TO THINK. SADIE HAD mumbled something that sounded a lot like "Love you too" last night. He wanted to think she'd been responding to him. But who the hell knew?

A guy with balls would out and out ask her. Hadn't he said he didn't like games? But he'd never played at something he couldn't afford to lose before.

Gear took risks with every new creation. Hell, he was taking a huge one with his new venture. But he couldn't afford to lose Sadie.

"I signed a lease," he said as they sat eating breakfast together. She'd made him blueberry pancakes, and had he not already been in love with her, he'd have fallen for her because of the pancakes, no question.

"A lease?" She toyed with her food, her appetite a little off.

"What's up? The baby making you too sick to eat?" he taunted.

"Asshole."

He grinned. "The lease for my new shop." He told her where it was, and she agreed the area sounded perfect. "You should come by and see it."

"Maybe I will." She added nastily, "That's if Harrison Jr. lets me get by without making me puke."

"Hey, I'm eating here."

"No kidding." She stared at him, and he loved that she liked his looks. "Where do you put it all?"

"My feet." They stared down at his size twelves. "I have big feet. Hey, another thing we have in common."

"I like having big feet," she said and picked at her pancakes, then pushed the plate aside. So maybe she didn't like blueberries. "These puppies let me run really fast, right over your back and up your ass if you aren't careful."

"Ohh. So scary. Maybe you should be a witch for Halloween."

"Ha-ha." She drank some coffee and smiled. "Since I was such a good girl last night…"

"You were. *So* good." The woman could swallow like nobody's business.

She snickered. "You're so easy. Anyway, you owe me. But I get some say in the costume, right?"

"Yeah. We could go meet my sister when you're done working today, if you want. She'd open the shop for us. You'll love Iris. She—"

"I already met her."

He paused. "You did?" What the hell had Iris done?

"Yeah. She came to scope me out, and I lured her to the dark side with cream puffs."

"Freakin' Iris. I told her to leave you alone."

"Embarrassed of me?"

"Yeah, that's exactly what I am. Embarrassed." He rolled his eyes. "More like my family tends to scare people away. They're not—ah—normal. Probably the only guy who wouldn't put you off is Thor. And I made sure I was present when you met."

"Oh? Why's that?"

"One, so he'd be on his best behavior with you. He's

got an IQ of a bazillion, and he can be a little preachy if you let him. Plus, some chicks dig the brainy type. I didn't want you to possibly be one of them."

"So you're saying I'm not brainy?"

"No, thank God."

Sadie threw a napkin at him, and he grinned. "Yeah, well, I liked your parents. And I like your brother and sister. Iris was cute. She was being protective. And the fact she owns a costume shop is a bonus. Halloween is my favorite holiday, but I loathe clothes shopping. This applies to costumes too."

"So you're saying you lucked out by meeting me. You owe me."

She frowned. "How did you get that? Since meeting you, I've been attacked by your vicious ex-fiancée."

"Um, you pounded her."

"I've been hounded by the press and nearly sued."

He loved the twinkle in her green eyes. "Again, you made the first move. Throwing water on a reporter? Oh, and that press is getting your shop a lot of popularity. I read an article about Sofa's the other day in a Best Of list online."

She wasn't done. "Then I had to deal with your family taking shots at me."

"My parents like you better than me."

"And I had to defend your honor at the gym. All in all, knowing you has proved to be really trying."

"Sac up, Sadie."

"Hate to break it to you, but I don't have a sac, thank you very much."

He laughed. "Yeah, not sure I'd be so hot for you if you did. Then again, I am a fan of that mouth."

She blushed, and he laughed harder.

"Shush," she said. "Now let's go. I have to get to work, and you have to do…whatever it is you do on Sundays. What are you doing today?"

He shrugged. "Going to head to the new shop and sketch out some ideas. I also need to talk to Iris about some rebranding, now that Motorcycle Madnezz isn't mine." It still hurt to say, but not as much anymore. Not when he had Sadie and a fresh start waiting for him.

As if sensing his fading grief, she gave him a hug and kissed his chest. Right over his heart.

He squeezed her. *Woman, you are it for me.* Now how the hell could he get her to see that? Because she'd panicked yesterday at the gym.

"Can't. Breathe."

"Oh, sorry. Sometimes I forget you're not as big as your mouth."

She grinned. "Come on."

"You know, you should give me a key," he offered. "Then I could come and go when I want to."

She froze. "A key?"

"Yeah, you know. They work on locks?"

"Smart ass." She went to grab a jacket, studiously not looking at him.

So weird to see Sadie flustered. He still didn't know if that was a good thing. He'd rattled her last night, but she hadn't run far. Just to the treadmill.

"And I could give you a key to my place. You know. So we're even."

She glanced up. "Even, huh?"

"Sure. Besides, I have a hot tub. Just think. You can use it whenever you want."

Her slow smile melted his heart. "Well, it would let me keep an eye on you."

"Hey, I'm an open book. I got nothing to hide, baby. It's just you and me. And more pancakes. And maybe something tasty from Sofa's, okay?"

"Everything from Sofa's is amazing," she argued.

And he wanted to breathe a sigh of relief that he'd made it past that hurdle.

They walked to their cars, and she stopped him. "So, ah, I'll get you a key later. I have to get one made, because Elliot and Rose have my spares."

"Sure. I have an extra one at home. Sleep over tonight and you can have it."

"And a soak in the hot tub?"

He grinned. "Sure. Why not? You earned it."

Her frosty glare took him aback.

"What did I say?"

"That I *earned* the hot tub? What? On my back?"

He snorted. "I would have said on your knees, because if you remember, I was mostly on my back. But no, I meant because of those blueberry pancakes you didn't eat. I'd marry you just for those."

He saw her pale at the word *marry*. Shit. He needed to talk to Elliot about her. Maybe her brother could give him some tips on how to win Sadie over permanently.

"Ha. I was kidding about being mad."

But not about being panicked over thoughts of marriage. "Yeah. I could tell."

"You could not."

"Quit bickering with me and go to work." He turned her in the direction of her car and gave her a gentle push and swat on her ass.

"Hey."

"I'll swing by here and pick you up at six, okay?"

"Fine. But I don't want to have to work hard for my costume. Have Iris pick it out."

"Sure."

"And no more warrior princesses. I did that. I need something else."

"For someone who doesn't care about what she's going to be, you're a little particular."

She opened her car door. "Hmm. Maybe something creepy. Sexy? I don't know. I'll think about it." She waved, shut the door, and left.

He stared after her, more in love with the little coward every damn time.

Gear spent the morning and afternoon at the new shop, taking measurements, looking around the area, spotting potential tie-ins and competition. He had plans to make the working area in the back visible. No hiding this garage. In front they'd have some room for supplies and products. Maybe some branding with clothing, like T-shirts or hats.

He smiled to himself, wondering if Smoke would ditch his Motorcycle Madnezz cap now that they were going to be called something else. But what? Gear came up with a blank every time he thought about what to name his shop.

Then he returned the calls Smoke had given him, rounding up four new clients and setting times to talk face-to-face. Making it all *real*.

After coming up with more plans, he drove home and

took a nice hot shower, changed into fresh clothes, and did menial chores to while away the hours until he saw Sadie again.

He still couldn't get over how right they fit. The sex was off-the-charts incredible. And despite them being new to each other, he'd never experienced that same connection with anyone else. Ever.

He felt like he knew her better than he should for such a quick courtship. She liked being in charge of her life. She liked to take charge in bed too, and he had no complaints about that either. But that caution when it came to permanence... They needed to deal with that.

He found the spare key he'd tied with a blue ribbon— blue, her favorite color—and had wrapped in a small box. He'd added a box of her favorite chocolates. Elliot had been most helpful with the name of the shop. But Gear needed to have a sit-down with the guy.

And soon. He knew he couldn't keep throwing out emotional grenades and not expect one to blow up in his face. They hadn't discussed him loving her. And though she'd accepted his key and planned to give him hers, which he could see would be a huge concession from the guarded woman, if he even tried spelling marriage in front of her, she'd bolt.

Then there was the matter of her father. Who didn't seem to like him much.

He sighed. *Why worry about this now? I have plenty of time to worm my way into her heart, right?*

He hoped. They argued all the time. Small, funny moments of contention that made being with her such a challenge. Gear would be bored with someone who agreed with him all the time. Sahara had liked the same things he had in the beginning, and he'd found out later she'd lied to reel him in. Sadie didn't seem to hold things back. She had no problem telling him what she thought.

It helped that they did like a lot of the same things, and in areas that mattered, they were on the same page. But what he really loved about her was her passion for being right. Not to the extent she was a pain in the ass to live with, but she had confidence in herself. She didn't need him to feel worthy. She had a life all her own, independent of him.

But she could need him a little more, and he wouldn't be bothered.

He still wondered how she'd really felt about them having sex without a condom, back in the car. It had been sexy as fuck, but totally not safe. He'd been alarmed because he wasn't normal for wanting to tie her to him with a kid. But why had Sadie—strong, impassioned Sadie—gone along with it? Had he been that good that he'd seduced her into accepting all of him sans protection?

He grinned, not upset with that idea at all.

After folding a load of laundry, he heard the doorbell ring. Thinking it was Sadie, he opened it without thinking.

And saw Brian standing there. The asshole's face still sported bruises, though makeup seemed to have covered much of it. Pussy.

He just stared at Brian.

Brian, who'd once been his best friend. They'd had sleepovers, gone on camping trips, and had been so tight he'd trusted his buddy when it came to signing away his rights to his livelihood.

Well, I know better now.

"Look, we need to talk." Brian gave him an apologetic

smile, and Gear saw what the cameras would. A handsome young guy, his sandy hair cut just right, not preppy short or metal-band long. He wore clean blue jeans and a dark leather jacket, and appealed with bright-blue eyes without a hint of malice.

Yeah, looks could be deceiving.

"No, we really don't." Gear didn't budge.

Brian sighed. "I know you hate me. And part of me deserves it."

"Part?"

"But there are things you don't know. For the sake of the friendship we once had, let me in to talk, would ya?"

Gear wanted to toss Brian out on his ass, yet he wanted to know what the hell had brought his ex–best friend over, when the guy clearly knew Gear hated him. So he'd hear Brian out. *Then* he'd toss him out on his can. "Fine. You say what you need to say, then we're done." Forever.

They both stood in his living room, neither conceding to sit.

"Talk."

Brian shoved his hands in his pockets, his remorse clear to see. But Gear wasn't buying it.

"Look, I'm sorry I slept with Sahara." Brian gauged Gear's response, and when Gear didn't give one, he continued with a frown. "She came on to me first, so you know. But I shouldn't have fucked her, not when she was yours."

Gear shrugged. "You wanted my hand-me-downs. Then again, you always did." Though Gear's family hadn't been wealthy, they'd always provided for him. Brian's parents had been lower middle class, caring for six kids. Brian hadn't often had new clothes or toys, or even clothes that fit. But Orchid had seen a little boy in need and helped him out, often giving him Gear's clothes once he grew out of them, and sometimes she just bought Brian new clothes because he needed them.

So it wasn't cool of Gear to bring up Brian's past. Then again, it hadn't been cool of Brian to sleep with Sahara.

Brian glared. "Maybe if you'd spent more time with your girlfriend and less getting your stones off in the shop, you'd have seen her looking."

"And maybe if you'd been in the shop with me instead of letting me do all the heavy lifting, we wouldn't be having this conversation. Oh yeah, and if you'd been my best friend, like you said, I'm sure you wouldn't have banged my fiancée. But you know, water under the bridge."

Brian flushed. "I was wrong. I said it. But Gear, I was doing my damnedest to keep the show going. You always told the network to kiss your ass, then did what you wanted your way. Why do you think you got away with so much? Because I was there cleaning up after you. I found ways to make the series run around your personality. We used Sahara's beauty to attract more viewers. Hell, man, we're the number one reality series on television. And I guarantee the minute we air that fight at the garage, we'll be rock solid for weeks."

"Yes, congratulations on your ratings for your show." Gear crossed his arms over his chest so he wouldn't be tempted to strangle Brian. "Why the fuck are you here?"

Brian groaned and finally sat. "It's not right without you. You were the heart of the show, and now that you're gone, everyone knows it. Finn is a mess."

"No shit." Taking pleasure in the fact Finn wasn't working? Priceless.

"But that's not why I'm here. I feel really bad about how it all happened."

"So you want to unburden yourself with the truth? Too little too late, pal."

"No. It's not like that." Brian ran a hand through his hair, aggravated. "Maybe it is. A year ago, Sahara started acting weird. She was moping around, losing weight. Remember?"

"Yeah. She was sick."

"She'd had a miscarriage."

Gear blinked. "What?"

Brian nodded. "She hadn't wanted to tell you about it, because you were so busy on that holiday special. We'd gone head-to-head with the then-network president. Remember? She hated the show, and we were all stressed."

"I don't remember that. I just remember having to do that stupid holiday bike." Sahara had been pregnant? No way.

"Right." Brian snorted. "Again, you worked on the bikes and bitched about the show while I handled the politics. And your girlfriend was the one suffering in silence."

Gear shook his head. "First of all, Sahara never suffered. In silence or out loud. That woman always looked out for number one—herself. We were already having problems back then. She wanted a bigger house, for us to live together in it. She kept buying expensive shit because we had an 'image' to maintain." He snorted. "What image? I built bikes. We were a fucking reality TV show. Not actors."

"But she did have an image to maintain. We had tons

of women tuning in to see what Sahara would wear. Her Instagram account was—is—massive."

"Whatever. Point is, buddy, Sahara and I were barely having sex back then. And I always wore a rubber."

Brian frowned. "That's not what she said."

"Yeah, well, she told me she was on the pill, but I never saw her take any. No way was I going to let her talk me into the baby she wanted. And before you go all pity party on her, she wanted the baby because it would be good for ratings. I think she wanted a dress-up doll and not a kid."

"That's not the Sahara I know."

"Dude, she full-out cheated on me with my best friend. You don't see any character flaws there?"

"Well, she's not perfect, but—"

Gear laughed, a harsh sound with little humor. "She's a narcissist and a bitch. She treats people like crap unless they're useful to her. She's always been nice to you because she needs you. But you know, Torch seems to have a real interest in your lady. I saw it last week at the garage. Might want to keep an eye on him."

Brian scowled. "Shut up."

"You done talking yet?"

"You're saying her miscarriage wasn't real."

"That's exactly what I'm saying. She played you for sympathy."

"If that's the case, why not use that for the show? She'd get the sympathy vote from viewers."

"Good point. I don't know why she made that up. Unless she really did have one from some other guy she cheated on me with. Or unless it was to get you two closer."

"I felt bad for her."

Yep. There it is.

"She'd been through something traumatic," Brian was saying. "She made me promise not to tell you, and you treated her horribly. I tried to get you to be nicer, but you never made time for her."

"Because she never wanted to hang out or do anything I wanted to. Do you have any idea how many stupid chick flicks and concerts I went to for her over the years? How many fashion shows while I sat on my ass and had to ignore models coming on to me? Yeah, Sahara loved that. That other women wanted me but I was devoted to *her*. Ironic then that she fucks me over with my best friend." Gear was tired of rehashing it all. "Is that it? Are you done now?"

"No." Brian stood. "Sahara didn't want me to cut you out of the show completely, but I had no choice. I knew you'd never let it all go, and if we'd kept you, the station would have axed us. You really pissed off the programming head with those comments about women knowing their place."

Gear gaped. "Are you kidding me? Sahara scripted that segment. I told her Orchid and Iris would skin me alive for saying that shit. She said it would be taken as funny. She made a joke of it on-screen."

"Yeah, well, not everyone liked it."

"And that was the start of women hating my guts. They either want a fuck or to tell me to fuck off. I can thank you and Sahara for that. Come on, Brian. You played me too. I was the uncultured, idiotic gearhead while you're the suave, sophisticated hero. And Sahara needed a better guy than me. In you came." Oddly enough, the more he talked to Brian about the past, the more Gear could feel himself letting it go. He didn't want Sahara. With Sadie, he had all he needed.

"It worked. For a long time it worked," Brian said. "But we need your expertise on the show. Finn's work is… Well, it sucks."

"No surprise there. The guy's a hack."

"He alienates people more than you do." Brian sighed. "With you leaving, Smoke followed. I figured he would. We lost Chains too."

"Huh."

"But you probably know that." When he didn't respond, Brian continued, "That fight at the shop was mostly for show."

"Oh. Is that why you didn't fight back?"

Brian's cheeks turned red. "Asshole. You always were better with your fists than your mouth." He took a deep breath, then let it out. "But I'm not here to fight anymore. We lost more guys after that. The mechanics always liked you best. They want you back."

"Fuck that."

"We'll give you most of your shares back. You get to keep Motorcycle Madnezz, and the show goes on. We're going international later in the season. It's gonna be epic."

"So take Finn." Gear didn't have any desire to go back. "I have my own plans, Brian. And none of them involve you." He didn't miss Brian's there-and-gone flinch. "You know what hurt the most? You. You turned on me."

"You turned on me first."

Gear stared. "How do you figure?"

"We used to do everything together. Always. Then

the show happened. And you got Sahara, and I was eased out."

"I got a girlfriend. You've had plenty of your own."

"But not like you guys. You burned hot, bro."

"Not your bro."

"You know what I mean. You and Sahara were a real item. You fit. You had chemistry."

An awkward sensation filled Gear's gut, a moment of fear that maybe he'd been doing the same song and dance with Sadie. But no. He'd never been so emotionally invested with Sahara.

"And remember, it was my idea to send in your video to the network. But somehow, what started out as the Gear and B-Man show turned into you, front and center with Sahara."

Gear frowned. "You liked working the desk, making things happen."

"No. I was forced to do that or be off the show. We both know my expertise was never with bikes. It's with making things happen, with networking, getting us orders. We worked so well as a team. And then it was all about you."

"And you never had the stones to tell me about it before now?" Gear refused to feel bad when he'd had no idea of Brian's resentments. "If you'd told me, I'd have fixed it."

"How? Sahara was there."

"I'd have fixed it," Gear said, knowing it to be the truth. "And if I couldn't, I'd have walked off the show."

"I didn't want that."

"No, but I would have put you first over a stupid TV show. You never gave me that choice. Instead, you made an ass out of me by sleeping with my girl. And man, you can have her. I'm happier now than I've been in a long time." He meant it. "I have a shop, a woman, and my family. I don't need fame and fortune, B-Man. That's your shtick."

Brian stared at him. "You found some other chick?"

"Yeah. And she tells me to my face when I'm an ass. She's not impressed by the show or by money. And she pretty much wants little to do with me." Gear smiled. "I'm having to convince her I'm worth a shot. So why the hell would I want to ruin that by going back to a show that's no longer mine?"

Brian considered him. "You really don't want Madnezz? It's your baby."

"It's just a show. I would have come back for my best friend, but I lost him a long time ago."

Brian looked frustrated and a little sad. But he hadn't given up. "Well, if you change your mind, call me. I can talk Sahara into whatever we need to do for the show."

"I thought you said this was her idea."

"Seriously? She hates your guts. It was mine." He shook his head and walked to the front door. He paused before leaving. "You know, for what it's worth, sometimes I miss the way we used to be."

Then he left.

Gear wondered if hell had indeed frozen over. Because he'd not only gotten closure with Brian, but he'd had a shot at getting Madnezz back.

And he'd tossed it over for Sadie without thinking twice.

Chapter 18

Monday evening, Sadie wondered why she kept feeling as if the roof was going to fall in on her. After a lovely Sunday night with Gear, when he'd been über romantic with rose petals, his *freakin' key*, and some of her favorite chocolates, they'd hung out at his place and made love instead of going to see his sister.

They had plans to meet Iris on Wednesday, late afternoon. Elliot and Rose had insisted she take the day off early, eager for Sadie to make a great impression on Gear's family.

"It's like you're all throwing me at him," she complained to Rose as they worked behind the counter serving customers.

"We like him for you," Rose said. "He's nice. Joe likes him too."

"Joe met him once."

"We both heard how Dad ripped him a new one at family dinner." Rose's dimples were showing. The brat. "He survived. Ava was really impressed."

"You talked to Ava?"

"Well, Elliot's accounting always needs a balance. He uses words like *true love* and *dramatic flair* and *oh my God, amazeballs*," Rose said drily, causing Sadie to chuckle. "Ava's more grounded."

Rose wiped the counters, saying no more.

"Well? What else did Ava say? Because she and

Landon like him, but Dad didn't seem to." And that still bothered her.

"Dad doesn't like anyone. And let's face it, no man will ever be good enough for his princess."

"Um, you married Joe."

"I mean you, doofus. You've always been Daddy's little girl. We knew it would be tough for him to let you go."

"Now hold on. I took Gear to dinner. That's it. There's no letting go."

"What are you so scared of, Sadie?" Rose asked, her voice soft. "Gear really likes you, Elliot said, and I see it every time he's with you. You like him too, don't you?"

"I guess."

"You guess?"

Sadie wished they'd get busier so she'd have an excuse not to talk to her sister. "He, um, gave me his house key. And I'm going to give him mine."

Rose's eyes grew huge. "Really?"

"Yeah. It's no big deal." So she kept telling herself. "We hang out a lot. And he has a hot tub. Now I can use it whenever I want. He said."

"Sadie. You're going to give Gear a key to your apartment?"

Sadie nodded, feeling hemmed in.

"Why?"

"Because he... I..." She grabbed the soapy rag from Rose and finished wiping everything again. "I don't know. I like him, okay? And it scares the piss out of me."

Rose gave her a hug, and Sadie held on. "Oh, sweetie, let yourself fall for the guy. It's okay to love someone."

"I did before." Sadie pulled away, missing her sister's calm the moment she did. "Adrian messed me up."

"And to be honest, you haven't had a lot of luck after him. But I don't think you'd let yourself."

Sadie frowned. "You've been spending too much time with Ava. That's what she says."

"She's right." Rose patted her tummy. "I got lucky with Joe. I had only dated a little bit and had some nice but not great experiences. Then I met Joe and fell in love. It's so worth it to have someone special in your life. Come on, Sadie. Give Gear a shot."

"I don't know." She felt sick at the thought of losing Gear. "He's almost perfect. We argue. We talk. We laugh. He's great in bed."

"And nice to look at." Rose grinned. "I'm pregnant, not dead."

"Hussy."

Rose laughed.

"We're moving kind of fast," Sadie said. "It scares me, because I like him so much. Adrian and I dated for years, and he crushed me."

"Do you think Gear will cheat on you?"

"Hell, no. Not if he wants to live."

"Okay. There's that."

Sadie sighed. "And he had the same thing happen to him. Sahara slept with his best friend."

"And they were engaged, right?"

"Yeah." Looking at their histories, Sadie knew she and Gear had so much in common. "It's weird. Sometimes it feels like he was tailor-made for me. But I don't trust that feeling." *I don't trust myself*.

"I like him. Elliot and Ava like him. And you love him."

"Love?" She scoffed, secretly horrified that she did. "Love made me weak. It's good for you and for Ava. But it hasn't worked for Elliot either. I think we're the unlucky-in-love types."

"You can fight it, but at the end of the day, where do you want to be? Making cupcakes, or hanging with Gear? You always say you're the boring one. But have you felt bored lately?"

"Not lately, no."

Rose nodded. "And you smile more. Oh, you're still a terror with our customers. Theo keeps begging to work the front with anyone but you."

"The punk." She grinned. Friggin' Theo.

"But we've seen the changes in you." Rose hugged her again. "I know you hate talking about mushy stuff, so thanks for bearing with me. This is the last thing I'm going to say about this—you love him. When you can accept that it's okay to love again, to open yourself to joy and pain and everything that comes with it, you'll truly be happy."

"That was totally mushy."

"I know."

"And your dimples are showing. Ack. I'm going into the back." She walked away on the heels of Rose's laughter.

She found Elliot fighting with a stubborn mound of dough. "Did you put Rose up to the talk out front?"

Elliot paused and looked up at her. "What talk? What did I miss?"

She groaned. "Never mind."

"Did she give you the 'you love him' talk? Because I was supposed to go first, but she pulled the *I'm pregnant* card, thinking it would mean more coming from her."

"What? You're all ganging up on me?"

"Sadie, you're a mess."

"Takes one to know one."

"Yeah, it does." Elliot pointed a dough-covered finger at her. "I've messed up a lot in my life. And being a screwup with relationships, and gay, ain't easy in this family."

"Who cares if you're gay?"

"Dad does. Did. He's over it now, but my point is we all try to be like Mom and Dad and their perfect relationship. They loved the crap out of each other. Now we have Rose and Joe. And even Cousin Ava has a guy she's keeping. That's a high bar for the love-challenged like you and me."

"Well, yeah."

"Adrian hosed you over. I mean, cheating on you with your best friend? And don't give me that crap that you and Annette weren't close. You like to lie to yourself about it, but she was your go-to, and she turned on you. I can't imagine what that's like. Oh, but you know who can? Gear. Your boyfriend. The guy you're gaga over and won't admit it."

"What do you people want from me?" Sadie wanted to pull her hair out.

"We want you to stop being such a weak, scared, girlie girl and tell the guy how you feel."

"Me? Why shouldn't he tell me first?"

"So he's never said anything about how he feels about you?"

She tried to think how to answer that.

"Ah-ha! What did he say?"

"Well, uh, we were at the gym a week ago. And he, all casually mind you, said he loved me."

Elliot gaped. "And?"

"And what? I went for a run on the treadmill, and we never talked about it again." *No, we only talked about making babies.* She wiped sweat off her forehead.

"Are you nuts? A man that fine tells you he loves you, and you go running? Did you even say it back or acknowledge he said it at all?"

"No."

"No. You're so stupid." He glared at her. "Stop letting Adrian ruin your life."

"This isn't about him."

"Of course it is. You had your heart broken. Treason, betrayal, you were cuckolded."

"Okay, stop."

"And now you'll never trust a man again. It's so sad."

"Well, guess what, Elliot? You don't know everything. Gear and I exchanged house keys."

Elliot stared at her. "Willingly?"

"Yes, willingly. What? You think I shook him down, demanding his key? He asked me for mine first."

"And he told you he loves you. Anything else?"

She didn't want to tell her brother, of all people, details about her sex life. "I like his parents."

"Dad liked him."

"Really? Were we not at the same dinner?"

"He did. For Dad, that's approval."

"He used the word *defiler*."

"And it was true. So what?" Elliot pounded the dough. "You've got a shot at something most of us would kill for. I've been trying forever to find someone. You all think I'm not able to commit. I just can't find the right guy to commit to. You've got Gear. In the words of Sadie Liberato, don't be a pussy. Go get what you want."

"Really? Quoting myself at me?"

"Hey, it fits. Now quit fooling around and—"

"Um, Sadie?" Rose stood in the doorway. "I think you'd better come out front."

Elliot and Sadie shared a glance. Rose sounded upset.

"You okay?" Sadie asked her.

"Yeah. But Sahara Blankenship is out here, and she wants to talk to you."

Elliot plucked his hands from the dough and raced to the sink. "Oh my God. Go, go. But wait until I get out there to talk to her. And please, do not, under any circumstances, hit the woman in our shop. Keep your hands to yourself."

Sadie walked out with Rose, curious as to what Gear's ex would want with her.

As usual, Sahara wore tight-fitting clothing: a dark-brown skirt over leather boots that must have cost a fortune. She had on a cream-colored sweater that showed off her assets and blended with her light-blond hair. She looked like any guy's fantasy and was surrounded by several cameramen keeping their distance to get the full shot.

Joy.

"You guys don't have the right to film in here," Sadie tried.

"They can film me wherever I go."

"But they can't film me for TV."

Sahara smiled. "Sure they can. And why wouldn't you want them to? Sofa's Spookville is pretty popular. We can only help draw in customers." So saying, she went to the pastry counter and chose a few treats. "To go, please."

Sadie held her thoughts to herself and grabbed Sahara's treats while a crowd gathered in the store, watching. Behind her, Rose and Elliot watched as well.

She felt like an albino gorilla on display. Ignoring the sense of dread building and wishing she had ice water to toss at these schmucks, she smiled. "That'll be ten bucks."

Sahara paid, but when Sadie returned her change, the woman closed a long-fingered hand over her wrist. She tugged Sadie closer, and Sadie went along because she didn't want to look like the bad guy. She towered over the petite Sahara, and God knew her looks couldn't compete.

"So you're Gear's new girlfriend."

Sadie tugged on her hand, and Sahara's nails bit into it. "Please let go."

"Uh-oh," Elliot said behind her.

"*You're* his new girlfriend?" Sahara laughed and released her, but not before leaving nail imprints on Sadie's hand. "What could you possibly offer Gear that I can't?" Before Sadie could answer, the woman's eyes welled with tears.

"Sweet Jesus, seriously?"

"He was mine. I loved him so much." Sahara wiped her eyes, but somehow kept her makeup from running. Sadie was impressed despite not wanting to be. "I would have given him anything. But he didn't love me enough."

Sadie glanced at the people around, many of them staring at Sahara with both fascination and empathy.

"Tell him… Tell him I want him to be happy," Sahara said, her breath hitching.

"I will." Sadie wanted nothing more than to pop this woman in the face again. "But you know, you could still have him back." Knowing Gear, this couldn't be further from the truth. But Sadie wanted to play.

Sahara froze, her gaze narrowed on Sadie. "Oh?"

"Well, it would mean breaking off with B-Man. And, you know, admitting that you cheated on Gear and basically made up all that crap about him with some other woman, all so you could swindle him out of his shares in the show."

And the cameras kept rolling. To Sadie's delight, she saw many in the crowd holding their phones up to record, so no matter what the network edited out, others would have copies of the entire conversation.

"That's all a lie."

"Not what I heard."

"Oh? When was that? When he was in bed with you, wishing you were me?"

"Oh no, she didn't," Elliot whispered super loudly.

Sadie leaned close to Sahara and whispered, "How's your face feel, Eve? I thought I'd smacked you into next week at the party." Then she pulled back and gave Sahara a wide smile. In a louder voice, she said, "It's too bad you're such a conniving backstabber. If you were as pretty on the inside as you are on the outside, you'd have a stellar show. Now all your talent is leaving, and you're stuck with a man not half as good as Gear. Oh, and I'm not talking about B-Man in bed. I mean your new front man, the mechanic. Fido or something."

Sahara's eyes glowed with hate. "I knew you looked

familiar!" She turned to the crowd. "She hit me. She's the one who punched me at the Halloween party. And Gear was in on it."

"Huh? Now you're blaming me for hitting you? So first I stole Gear, then I smacked you? Or is it the other way around?"

"You didn't steal shit. You're nothing. You're ugly and look more like a man than a woman should, anyway. I don't know what he sees in you."

"Ouch. That hurts coming from a shallow, mean-spirited, betraying witch." Sadie shook her head, enjoying herself. "You came between best friends. Man, that is low."

"Shut up," Sahara screeched. "What would you know? You're stuck in this crappy little shop, serving coffee and donuts." She snorted. "You look as if you haven't seen a hairdresser in ages."

"Yeah, but it's clean. Doesn't a shower count for anything?"

She heard several in the crowd laugh.

"Say what you want. But Gear won't want you for long." Sahara shot Sadie a mean smile. "He's already getting in trouble with a pretty redhead at that new gym he's going to. I hear he assaulted her. That won't go over well with fans, I can tell you that. Tell him he'll be hearing from her lawyer. And from mine. I kept quiet about the abuse I suffered, but—"

"Lady, please. First of all, that redhead at the gym grabbed him. And we have witnesses. Oh, and the owner banned her from the place." Go Mac. "So I guess I'll be telling Gear he should sue her after all for pain and suffering. Oh, and trying to blame him for assaulting *you*?

Unless you guys were living in a bubble and have the hospital reports to prove it, all you did by just accusing him of something he didn't do—on national TV—is set yourself up for a slander lawsuit. And all of the people behind you have you on video. Why don't you take your skanky ass out of my quality baked goods shop?"

"You haven't seen the last of me." Sahara gave Sadie the finger. "I'll see you in court."

"Well, before you do, make sure to get some touch-ups. Your boobs are sagging, and your forehead could do with some more Botox."

Sahara stared at her, then flew into a rage. Sadie saw it coming and did nothing to stop the woman from darting around the counter to smack her in the face.

Everyone stared, the shop silent.

"Oh, Sadie," Elliot cried, the drama on thick. "Quick, Rose. Call the police. Sadie's been assaulted."

The crowd started talking in low murmurs, then grew louder.

All while Sahara stared at Sadie in shock, then in growing anger as she realized she'd ruined her chances at revenge on Gear. She screamed and cried and continued to whale on Sadie, who did no more than turn her head and try to protect her face from the crazy woman's nails.

Finally, after what seemed like forever, the camera guys pulled Sahara away.

By that point, police entered the scene and took statements, plus video for proof, and asked if Sadie wanted to press charges.

"I sure the hell do."

Her face hurt a little. Not all that much, since the

woman didn't have much power behind that one open-handed slap, just tiny-girl rage and screams.

But making her lose it in front of her adoring public?

"That was epic," Elliot whispered as he handed her an ice pack. "You're my new hero. If Gear didn't love you already, he does now."

Sadie only knew she'd come too far to quit now. But what that would mean from Gear, she didn't yet know.

"It was the punch heard 'round the world again, Katie. Today at Sofa's, a popular bakery in Green Lake, Sahara Blankenship assaulted Gear Blackstone's new girlfriend. No one could quite believe the scene."

"I'm still wondering if this is part of the new show. Then again, this was crazy. You can't make this kind of stuff up!"

"But if it was for the show, why didn't Sahara's team release the footage? We only have spectator videos of what's taking the internet by storm. No, I think we've got some real girl drama here, Katie, and all over that hunky Gear Blackstone."

Three days after Sadie had been assaulted, Gear stared in horror at his phone, still not comprehending how everything had gone to shit so fast.

He understood why Sadie hadn't wanted to see him since it had happened. *Jesus.* She'd been attacked, on film, in her store. All the publicity she hated, plus a huge helping of Sahara.

He grimaced.

Even worse, she'd stood up for him, defending him, even after that April chick had tried blaming him for attacking her. The bald-faced liar. And that bit from Sahara about abuse? How could she sink that low? Brian thought Gear might come back to deal with that?

No way in hell.

The only good thing to come from the altercation was that April's case had no merit and had already been scorned by public opinion. Sahara came off as a crazy woman. Her prior claims against him now had doubt, all thanks to Sadie, who'd gotten slapped and mauled for her efforts.

He groaned and texted her again. No answer.

She was likely majorly pissed about her face being spread all over the news.

But even bad press was good press. *Motorcycle Madnezz* would be airing its first episode of the new season in just a few days, on Halloween, and he had a feeling they'd show the fight footage from the time he'd tried to grab his stuff from the shop.

Between him and Sadie, they'd end up remaining in the spotlight if they weren't careful.

Sofa's had gotten a great bit of added press. At this rate, he could see them opening up a second store. With the amazing Sofa's Spookville ongoing, his name associated with the place, and now Sadie's new fame, the store had been packed since Tuesday morning, the day after the fight.

Yet Thor told him Sadie had been absent, and Gear regretted that anything he'd done had impacted her job. He had called her, worried and sorry as hell. But she hadn't responded yet.

Well, fuck that. She could tell him he'd ruined her life in person. But when he got to her apartment again, as he'd been going daily since Monday, she didn't answer. Since she had yet to give him a key, he had no way to get in unless he broke through her door. And he'd done enough damage.

Dejected, he went back home and found Elliot waiting for him.

"Hey, Gear. Did you—?"

Gear dragged him inside and shut the door, in the event reporters started hanging around again. He'd found a few Tuesday, but by this afternoon they'd started to trickle away.

"Is she okay?"

"Who, Sadie?" Elliot looked around, not paying Gear much mind.

"No, the queen. Of course I mean Sadie."

Elliot waved away his concern. "She's fine. Took a punch for you, man. I think she's in love."

"I wish she was," he muttered. Gear sighed and plopped onto his couch. "Elliot, I need help."

"Not really. I love what you've done with this room."

"Hey, focus. Your sister."

Elliot sighed. "Yes, I know. Sadie's miserable without you. She loves you but is afraid to commit. Blah, blah, blah."

"Really? You think she loves me?" As sick as he was about what she'd suffered because of his association with Sahara, the notion she truly cared brightened his whole world.

"I know my sister, and she's a sucker for big muscles, big hands, and a small brain."

Gear laughed, then groaned. "Elliot, what do I do? I brought a lot of trouble to Sadie's door. Now she won't talk to me. She texted that she needed some time and space, but come on. I just want to talk to her."

"No can do, my friend. She's in hiding. Witness protection."

"*What?*"

"Reporters were all over her Tuesday, so she went home. Then a few followed her to her building, so she's hanging at Dad's."

Gear swore. "Great. He hates me."

"You might be right on that." Elliot sat and kicked back. "Got anything to drink?"

Gear fetched him a soda and rejoined him. "What can I do to make her okay?"

"Nothing. This is Sadie we're talking about. She'll be okay when she's ready, and not before."

"Yeah, but what can I do to help?"

"Well, you could send her a big, lovey-dovey care package."

"Tell me."

"Chocolates, stuff she likes, that kind of thing. And send it to Dad's."

"I can do that." He already knew what he'd put in the basket. "What else?"

"Tell her how you feel." Elliot's gaze seemed to burn a hole through Gear's head.

"I did that. She ran away. Literally. We were at the gym. I let slip I love her. She ran to the treadmill."

"That's my sister." Elliot sighed. "Pathetic." After a pause he said, "I don't know how much she told you about Adrian."

"Enough. The dick slept with her best friend."

"Yes, he did. The sad thing is Sadie has always been

superconfident and open. She fell for Adrian hard. And he took advantage. He was always trying to make her into something she's not."

"I don't want her to be anything but Sadie."

"Then you have to know she'll freak out if she thinks she's falling for you."

"I get that. That's why I let it go after I told her and she ran. It's not easy for me either. I trusted Brian, and he slept with Sahara. Then he stole my shop. My work. All of it. I didn't expect your sister, and I for sure didn't want to fall in love. But somehow, her big mouth and big feet ran me over without me realizing it."

"She has that effect on people."

"She's great. We're so much alike. She's funny, smart, snarky, hot—"

"I'll stop you right there." Elliot slurped from his soda can. "I know my sister has some fine qualities. But the one she's going to need from you is patience. She's stubborn and can be a real pain. If you have what it takes to handle that, then you'll be the luckiest guy I know."

"I could use some luck."

"Start with the presents. And try to think of things she'll like. I could tell you, but that would be cheating. If she doesn't text you back by Halloween, you let me know. Don't worry. I'll drag her to your family party if I have to. Like déjà vu," he muttered and stood. "I'm keeping this." He swooshed the can.

"Fine. Just let me know if I can do anything to help her. Or you. I'm really sorry Sahara was such a bitch."

"Seriously? We're selling out of everything every day." Elliot beamed. "I gave Theo extra hours. People are talking about us, and if everything goes well with the

Food Network spot, I might be looking at a cookbook deal. Well, that's a dream, but I'm going to work hard to make that happen."

"Good for you."

"Oh, and tell your brother I'll talk to him at the party. He invited a bunch of us, just so you know. Explain to him I was busy with the Sahara fallout, would you? I texted him, but I want him to know we're still on board to cater the university shindig."

"Catering. Right." He showed Elliot out, his mind on gifts for Sadie.

He made a list and smiled, feeling better about things. Still, he wished they could have a face-to-face conversation about the love bubble in the room. Oh well. That would have to keep. He had some time before the party. With any luck, he'd make headway before then.

Sadie, baby, I love you. Now quit running away!

Chapter 19

HER FATHER STARED FROM HIS LAPTOP TO SADIE. "You're viral, Daughter."

She groaned and hid her face beneath a couch pillow. It had been four days since the *punch heard 'round the world again*. "You'd think a woman had never been in a fight before."

"Well, I know you're better than that. She really took you down with that feather slap to the face?"

"Dad." She flushed, not liking her father's disapproval.

"She hit you. How do you let a woman that tiny leave a mark?"

Relieved he wasn't upset about more than Sahara getting a few licks in, Sadie eased the pillow off her face and stared at the blue running compression socks she'd been given yesterday.

Gear, that asshole of a sweetheart, had been sending gifts to her father's house. So far, she'd received a box of her favorite truffles, a DVD of her favorite Halloween anthology, *Trick 'r Treat*, and a plastic pumpkin full of Halloween candy. She'd been so out of sorts and depressed that even candy shopping hadn't done more than make her want to cry.

And who the hell cried choosing chocolates over Skittles?

"He's trying to make you fat," her father complained,

staring at the pumpkin on the coffee table. He reached in and grabbed a snack-sized Baby Ruth. "What do you think?" He added to the mound of wrappers building next to the laptop.

"I don't miss the gym." *But I miss Gear* so *much*.

"Don't stay away too long. It's one thing to lick your wounds. Another to come off as scared and weak."

"Thank you, Dad. Inspiring, as always."

Tony harrumphed. "You know what I'm saying."

"Are you sure you aren't *connected*?"

He laughed. "Are you still on the mob kick? Really? Look at me. I'm fifty-six years old and an accountant. My biggest thrill is cross-country skiing when I visit the mountains. How does that make me a mob guy?"

"I don't know. You're always going on about loyalty. *La famiglia e tutto*. Family is everything. Bada-bing, bada-boom. What should I think?"

"That I talk a big game and watched *The Sopranos* religiously?" He popped the candy bar in his mouth.

She sighed, wiggling her toes. "He gave me blue compression socks."

Her father rolled with her change in subject. "Because he knows blue is your favorite color and that you like to run."

"Yeah." She sighed. "Dad, how did you know about Mom? I mean, that she would be your forever wife?" Her father had loved her mother dearly. And though he'd done his fair share of dating since her passing twenty years ago, he claimed he'd never find another to fit him as well as Marina.

Tony sat up straighter and studied her. "Your mother... I fell in love with her at first sight. She was

a beauty, studying so hard in the university library."
He smiled, lost in the memory. "I just watched her. For
hours. And when she left, I offered to carry her books.
Unlike *some* people, she liked to read." He gave her a
knowing look.

"Dad." Sadie sat up.

"She didn't fall for me as fast as I fell for her. But I
won her over." He smiled at Sadie's socks. "She liked
pink, so I bought her some pink hair bands. That got me
a first date, and the rest is history."

Sadie knew her mother would have liked Gear.
Marina had only cared about what was in a person's
heart. Not looks, fame, or money, but truth of spirit—
that's what drew her mother to people. "I think I really
like Gear."

Her father sighed. "I know. You keep mooning over
the man."

"We have so much in common. He works so hard,
and he's been screwed over royally."

"So you have infidelity in common, and you're in love?"

"No. Yes. Kind of." She blushed. "He's the first real,
good man I've met since Adrian."

"Since before Adrian, you mean. That piece of trash
didn't deserve you."

"Right." She stared at her toes. "Gear kind of reminds
me of you."

"He does?"

Her father's look of incredulity made her laugh.
"Yeah. He's a hard-ass. He doesn't have time for stupidity, and he protects his own. He really loves his brother
and sister, and he respects his mom and dad, even if he
had to go his own way." She paused. "Plus, he's never

been intimidated by me. He respects me, and he treats me right."

"Well, now. That's something to think about." Tony leaned close, riffled through more chocolate bars, and ate a Snickers. "But he's under scrutiny by the media, and you hate that."

"I do, but I know it's not his fault, and it won't last forever."

"He has a job, then?"

"Yes, his own new job, not on the show." She told him about the place Gear had leased. "He's super talented, Dad." She turned his laptop toward her and typed in Gear's name. Then she clicked on Gear's old website.

"Oh. These are good." Her father leaned closer, scrolling through images of Gear and his crew working on projects. "I thought he was just a mechanic with delusions of grandeur. He looks like a thug."

"Yeah." She sighed in pleasure, missing him so much she teared up.

"For God's sake, Sadie. If you like him so much, go see him."

"I thought taking some time to see how I feel would be a good idea. But I… I think I might really love him."

Her father said nothing, just watched her.

"It feels weird because we met not long ago. But everything about him, even his motorcycle show, fits him. And it fits me. Dad, he gave me the key to his place." She showed her father the house key she kept in her pocket.

"So let me get this straight. This man who gave you his key, is sending you socks and chocolates, and who got you involved with the tawdry world of bikers and brawls is who you'd choose to be your husband?"

She blew out a breath. "I'm not talking marriage or anything. I just know I love him."

"Where do you see this going with *Gear*?" he emphasized the name.

"I don't know. He makes me happy. I think we should take things one day at a time."

"Okay."

She blinked. "Just okay?"

"Sadie, be happy. This man, no matter what I might think of him, has you more alive than you've been in years. Do you think he could hurt you?"

"I don't think he'd ever try to. But if he did something like Adrian did, I might never recover."

"But you recovered from Adrian."

"That was different."

"Why?"

She wanted to put it into words. "I don't know. I loved Adrian, but life existed without him. I feel so much with Gear. He's real, and he never wants me to be anything but me around him. With Gear, I'm enough."

Her father looked at her. "Enough is exactly right. Your mother was enough for me, and I was enough for her. Expectations can fall flat. If he truly accepts you for who you are, and you can accept him, I would ask how much time you think you really need, and for what?"

"Huh. Good point."

"My daughter isn't the type to let fear rule her. Your Gear didn't let me get in his way of pursuing you. He came to dinner. He tolerated my rudeness."

"So you admit you were rude."

"And he was certainly no pushover."

"He's not." She smiled. "So you think I should go after him?"

"If you want him. You're a Liberato, Sadie. We go after what we want."

"Huh. That's his family's motto too."

"I really do have to meet these people."

"I bet I can get you an invitation to a Halloween party, Dad. Are you game?"

"Do I have to wear a costume?"

"Yes."

He groaned. "Oh fine. The things I'll do to make sure my daughter isn't getting involved with a group of rowdy biker thugs."

"Thanks, Dad."

"Now go see what else is in that basket he sent. Any more Baby Ruths, by chance?"

Smoke seemed to like the idea Gear proposed for the new shop. They stood in the space, measuring it out as Gear wrote down notes.

"So you want us to work where everyone can see." Smoke scratched his head. "Kind of like that dog-and-pony bullshit from Madnezz, man. Just sayin'."

"The idea for this place is that it's more than a garage. There's an art to crafting a bike. And we can make some kind of shades or something to cover up when we just want to work without being watched. It's just a thought at this point. Plus, we do it right, we sell the brand merchandise up front, but on a much smaller scale than Madnezz."

Smoke seemed to consider that. "So we're going a little more upscale. That's cool. Do I have to wear a uniform?"

"Hell no. We're not in private school. We're fuckin' mechanics."

"Good. For a minute you reminded me a little too much of B-Man." Smoke ignored the finger Gear shot him and laughed.

"Funny." Gear shook his head. "Can you believe they tried getting me to come back to the show?"

"That place is poison. And yeah, Torch is totally doing Sahara."

"I get the feeling everyone knows but Brian. Sad. But you reap what you sow. Or so my mom is always harping."

"Hello?" A husky feminine voice came from the front of the shop.

"Yo, Iris. Back here."

She walked back past stacks of leftover pallets and stopped. "This is it? This is all you have so far?"

He looked around, seeing nothing but wooden pallets and the lone bar table left over from the previous tenants. "Yeah. Consider it a blank slate."

Smoke took a hard look at Iris.

"Oh, hello." She looked up, and up, at Smoke. "Didn't you used to be on the show?"

"Yep." Smoke just stared at her from beneath the brim of his new Seahawks ball cap.

"O-kay. Chatty fellow. So Gear, I came up with some ideas." She opened her bag and placed it on the lone piece of furniture in the place. Then she powered her laptop and waited while Gear and Smoke loomed over her.

Smoke kept looking at her. "This is your sister? She's so little."

"I know. But she has a big mouth."

"Hey," Iris barked. "Shut it and be positive."

"See?"

Gear saw Smoke smile, then give his sister a thorough once-over. Smoke looked at Gear, saw him noticing, and shrugged. "Just lookin' is all."

"Yeah, is all." Gear glared.

"So, what do you think?" Iris asked, oblivious to them.

Gear looked at several options for color choices, names, and logos, and tended to veer toward the last one she'd designed.

Smoke nodded. "Why not? It's your place."

"Blackstone Bikes, with a BB logo?" Iris typed. "Colors?"

"I don't know. Maybe blue." Gear hadn't stopped thinking about Sadie, wondering if she'd liked his gifts. He also wondered if her dad had been talking her out of giving him a chance, and it killed him not to storm over there and demand they speak. He had one more day before he'd decided to stop giving her time apart. "Before I commit, I need to think on it. Can you email me a copy of that?" When she nodded, he realized he had a new reason to see Sadie. He wanted her opinion on Iris's ideas.

Iris narrowed her eyes at him. "You're going to ask Sadie what she thinks, aren't you?"

He flushed, wishing he wasn't so easy to read. "Maybe."

Smoke asked, "Who's Sadie?"

"A good friend of mine."

Iris smiled. "Gear's in *lurrvvve*."

"I'm not afraid to put you in a headlock," he warned her.

"Yeah, right." She looked up at Smoke. "Don't mind him. He's turned all caveman on us lately."

"Lately?" Smoke snorted. "Dude has been straight up Neanderthal since I met him."

Gear just stared.

"What?"

"You're awfully chatty today. Like, we're having conversations that don't involve engines. You feeling okay?"

Smoke shrugged. "I didn't like the vibe at the old place once the network jumped on. Negative atmosphere. I didn't want to add to it."

Iris nodded, approving. "Yes. You really can feel the difference, can't you? Gear is now positive. With Sahara, he was nothing but bad energy."

"Totally bad," Smoke said, somehow with a straight face.

"Yeah, well, if I don't get back with Sadie soon, I'm gonna be full of bad energy." Gear sighed. "Now let's see if Joaquin's ready to place an order. He called this morning. Iris, let me know how long it'll take you to put together a new brand package like the first one you did for me. Oh, and I need two costumes for tomorrow night. One for me and one for Sadie."

"You're just telling me this now?" She fumed. "I do have a life, you know."

"Sorry. I meant to tell you last week, but then a lot of stuff went down."

She patted his arm, her sympathy more than welcome. "A week is still not much time to get things ready, but I figured you'd need my help so I set some things aside. I know you're having a hard time, sweetie. Sure, I'll help." She turned to Smoke. "You should come too. My parents throw a big Halloween party each year. Friends and family. And if you're going to continue to be a part of all this, then that makes you family."

"Yep." Gear slapped Smoke on the back. "It's a costume party. Mandatory dress-up."

"Hell."

"I could try to find you something to wear," Iris offered. "Maybe. You're pretty big, aren't you?"

Gear shot Smoke a look, and the big guy choked down the inappropriate response Gear could see on his face.

"Yep. Like, six-five."

"Wow." Iris put her things back into her bag, then tugged Smoke with her. "Bye, Gear. See you tomorrow night at the party. Come on, Smoke. You come with me."

"Yes, ma'am." He grinned at Gear. "Later, boss."

"Touch her and die," he warned.

To which Iris said, "Ignore him."

"I normally do," Smoke quipped.

The shop emptied, leaving Gear to his thoughts. As usual, they dwelled on Sadie. He locked up, still not sure what to do about her. He had nothing but time, yet he hated waiting when he could be proactive. He'd send her another gift tomorrow. He had no idea if she'd liked his gifts, because she hadn't texted or called, and he'd been trying to give her the "space" she wanted.

Man, he hated that fucking word.

He pulled into his driveway and entered the house, then froze at the low sound of music coming from the back.

He dropped his notepad and keys and tossed his jacket on the couch, then followed the chill alt rock music upstairs. His pulse raced, and he prayed Sadie had used her key.

"Hello?" He got no response. "Sadie?"

When she didn't answer, his imagination went into overdrive. What if it wasn't Sadie? What if Brian or Sahara had managed to get in, and the music was to cover their eventual murder scheme? Something similar had happened just the previous night on true crime TV.

He frowned, thinking he should have kept his baseball bat in the house for protection instead of shoving it in a sports locker in the garage. He walked cautiously, peering into the bedroom but seeing it dark.

"Huh."

He still heard music. Wary, he followed it to the media room and saw Sadie kicked back on the couch engrossed in a horror movie while also listening to music. Strange and perfect. And so very Sadie.

She looked good. Her hair was down over a long-sleeved Seahawks tee. She wore jeans and some fuzzy socks, and he thought about yanking her to him and never letting go.

"Hey." Brilliant beginning. He wanted to smack himself.

She started and sat up, her hair sliding like silk over her face. She pushed it back and blew out a breath. "Oh my God. I thought you were the devil." On-screen, Satan was devouring someone's guts.

"Well, I was at one time, if you remember."

She grinned. "That's true." She looked him over as intently as he studied her. "You look tired."

"Thanks. You look great."

"I know."

He chuckled, trying to figure out how to play it. Cool, easy. No point in scaring her away again. "Nice of you to finally fucking stop by." *Great job, Gear. The anger was supposed to keep.*

She raised a brow. "I'd think you'd be happy to see me."

"I am." He shoved his hands in his pockets, trying to get it together. "So, ah, what brought you by?"

She frowned. "Are you in love with me?"

He blinked. "What?"

"I asked if you're in love with me. Do. You. Love. Me?"

He shrugged, his heart hammering so hard it threatened to pound through his chest. "So what if I am?" Did she expect him to just lay his heart on the line while she watched in judgment and debated trampling it? Could he keep it to himself any longer? Shit, no. "Fuck, you know I am."

She flushed. "How do I know?"

"I told you. At Jameson's Gym. Then you ran away."

"I was going to the treadmill to work out."

"Bullshit. We don't lie to each other, so let's not start now. I scared you. Admit it." He took his hands out of his pockets and ran his fingers through his hair. His nerves were jumping all over the place, because he knew, deep down, that this would be a defining moment in his relationship with Sadie. Where he either got the girl or fucked everything up.

Sadie blew out a breath. "Fine. You scared me."

"I knew it. I said it too soon. I didn't mean to, but—"

"*BecauseIwasfeelingthesamething*" came out in a rush.

He stared, not sure he'd heard right. "Huh?"

She glared at him. "You heard me. I was freaking out because you said what I'd been feeling. I mean, my track record with guys isn't great. I wasn't looking for a relationship, you know. Just a quick bang at the party.

Then you snuck your way into my heart." To his shock, her eyes were bright with unshed tears.

"Sadie?"

"Shut up. I need to say this."

He waited, wanting to hug her and kiss her and tell her it would all work out.

"I really loved Adrian. I know it was a while ago, but he broke my heart. Ever since, I've dated losers or guys that just didn't do it for me. Then there's you.

"You're coarse, obnoxious, have baggage out the ass, and gave me your friggin' key." She sniffed and seemed oblivious to the tear tracking down one cheek. "I fell hard for you from the beginning. And I didn't want to. But damn it. Everything we do is, like, the same. You're as boring as I am."

He grinned. "And I hate people."

"Yeah. I love that about you." She smiled and wiped her cheeks. "When we were together in the car, just us without protection, I…" She turned bright red.

"Sadie, tell me. Remember, it's us. We don't play games."

She nodded. "And we don't lie to each other. So the truth is, when we didn't use a condom, I wanted a baby. And before you tell me I sound psycho, I know I sound psycho. It's not like I want to get pregnant right now or anything."

"Man, are you red." He didn't know how to feel about her wanting his kid. *Alarmed* was the correct word, what he should have felt, but *ecstatic* came to mind instead.

She glared. "I feel like an idiot. I'm not a *Madnezz* groupie wanting to carry the mighty Gear Blackstone's love child. I'm a normal woman who wants a husband

and family, but not while the world looks on. I'm not a fan of the TV show, Gear."

"Yeah, I get that." He was dying to hold her. "Can I hug you now?"

"No." She fought a smile. "Idiot. I'm trying to tell you I was baby-crazy for you, and you want to hug me? A normal guy would be running for the door. I barely know you and I love you. That's insane."

He said, "Screw it," and dragged her close for a big hug. "Sadie, I love you too. So much. It's crazy. Makes no sense. Shouldn't be. But there it is."

She hugged him back as tightly. Then they kissed, and everything was right with the world.

Sadie caressed his nape, and he shivered. "I don't know how, but you get me. I just worry that I won't be enough for you. Gear, I want to get married and have kids. I don't want a billion dollars, a hit TV show, or a cookbook deal. I just want to do what I'm doing with the man I love."

"And what's wrong with that?" he asked. "The TV show was a fluke. All I ever wanted to do was build bikes. So, to kind of quote you, 'I just want to do what I'm doing with the woman I love.' You're that woman. I can't understand it. *You* didn't want a relationship? I sure the hell didn't. My best friend and my fiancée royally fucked me over. I spent two months before you wanting to kick both their asses and had to settle for kicking Brian's. Women. Nothing but trouble, I thought."

He kissed her again. "And I was right. You are nothing but trouble. I can see I'm going to have to up my workouts or get fat. And I'll have to keep an eye on you to keep you out of fights." He brought her closer, so that she couldn't possibly miss his erection. "Do you have any idea how hard you make me? All the time, baby. When you're smiling, laughing, being tough. I want to be with you, because you bring me joy." He wiped her cheeks. "And no offense, but you're an ugly crier. And I'm still hard and can't stop staring at you."

"Oh. Stop." She chuckled. "Yeah, well, you're no prince. I'm constantly measured against perfect Sahara. And we both know I'm not nearly as pretty as she is."

"Nope. She was gorgeous."

She glared. "Not helping."

"But you're beautiful. With my eyes open or closed, you're the most beautiful thing I've ever seen. She's nothing but a memory, and a bad one at that." He brought her hand between them and kissed it. "It won't always be easy, you and me. But I like when we argue. And I know I can trust you. That might not mean much to most people, but to me it's everything."

She nodded. "Me too."

"No games."

She shook her head.

"I want it all with you. Marriage, kids, us living together. But maybe not in that order, because you look ready to pass out."

She laughed, tucked her head into his chest, and groaned. "Man, I think you're it for me. Like, if this get screwed up, I'm done. Forever."

"Yep. Me too."

"It's all too soon."

"I agree."

"And I never gave you my key."

"You can keep it. You know, for storing your stuff that won't fit in here."

She raised her head so fast they nearly collided. "You want me to live *here*? With you?"

"No, I want you to live in my garage, chained to the floor where you'll spend all day every day cleaning my tools." He leered at her. She didn't smile. "Of course I want you to live here, moron. I love you."

"But, uh…"

"But, uh, what?"

She expelled a heavy breath. "I like your kitchen. I'll want to take over."

"Go for it."

"I might want to repaint your bedroom. I'm partial to blue."

"Go ahead."

She frowned. "What if I want to change other stuff?"

He shrugged. "I don't care. I just want you."

She sighed. "Man, you make it difficult to argue." She sounded put out. "And I hate that I love your house. Because I'd want to live here even if you weren't here. And I just know I probably like some of the parts Sahara designed." She looked horrified by that idea.

"So we'll change them. The house is great."

"But the location sucks," she pointed out.

Wanting to cheer her up, he nodded. "It does if you work in Green Lake. Man, think of all the bitching you could do to and from work every day."

She smiled. "Yeah. You'd really owe me if I moved in with you."

He kissed her, this time giving her something more to think about with his lips and tongue. When they broke apart, they were both panting. "I'm gonna want more, Sadie. Like, sex all the time. The right to show you off to my friends. Well, to Smoke. He's a friend and going to be working at the garage. And you'll have to deal with Iris wanting to be around you all the time. And Thor too. Orchid will do tarot readings for you, and Otis will probably ask you to spar, to see what you're made of."

"I love your family." She kissed him back, and he wanted nothing more than to get rid of her clothes. "My family loves you too." She nibbled down his throat, and one of her hands found its way under his jeans.

He sucked in a breath, then moaned. "Liar."

"Nah. My dad's seen the light. He thinks you'll be good for me."

"Can we not talk about him when—*God*. Stop or I'll come. I missed you so much."

She kissed him. "Not more than I missed you."

"Is this a contest?" He walked them behind the couch, doing his best not to come as she pumped him with nimble fingers. Then he slid his jeans and underwear down and turned her around, her back to him.

He wrapped his arms around her and kissed her neck until she turned her head, then he took her mouth. All the while, his busy hands made short work of her jeans and panties. Once he had them pushed down her legs, he bent her over.

"I have wanted to do you like this forever. Right here, over this couch."

"Really?"

He slid his fingers between her legs, then shoved a finger inside her.

"Oh yeah. You're ready."

She moaned in time with the horror movie on television. "So romantic…you devil."

On screen, a demon smiled at the woman in his clutches.

Just as Gear looked down at his warrior princess. "Well, Xena, think you can handle me?"

"You going to talk me to death or—*Oh, damn*."

He'd shoved home and loved her with thorough, brutal strokes. She came in seconds and took him with her. The sexiest, most pathetic sex they'd had to date.

"Man, you're like a two-second wonder," she panted.

"Back at ya, Ms. Easy." He couldn't see past the sparks going off in front of his eyes. "And I hate to tell you, but if you weren't on birth control, that right there would have been a baby."

"We need more practice."

He withdrew and turned her around.

"Hurry. I'm messy."

He chuckled. "I love you, Xena."

"I love you, Satan."

A round of evil laughter and screams came from the sound system before a burst of techno chill eased the vibe.

They stared at each other and burst into laughter. "I'm so telling our kids about this one day," Sadie said. "Well, minus the sex parts."

His heart too full, Gear could only nod and kiss her again. *Our kids*. The future had never looked so bright.

Chapter 20

"NOW THIS IS HOW YOU DO HALLOWEEN," ELLIOT announced as he stared around him at Gear's parents' place.

Sadie nodded, her hand entwined with Gear's. "Oh yeah. Gear, your parents are awesome." She plucked at his lace sleeve and grinned. "And so is Iris."

He laughed. "If you say so. I don't know what I think about my sister pairing us up as Lord and Queen of the Underworld. She's got a fixation on me as the devil for some reason."

Elliot snorted. "Maybe because you're leading my sister into sin?"

"You should talk, Gabriel. What the hell?" Sadie flicked the angelic wings at Elliot's back. "You are *for sure* no angel."

"Ah, my children." Her father approached, with Rose and Joe by his side. He raised a brow at Gear. Sadie knew they'd had a talk late last night, and Gear seemed much more at ease about dealing with her dad now. "Ah, are you Hades or Pluto?"

"Hades, I think. Iris prefers Greek over Roman." Gear shrugged. "Not my call."

"Because the Greek gods are easier to recognize," Sadie murmured, staring at her father. "Really, Dad? This is your costume?"

He shrugged and held his plastic tommy gun by his shoulder. "You inspired me."

Elliot whispered in a loud voice, "He's a genius. *Pretending* to be gangsta."

Rose gaped. "I knew it. I told you guys he wasn't just an accountant."

"Rose, don't get too excited." Joe patted her belly.

Sadie cringed. "I love that you guys are in a couples costume, but Raggedy Ann and Raggedy Andy having a baby kind of creeps me out."

"Me too." Gear grimaced. "Iris did you no favors there. Where is she, anyway?"

They glanced around. Sadie saw Orchid and Otis arm in arm. Orchid looked like a wood sprite, and Otis was a zombie biker. Not too original, but he did appear authentic. Iris stood in the shadow of an incredibly attractive man dressed in a business suit, holding a briefcase.

"Who is that with Iris?" she asked. "Because...just, wow."

Rose craned her neck around Joe to see and agreed.

Gear tugged her closer to him. "Okay, that's your one and only wow for the night."

"Gotcha." She gave her underworld lord a kiss on the cheek. "You still have one to use."

"I'm saving it for later," he said, then whispered in her ear, "for when you show me what you're wearing underneath that dress."

She smiled and gave him another kiss. "Oh, you earned that." She paused and whispered into his ear, "Harrison *Moonchild* Blackstone."

He covered his face with his hand, and she laughed so

hard she cried. She'd finally weaseled his middle name out of his father, and she was so excited to have that kind of ammunition over him she didn't know what to do with herself.

"I could kill my dad," Gear gritted out.

"What? What's so funny?" Elliot wanted to know.

Gear squeezed her waist so hard she squeaked. "Nothing. Just a private joke between me and Hades."

"Yeah, that's right," he growled, then gave a frustrated laugh. "I know I'm going to be paying for this for the rest of my life."

Sadie grinned. "You got that right."

Iris and her giant hottie saw them and came over. A decent crowd had filled the party, and Otis and Orchid's house accommodated everyone with ease. They'd planned their party to the nines, using a caterer Elliot swore was out to get him.

"Hi, guys." Iris looked amazing in a medieval costume. She wore a brown velvet dress—square at the neckline but hinting at a full bosom—that fell to the brown slippers on her feet. Lined in gold, with formfitting sleeves draped at the wrist, a corset belt, and a matching squared headpiece, Iris's costume guaranteed she could have passed for a real medieval lady.

Unlike Sadie, who was pretty sure her odd resemblance to Maleficent wouldn't win her any true-to-life awards.

"Who's your friend?" Rose asked.

"Smoke, meet—"

Next to her, Gear and Elliot gaped. "Smoke?" they said at the same time.

"So much hotness under that hat," Elliot whispered. "You look so, so…"

"Civilized," Iris offered.

"Thanks," Smoke grumbled, glaring at them. "It was her idea."

"Well, I didn't have anything that fit him. He had a suit he hadn't worn in forever, so I let him borrow the briefcase and glasses." The black frames had no glass in them and turned him into sexy businessman personified.

"Don't wear that to Blackstone Bikes," Gear said. "You'll scare our customers."

Smoke chuffed. "Yeah, right."

Blackstone Bikes was Gear's new baby. His business would take off, Sadie knew it. He'd shared so much with her last night, from Brian's surprising confession and invitation to rejoin the crew, to what he wanted to do with his business. She'd agreed on his choice of logo, but had added black to the blue color motif.

He seemed so upbeat and happy that she hadn't been able to resist smiling or laughing all day. She'd never been so pleased with life, and she worried she might be dreaming it.

She knew they'd have hard times. That sometimes little fights would flare into bigger ones. But the important parts stayed with her. His kindness and thoughtfulness, and their shared sexual chemistry, drew them closer with every intimate encounter.

She'd been so alone for so long. And though he'd had a partner, Gear had admitted he felt the same. But now, with Sadie, he felt complete.

Out of the corner of her eye, she saw him mouth to her, making a heart in the air with his fingers: "*You complete me*."

"Idiot." She kissed him, leaving black lipstick on

his lips. She smeared it on, wanting her mark there for everyone to see.

A glance at the group showed everyone focused on them.

"What?" she snapped. "Can't I kiss Hades without it being a huge deal?"

"There's my Xena," Gear said with a laugh. "Always ready to fight."

"Did someone say *fight*?" Thor asked in a booming voice as he joined them, dressed as…Thor. Handsome yet somewhat smaller than the Norse god in stature if not attitude. "Bring it, oh angelic host, underworld king, and Tony Soprano!" He did a double take at Joe and Rose. "And the Raggedy family?"

"That's so lame," Smoke said and snickered.

Thor glared at Smoke, but Sadie saw the humor in his eyes. "Lame? Nice suit, Mr. Mundane. Clark Kent wannabe." Thor held out his mighty Styrofoam hammer at Smoke and swore he'd smite him but good. "A business suit? Really? Ugh."

Elliot just stared.

"Close your mouth, or you'll catch flies," Sadie said in a low voice and watched his jaw snap shut.

He glared at her. Then, not to be outdone by Thor, he started in on the Norse pantheon. The guys laughed and teased. Her father pretended to threaten people with mob hits, laughing and enjoying himself. And Otis and Orchid headed over to join the fun.

Sadie stood with her loved ones—and her own private demon she loved to distraction—and knew she'd never forget this Halloween.

The day she'd finally dared the devil to love.

And he'd accepted.

Please read on for a sneak peek of Marie Harte's

COLLISION COURSE

"TWO DOZEN RED ROSES AND I'M SORRY I SCREWED your sister?" Josephine "Joey" Reeves stared at the thirtysomething guy in front of her counter, thinking she must have misheard him.

"Yeah, that doesn't sound so good." He sighed, finger-combed back his trendy bangs, and frowned. "I was going to go with 'Sorry I fucked your sister,' but that's a little crude. Probably just 'I slept with your sister,' right? That's better."

She blinked, wondering at his level of stupidity. "Um, well, how about ending at just 'I'm sorry'?"

He considered that and nodded. "Hey, yeah. That'll work. Do I need to sign the card? Maybe you could write that for me. My handwriting sucks."

So does your ability to be in a committed relationship. Joey shrugged. "It's your call. But if it were me, I'd prefer a note from the person who's sorry, not from the woman selling him flowers."

Her customer brightened and chose a note card from the stack on the counter. "Good call. Hey, add another dozen while you're at it. She loves roses."

Joey tallied up the order while he signed the card,

then took it from him. The guy really did have crappy handwriting. After he paid and left, she tucked the note into the folder of orders due to go out in another hour. For a Monday afternoon, the day had gone as expected and then some. The store hadn't been chock-full of customers, but it hadn't been empty either. Late spring in Seattle had most people out and about working on their gardens, not inside shopping for hothouse blooms.

Still, enough anniversaries, birthdays, and relationship disasters had brought a consistent flow of customers into S&J Floral to make Stef, Joey's boss, more than happy.

Joey hummed as she organized, thrilled that she'd gotten the hoped-for promotion to manager that morning. She'd worked her butt off for it, and that diligence had paid off. She wanted to sing and dance, proclaim her triumph to the masses.

Except it was just her, Tonya in the back putting together floral arrangements, and a random half-dozen shoppers perusing the store. It had been Joey's idea to add some upscale gifts to their merchandise. Buying teddy bears, pretty glass ornaments, and knickknacks went hand in hand with buying flowers. S&J had seen a boost in revenue since last December when they'd implemented the big change.

Thank God it had worked. Joey appreciated Stef taking a risk by believing in her. And now…a promotion to manager and a $50K salary! With this money, she and Brandon could finally move out of her parents' place and start fresh, away from the history of mistakes her family never let her forget. She couldn't wait to tell her best friend Becky the good news.

Determined to start over again, Joey dug into her

orders and updated delivery times, getting in touch with their new delivery guy, a cute twenty-year-old who'd no doubt soon be rolling in tips.

"Well, hello there."

She glanced up from the counter and froze.

"You work here?" A large grin creased a face she'd tried hard to forget.

The man who'd been haunting her sleep, who'd dogged her through a wedding and sizzled her already-frazzled nerves, looked even better in the hard light of day.

"H-hello." She coughed, trying to hide the fact that her voice shook. When she could breathe without hyperventilating, she said, "Sorry. What can I do for you today?"

The look he shot her had her ovaries doing somersaults and her brain shutting clean off.

The first time she'd seen him had been on a visit to her first wedding client ever, and she'd been *floored*. The guys who worked at Webster's Garage all looked larger than life, covered in tattoos, muscles, and that indefinable sense of danger they wore like a second skin. But it had been this guy. Webster's paint specialist. The tall Latin lover with dark-brown eyes and lips made for kissing, who had snared her.

He had a way of raising one brow in question or command that turned her entire body into his personal cheering section.

"...for some flowers. I dunno. Something that looks like I put thought into it?"

Focus, Joey. Be professional. This isn't personal. Don't get all gooey on the man. "Ah, budget?"

He sighed. "For Stella, it has to be decent. Girl is like a human calculator when it comes to anything with value. If I skimp, she'll know," he said, still grinning. He took the binder she slid to him and leafed through the floral selections. "I'm Lou Cortez, by the way."

"I remember." He'd only introduced himself once, months ago in the garage while she'd been going over flower choices with his boss. But Joey had never forgotten those broad shoulders, chiseled chin, or bright white smile. Wow, was he too hot to handle.

She'd kept her distance—or at least tried to. She'd been invited to the wedding, having become friends with the bride. Of course, all the woman's employees had been invited as well. Joey had done her best to steer clear of the man women seemed to drool over. Talk about trouble she didn't need.

She realized he'd stopped looking through the binder and was staring straight at her. More like through her. Wow. How did he do that? Bring so much concentration and intensity she felt as if his gaze reached out and wrapped around her, holding her still?

And why, when confronted with all that masculinity, did she want to stammer and obey any darn thing he said? She had to force herself to be strong, to speak. But she just stared, mute, at so much male prettiness.

His smile deepened. "And *your* name would be…?" God, a dimple appeared on his left cheek.

A dimple. Kill me now. Breathe, dummy. You can handle this. It's business. "Oh, right. I'm Joey."

"You don't look like a Joey," he murmured.

Her heart raced, and she forced herself to maintain eye contact. "Short for Josephine. So the flowers. Did you find anything you like?"

A loaded question, because his slow grin widened as

he looked her over. Then he turned back to the binder and shook his head. "Nah. I need something original. Do you design bouquets?"

"Yes." More comfortable on a professional level, she nodded. "We have some amazing florists and—"

"No. *You*. Do you put flowers together?"

"Yes."

"Good. I want you to do it." He shrugged. "Del, my boss at Webster's, you remember her?"

She nodded. How could she forget the woman with such cold gray eyes, tattoo sleeves, and funky ash-blond hair braided in twists? The same woman she'd made friends with not long after meeting. Heck, she'd attended Del's wedding.

"She said you were amazing. My sister needs something amazing right now."

The flowers were for his sister. *Oh man. He's sexy as sin, he has a body to die for, and now he's buying flowers for* his sister?

She softened toward him. "Do you know her favorite flower or color? A scent maybe? Did you want sophisticated or simple? How old is she?"

"Ah, something cool. I don't know. She's gonna be twenty-three." He rattled off a few ideas, and she made quick notes.

"I can have this for you by…" She paused to check the computer. "Tomorrow. Would that work?"

"Hell. I really need them today. Her birthday isn't until Friday, but she got some shitty news, so I wanted to give them to her when I see her later. I'm willing to pay extra, no problem."

Adding *charming* and *thoughtful* to the Lou List, Joey

did her best not to moon over the man and kept a straight face. "Well, if you can wait until the end of the day, I'll try to fit them in. We close at seven. Is that okay?"

His face broke out into a relieved smile. "*Gracias*, Joey. You're doing me a huge favor."

Ignoring his smile, she called on her inner manager. "Well, you're doing something nice for your sister. And I know all about crappy days."

"Yeah?" He leaned closer, and she caught a waft of motor oil and crisp cologne, an odd blend of manly and sexy that nearly knocked her on her ass. "Who tried to ruin your day, sweetheart? I can fix that."

She blew out a shaky breath and gave a nervous laugh. "Ah, I just meant I've had those kinds of days before. Not now. It's just a regular Monday for me." A great Monday, considering her promotion.

He didn't blink, and she felt positively hunted.

"Well, if anyone gives you any trouble, you let me know, and I can talk to them for you. Nobody should mess with a woman as pretty and nice as you." He stroked her cheek with a rough finger before she could unglue herself from the floor and move away.

Then he glanced at the clock behind her, straightened, and said something in Spanish. "Sorry, Joey." Her name on his lips sounded like a caress. "Gotta go. I'll be back at seven to pick them up, okay? Thanks. I owe you."

"You don't owe me anything. I mean, I'll probably have to charge you extra for the sudden notice. It's a rush order," she blurted, not wanting him to think she was giving him special favors.

"I'll pay, no problem." He slid a card toward her. "My number in case something comes up with the flowers. Or a customer bothers you." He nodded to it. "You're a sweetheart. I'll see you soon."

He left, and she could breathe again. Still processing the overwhelming presence that had been Lou Cortez—mechanic, paint expert, and all-around heartthrob—Joey tried to calm her racing heart.

One of their regulars plunked a few items on the counter, her blue eyes twinkling, her white hair artfully arranged around her face. "Don't know how you let that one get away. If I was a few years younger, I'd have been all over him." She waggled her brows. "Then again, he looked like he might be open to an octogenarian with loads of experience. Think he'd mind if you gave me his number?"

They both laughed, even as Joey tucked the card into her pocket and rang up Mrs. Packard's items. The thing burned in her pocket, a link to a man she knew better than to step a foot near. She'd throw it away after he picked up his flowers. Joey had made mistakes with a charmer a long time ago, and she had no intention of ever going down that road again.

"Aw. Come on, baby. Don't be like that." Silence, then the groveling of a man who'd done wrong echoed through the garage bay, adding a jolt of much-needed humor to Lou's late Monday misery. Sam continued to apologize into his cell phone. "Okay, okay. I swear I'll take you to that stupid party. Ivy…" Sam sighed. "Yeah, I know. I'm sorry."

Lou snorted. Some men didn't know a thing about women. Like the dickhead who'd just dumped his younger sister. Lou wanted to bend the guy into a pretzel, and he hadn't liked the SOB to begin with. Good riddance. Then take his buddy Sam, still groveling into the phone. Before the guy had hooked up with his girlfriend, he couldn't talk to, compliment, or even look at a woman without sounding like a Neanderthal. Thank God Ivy had managed to kick his ass into gear. Now the giant with a jaw like granite was apologizing—with sincerity.

Lou glanced out from under the hood of his current project, wishing they weren't down two mechanics this afternoon. But with one guy helping his mother with something and the other at the dentist, it was up to Lou and Sam to take care of the afternoon schedule. Three rush jobs didn't help either, but at least oil changes didn't take as much time as this shitty Chrysler he'd swear was possessed. And, lucky him, its owner had asked for Lou by name.

Sam finished his phone call and disconnected, tossing his cell on his cluttered workbench. He glanced around, saw that Lou had been listening to every pathetic word he'd uttered, and flushed.

"Yo, jackass. Get the lead out," Sam barked. "Del said we have to finish the LeBaron and Grand Am by the end of the day if we want to stick Foley on Blue Altima tomorrow."

Blue Altima—a car he loathed like nobody's business. The damn thing had been in and out of the shop three times in the past six months, and no one liked working on it or dealing with the pain-in-the-ass owner. An old woman who ate bitch pills for breakfast.

"I'm all over it," he muttered.

Lou had been raised by his mother, his grandmother,

and five aunts. He had five sisters and thirteen female cousins—who lived *way* too close by—and he'd been working for Delilah McCauley since her father had all but retired.

Lou respected women. He *loved* women.

Yet Patsy Sidel did nothing but bitch about her car, no matter how many times the crew and Del had begged her to trade it in for one that worked.

No, he had no urge to deal with Mrs. Sidel. Not when he had his mind full of another woman with no time for him or his charming ways, which frankly baffled him.

He swore as he busted his knuckles against a stubborn bolt, the pain right up there with the headache brewing anytime he thought about Josephine—Joey—Reeves.

It continued to confuse the hell out of him that the one woman he'd had his eye on for months still refused to respond to his obvious appeal, handsome good looks, and killer grin.

He swore to himself as he fought with the spark plugs on his current project, his thoughts on a sexy brunette who spooked if he so much as took a step in her direction.

What the hell had happened? It was like he'd fallen into an alternate reality. His badass boss had snagged a decent guy, complete with a kid and a dog. His fellow mechanics, all gruff, tatted, and coarse, had scored sweethearts. Even the boss's dad had a fine woman who thought he hung the moon. And Liam was an all-around bruiser.

But Lou—the best-looking and smartest of the bunch—could barely get a smile from the chick he'd been digging?

He'd first seen her when she'd timidly stepped into

the garage, months ago, asking for Del. His entire world had centered on that one moment, and it was like the fucking sun had spotlighted the petite brunette, showcasing the perfect woman in the center of his world.

Then she'd scurried by him, not looking much at any of the guys, as a matter of fact, and disappeared into Del's office. Joey had come by a few times after that to deal with Del and flowers for her wedding. But somehow she managed to avoid being anywhere near Lou.

The guys thought it hilarious, since he'd made his interest clear. Even Del questioned what had happened to Lou's famous ability to charm women. What made it even worse? Del liked the chick, and she'd invited Joey to hang at the wedding as a guest.

Again, he'd been denied. He'd tried talking to her only to have her stammer and light out as if her hair had caught fire. Then she'd disappeared when he'd tried to ask if she was okay.

Sheer luck had brought him into her shop today, inspired by the idea of getting his sister flowers to celebrate her breakup with a major asshole. Of course, Stella wouldn't see it that way. But he did.

He sighed. Josephine Reeves. Demure. Sleek and pretty. *Joey* had a tiny frame, gently curved in all the right places though. Her mink-brown hair curled around her shoulders, long and thick. She had pretty features, nothing too remarkable. Lou had been with knockouts. Women with huge breasts and round asses, thick thighs, muscular frames, blonds, redheads, you name it.

But for some reason, Joey Reeves and her tiny hands, less-than-a-handful breasts, and slender figure got him harder than steel. Just thinking about her brought out all the dominant instincts he'd made good use of since he'd first taken a woman to bed.

Man, the thought of all he wanted to do to her... Touching her in the store hadn't been smart, but he hadn't been able to stop himself. Finally, they'd had a face-to-face conversation. More than the physical attraction, just being around her made his heart do weird somersaults. He'd felt happy just being near all that sweetness.

And he had another couple of hours until he'd get to see her again.

He smiled and chuckled, wondering if she'd try to pawn him off on another employee. Not that it mattered. He planned to seduce the woman into a date if it was the last thing he ever—

"Shoot, Lou." A husky female voice jarred him from his fantasies. "My father works faster than you anymore."

He jolted and swore, scraping across that damn bolt again and bleeding over the engine. "You need to wear a bell."

"No kidding." Liam, Del's father, didn't sound happy. No doubt insulted that his daughter had compared him to Lou. "For the record, I'm still a better mechanic than any of the dickheads in here." He flashed a satisfied smile. "No offense, Lou, Sam."

Sam grunted.

"What he said." Lou swore under his breath, cradling his stinging hand.

Like the rest of the guys who worked in the shop, Liam Webster wore his brawn well. Six-two and built like a brick, the guy looked and acted a decade younger than his sixty years. Hell, Lou was no pushover, but he had no intention of ever going up against Liam. The old man looked like the type to fight dirty. With a daughter like Del, he no doubt knew how to handle conflict.

On a regular basis.

Del *McCauley*, now that she'd married Mr. White Picket Fence, looked good wearing a gold band on her finger. Other than the ring, going home daily at five, and smiling all the damn time, his boss hadn't much changed. Then again, it had only been a week since she'd officially become a Mrs.

Lou realized Liam had used the word *dickhead* and Del hadn't laid into him. "So we can swear again?"

"Yeah." Liam blew out a breath. "Now that my princess snagged herself a man and is living in wedded bliss, the rest of us are free to talk like normal people."

Prior to her wedding, Del had pronounced the garage "swear-free" for months in an effort not to swear at her own wedding.

"It worked, Dad." Del grinned. "I didn't say one fucking thing wrong."

"Ah, there's my girl." Liam hefted a beefy arm over her shoulder and squeezed until she squeaked.

Lou grinned. Del really was a cute Amazon. "You two taking off?" The time had reached five already.

Only two more hours until he got to visit his own *princesa*.

"Yep. Time for this old man and his daughter to go home. I'm eating at the McCauleys' tonight." Liam beamed.

Must be a great thing to see his daughter married to a decent guy and into a hella nice family. Lou constantly struggled to keep his sisters in line and his cousins from going off the deep end when it came to men and bad choices.

"Oh?" Lou wiped his hands on a dirty rag to stanch the bleeding.

"God, Lou. Stop." Del marched off and returned with a clean rag and bandage. "Use these."

Lou used the rag to take care of the excess blood, then slapped the bandage on his throbbing knuckle. "Check that, Liam. Your baby girl is all domesticated. Want to kiss it and make it better, Del?"

She flipped him off, and they laughed. "Don't work too hard, Lou." Del shook her head and darted a sly look his way. "Wouldn't want to be too late when you pick up those flowers for your sister."

"How the hell do you know that?"

She shrugged. "I know all and see all, Cortez. Remember that." She huffed. "And make sure to tell Heller to stop hogging all your time when you see him tomorrow. I need you in here too, you know."

"Yeah, yeah." Lou worked for Del mostly, but his paint work he did through Heller's shop. Heller's Paint and Body—which had read Heller's Paint and Auto Body before the *Auto* fell off the sign—specialized in high-end paint jobs, and Lou got a real kick out of creating works of art with wheels.

"I'm not kidding. I don't care how big or mean Heller thinks he is. You belong to me." She scowled, then turned on her heel and stalked back to the office.

Liam shook his head. "Be nice when you tell him that."

"Oh, I will." Only a man courting death mouthed off to Heller.

Liam followed his daughter out of the garage.

"Tell Heller what to do? I don't think so." Lou snorted, heard Sam's mumble of agreement, and got back to work.

"He's not a bad guy." Sam didn't say any more.

—◊—

Done with his project, Lou drove the Chrysler outside, took the Grand Am into the bay, and readied it for an oil change.

Sam looked away from the engine he was working on. "Make sure to tell Heller the next beer at Ray's is on me. The plan is to head there Friday night."

"Nobody told me." Lou scowled.

"I'm telling you now, Romeo. Try to get a life and show up. Or is your mom still keeping you in on curfew?"

Lou cursed him in Spanish, getting an honest-to-God laugh out of Sam. Freaky. "Are you on drugs? What's with all the cheer, man?"

"It's called love, Lou. You ought to give it a try. With just one woman, I mean."

"Funny." Lou changed out the filter, then took the oil pan and dumped it in the drum in the back. He returned, put on the new filter, cleaned up the undercarriage, then finished refilling the oil and putting the vehicle to rights.

Sam, being Sam, refused to let it go. "Of course, since you're still panting after Del's flower chick, maybe you're actually gonna follow my advice, huh? Doing your best to find some love, Casanova? Except the chick is smart and sees right through all that charming shit that normally works." Sam smiled. Again.

"You got a point to make, Mr. Mouth?"

"Nope. I'm done. Heading home to Ivy for dinner."

Sam sounded satisfied, and Lou couldn't blame him. He liked Ivy, the sweet thing. Though he still had no idea what a cutie like her was doing with a thug like Sam.

Sam left the bay to hang up his coveralls and grab his jacket. He returned to the bay, then parted with, "Hey Lou, you ever find a date, we'll double. How about that?"

"Fuck off, Hamilton."

"Eat shit and die, Cortez." Sam left, whistling.

The bastard.

Noting the time, Lou hustled to finish his last oil change. He cleaned then locked up after himself. Nothing he could do about the bloody bandage or smell of oil coating him like cheap cologne.

He raced to the flower shop, praying she'd waited an extra ten minutes past closing.

Not that it mattered. He'd still give Stella a shoulder to cry on, even without the flowers. If Joey had gone home, he'd have to swing by the next day. Or the next. Not that Lou would resort to harassing the woman. But if she'd just give him a chance to show her how much fun he could be, he knew he'd have a shot at seeing the real Joey Reeves.

Preferably in just the skin God gave her.

He groaned, now aroused again, and did his best to think clean thoughts as he motored through traffic to win a certain *princesa* needing a white knight. Or, at least, a slightly tarnished one.

Chapter 2

JOEY GLARED AT HER PHONE, NOT PLEASED TO STILL BE stuck hanging around the shop fifteen minutes past closing. She'd already texted her mother, but since Brandon had been invited to dinner with a friend, she didn't have to pick him up until eight anyway. She would have texted Lou to see what had held him up, but if she did that, he'd have her personal number.

What to do, what to do... Oh, screw it. Lou Cortez could just—

A car zoomed into the parking lot in front of the store. A sleek, highly polished dark-purple muscle car. A Camaro maybe? She had no idea. But the thing had been custom designed for sure. She stared in wonder at the lifelike cobra subtly shimmering on the back side panel before the car turned to park and she couldn't see the image anymore. Artwork like that had to cost a fortune. No amateur spray painting. Lou's car would look totally at home at a car show.

He stepped out in the same jeans and gray tee he'd been wearing earlier, complete with black boots and a black denim jacket. What would look casual on anyone else looked spectacular on Lou. All he needed to turn himself into an advertisement for the ideal man's man would be a woman on each arm, a beer in hand, and that amazing smile he'd turned on her earlier.

He hustled up to the front door and knocked,

peering inside past the closed sign and tugging at the locked door.

She sighed, went to the front, and opened the door. "You're late." Oh yeah. Manager Joey was sticking to her guns. Joey had no time for those who didn't stick to her schedule, sexy smile or not.

He held up his hands in surrender, and she noticed a big bandage on one that hadn't been there before. "*Lo siento*. I'm so sorry. Totally my fault, but the sludge in Johnson's car made the oil take forever to come out. And my boss is a total hardass. If I hadn't gotten that last oil job done, I'd be working on Blue Altima tomorrow, and that car is straight-up cursed." He spoke fast, his accent thick.

"Blue Altima?"

He shivered. "You have no idea how many fingers, wrists, and arms I've busted with that thing." He held up his bandaged hand. "This is nothing. I'm really, really sorry I'm late. I swear. I broke a few speeding records to get here."

Familiar with the city traffic, she well knew it could take twenty minutes to go a mile in this town, even after rush hour on a Monday. She tried to hold onto her mad, but he'd talked so fast and looked so earnest she couldn't. "Come on. I'll get you the flowers." *And then you can leave and not come back.*

Behind her, he seemed to loom. Joey was on the short side, and Lou had to stand a few inches over six feet. He made her feel downright tiny. When she reached the counter, he started to follow her behind it.

She turned and automatically put a hand out before she could think about it.

He took an extra step before stopping, so that his warm, broad chest pressed against her palm. He glanced from the contact to her face, his expression impossible to read. But *intense* seemed to describe it well enough.

She blew out a breath and quickly lowered her hand. "Nobody goes behind the counter unless Stef says it's okay." Stef's orders, and Joey was nothing if not a stickler for the rules.

He took a step back and crossed his massive arms over his chest. "Stef?"

"My boss." And friend. The woman had taken a chance on a teenager, and unlike Joey's parents, Stef had never judged her for her choices. "There you go." She pointed to the flowers she'd put together in a square glass vase, sitting on the back counter.

"Oh man. Are those for Stella? They're perfect."

Seeing that he made no move to follow her back and that he seemed thrilled with her arrangement, she relaxed. "Purples, whites, and a few sprigs of pink to mix it up. It's lightly scented, a hint of lavender. You said she'd like that."

"Yeah." He whistled. "This should help ease the sting from the jackass who dumped her."

She cringed. "Ouch."

He looked back at her and smiled. "Nah. He was a jerk. She'll be much better off with someone else." He dug in his back pocket, pulled out his wallet, and slapped a card down. "Whatever it costs, it's worth it."

Joey rang him up, making no mention of the fact she hadn't charged him extra. As much as he bothered her, she couldn't hold being a good brother against him. She handed his card back, then waited for him to sign and *leave*.

He signed then handed her back the slip.

But he didn't move, didn't even reach for the bouquet. "So, Joey."

Those eyes mesmerized her, and she quickly looked down and fiddled with his ticket. He had that bedroom stare she'd seen before, the one that invited a girl to take all her clothes off, lie back, and wait for the good times to roll. How sad that anytime she saw this man she barely knew she thought of sex. Talk about needing to get back into the dating scene to cool her jets. Desperation did not a pretty girl make.

She wanted to look him back in the eye, to mouth something smart. She'd say, "So, Lou," and just pause the way he had. Except Manager Joey had left the building, and girlie, stupid, shy Joey took her place. She felt tongue-tied. *Crap*.

A regular customer, a person she talked to without fear of complication, and she had no problem conversing. The moment she felt that something intimate, that spark of desire for a man or a relationship, she turned shy. It was so weird and totally unlike the real Joey. And also a telling sign of whom she should steer clear of.

She blew out a breath, grabbed his flowers, then held them out to him, looking at him from under her lashes. Determined to be pleasant and get him out of the shop before she made a fool of herself, she forced a polite smile. "Here you go."

About the Author

Caffeine addict, boy referee, and romance aficionado, *New York Times* and *USA Today* bestselling author Marie Harte is a confessed bibliophile and devotee of action movies. Whether hiking in Central Oregon, biking around town, or hanging at the local tea shop, she's constantly plotting to give everyone a happily ever after. Visit marieharte.com and fall in love.